Praise for Meg Benjamin's
Long Time Gone

2011 Romantic Times Reviewer's Choice Award
~ Indie Press Romance

"This fourth story set in Konigsburg, Tex., has a soupçon of humor, delightful human and animal characters, an excellent romance and a bit of a mystery. A wonderful story that readers will be sorry to see end."
~ *Romantic Times (Top Pick, Contemporary Romance)*

"Meg Benjamin relates an appealing story about two people at a crossroads in life, living with the problems of the past and trying to forge a stronger future for themselves."
~ *Romance Book Scene*

"I could go on and on about how much this book works for me. I will stop here and say hands down this is a must read series and Long Time Gone is a perfect addition to the Konigsburg set of books."
~ *Erotic Horizon*

"Ms. Benjamin's words drew me in and I felt connected to Erik and Morgan. I loved this book and would recommend it to any reader who loves sparks and happy ends."
~ *Fallen Angel Reviews*

"Ms. Benjamin did a fabulous job in letting the romance grow, and once our hero and heroine finally got together, the heat was definitely on. Do these two manage to solve the mystery and find a happy ever after? With hot sex with mango sherbet, crooked politicians, yuppie bikers, Bored Ducks, and a Maine Coon Cat with attitude, they manage."
~ *Whipped Cream Reviews*

"I loved the way that Erik and Morgan's relationship was allowed to develop gradually. No big misunderstanding, just two adults, attracted to one another and making the transition from friends to lovers. Their ease with one another made their difficulties dealing with their respective families seem even more fraught."

~ *Manda Collins*

"Meg Benjamin has finished this series in a way that makes it just right for all the Toleffsons. Erik is like a fallen angel and Meg Benjamin did a great job in showing us that every man deserves a second chance. The whole gang is back and Ms. Benjamin shows us how they have grown from single life to happily ever after marriages. Loved it."

~ *BlackRaven's Reviews*

Look for these titles by *Meg Benjamin*

Now Available:

Konigsburg, Texas Series
Venus in Blue Jeans
Wedding Bell Blues
Be My Baby
Long Time Gone
Brand New Me

Long Time Gone

Meg Benjamin

SAMHAIN
PUBLISHING

Samhain Publishing, Ltd.
11821 Mason Montgomery Rd., 4B
Cincinnati, OH 45249
www.samhainpublishing.com

Long Time Gone
Copyright © 2011 by Meg Benjamin
Print ISBN: 978-1-60928-129-8
Digital ISBN: 978-1-60928-108-3

Editing by Lindsey Faber
Cover by Mandy M. Roth

First Samhain Publishing, Ltd. electronic publication: July 2010
First Samhain Publishing, Ltd. print publication: August 2011

Dedication

For the usual suspects—Bill, Josh and Ben. And for all the great Texas winemakers who gave me their time and expertise, especially Jim and Karen Johnson of Alamosa, Madeline and Ed Mangold of Spicewood, Gary Gilstrap of Texas Hills, and John Otis of Crossroads. Thanks, guys!

Chapter One

Erik Toleffson hated the Dew Drop Inn in downtown Konigsburg, Texas, with a loathing that was deep and abiding. It wasn't just because he didn't drink—he could tolerate most bars without any problem. But the Dew Drop wasn't most bars.

It was so dark it reminded him of a cave—he half-expected to see bats hanging from the rafters. And bats might have been an improvement over some of the bar's customers, particularly considering that Erik, one of Konigsburg's limited supply of cops, had had professional interactions with several of them. There was Otto Friedrich, the high school football coach, whom he'd decked a couple of years ago for attempting to assault Erik's future sister-in-law. And Billy Jo Slidell, who'd had a couple of DUIs in the last month that ended with Erik tossing him into what passed for a drunk tank in the Konigsburg jail. And Brendan Fowler, who'd had to bail out Mrs. Fowler, Marlene, after she'd thrown a punch at Ethel Overmeyer. Erik wasn't sure what the origin of the fight had been, but Ethel outweighed Marlene by about fifty pounds and was just getting ready to throw her own punch when he intervened, so he figured Marlene was lucky to have gotten off with a fine.

Given his choice, he'd have hung out at the Coffee Corral or even Brenner's Restaurant down the street, although he couldn't afford to eat much more than a couple of dinner rolls there. But his brothers liked the Dew Drop, and Erik wasn't ready to complain about it now that they'd started including him in their five o'clock get-togethers. It hadn't been all that long ago they'd have been running in the other direction if they saw him coming, given his standard practice of beating the crap out of them until they'd been old enough to fight him off singly and in a group.

Not that he blamed them for that. In their place, he would have done the same thing. He'd even be willing to let them beat him to a bloody pulp now if they'd like to take him on, assuming it might help to even the score from their childhood.

Erik watched as his brother Pete tried to flag down a barmaid from their booth in the corner. All four brothers were about the same size, with the same brown hair and eyes, but Pete was maybe an inch or two shorter than the others. Which meant he was around six-three. Lars and Cal were scrunched into the other side of the booth, trying to find room for their feet in the limited space. It was best to be the last one to arrive at these get-togethers. Being late meant you got the outside seat, which meant being able to extend your legs out into the floor space instead of trying to reduce yourself to booth-size.

With other people the customers might have objected, but nobody made much of a fuss about the Toleffsons, and not just because they were bigger than most of the men in the bar. With the exception of Erik, all the Toleffsons were popular people in Konigsburg. Nice guys, upstanding citizens, a veterinarian, an accountant and an assistant county attorney. All of them well-liked, with the exception of him. But then he'd often been the exception in cases like that. "Nice" and "upstanding" weren't words that anybody had ever used to describe him.

Pete scowled toward the bar, where the owner, Ingstrom, was ignoring him. Both barmaids were at the other end of the room, giggling with a couple of cowboy wannabes whose Stetsons looked brand new.

Time was when the barmaids would have been hanging around the Toleffson booth, but now three out of the four brothers were married, and Erik figured nobody thought of him as worth flirting with. The only reason the four of them could get together at all was that the Toleffson wives had a girls-only dinner on Wednesday. Knowing his sisters-in-law, Erik assumed they were probably trading war stories or plotting battle strategy. Not that any of his brothers stood a chance against their wives, either singly or in concert, strategy or no strategy.

"What the hell does it take to get served around here anymore," Pete growled, "divine intervention?"

"Forget it." Lars pushed himself to his feet. "I'll go to the bar myself."

"I'll help." Cal glanced at Erik. "Dr. Pepper okay? Ingstrom switched distributors."

"Sure. Anything."

Pete glanced his way as the other two headed toward Ingstrom. "What do you hear about the chief's job?"

Erik sighed. If he'd had any glimmer of a good mood, it promptly vaporized. "City council meeting tomorrow afternoon. They're supposed to announce their decision then."

"Any hope it won't be Ham Linklatter?"

Erik shrugged. "Anything's possible. But Mayor Pittman wants Linklatter and the council's not famous for standing up to him."

"Linklatter's an idiot. I've seen cheese with a higher IQ."

"Ham's a little...unfocused. He's got seniority, though. And he's the only full-time cop in town."

Pete grimaced. "He was hired by a psychopath and promoted by a screwup. That doesn't sound like much of a recommendation."

Erik sighed again. Konigsburg's former police chief, Claude Olema, had been fired a couple of months ago for gross incompetence after a high-risk prisoner had escaped from the jail. Erik hadn't been impressed with Olema's skills, but at least the chief had been reasonably honest. The chief before Olema, Brody, had tried to kill Cal's wife, Docia, but that had been before Erik's time. Good thing, too, considering what Erik would have felt like doing to Brody himself if he'd known him then. "The town hasn't been all that lucky in terms of police chiefs. I'll grant you that."

"What have you been doing for a chief since Olema left?"

"Sheriff Friesenhahn's sent over a couple of his deputies to keep an eye on things. Pittman wanted to make Ham acting chief, but the council wouldn't back him on it."

Pete grinned. "You mean Horace wouldn't. Thank god we've got one hard-ass who isn't afraid of the mayor."

Horace Rankin was Cal's partner in the veterinary clinic. He was also president of the city council and currently Erik's only hope. If anybody could come up with an alternative to Ham Linklatter, it would be Horace.

"Did you apply for the job?"

"Sure." Erik's mouth twisted slightly. "We all did—me and Nando and Curtis Peavey. Won't mean anything, though. Pittman's already chosen the next chief."

Pete leaned back against the booth. "What will you do if they promote Linklatter to chief? Could you work for him?"

Erik shrugged again. "I'll figure something out."

Actually, he'd already figured out there was no way he'd work for Ham Linklatter, although he wasn't ready to discuss it with the family yet. He'd worked for incompetents before—he'd gotten along with Olema, even though he didn't hold his skills in much regard. But he'd never yet worked for a moron, and he wasn't eager to try.

He liked Konigsburg, Texas, and he didn't really want to stick around to watch what happened when Ham started screwing up. Which made it doubly hard—he'd have to leave the town he'd grown to like and his family just when it seemed they might actually be willing to forgive him. That forgiveness hadn't come easily, and he still wondered sometimes if he deserved it.

Cal slid into the booth opposite, pushing a glass of soda across the table to Erik and a bottle of Lonestar to Pete. "Have you seen Wonder? I need to tell him about dinner on Friday." He raised an eyebrow at Erik. "You're coming, right?"

"For an hour or so. I'm on duty at eight. I'll bring the soda."

Pete gestured across the room. "Wonder's over there at the booth with Allie and Morgan."

Erik glanced at a booth at the other end of the row. Cal's friend Steve Kleinschmidt, aka Wonder Dentist, sat opposite his fiancée Allie Maldonado, a buxom brunette baker who made the best scones on the planet. On Allie's other side, a woman cradled her head in her arms on the tabletop. Erik sighed. Probably another drunk, not that he was going to do anything about it as long as she stayed quiet. With only a few available jail cells, the law in Konigsburg had to be discriminating about who got swept up. On the other hand, she'd probably be a more pleasant cell occupant than somebody like Terrell Biedermeier, currently knocking back boilermakers at the bar and long overdue for a trip to the drunk tank.

The woman raised her head, and Erik felt as if he'd been kicked in the gut.

Her eyes were huge, liquid brown. Like melted chocolate. Like coffee beans. Like Bambi.

Erik swiveled back to the table and grabbed his Dr. Pepper. *Like Bambi? Jesus, Toleffson, get a grip.*

Morgan Barrett just needed some sleep. That was all. She tried to remember how long she'd slept last night. Four hours? Maybe. She hadn't expected the truck with the grapes from Lubbock to show up at three in the morning, that's for sure.

The good news was that the truck was ahead of schedule, which meant they could start the crush a few days early, according to Ciro. The bad news was, well, it was freakin' three in the morning and she had to stay down there until all the grapes were unloaded.

She'd spent the rest of the day helping Ciro and Esteban run the destemmer and the crusher, draining the juice and pulp off into the holding tank. At least it was a cabernet franc so they didn't have to filter off the skins, as they did with the viognier.

Over the course of the past year, she'd discovered that white wine was a total nightmare.

Next week they'd have to start picking the sauvignon blanc grapes in their own vineyard, even though it was early, because the heat had made the grapes ripen before her father and Ciro had originally figured they would. And Dad was pissed because he wouldn't be there to oversee the crush. And Ciro was pissed because he hated using volunteer pickers. And Morgan promised herself she'd find something to be pissed about too, as soon as she got a spare millisecond.

Actually, she could always be pissed about the way her existence had been gobbled up by Cedar Creek Winery. It all seemed so simple when she'd agreed to take over for Dad after his accident. She'd go to the winery, learn what she needed to learn about wine production and put together a marketing plan on the side. And when she was through with all that, she'd start making plans to get the winery the recognition it deserved.

Simple. *Right.* And Hurricane Rita was a bad rainstorm. She probably shouldn't be wasting time in the Dew Drop instead of reviewing the barrel room records, but she wanted to at least pretend she had a social life.

If she could just hold everything together until next

weekend, maybe Dad... Morgan felt her head droop. Just five minutes. She'd put her head down on the table for five minutes and then she'd be good to go. Power-napping. The mark of a successful businesswoman. And she was a successful...business...woman...

"Morgan." Someone shook her shoulder, gently. "Morgan, honey."

"Mom?" Morgan murmured. And then felt like a moron. She was seated in the Dew Drop Inn in downtown Konigsburg. Her mother had better taste.

"Morgan?" Allie Maldonado gave her a slightly concerned look, eyebrows raised. "Okay?"

"Yeah," Morgan groaned, pushing her hair out of her eyes. Just five minutes of sleep. That's all she needed, honestly.

A man across the room scowled at her.

She blinked. What had she done now? Was putting your head down on a table to grab five minutes of shut-eye some kind of honky-tonk *faux pas*? Had she violated the health code, assuming the Dew Drop had a health code to violate?

The man turned away quickly. She had an impression of dark hair and eyes, broad shoulders, a face that looked like he'd lived through a lot, not all of it pleasant.

"Who's that?" Morgan turned to Allie. Allie always knew everything. Except that Allie was slightly distracted these days. Not that Morgan blamed her. Trying to arrange a wedding to Wonder Dentist would try anybody's patience.

Allie looked up from Wonder briefly and checked the booth at the far end of the room. "Toleffsons. All four of them. Did you have a particular one in mind?"

"Oh. I couldn't see that far." Morgan leaned back against the booth, trying to get another look at the men across the room without being too obvious about it. "Which one is the one on the end?"

"Erik." Allie took a swallow of wine. "The cop. You might not have seen him as much as the others. He's always working. They all look alike, though, more or less."

Morgan narrowed her eyes, surreptitiously studying the back of Erik Toleffson's head. "Maybe. He doesn't look much like Cal, though. He needs to smile."

"No, he doesn't." Wonder set down his bottle of beer. "When Erik smiles it means he's getting ready to tear somebody a new one. Scariest sucker I've ever known."

Allie grinned and put her hand over his on the table. "You're such a poetic SOB. Tell them to join us. I need to give Cal a message for Docia."

Wonder grimaced, pushing himself to his feet. "Okay, but if the Toleffsons are joining us, we're getting a table. I'm not letting those elephants scrunch me up against the wall again."

Wonder Dentist was one of the least formidable-looking men Erik had ever met. He stood maybe five-eight, with a slightly concave chest, horn-rims and thinning hair. Combined with his habitually smart-assed personality, he was not someone Erik would consider a great catch. Yet he'd somehow managed to snare one of the best cooks in town for his bride-to-be. Just another example of how the universe didn't always play fair.

Cal and Lars pulled a couple of tables together, while he helped Pete corral chairs, ignoring Ingstrom's scowl as they rearranged his floor space.

"Have a seat, Erik. There's room over here beside us." Allie Maldonado put a hand on the shoulder of the woman next to her, Ms. Bambi-Eyes.

A set-up? Allie Maldonado actually thought he was worthy of a setup? Erik almost felt like shaking his head to clear it. Nobody wanted to hook up with him.

"This is Morgan Barrett. I don't know if you've met. Her dad's a partner in the Cedar Creek Winery outside town."

Morgan Barrett raised those remarkable eyes once again. Erik's jaw tightened. Aside from the eyes she looked a little like she'd been dragged through a knothole. Rumpled clothes, mussed hair. Very sexy mussed hair.

If she wasn't a drunk, she was one of the tiredest individuals he'd ever seen.

"Pleased to meet you." She yawned in his face. Well, okay then, not a drunk.

"I'm sorry." She shook her head. "We got a shipment of grapes last night. I'm usually more alert than this. I need to go home and sleep until the next load comes in, preferably in another week."

Allie nodded. "Harvest season. I remember. You going to have a new wine for the Hill Country Wine and Food Festival?"

"Yes." Morgan paused, then shook her head. "No. Maybe."

"Well, that seems to take care of the possibilities." Cal grinned.

Morgan sighed. "Esteban's got one ready to go, but ATF hasn't approved the label yet. We've been waiting on it for weeks now, but with Homeland Security it takes forever."

"Homeland Security?" Erik set his Dr. Pepper down on the table and pulled up his chair. "Wine is now considered a lethal weapon?"

"You haven't tasted the wine from Castleberry's, have you?" Morgan shook her head. "Sorry. I shouldn't be dissing the truly lousy wine being produced by our competitors. ATF, which is now part of Homeland Security, has to approve the text on wine labels and wine labels are not high on their list of priorities."

"So what are you going to call it?" Allie asked. "Is it red or white?"

"Red. It's Esteban Avrogado's first blend. He asked me for some advice, and I came up with a new name so we can market it."

Erik couldn't tell for sure in the gloom of the Dew Drop, but it almost looked like she was blushing.

"It's a Bordeaux blend—cabernet, merlot and cabernet franc. Only we can't call it Bordeaux because of the EU rules since it's not *from* Bordeaux."

"So you're calling it..." Allie gave her an encouraging smile.

"Bored Ducks." Morgan looked around the table expectantly.

Six faces stared blankly back.

"Well, because it's... I mean, people don't always know how to pronounce..." Morgan's lips thinned to a taut line. For a moment, she looked close to tears.

Erik had a sudden, unaccountable urge to get that look off her face. "That's funny," he said, pushing his lips into something that was in the neighborhood of a grin. "Bordeaux, Bored Ducks. Funny."

Wonder narrowed his eyes. "Funny?"

Allie gave him an elbow to the ribs. Wonder winced and settled back in his chair.

"Bored ducks." Cal grinned. "Sorry. Took me a minute. Now I see it."

Lars nodded. "We Toleffsons may not be swift, but we usually get there eventually. I think it's funny too."

Allie reached for her glass. "Novelty wine labels are a good marketing tool. It'll get the browsers' attention."

"It will indeed," Wonder intoned. "All across the state, the aisles of the wine sections will be clogged with shoppers muttering 'What the hell?'"

He winced again. For a small woman, Allie Maldonado appeared to wield a mighty elbow.

"I like it. And I'll bet the wine tastes terrific. All the Cedar Creek wines are good, Morgan."

Morgan grimaced. "I just hope it doesn't take people so long to figure out the name that they forget to buy the wine."

"Steve will buy a case." Allie turned narrowed eyes on Wonder. "Won't you, sweetie?"

"Sure," Wonder croaked, rubbing his side. "Wouldn't miss it."

Morgan yawned again. "I need to go back home and get some sleep before the next crisis."

"Morgan, you shouldn't drive." Cal's face was serious. "You're too tired. Stay over with us."

She shook her head. "It's okay, I'm not driving. Ciro is having dinner with Nando. He said he'd give me a ride back if I hike over to the station."

Erik blinked at her. The police station? Where he'd just left? What the hell was going on there now? The last thing the Konigsburg PD needed was another crisis. "I can give you a ride to the station. I need to check on a few things before I go home."

Not exactly true, but close enough. If people were dining at the station, Erik figured he should know about it. Nando Avrogado was another of the part-time officers, and the only Konigsburg cop Erik would depend on to be able to find the keys to the cruiser in less than ten minutes. If anything happened that got Nando thrown off the force, Erik would be on the first thing heading out of town.

"Oh." Morgan Barrett gave him a slightly dazed look, as if she were trying to remember just who he was. Then she nodded. "Okay. Thanks."

Officer Grouch, aka Officer Toleffson, opened the door to the passenger side of his oversized pickup, and Morgan wondered if she had enough energy left to climb in.

Oh, guts up. She pulled herself laboriously onto the seat and plumped down.

Officer Grouch climbed into the driver's seat and started the engine. Morgan tried to study him without staring. He resembled his brothers, but not exactly. In profile, his face looked as if it had been carved out of some very sturdy material, probably concrete. His jaw was squarish, firm, his eyes deep-set and dark. The creases around his eyes looked like canyons, as if he'd spent a lot of time staring directly at the sun.

He didn't look at her as he pulled away. Morgan wondered if he'd forgotten about her already. Then he glanced in her direction. "How'd you end up running a winery?"

Morgan shrugged. "I'm not really running it. My dad is part owner, but he's laid up with a broken leg and some cracked ribs from an accident. I'm filling in until he's back on his feet. It gives me a chance to learn the business." At least that was the current party line.

"What about your mother?"

"My mom works in Austin. She's a real estate agent." Morgan grimaced. "My parents are separated."

Not, of course, that her mother would have helped out at the winery even if they hadn't been separated. Her mother was too smart to get roped in.

"Must be tough." Erik's voice didn't sound like he really thought it was tough—he didn't sound like he thought much about it one way or the other.

Morgan slid down in her seat to rest her chin on her chest. "It's okay."

He glanced at her again, then slowed at the stoplight on Highway 16. Just as he started to turn left, an SUV sped through the intersection, running the light.

Morgan jerked upright and grasped the panic handle as Erik hit the brakes.

"Aw, hell," he muttered. "Hang on."

The truck accelerated so quickly that Morgan was thrown

back against the seat. Erik fumbled in the console and pulled out a red blinker. "Hold that on the dashboard, will you?" He flipped a switch and the blinker began to flash.

Morgan held the blinker in the middle of the dashboard, bracing herself on the door with her other hand. Erik cut hard to the right, following the taillights of the SUV. Within a few minutes the SUV slowed down and stopped in the middle of the street. Erik pulled in behind.

He reached into the glove compartment and pulled out a gun in a holster, then turned to Morgan. "Stay in the truck. Keep the door locked." He climbed out, heading toward the SUV.

Morgan's heart hammered against her ribs. Erik stepped up slightly behind the door, talking to the driver through the window, one hand resting on the gun at his hip. After a moment, the driver's door opened and a man in a baseball cap poured himself onto the street.

Of course he was drunk. Erik's least favorite misdemeanor—Driving While Stupid. On the other hand, if he were to pick up everybody in Konigsburg who was guilty, he'd have at least half the town in jail. He pulled out his cell and dialed the station.

When Nando picked up, Erik could hear Tejano music playing softly in the background. "Konigsburg Police, this is Officer Avrogado."

"Hey, Officer, I need your assistance," Erik growled.

"Toleffson? I thought you went home."

"I did. Some idiot ran the light on Highway 16 in front of me." He sighed. "I've got a civilian in my truck. I can't bring him in myself."

"Is he giving you trouble?" Nando's voice sounded wary.

"Nah, he's plastered. He'd probably sleep it off if I left him lying in the street, but the citizens might complain."

"Okay, let me get set up here." Nando murmured to someone in the background.

Please, god, don't let him have a woman there. If they lost Nando, Erik would be stuck with Ham Linklatter and Curtis Peavey. He might as well eat his gun.

19

"Okay," Nando came back. "My dad will stay here in case anybody needs a cop while we're gone. I'll come meet you in the cruiser."

Thirty minutes later, the drunk was locked in the cell, and Nando's father was giving Erik the third degree.

"How come you had Morgan out there? She could've gotten hurt." He was about Nando's size and weight, maybe six feet and stocky. He had the look of someone who spent a lot of time outside, his face burned bronze from the sun, with permanent squint lines around his eyes. He also looked like a man who didn't take much crap. Erik decided not to give him any.

"I didn't intend Miss Barrett to be in the middle of it. The guy cut in front of us."

Morgan laid her hand on Nando's father's arm. "It's okay, Ciro. Officer Toleffson was giving me a ride over here so I wouldn't have to walk. It was all just lousy timing."

Avrogado sniffed, clearly not satisfied. "So you say."

"So I say." Morgan's eyes looked brighter than they had at the Dew Drop, and she was smiling. "Can we go back home now?"

After another moment, Avrogado shrugged. "Yeah, why not. You get anything to eat?"

Morgan paused to think. "I guess not. I forgot all about it."

"Here." Avrogado picked up a paper sack off Nando's desk. "Carmen's chicken. You can eat it in the truck."

Nando cast a mournful look at the sack. Avrogado narrowed his eyes. "Go see your mama if you want more. She'll be glad to whip some up for you when you come by home. Which I'll expect you to do within the next two days."

Morgan turned back to Erik with a half-smile. Her face was heart-shaped, he noticed for the first time. Curling brown hair the color of toasted pecans. "Thanks for the ride, Officer."

"Any time." Erik found the corners of his mouth edging up for reasons he didn't really want to examine. "Sorry about all the excitement."

"I'm not." The half-smile turned full, and he got a hint of what her face must look like when she wasn't exhausted. "It's the first time I've been all-the-way awake for two days."

"Come on, Morgan. We've got stuff to do." Avrogado's voice was impatient. Morgan's smile faded as she followed him out the door to the parking lot.

Nando sighed. "Okay, I'll flip you for who gets to spend the night here with the drunk. At least one of us won't have to go to the council meeting tomorrow."

Erik closed his eyes. Ham Linklatter. The Hand of Doom. He'd been able to forget about it for the past hour, courtesy of Morgan Barrett, who'd be staying around Konigsburg no matter who the next chief of police was.

Yet another reason to be pissed at fate.

Chapter Two

Mayor Hilton Pittman climbed the stairs to the Konigsburg city council chambers, keeping his most benign smile firmly in place. It wouldn't do to let the council know just how triumphant he really felt. He was on the verge of taking care of the town's police problems, without getting dragged down with them back when the problems went nuclear. He'd had a feeling Olema was going to be trouble when the city council hired him, but he'd let them go ahead with it. Spectacular failures could be useful, as long as they weren't his.

They'd listen to him now. And he'd make sure things worked out correctly this time.

Brinkman trailed along behind him, carrying his briefcase like a good assistant so that Hilton would have his hands free to greet any potential voter who might be hanging around the chambers. Not that many people would be hanging around today since the council was in closed session considering the applicants for chief of police. Nonetheless, as Hilton arrived at the top of the stairs, he wasn't completely surprised to see the entire Konigsburg police force seated in a row of chairs outside the door to the chamber. Since the entire force consisted of four men, one full-time and the others part-time, they didn't constitute much of a crowd. Pittman frowned slightly, wondering who was taking care of things in town while the men were sitting there. Probably the dispatcher, Helen Kretschmer.

Just as well Helen hadn't come along. One look from her gave Hilton instant indigestion.

Hilton nodded at Ham Linklatter, the next chief of police, his smile warming. Linklatter wore a stiffly pressed khaki uniform, resting a new white Stetson on his knee. The bright pink flesh of his face always seemed too thin, showing the shape of the skull underneath. His pale blond hair was damp, probably from his morning shower, and he wore it plastered across the bald spot that was developing in the middle. He was smiling broadly, revealing squarish white teeth that made him look even more like a walking skeleton. Linklatter was not a prepossessing specimen.

Plus, of course, he was a moron.

On the other hand, he took orders well. And he knew all about sharing. Those were Hilton's two main requirements for a chief of police, and Ham fulfilled both of them one hundred percent.

Hilton glanced down the row at the other cops. Curtis Peavey had placed his hat under his chair and sat with his eyes closed, his head drooping. Peavey usually worked nights so he could help his son-in-law with his peach orchard during the day—Hilton figured he wasn't used to being in uniform when the sun was shining. He'd probably stick around after Ham took over because he was only a couple of years from retirement, although god only knew what his retirement pay would be like, given the miniscule salary the part-timers pulled down.

Next to Peavey, Nando Avrogado leaned back in his chair, studying the hall through half-closed eyes. He glanced at Hilton without much interest. His beefy arms were folded across his chest, his long legs stretched out in front of him. Hilton had once seen Avrogado bring down a rampaging drunk with a single punch. He was a good enough cop, but a potential troublemaker, given that, unlike Linklatter, he actually knew what he was doing. But he had family in town since his father was part owner of one of the wineries, and he'd probably want to stick around even with Linklatter as chief. Chances were he'd bite the bullet and take orders from Ham.

Which was more than Hilton could say for Erik Toleffson, the last man in the row. Toleffson was a wild card as far as Hilton could tell. If Avrogado could bring down a drunk with a single punch, Toleffson could do it with a single piercing stare. And he had the singular effect of making Nando Avrogado look average-sized. All the Toleffsons were huge, but Officer Erik Toleffson was the biggest. He seemed to cast a shadow over Hilton every time they'd spoken, which was as infrequently as Hilton could manage. No matter how hard he tried, he couldn't picture Toleffson taking orders from Ham Linklatter. Which meant Toleffson would probably need to hit the road. If he didn't go of his own accord, he might have to be helped along his way.

Not that Hilton found that prospect all that troubling. Given his choice, he'd prefer that Toleffson hit the road ASAP since Toleffson was undoubtedly the smartest cop on the force. But getting him out the door might require some help, preferably from somebody more menacing than Linklatter. A problem Hilton would have to address at a later time. He pushed through the door to the chamber.

Horace Rankin, the city council president, had taken his seat at the end of the council table. He rapped his gavel against the tabletop as soon as he saw Hilton enter the room. "Okay, everybody, we're all here. Let's get settled now. We've got business to conduct."

Hilton slid his benign smile, momentarily displaced by the sight of Erik Toleffson, back into place. Showtime.

Horace pushed his wire-frame glasses up his nose, chewing reflectively on the ends of his walrus moustache as he contemplated the meeting agenda. "Since we've got some people outside waiting to hear about the chief of police decision, I'm going to suggest we change the order of items, move the reading of the minutes down to item four or so. Any objections?"

One of the council members shrugged. The other two seemed to be occupied pouring water or digging through the piles of paper in front of them.

Hilton thought about objecting. He wouldn't have minded if the cops became bored and left before they got to the chief of police item. The whole Ham Linklatter thing wasn't going to be a popular decision. Fortunately, it was a done deal no matter what the other police officers might think.

Horace plowed ahead. "Okay, then, first order of business is hiring a new chief of police. Mayor Pittman has asked for five minutes to address the council. That okay with everyone?"

Portia Grandview gave Hilton a narrow-eyed look, while Dan Albaniz rubbed his eyes. Arthur Craven stared down at his hands. Hilton smiled back benignly.

"Not hearing any objections, you have the floor, Mr. Mayor." Rankin's voice dripped sarcasm.

Hilton chose to ignore it as he stepped to the lectern at the other end of the table, collecting his notes from Brinkman on the way by. Not that he needed notes, but it looked more professional if he had them. "Dr. Rankin, members of the council." He nodded in their direction. "While the choice of a new chief of police is your decision, I'd like to give you my input on this most important personnel matter. You all know Ham Linklatter. He's a Konigsburg boy, born and bred. Moreover, he's been with the force for four years, rising from part-time to full-time status. He brings a wealth of experience to the job."

At least two of the council members looked like they'd just bitten into something sour. They were probably remembering that most of Linklatter's experience had been with a chief of police who'd been crooked as a dog's hind leg. Fortunately, Linklatter had been involved in arresting the other crooked cop who'd been the chief's assistant. The chief himself had gotten away to parts unknown. Not one of Konigsburg's finest hours.

"He's been with the force in good times and bad. And he's shown his honesty and integrity throughout those times." Probably because he wasn't smart enough to be a crook, but that was neither here nor there.

"I'm pleased and very, very proud to recommend Ham Linklatter for the position of Konigsburg Chief of Police. I hope you'll all agree he's the best man we have available." Hilton smiled at each council member in turn. No one smiled back.

Rankin pulled a large white handkerchief from his pocket and blew his nose with a loud honk. "Thank you for your input, Mr. Mayor. You can take your seat now."

Hilton managed not to lose his smile entirely, but he did it through gritted teeth. Last council election, he'd canvassed to see if he could find an opponent for Rankin, but no one had been willing to take the old coot on. Next time Hilton would have to dig a little deeper.

Rankin balled up his handkerchief and stuffed it back in his pants pocket. "As we were going through candidates for this job, it struck me we needed to hear from someone with a little more law enforcement experience than we had on the council. I asked Sheriff Friesenhahn to do an evaluation of the department for us. Go see if he's out there yet." He nodded at Brinkman, who was rearranging Hilton's notes.

Brinkman blinked at him. Normally, he only took orders from Hilton, but this appeared to be a special case. He rose to

25

his feet and started toward the door.

Hilton gritted his teeth again. Rankin was trying an end run, using Ozzie Friesenhahn to get around him and Ham Linklatter. It wouldn't work, of course, but it was an unnecessary complication. Friesenhahn was a legend in Kramer County, having been re-elected more times than any other individual in county history. He was also completely outside his influence, which made him a very dangerous man indeed.

Brinkman opened the door and the sheriff stepped into the room, one floorboard creaking ominously beneath him.

Friesenhahn weighed somewhere in the neighborhood of three hundred pounds. He moved with all the grace of a lumbering bull elephant, the seams of his dark uniform pants straining to contain the bulk at his waist. When he arrived at the table, he removed his white Stetson with its leather hatband and silver star, placing it in front of him.

"Afternoon everybody." Friesenhahn nodded around the table, rubbing a hand across his bristle of crew-cut hair.

He pulled a pair of half-glasses from his pocket. They were probably supposed to make the sheriff look as genial as somebody's grandpa. In reality, he was about as genial as a coral snake. Friesenhahn took a file from his briefcase and rested it on the lectern in front of him.

"Your boys have a chance to check the department out?" Rankin asked.

Friesenhahn nodded. "They've been keeping an eye on the place since y'all haven't had a chief of police to speak of for the last several weeks."

Hilton narrowed his eyes. He'd done his best to get the council to appoint Linklatter as soon as they fired Olema, but he couldn't manage to pin them down. Instead they'd had sheriff's deputies wandering through, potentially stirring up trouble for everybody, particularly him.

"So what's the verdict?" Rankin settled back in his chair, folding his hands across his own not-inconsiderable belly.

"You got some good men here. But both my deputies said you've only got one man who could handle the chief's job. I checked his record, and I'm inclined to agree."

Hilton licked his lips. They could still be talking about Linklatter, with any luck. After all, his record didn't look too bad, at least on paper.

"And that man is..." Rankin prompted.

"Erik Toleffson."

His jaw was clenched so tightly it hurt. This was intolerable. He needed to do a quick end run around Friesenhahn. He managed to push his lips into the semblance of a benign smile again as he leaned forward. "Sheriff, I'm sure we all appreciate your expertise and the time you've taken to evaluate our situation. But you've been misinformed. Ham Linklatter is the most experienced applicant."

He took a quick check of the council members. He'd talked to all of them, and except for Rankin, they'd all been on board with Linklatter before the meeting. Not happy maybe, but on board.

Friesenhahn shuffled his papers, peering through his half-glasses. "Linklatter's got more time with the Konigsburg cops, but Toleffson's got three years with the MPs, plus another three in Iowa. And he's got a degree in Criminal Justice. As I recall—" he shuffled the papers again, "—Linklatter doesn't have any college hours."

Hilton's jaw ached. Of course, Linklatter didn't have any college hours. He'd been lucky to make it through high school from what Hilton could remember. "Sometimes life experience is more important than school, Sheriff."

"Yeah, and sometimes it ain't." Friesenhahn fixed him with a piercing blue gaze. His eyes were the color of glacial ice and just about as warm. "Compare Linklatter's time on the street in Konigsburg with Toleffson's time on the street in Baghdad. You want to argue that, Pittman?"

He could feel his own face flushing. Time to play his trump card. "Whatever Toleffson's experience may be, he's only a part-time officer. Ham Linklatter has been full-time for two years. You can't just leapfrog over seniority that way, Sheriff. Sets a bad precedent."

"Yeah, well, your whole personnel policy with this police department stinks to high heaven, Pittman. Town the size of Konigsburg can't get by with a part-time force. I don't know why Toleffson was willing to come on as a part-timer. I hear he's got family around here or something, but anywhere else he'd have been hired as full-time straight out. Hell, right now you could hire all three of your part-timers on as full time and still need more part-timers."

Hilton didn't bother smiling anymore—clearly, it was wasted on Friesenhahn. "Maybe the county has unlimited funds for personnel, Sheriff, but Konigsburg has to live within its means. We have the best police force we can afford."

"Pittman, this town's a disaster waiting to happen. You can pay for police salaries now or you can pay off the lawsuits later." Friesenhahn turned back to the council table. "Y'all got any questions?"

"You're saying that Ham Linklatter's not qualified?" Portia Grandview's voice was cool.

Hilton perked up. Grandview wasn't a sure thing. He knew she didn't like him, but he figured she didn't like Friesenhahn any better.

The sheriff shrugged. "He's qualified for what he's doing now. Good man on traffic. You don't want to promote him above what he can do, though."

"Anybody else have any questions?" Rankin glanced around the table, weighing the silence. Nobody moved. Rankin nodded at Friesenhahn. "Thanks, Ozzie."

Friesenhahn replaced his white Stetson on his head. "Any time."

He listened to the sound of the sheriff's heavy footsteps heading back toward the door and tried to think of a last-minute strategy. Was Friesenhahn enough to turn the tide against Linklatter? Could he come up with a quick "Come to Hilton" speech that would bring them back on board?

He glanced at Rankin. "Mr. Chairman, I wonder if I might…"

Rankin stared back, unsmiling. "You had your say already, Mayor, now it's time for our discussion. We'll have to ask you to leave."

Hilton narrowed his eyes. "I understood that I'd be allowed to remain in chambers for the vote."

Rankin gave him a bland smile. "Nope. Sorry. Rules are clear. Council members only for personnel decisions unless there's been a request for an open meeting."

Hilton's jaw ached again. He should have had Brinkman check the rules more closely. If he demanded time to look at them now, everybody would be pissed at him for holding things up. He managed to push his lips into one more supremely insincere smile. "All right, then. I'll trust to the wisdom of your deliberations."

Actually, of course, he didn't trust their wisdom at all. Somehow, although Rankin and Friesenhahn had gotten into bed together, it was Hilton who'd gotten screwed.

Morgan arranged one last load of glasses in the tasting room dishwasher. Summer was a busy season, with tourists showing up for three-day vacations and antique runs. She'd been pouring wine since eleven in the morning, giving her spiel and smiling until her cheeks were numb. At least half of the people said they weren't wine drinkers and only wanted tastes of Bluebonnet Sue, Cedar Creek's dessert wine. Morgan had tried to push a little Muscat Canelli, too, but for a lot of the drinkers even Muscat was too dry.

She sighed. They'd sold a lot of Bluebonnet, but that wouldn't make Ciro happy. Of course, not much made Ciro happy where she was concerned. Right now he was checking the receipts.

"Nobody bought any Malbec." Ciro raised an eyebrow. "You give them any tastes?"

Morgan shrugged. "I tried, but a lot of them won't drink red wine unless it's sweet. They think the Malbec's too heavy."

Ciro grimaced. "It's not heavy. The balance is great. Cliff and I worked on that sucker for a year to get the balance right."

"You know it and I know it. But we're still drawing a lot of new wine drinkers, Ciro. They're afraid of dry reds." She pushed a few more glasses onto the shelf, trying to sound nonchalant. "You know, we could probably sell more dessert wines—reach a few more customers. Maybe we should try a port."

Ciro narrowed his eyes. "I'm not wasting any of our grapes on port wine."

"We could always buy some juice from California and use that."

"Bite your tongue," Ciro snapped. "We're a Texas winery. We use Texas grapes. Period."

"Other people are buying from California, even from Australia and South America. There's a grape glut. Maybe we could put out a line of cheaper stuff—Castleberry has a whole house-wine line based on California juice."

Ciro threw the receipts back into the drawer. "Did you hear what I just said? We're not Castleberry, goddamn it. We're a premium winery, Morgan. Don't you understand what that means? And don't even mention that to your daddy. You'll give him a relapse."

Morgan wasn't sure how you could get a relapse with a broken leg, but she knew her father would probably agree with Ciro. And she needed to do more research before she talked to Dad about it. "Don't worry—I won't say anything. I'll finish closing up. You can go on to dinner."

Ciro folded his arms across his chest. "Carmen says you should come over and get a meal. She'll have the food on the table in fifteen minutes."

"Thank her for me." Morgan fitted the last glass onto the shelf. "I've got some stuff I have to do in town. I'll grab dinner there." The last thing she wanted to do was spend dinner hearing a catalog of all the mistakes she'd made over the past week, in stereo.

"You going back to the Dew Drop?" Ciro's voice simmered with disapproval.

You are not *my father, damn it.* "I'm meeting with Allie Maldonado about the volunteers' luncheon. I don't know where we'll end up." She held his gaze for a long moment, willing herself not to blink.

Ciro looked away first. "Yeah, well, make sure you get a meal someplace. You got a lot of work ahead of you tomorrow. Can't have you getting sick." He turned and walked out of the tasting room, heading toward his sprawling ranch-style house on the far side of the west vineyard.

Morgan blew out a breath she hadn't realized she was holding. At least she'd been spared an evening being picked apart by both Ciro and Carmen. She might even go into town and see Allie—she actually did have some details of the volunteers' luncheon to work out.

And maybe Officer Grouch would be around to glare at her, although she couldn't think why she needed somebody else to disapprove of her choices.

Of course, he hadn't actually glared last time. And he had been the first one to understand the whole "Bored Ducks" thing. And he'd been really...competent when he'd been taking care of the drunken driver.

In fact, there'd been something sort of sexy about that. About the commanding way he'd dealt with a troublemaker. Morgan didn't really need protecting, but if she ever did, Erik Toleffson looked like the right man for the job.

She wondered how competent he was in other areas.

Okay, enough. Clearly, she'd been celibate for far too long. Unfortunately, it didn't look like she was going to be changing that situation anytime soon.

Certainly not with Officer Grouch.

Erik sat in his booth at the Dew Drop, waiting for his brothers and staring at the bar. For one of the few times since he'd quit drinking, he felt like jumping off the wagon. Hiding in a bottle had a certain attraction right now.

Chief of police. Of Konigsburg, Texas.

Acting chief of police, actually. Rankin and the other council members had made it clear—he was on probation for now. But if he didn't screw up, after a couple of months he'd have the job for real.

The question was, did he want the job for real?

He'd be the first to admit he hadn't been thinking of actually being hired as chief when he'd submitted his application. It was just a last-minute attempt to keep Linklatter from taking over—he and Nando had both applied, and he found out later that Peavey had too. Hell, Helen Kretschmer might have put in her own application. He and Nando had figured the more applications the council had to go through, the more they could slow down the process, maybe get enough time for somebody from outside Konigsburg to apply. But Hilton Pittman had tried his best to move things along at light speed.

They'd all known what would happen if Linklatter took over, but they'd also known they had almost no chance in hell of stopping him, short of some kind of miracle.

But now here he was, chief of police. He'd be in charge of the whole damn department, people would be depending on him. He tried to think of a time when he'd been in charge of anything anywhere, but he came up dry. He was everybody's favorite second in command, somebody who could work on his own and get the job done, then come back for another assignment. The idea of keeping track of other people and

31

making his own assignments so they could get jobs done for him made his stomach contract into a knot.

Ham hadn't taken it well. When Rankin had opened the door to the council chamber, Ham had clearly expected to be invited inside. Instead, Rankin had nodded in Erik's direction. "Come on in, Toleffson, we got some things to discuss."

The last thing Erik had seen as he turned toward the door had been Ham's rigid face, the crown of his new Stetson crumpled in his fist.

Pete slid into the booth across from him. "Is it true?"

Erik thought about asking him what he meant but decided not to be an asshole. He nodded. "Yeah."

Pete smiled a little cautiously. Of Erik's three brothers, he was the only one who still seemed to see through him to the full-on bully he'd once been. Possibly because Pete was the one who'd ended up on the wrong end of his big brother's fists more often than Lars or Cal. "Good deal."

"Don't start celebrating yet," Erik said drily. "I'm only acting chief for now. There's a two-month probation."

Someone pounded on his shoulder and he looked up to see Cal grinning down at him. "Way to go, Bro. Horace told me when he got back to the clinic. Sounds like Friesenhahn came down on your side all the way."

Erik shook his head, sliding out of the booth to let Cal in. "I don't know why he would. I've never talked to Friesenhahn. I just know him by sight."

"Considering the competition, that may have been enough," Pete muttered.

Lars arrived and gave Pete an absent-minded shove to move him to the inside of the booth before he sat. "Erik, I just heard the damndest thing."

"If you heard that I'm the new chief of police, it's true. If you heard something else, I probably don't know anything about it."

Lars broke into an exact copy of Cal's grin. "Okay! Way to go, Bro."

"Why isn't this man smiling?" Cal said after a moment.

Erik pinched the bridge of his nose. "Because I'm still in shock. I just applied for the chief's job to try to head Linklatter off. I never thought they'd actually give it to me."

Cal frowned. "But you're qualified. Horace said you had three years with the MPs. In Baghdad."

"It wasn't all in Baghdad." Erik shrugged. "Mostly Kuwait."

All three of his brothers were watching him. "You were in the army? In Iraq?" Lars said. "I never knew that."

Erik stared down at his hands. He desperately wanted this conversation to end. Talking about the past with his brothers was about as much fun as patrolling Fallujah. Most of their childhood memories were better left alone. "I didn't tell anybody at the time."

"Not even Mom and Dad?"

"I wrote them about it after I got over there. I didn't want them to worry." Which was a crock and a half, but maybe they'd let him get by with it.

"And you were a cop in Iowa?" Cal raised a questioning eyebrow. "I thought you worked for a private security company."

"I did. Until I finished my degree in Criminal Justice. Then I worked for the Davenport police." Erik wondered what Rankin had thought when he'd discovered Cal didn't know anything about his older brother's life. On the other hand, Rankin might know a bit about Cal's life, which would explain why his little brother knew nothing about Erik, largely by choice.

Pete was the first one to look away. "I'll be damned."

"I hope not." Erik signaled at the barmaid. "I'll get this."

"Like hell." Lars slapped his wallet on the table. "You don't pay for your own celebration around here."

The next two hours were taken up with people Erik knew only slightly slapping him on the shoulder and shaking his hand. He began to get the feeling that nobody in town had wanted Ham Linklatter to take over, with the exception of Hilton Pittman.

Several people wanted to buy him a beer, and he passed them on to his brothers. Some seemed vaguely annoyed that he didn't drink, but others gave him an approving nod, as if a non-drinking chief of police were a plus. Erik felt like telling them it wasn't much of a moral decision, given that nobody wanted to spend time with Mr. Hyde, least of all him.

After an hour or so, Lars and Cal staggered off to their wives and children. A few minutes later, Pete's wife, Janie, showed up to drag him home, but stayed to toast Erik.

"I knew the good guys would win," she said, grinning. "I knew they'd pick you."

Erik shook his head. "You knew more than I did, then. I'm still getting used to the idea." He thought about questioning her definition of "good guys" but didn't. He liked his sisters-in-law—they were one of the chief reasons he envied his brothers. And they seemed to like him back. Of course, the fact that he'd flattened one of Janie's ex-boyfriends who'd tried to take a few liberties with her had helped shape her opinion of him.

"Everybody seems really happy about it."

"I'm sure Pittman would have a few things to say about that."

Janie frowned, staring at the doorway. "We may be about to find out."

Erik turned to follow her gaze. Hilton Pittman was making an entrance, dressed to impress. He wore a dark suit that probably cost a lot, although Erik would guess it didn't cost too much since Hilton wouldn't want people to think he had any extra cash to spend on clothes. His hair looked a little like some new kind of plastic, perfectly groomed and unlikely to move, just the right shade of brown flecked with gray. His smile snapped into place automatically, as his right hand shot out to grip the hand of the nearest man at the bar. The astonished drinker put down his beer and started to say something, but Hilton had already moved on, pumping the next hand, grinning firmly.

"Look at him work that crowd." Pete shook his head. "A real pro."

"Yeah, but a pro what?" Janie took a sip of her beer. "I wish somebody would run against that man sometime."

"Why doesn't anybody do that?" Erik picked up one of several Dr. Peppers in front of him.

"Because nobody else wants to be mayor. It's a lot of work and the salary is ridiculous. Hilton has pretty much gotten it by default for the past five years."

Erik studied Pittman as he worked his way around the bar. For somebody who wasn't making much salary, he looked pretty well kept. Erik glanced at Pete, the Assistant County Attorney.

His lips were set in a grim line. "Whatever he's doing, he's good enough at it that he hasn't popped up on anybody's radar.

Yet. Supposedly he's still running his car dealership."

Pittman was rounding the corner of the bar, heading roughly in their direction. Erik tried to remember if he'd ever seen him in the Dew Drop before. He didn't think so, but then he hadn't spent as much time in the Dew Drop as his brothers had.

Pittman came to a stop beside their table, his smile glowing in the dimness of the bar. "Toleffson, I guess I'm not the first to congratulate you today."

"No sir, but thanks anyway." Erik shook the mayor's hand, watching his eyes. Maybe he could pick up some pointers on talking to people he'd rather fillet.

"Quite a step up—from part-time officer to chief."

"Yes sir."

"Here's hoping it works out for you. Not everyone could handle that much responsibility." Pittman was still beaming, but his eyes had turned to smoldering cinders.

From the corner of his eye, Erik saw Janie stiffen. He leaned forward quickly. "I intend to give it my best shot, Mr. Mayor."

"I'm sure you will. I just hope that'll be enough." Pittman nodded at the table, his smile flattening slightly. "Good night, y'all."

"Fuckin' asshole," Pete muttered, watching the mayor work his way back to the door.

"Always has been. Don't take it seriously." Janie pushed her beer away, turning to Erik. "Come to Brenner's with us. We'll buy you dinner to celebrate."

"Thanks anyway. I think I'd better head home. I've got work tomorrow."

Janie frowned. "They're not making you start now, are they?"

"Sure." Erik managed a grim smile. "They haven't had a real chief of police since March, when Olema finally gave up on his appeals and hit the road."

Pete shook his head. "Holy crap. You don't even get a day off?"

Erik pushed himself to his feet. "There are no days off in my business. Thanks for the support. See y'all later."

As he shambled toward the door, he was aware of several

dozen pairs of eyes boring into his back. He had a feeling that would be par for the course, at least for the foreseeable future.

Chapter Three

After two days of tasting room duty, Morgan was supremely grateful when she turned the place over to Kit Maldonado. Kit was Allie's niece, taking time out from her studies at UTSA. Morgan felt a little guilty about hiring her away from Allie's bakery, but both Allie and Kit assured her it was okay, and Kit handled her duties at the winery like a pro. Of course, her main duties were smiling, pouring and talking, but she was a whiz at all three, plus she was drop-dead gorgeous, with straight black hair and eyes like obsidian. At least the number of male visitors coming to the tasting room should pick up.

If only she looked a little older. Just glancing at her, Morgan would have pegged her age at maybe eighteen. She had a feeling Kit would need to keep her ID on hand in case a wandering Texas Alcohol and Beverage Commission agent should happen through.

"You may be able to taste hints of grapefruit in this viognier," Kit cooed to a couple of tourists sitting at the tasting room counter as Morgan walked through.

Morgan herself tasted nothing but grapes in the viognier, but it wasn't really lying to say otherwise. People tasted what they wanted to taste. Or sometimes what they'd been told to taste.

Outside on the covered patio, a group of enthusiastic, sweaty volunteer pickers drank bottled water to cool off. Cooling off was necessary—by ten, it was at least eighty-five degrees in the shade.

A new group of pickers stood underneath the live oaks, rubbing on sunblock and adjusting their hats before they headed for the vineyard. Morgan gave everyone garden snips and led the way to the nearest group of vines. She ran through her spiel about how grateful the winery was for their help and then showed them how to clip the grape clusters off the vines.

Ciro was there too, of course, directing the professional vineyard crew as they picked up the crates of grapes the volunteers had filled and dumped them into a container to be carried to the destemmer. He gave the volunteers a narrow-eyed glare, but at least he didn't tell this group to stay the hell out of the way, as he had with the first group in the morning.

Morgan took a deep breath and tried to relax her shoulders. The volunteer pickers were her idea, yet another reason for Ciro to complain about her performance.

She breezed back through the almost-cleared vines, smiling at the pickers and the perpetually scowling Ciro. Then she headed back to the winery building, where she escorted some of the volunteers out to watch the destemmer and the crusher while Kit poured malbec and chardonnay for the others and babbled on about tannins and balance and berry overtones as if she really knew what she was talking about. Maybe she did.

At eleven, Allie showed up with the catering truck. "Having fun? Did they actually pick anything?" She cocked an eyebrow at the milling groups of pickers, now mostly gathered in the shade around the patio.

"They pretty much did it all, actually. Ciro and the pros will go through and get any clusters they missed, but we got all the sauvignon blanc done."

"Better you than me, kid—the temperature's up in the nineties." Allie grabbed a bottle of water from the cooler on the patio, then started unloading the catering truck with some help from the winery crew and Ciro's son, Esteban.

Morgan ambled back to the cement slab outside the holding-tank room. The grapes tumbled through the augur on the destemmer, fruit separating from stems and leaves, then passed into the crusher. Some beaming volunteers watched the machines. Most of them had already had at least one glass of wine, and they were perfectly happy to watch the grapes they'd picked being turned into juice.

She watched the bellows move in and out on the crusher. Not exactly thrilling. When she'd first visited her father at the winery as a kid, she'd expected a big vat of grapes with Lucy and Ethel stomping around in their scarves and peasant blouses. The real thing was a lot less romantic.

Allie corralled her a few minutes later to help set up tables on the covered patio that had a view of the Cynthiana vineyard and the hills beyond. Morgan poured water and wine and reminded herself that she wasn't really being a waitress, praise be, since she was more or less running the show.

Once the volunteers had taken their seats around the tables, she went into marketing mode again. She helped serve. She wandered from table to table to talk to the volunteers. She gave a toast after the meal was over to thank everyone for coming, making them feel like guests instead of volunteer pickers who took home a free bottle of wine as payment.

Finally, as the volunteers wandered out, some stopping in the tasting room to pick up a few more bottles to take with them, Allie pushed Morgan into a chair and handed her a plate with a sandwich and a scoop of fruit salad. If she hadn't, Morgan would probably have forgotten to have any lunch at all, as she had for the last two days.

She shook hands and said goodbye to the last of the pickers, then allowed herself to settle back into one of the easy chairs in the office. She wondered if they'd made any money from extra sales today. They could use it. It cost a heap to run a good winery. And Cedar Creek was good. Everybody who entered the tasting room could see that, just based on the medals hanging from wine bottles on the trophy shelf.

If they could just increase their sales a little, maybe they could expand beyond Texas and then bring in more people to help run the daily operations. She bet Dr. Castleberry didn't manage his own winery, judging from the pictures she'd seen of him at society events in Dallas. Castleberry probably had a whole raft of people to make sure the tasting room did okay and that the on-site sales were brisk. Instead, Cedar Creek had Morgan, who not only did that but all the other day-to-day scut work too. And didn't do it nearly well enough to suit Ciro and Carmen.

Morgan sighed. *Right. Guts up, kid.* They'd have to sell a whole lot of wine before Dad and Ciro considered expanding their sales or bringing in anybody other than family to manage the daily operation of the winery.

Gee, being an independent businesswoman was fun.

Erik came back to the office from his morning patrol a little after one. He stood at the front sorting through the mail that the dispatcher had left for him. So far his first week in charge hadn't been that bad.

A little weird, maybe, but not bad.

Every once in a while, Ham Linklatter shot him a poisonous look from his desk at the front of the room. He didn't bother Erik much, although he did provide occasional entertainment.

Linklatter was the dumbest human being he'd ever met, and that included the bank robber who'd written a note to the teller on a deposit slip that included his name and address. Linklatter brought new meaning to the word "dumb".

And the dumbest thing Linklatter was currently doing was trying to sabotage Erik. He hadn't yet stooped to leaving thumbtacks on his chair, but Erik figured it was only a matter of time. After five days with Erik as chief of police, Ham's creativity was beginning to run low.

So far Linklatter's sabotage was more irritating than dangerous. It had actually started a couple of weeks ago when Ham had lost the key to the police cruiser and then pretended Erik had misplaced it. Unfortunately, he'd mentioned the fact that he'd lost it in front of Nando, who publicly reminded him. Now Erik kept the extra keys at the front desk where Ham couldn't get at them without permission.

Earlier this week, Linklatter had hidden the extra paper for the printer and told the dispatcher Erik had forgotten to order any. The dispatcher, Helen Kretschmer—one of the scariest women Erik had ever met—gave Linklatter five minutes to produce the paper before she skinned him. Linklatter had complied.

Since then, he'd confined himself to muttering behind Erik's back, although not so far behind that Erik couldn't hear him. Now Linklatter sat at his desk at the front of the station, writing up a traffic report and scowling.

Erik sighed. Amusing though it was to watch Linklatter trying to plot, somebody needed to be out on the street.

"Linklatter," he called, "aren't you supposed to be on patrol?"

Linklatter gave him another scowl. "Soon as I finish this report. And check out the keys to the cruiser. Be a lot easier if they were someplace where I could just pick 'em up on my way out."

Behind the counter, Helen Kretschmer snorted.

Erik sighed again and walked back to his office.

Olema had done at least one thing right in his time as chief—he'd fixed up the chief's office. The station house had been built in the sixties, and not much had been done to it since, beyond adding air-conditioning and a couple of computers. But the chief's office took up half the width of the building, and the desk looked like it belonged in a corporate headquarters somewhere.

Of course, given the former chief's level of competence, that corporation might be Enron.

Olema had cleaned out his desk before he'd gone, and neither of the sheriff's deputies who'd filled in had brought anything with them, so Erik had lots of space for his two legal pads and three ballpoints.

He rummaged through his desk drawer, looking for the spare set of keys he'd had made up for the cruiser, until he heard a loud male voice from the front.

"Well, then, who can I talk to?"

Helen's voice rumbled in the background as Erik walked out to her desk. She wasn't loud, but then she didn't need to be. Most people dove for cover whenever she turned her gimlet gaze their way. This guy, whoever he was, seemed more intrepid than most.

"Goddamn it, Helen," he bellowed, "I ain't talking to Linklatter. I need somebody who can actually do something."

Erik sped up slightly, rounding the corner in time to see Helen narrowing her eyes, probably preparing to turn whoever it was into stone. "What seems to be the problem, Helen?"

The man who stood in front of Helen's desk was smaller than his voice. He wore jeans and a faded work shirt. His buff-colored Stetson sat on the counter in front of the desk.

Helen stood with her sturdy arms folded across the breadth of her chest. She wasn't a tall woman—Erik figured maybe five foot four—but she was built like a fireplug, and every inch was muscle. Although he'd never seen her in anything but long sleeves, he was willing to bet she had a skull tattooed on her bicep. Her short, graying red hair frizzed around her head in the kind of permanent his granny used to wear. Her eyes were gunmetal gray, and he'd seen one look freeze a shouting drunk in his tracks. Give her a Glock and she'd be unstoppable.

"Mr. Powell here has a problem," Helen said, her voice shimmering with disdain. "I don't know what, except that he doesn't know how to use a normal tone of voice or how to talk to a lady."

Erik figured the lady in question was Helen, no matter how unlikely that seemed. "What can we do for you, Mr. Powell?"

"You can find out who's poisoning my stock, that's what you can do, goddamn it!" Powell folded his arms across his chest, like a mirror image of Helen, despite the fact that she had fifty pounds on him.

Erik sighed. "Come on into my office and tell me about it." He heard Linklatter sniff as he headed back up the hall.

It took a few minutes to calm down Powell enough to get to the point, but Erik figured that was par for the course with Powell, who struck him as a man who needed to talk himself out before he got to the point.

"So far I've lost a couple of kids," Powell grumbled. "And the mother's pretty sick too."

Erik blinked. "You've got a lost child?"

Powell snorted. "No, goddamn it! Kids. Goats. Two of my goats died after they drank the water in my stock tank, and another one's sick. Somebody poisoned my tank!"

Goats. Right. Konigsburg, where there were more goats than people. Erik put down his pen. "Maybe the water went bad."

"No, sir! No, it did not." Powell shook his head vigorously. "The water was just fine two days ago, and then this morning I found those goats. Got Dr. Toleffson out there looking after the nanny now." He squinted at Erik suddenly, as if he'd just made the Toleffson connection.

Erik wrote himself a quick note. *Goats. Sick. Cal.* "Did you call the TCEQ?"

"What the hell is TCEQ? No, sir, I called you. This here's a crime, goddamn it!" Powell pursed his lips. He looked like he had a bad case of heartburn.

"TCEQ is the Texas Commission on Environmental Quality. They'll test your water to see what's wrong. They can tell us whether it's a natural problem or not." Erik flipped through the Rolodex on the desk, looking for the TCEQ card.

"Does that mean you're not gonna come out and have a look-see?" Powell's heartburn appeared to have gotten worse.

Erik took a deep breath. The town had every reason to distrust its own police department. One former chief had been a gold-plated crook and the other had been a blockhead. Part of his job was to try to repair that damage.

And if he wanted to hold on to the job for real, he needed to get Konigsburg straightened out and running right.

He nodded. "I'll come take a look later this afternoon."

Morgan sat on the patio, shaded from the late-afternoon sun, and tried to stay awake. She'd been up since four in the morning, getting ready to meet the volunteers, then running the harvest, giving winery tours, serving lunch, and finally, thank god, selling the pickers a whole bunch of wine.

Using volunteers to pick the grapes during small-crop years wasn't all that efficient, but it did have its compensations. Mainly, it was cheap. Ciro might snarl about it, but he'd let her go ahead, after she'd explained that other wineries were doing it successfully.

Suck it up, Morg. Great marketing, and you know it. Now if she could only convince her father that doing some actual planned marketing was as important as watching the destemmer. And that she could do both.

Across the patio, the winery dogs, Skeeter and Fred, looked longingly at the door to the tasting room. They were hot, poor babies, and tired and they wanted to go inside.

But Arthur, as usual, was draped across the step, blocking the pet door.

One of Skeeter's parents had had at least a nodding acquaintance with a Great Dane. Fred was mostly terrier, although god only knew what kind. They'd been running around the vineyard all day, chasing lizards and having a wonderful time conning the volunteers out of snacks.

Arthur hadn't done anything but sleep, not that he ever did much during the daytime anyway. He was too smart to work during the heat, particularly when night was his preferred hunting time. Now he was enjoying himself, keeping Skeeter and Fred away from the door and the air-conditioning.

"Arthur, cut it out," Morgan called.

Arthur raised his head to gaze at her through slitted eyes. Tufts of fur prickled at the points of his golden ears. He stretched his paws out in front of him, yawning widely.

Morgan sighed and walked over to the door. "Come on. Move it."

Arthur pulled his paws underneath him languidly and stood. Morgan was virtually certain he had no cougar or bobcat in his background, just a bit of Maine coon cat, but sometimes when he stretched she had her doubts.

As soon as Arthur moved, the dogs trotted swiftly across the tile. Arthur squinted at them but stepped aside as Morgan opened the door.

Inside, she could hear Kit extolling the virtues of the malbec to a bunch of tourists from Tyler. Morgan groaned inwardly. She'd had almost as much congeniality as she could stand for one day. Maybe she could slip by without being noticed.

"You may be able to taste hints of blackberries," Kit trilled. "I can taste cranberries, too. This wine would be great at Thanksgiving."

Nice one. Cranberries were new. Morgan backed out of the tasting room quickly before she could be roped into pouring.

Once upon a time, she'd had scheduled appointments. Once upon a time, her work day had started at eight thirty and ended at five thirty. Once upon a time, she'd averaged more than six hours of sleep a night.

Ah, memories, memories.

She ran a mental checklist of the things she needed to do for Ciro and for herself before she could legitimately call it a day. She had some paperwork to get ready for the Wine and Food Festival. She needed to call ATF about Bored Ducks and probably spend a merry couple of hours on hold. She had to check in with Dad, who undoubtedly wanted all the details about the day's sauvignon blanc crush.

And she needed to go look at a potential vineyard. All of a sudden getting away from Cedar Creek for an hour looked better than any of the other chores she had to do. Morgan grabbed her purse and headed for her SUV.

Ciro had already scouted this particular property. Good drainage and soil depth. Not too alkaline. Currently being used as a goat pasture. Ciro knew vineyards. His own two already produced some of Cedar Creek's best sangiovese grapes. According to what he'd said, the lease rate didn't sound too high, considering where the land was. Best of all, it was fairly close to Cedar Creek as the crow flew.

Dad wanted her to look at it, although Morgan suspected she wouldn't be able to tell him anything Ciro couldn't. But he'd want her play-by-play on the starry-eyed assumption that she'd get to know what she was doing—and that she'd like it when she did.

After she finished checking the vineyard out, it would be close to six and she could drive to the Dew Drop to see Pete and Allie and Cal and Wonder.

And Chief Toleffson. Not that she would make the trip on his account or anything.

Morgan flipped open her state atlas as she bounced down Blumberg Road. Ciro had told her to turn right at Cuevas and then left at an unmarked farm road with a goat crossing. Morgan felt the SUV switch into four-wheel as she started up the hill.

Twenty bone-jolting minutes later, she parked beside a mesquite tree, pulled on the emergency brake and climbed out. The hillside looked steep, but not too steep for planting. Tufts of cedar and brush led to a distant stand of live oaks at the crest. Getting trucks in here for harvest would be a bitch. She wondered if they could talk the owner into grading the road for them.

She walked along the ridge, looking down at her feet. Lots of limestone. But Ciro had seen the soil analysis and said the alkalinity was within the upward limits. Morgan knelt and picked up a handful of dirt, crumbling the clods in her fingers, then poked a finger deeper to dig below the topsoil. Good red dirt stretched down toward subsoil depth.

She turned to look back up the hill and stopped. A dual tire track ran through the dirt above her. It looked heavier than a pickup.

She frowned slightly, squinting against the late-afternoon sunshine. Ciro had said the land wasn't used for much besides grazing goats, but it looked like a truck had been driving around up there. Could somebody else be checking out the property?

She dusted her hands against her thighs and began to

work her way farther across the ridge, studying the tracks. They looked fresh. Morgan bit her lip. Maybe somebody else was interested in the lease.

Please, god, don't let it be Noah Castleberry! Bad enough to lose sales to that snake, let alone an entire vineyard. Dad would never let her forget it if she somehow let the lease slip through their fingers.

Morgan glanced up the hill again. Toward the top she could see a couple of goats drinking from a sinkhole. The stock tank behind them was surrounded by wire fencing for some reason, keeping them away from it. Morgan craned her neck, looking for a truck or an SUV.

She saw a quick flash of something beside a mesquite grove a few hundred yards up the slope, maybe the reflection of a window or a mirror. She started to walk toward it, then slowed. If Castleberry's people were out here, she didn't want them to notice her. Knowing that Cedar Creek was interested might be all he'd need to lease the land on the spot. She redirected her route to the side of the tank, stepping behind a mesquite clump.

The goats paid her no attention. Morgan started forward again, cautiously. Somewhere to her right she heard a boot crunch on gravel.

She started to turn toward the sound, but then someone grabbed her shoulders from behind. Rough hands shoved her toward the edge of the ridge. With a startled yell, she went flying through space.

The toe of one boot caught in a tree root, sending her rolling. She tried to grab hold of a grass tuft to slow herself down before she reached the lip of the ridge, feeling the stems slip through her fingers. Her knee hit a stone, sending a sharp jolt of pain through her leg. One cheek scraped along a length of limestone, and she yelped. Morgan dug her fingers into the ground desperately, grasping at whatever slapped against her palms. Clods of dirt, limestone, bits of mesquite. Brush and cedar scraped her arms, throwing her from side to side.

At the very edge of the ridge, her body slowed, and she tried again to stop her fall, grabbing at tufts of grass that gave way in her hand. And then she was dropping, arms windmilling, until her head connected with something very hard.

For a moment, the lights went out.

Erik put the truck into four-wheel and headed up the road toward the stock tank. He didn't know what he was supposed to do when he got there, except verify that it was, indeed, a stock tank. He had a call in to a contact at TCEQ. As soon as he found out how they wanted him to take the sample, he'd send it off to be analyzed.

At least Cal had already been planning to go to Powell's ranch to check the goats and had offered to direct him up to the tank.

"I don't suppose you've got any idea what the hell happened to those goats," he said after they'd bounced over another stretch of washboard.

"Ate or drank something nasty—that's all I can tell you." Cal grabbed hold of the panic handle over his door. "Believe it or not, the road gets worse after this."

Erik sighed. "We better pull over and hike the rest of the way. No way the city would pay to fix my suspension." He parked under some oak trees beside the goat track that passed for the road, then followed Cal along a rocky trail to the top of the hill and the stock tank.

It was large, round, and made of galvanized steel. Powell or somebody working for him had tacked a length of chicken-wire around the top to keep the goats from drinking.

Cal glanced at Erik and shrugged. "Stock tank."

"No shit." Erik sighed. Complete waste of time, as promised. He did a quick survey of the area around the tank, looking for footprints or tire tracks, but all he saw were goat hoof-prints. A rainbow sheen floated on the surface of the tank water. "Looks oily."

Cal squinted. "Yep."

"Would oil make the goats sick?"

"It wouldn't do them any good. I need to head back now. Horace is holding down the clinic by himself."

Erik waited a moment longer, so that if anything interesting were going to happen—like the Creature from the Black Lagoon rising from the stock tank—it had a chance. Then he started back the way they'd come.

Something red flashed below him on the hillside.

Erik paused, frowning. "Did you see that?"

Cal turned back, squinting down the hill.

It was probably just trash, blown there from the ranch—or maybe a cardinal. Erik stepped toward the edge of the incline and looked down.

A brunette in a red blouse lay sprawled on a ledge below them. As he watched, she began to sit up slowly.

"Aw, shit," Erik muttered and started down the hillside toward her. He could hear Cal behind him. "Get the first-aid kit," he called. "It's in the glove compartment."

When he was a couple of yards above the woman, trying hard not to send pebbles skittering her way, she turned her head slightly toward him.

His throat tightened. *Morgan Barrett.*

He slid the last few feet and dropped to his knees beside her. "Fancy meeting you here." *Keep it light.*

Morgan stared, her eyes dazed.

"Lie still." He reached to cradle her head. "Cal's coming with the first-aid kit. Where do you hurt?"

"All over," she groaned, holding out her hands. "I left most of my skin on that hillside."

"How about your head and neck—any pain there?"

She shook her head, then winced. "You mean besides the mondo headache? No. I don't think anything's broken."

He wrapped an arm around her shoulders to prop her up. She felt fragile. Hell, maybe some Blue Norther blew her off the hillside. Her eyelids started to flutter again. "Come on, Bambi, stay here with me."

Morgan's eyes flew open. "Bambi?"

He smiled tightly. "Can you move your arms and legs? Nasty scrapes on your hands. Anything sprained?"

She flexed her arms slowly as Cal slid to a stop beside them. "Morgan. Jesus! What happened?"

Erik dropped his arm to her waist, propping her up. "Help me move her."

Cal leaned down and scooped her easily into his arms. "Let's get you up to the top of the slope."

Erik felt an unreasonable shot of resentment as he watched his brother carry her away, then shook his head. *Get back in the game.* He grabbed the first-aid kit and climbed up behind them.

"Did you trip?" Cal's voice sounded amazingly calm. "The ground's pretty uneven up there."

"I guess," Morgan said slowly. "Yeah. I mean, that makes sense."

Something about her voice sent a trickle of alarm down the back of Erik's neck. He winced as her head bobbed with Cal's steps. "You're not sure? Don't you remember?"

"No. Well, maybe." She gazed at him over Cal's shoulder with troubled eyes. "I mean the whole thing's a little blurry. I'm not exactly firing on all cylinders here."

"What's blurry?" Erik kept his voice calm, fighting down the hollow feeling in his gut. He suddenly realized it was the voice he used with crime victims. "What do you think happened?"

Her eyes widened. "I think somebody pushed me."

Chapter Four

Cal drove Morgan's SUV back to Cedar Creek while Erik brought Morgan herself in his truck. Morgan argued that she was perfectly able to drive, but both he and Cal had ignored her.

Erik couldn't decide what to ask her about being pushed down the hill. It was possible that she was suffering from the aftereffects of a concussion. On the other hand, she could be telling the truth. For some reason, he was inclined to believe her. Still, he figured he'd have more time to ask her questions later on, after a doctor certified that she wasn't hallucinating.

Cal said he'd call a doctor when he got back in cell range. At least he knew the name of one—Erik didn't have a clue.

He kept an eye on her to make sure she didn't pass out as he drove back down the road from the goat pasture. After a few minutes, Morgan turned back to look at him rather than watching the hillside roll by. "I'm okay, really. Shaken up and bruised and scraped. No broken bones. No concussion. Just a headache. Otherwise okay."

He steered around a particularly vicious pothole. "Concussions are tricky. Best to see a doctor before you decide you're okay. In fact, why don't I take you on to the ER at the county hospital right now?"

"Just take me back to Cedar Creek, Chief. I don't want to make a big thing out of this. If Doctor Fleisher is in the neighborhood, he can swing by."

She leaned her head back against the seat, closing her eyes. He really hoped she wouldn't start to fall asleep because then he'd have to yell to wake her up, and she didn't look like she'd enjoy being yelled at. "Could it have been a goat?" he asked.

She didn't open her eyes. "No. I thought of that. A couple of goats were drinking out of a sink hole, but they weren't that close. And they weren't interested in me. Besides, it didn't feel like a goat."

He raised an eyebrow. "Feel like a goat?"

"You know—like horns."

He kept his eyes on the road as they jounced down the hillside. "So you think it was a person?"

She opened her eyes then, giving him one of those *what kind of a moron are you* looks. "Well, it wasn't a goat and it wasn't a disembodied spirit, so yeah, I think it was a person. Besides, it felt like hands on my shoulders. And before you ask, no, I haven't a clue who it was or why they pushed me."

"You see anybody out there while you were looking around?" He turned onto Cuevas, bouncing along toward the highway.

She frowned again. "I'm not sure."

"Meaning?"

"I saw some tire tracks. And I thought I saw something parked up in the trees. There was a flash from some glass. But I didn't see any people close by." She leaned back against the seat again. "I did hear a footstep just before somebody shoved me, though, and I could swear I heard a truck driving off as I was rolling down that hillside."

Erik glanced into the rearview mirror. He and Cal hadn't met anyone as they were coming in, but there could be other roads back into the brush, particularly for a four-wheel drive. The hills were full of goat trails and wagon ruts.

Beside him, Morgan's eyelids began to droop.

"Don't you go to sleep now." He made his voice sharp. "You need to stay awake."

She ignored him for a moment, then opened her eyes. "You called me Bambi."

Erik stared resolutely at the road ahead. Just his luck she'd remember that part of it.

"Back there on the hill." She squinted at him. "You called me Bambi. Why?"

"Trying to keep you awake. If you have a concussion, you shouldn't sleep." He turned onto the highway and headed toward the winery.

"But why Bambi? Why not Morgan? Or Miz Barrett? Or 'hey, you'?"

"Caught your interest, didn't it?" He shrugged. "Kept you awake." He turned in at a road next to a hanging sign with *Cedar Creek Winery* written in elaborate script, then pulled up in front of a limestone building with a silvery tin roof—traditional Texas with a few contemporary twists. A covered patio sat at the side with umbrella-topped cedar tables and chairs. Vineyards stretched out over the hills in orderly rows of grapevines.

After a moment, Erik remembered it. Cal and Docia had been married on that patio. How the hell had he forgotten that? It looked so damned picturesque he almost felt like drinking some wine himself.

A man he recognized as Ciro Avrogado came striding through the door as soon as Erik put on the parking brake. A broad, dark-haired woman in jeans and a bright pink T-shirt stood on the porch, watching.

"Oh god," Morgan moaned. "Not Carmen too."

Avrogado stopped at the side of the truck, waiting. "Cal Toleffson called and told us what happened. Why'd you bring her here? Why didn't you take her to the ER?"

"I don't need to go to the ER. I just needed to get back here and lie down," Morgan said through gritted teeth. As she opened the door, Avrogado reached in to help her. She stuck out a hand to stop him, wincing. "It's okay, I can walk."

The woman in the pink T-shirt gave Erik a narrow-eyed look. "So you're the new police chief?"

"Yes, ma'am." He started up the walk, keeping an eye on Morgan as she limped toward the porch. "Erik Toleffson."

"Carmen Avrogado. Nando's my boy." Her eyes were still narrowed.

Erik didn't know what test he was taking, but he was pretty sure he hadn't passed it yet. "Nando's a good man. We're lucky to have him."

Carmen gave him a curt nod, then turned back to Morgan. "And you, missy, what would have happened to you if the chief hadn't been there? You think about that yet? Why'd you just take off without letting anybody know where you were? You think we're psychic down here or something?"

Erik saw Morgan wince, but he didn't know if it was from Carmen or the effort of climbing the fieldstone stairs. He stepped forward and took her arm, putting it across his shoulders.

On the porch, Carmen raised her eyebrows. "Well? What did you think you were doing out there?"

"I didn't break any bones," Morgan said, lifting her foot to the first step. "I didn't pass out. The fall knocked the wind out of me. I would have gotten up and walked back up the hill in another few minutes. Everybody's making too much out of this."

Carmen snorted, shaking her head. "We're not making too much out of this. Your daddy ain't gonna be happy."

Morgan skidded to a halt, bumping her shoulder against Erik's chest. She turned back to Avrogado. "You can't tell him, Ciro, you really can't. Please!"

Avrogado rubbed the back of his neck, frowning. Erik had the feeling he was trying not to look at either of the women. "We have to tell him, Morgan. You know that."

"No." Morgan dropped her arm from Erik's shoulder. "You don't. You know what'll happen if you tell him. He'll decide he has to come back here to make sure everything's okay, and he isn't strong enough yet. The doctor said another couple of weeks at least before he can start moving around again. I don't want him to hurt himself. Please, I'm begging you."

Avrogado folded his arms across his chest, scowling. "He'll be mad as hell if he finds out."

"*When* he finds out," Carmen corrected, her lips a thin line. "You've got to tell him sometime."

Morgan turned back to her quickly. "I'll tell him. I promise. But not right now."

Erik could see her shoulders beginning to droop. Her reserves must be almost used up. One of the warm breezes that came off the vineyards could probably blow her over. He leaned down quickly and swept her up into his arms before she could object.

Morgan gave a soft "hmph" against his shoulder. Behind him he could feel eyes boring into his back again. He pushed the door with his shoulder, stepping through into what turned out to be the tasting room.

And realized suddenly he had no idea what he was supposed to do next.

"Where am I taking you?" he muttered.

Morgan nodded at a door on the other side of the room. "My apartment opens off the office, but I can walk there myself if you'll please put me down again."

"Indulge me." Erik headed for a door with a *Private* sign.

A stunning girl with long dark hair was standing behind the bar pouring wine for some tourists. All of them stared at Erik and Morgan with rapt attention. The girl glanced up and then down again quickly.

He narrowed his eyes. The pourer looked underage, but he'd deal with that later.

"She's twenty-one." Morgan smiled faintly. "But you can check. She's used to it by now. She's Allie's niece."

Erik opened the door and stepped into an office with a desk and computer. Another door opened in front of him. He nudged it with his shoulder and walked into a snug, warm room. Plastered walls, a small limestone fireplace at the far end, pegged pine floors like his apartment in town.

Correction—like Docia's apartment in town. He was just renting it from her.

He deposited Morgan onto an overstuffed couch with a brown afghan across the back.

She gave him a thin smile. "I think there's iced tea in the refrigerator. And soda. And wine. No beer, though, sorry."

"That's okay, I didn't figure you'd be entertaining me." He stared out the window behind the couch. Rows upon rows of grapevines marched up the hillside to a stand of live oaks at the top.

"Cynthiana. Native American grapes." She stretched out on the couch, resting her head on the padded arm. "They're also called Norton, but Cynthiana sounds more uppity, so that's what Texas winery people call them. In Missouri, it's Norton." She pressed a hand to her mouth to stifle a yawn.

The rich sunlight of late afternoon cast long shadows across the vines, the heavy grape clusters glowing golden in the distance. "It's beautiful," Erik murmured.

Morgan opened her eyes, nodding. "Yeah. Picturesque as hell. Believe me, you love it right up until you have to climb up there and pick those suckers."

She grinned at him, and he felt a quick twinge somewhere

south of his diaphragm. She was dusty and bruised and there was a nasty cut running along her cheekbone. But her cocoa eyes still sent a bolt of warmth straight to his groin.

He cleared his throat. "You heard a truck when you fell. Not a car?"

Her smile turned wry. "I didn't think you were listening back there. Yeah, I heard some kind of motor. It sounded too heavy to be a car—louder."

He nodded. He could hear voices now in the winery office. Probably the doctor. Maybe Cal.

"Do you believe me?" Morgan wasn't smiling anymore. Her eyes had gone all Bambi again. "Nobody else will when they hear about it."

Erik's chest tightened. "Yeah. On the whole, I do."

"Are you going to do anything about it?" She watched him steadily, probably waiting to see if he'd back down.

He sighed. "Eventually. First, I have to figure out who might have been up there."

"Morgan?" A short, balding man in a rumpled seersucker suit walked into the room, blocking Erik's view of Bambi. "Cal said you hurt yourself." He set his medical bag on the table. "You're lucky I was already out here. I don't make house calls as a rule."

Morgan's lips spread in a tired grin. "That's okay, Doc, I won't make a habit of it. I promise."

Erik took his cue to leave and headed back toward his truck.

When Morgan woke up, it was dark outside. She hadn't really meant to sleep, but after the doctor had confirmed no broken bones or concussion, and after Carmen had agreed, grudgingly, to leave her alone, she'd drifted off.

She stumbled to the bathroom to splash some cool water on her face, then stared at herself in the mirror. Scratched cheek and hair that looked like it could be used to clean a skillet, but nothing a couple of days with her feet up couldn't cure.

Of course, the chances of her being able to put her feet up at any point in the near future were somewhere south of slim.

She sighed. Too late to go to the Dew Drop, even assuming she could haul her aching body out to the SUV.

Instead, she limped to the refrigerator in the tasting room. At least Allie had left the remains of the volunteers' lunch. Morgan plopped a spoonful of King Ranch chicken onto a plate and pushed it into the microwave just as someone knocked on the patio door.

"Morgan?" Ciro called.

Fred and Skeeter ran to the door, yipping ecstatically. Morgan undid the latch and let him in.

"You okay? Carmen sent you dinner." He handed her a foil-covered plate. "Gorditas."

She slid the plate into the refrigerator. "Thanks. Between Carmen and Allie I shouldn't have to cook for the next week."

Ciro helped himself to some fruit salad and settled onto one of the barstools. "Did you get a chance to look at that vineyard site before you fell down the hill?"

Morgan considered telling him she'd been pushed, and then decided against it. Chances were he probably wouldn't believe her if she did. "It looks good to me, but I know I'm the new kid around here, so my judgment doesn't count for much." She took a forkful of chicken. "I'll tell Dad about it. Since you're the one recommending it, I'm sure he'll agree."

"Good for cabernet franc, maybe mourvedre, maybe even primitivo or barbera if we want to go to the trouble." He stared at the ceiling, figuring. "Should be ready in five years or so if we can plant this year. The market for all of that is really expanding."

Morgan looked down at her plate, trying to figure out how to ask the next question without making Ciro overly curious. "Is anybody else interested in leasing that land?"

He frowned. "Like who?"

"I don't know. Maybe Castleberry's just got me spooked. If somebody else is interested, wouldn't we want to move quickly?"

"Haven't heard anything." He chased a grape with his fork, keeping his eyes on his plate. "I wanted Nando to look at it, but I don't think he ever got around to doing it."

"Nando?"

"Good place to get started in the vineyard business. Let the boy get his feet wet." He was still avoiding her gaze.

Morgan took a breath. Nando was old enough to take care of himself. Ciro was her father's best friend and the man who was making most of the decisions at the winery. This was definitely not a fight she wanted to get involved in. "So Nando's decided to start working in the vineyards?"

His lips thinned. "Boy doesn't know what he wants. Thinks he wants to be a cop. Here—in Konigsburg. Damn fool nonsense. He'll never make a living that way."

She took another careful step into the minefield. "They really need good cops in Konigsburg. After Chief Olema, that is. Nando might be able to get somewhere now that Erik Toleffson's the chief."

Ciro looked up at her, eyes blazing. "I didn't raise that boy to be a cop. He's got two generations of farmers in his blood. Vineyards are booming. I don't know what the hell he's thinking of."

She touched his hand quickly. "I know. It's a good industry to get into in Texas. I'm really grateful for the opportunity, although I wish I hadn't gotten it just because Dad got hurt." Which was true—more or less. She turned back to the refrigerator. "Want some sauvignon blanc? Looks like there's an opened bottle from the tasting room to finish up."

He shook his head. "Nah. Gotta get home. You take care of yourself, Morgan. Get some rest."

Good advice. A half hour later, she wondered why she couldn't get herself to take it. In fact, she hadn't felt so wide awake in weeks. Outside she could hear cicadas buzzing and a few frogs chirping near the creek.

Stupid to feel nervous just because she'd taken a tumble down a hill. Particularly when she had all this protection. Fred and Skeeter lolled under the bar. Arthur sat in front of the door, waiting for some tasty critter to be stupid enough to come within puncturing range.

She poured herself a glass of sauvignon blanc. She didn't usually finish up the leftover wine from the tasting room since they had so much of it, but maybe tonight she'd make an exception.

Fred and Skeeter suddenly came to attention as headlights swept across the road outside. Arthur got to his feet. A truck pulled up in the parking lot.

Morgan took hold of Skeeter's collar for luck, not that Skeeter would attack anything larger than a gecko. A man walked up the stairs into the reflected yard lights.

Chief Erik Toleffson. Still in uniform. Looking...really hot.

Her breath came out in a whoosh. She let go of Skeeter and opened the door almost before he had a chance to knock.

He stood in the doorway, blinking. "Hi."

"Hi. Come in." She stepped back, warding off Skeeter and Fred who approached in tail-wagging frenzy. Arthur planted himself in Erik's path with a challenging stare.

Erik stared back. "Is that a bobcat?"

"No, it's just Arthur. Ignore him." Arthur swung his head to give Fred a monitory hiss before stalking off toward the apartment and his food bowl. "Would you like a glass of sauvignon blanc? There's some left over from the tasting room." Morgan knew she was babbling, but she couldn't seem to stop.

Erik Toleffson turned his molasses gaze her way and smiled.

Erik placed his hat on the bar. "Thanks, I'll pass."

Technically, he was still on duty, assuming that the call forward worked on his cell, of course. A new way to get around not having enough people for night duty since it was Peavey's day off. "I just wanted to check on you. To tell you the truth, I didn't expect you to be awake."

He'd hoped she would be, though. *Bingo.*

Morgan walked behind the bar and opened the refrigerator. "Water? Soda? Fruit salad? I've got a little of everything."

"Soda. Thanks."

He watched her reach into the refrigerator. She had on jeans and a white tank top that showed a lot of her chest and did interesting things to his solar plexus. When she turned to set the can down in front of him, he saw the clear outline of her nipples against the white ribbing.

No bra. His lungs contracted. *Down boy!*

"Actually, I slept most of the afternoon." She pushed a hand through her hair, sending short curls tumbling around her ears.

The shadowy disks of her nipples peaked against the thin

cotton. He wondered if the feeling in his chest was heart palpitations.

"So now I'm wide awake." She grinned in his general direction.

He tried to remember what she was talking about. *Oh yeah, sleeping.*

He pulled up a bar stool on the other side of the counter. Better than standing there with his pulse thundering in his ears. "Nice place. How long has it been open?"

"The winery? Dad started off in a Quonset hut around 1994. He and Ciro finished this building a few years ago." She looked up at the vaulted ceiling over her head, smiling. "I've always liked it."

"How long have you lived here?"

Her smile faded slightly. "I moved in after my dad got hurt. Before that I just came down on weekends. But I needed to be on-site so I could help Ciro."

"Does your mom come down to help you out sometimes?"

Her smile disappeared entirely. "My mom doesn't like wine."

"Must have made for interesting dinner conversation." He picked up his soda.

"Oh, it did that." Her lips stayed flat. "Like I told you, my folks are separated. Not legally, but practically."

"Where do they live?"

"Austin. My mom's there full-time. My dad was there in a rehab facility, getting his leg back in shape. My mom let him move back in when they released him, so maybe some good came out of the whole wretched mess. Maybe they'll work out their differences. What about your folks?"

Erik frowned, not sure what she was asking. "They're still in Iowa."

"Are they thinking of moving down since all of you are here?"

"They threaten to every once in a while. We might be able to lure them down for the winter, but my mom's not big on heat."

A moment of silence stretched between them. He tried to think of something to fill it. "Remembered anything else about what happened on the hill?"

She gave him a dry smile. "No. In fact, I'm looking forward

to forgetting the whole thing."

Not as great a smile as before, but he'd take what he could get. He mentally told his nether regions to cool it. "I'll try to get back up there tomorrow to see if I can find the tracks you talked about."

"Good idea. At least I'll know I didn't imagine them." She leaned on the counter next to him, letting the scoop neck of her tank slide down a little more. "So what were you doing up on that ridge this afternoon when you so kindly saved my butt?"

Erik gave up trying to calm his unruly body. As long as she was leaning against the counter like that it was a lost cause. "I was looking at the stock tank. Rancher who owns the land had some sick goats. Claimed it was because somebody poisoned his tank. We need to have the water tested."

Her head snapped up. "Oh shit."

He raised an eyebrow. "I didn't think the situation was good, but I didn't think it was that bad."

"It is if we're thinking of planting a vineyard there." Morgan rubbed her hand across her forehead. She looked like her headache was back. "Ciro is going to freak. And I told him I'd pitch the vineyard to Dad."

"Take it easy. We don't know what's wrong up there yet. The water could be bad, but it could just be something that was dumped in the stock tank. Particularly since somebody also pushed you down that hill."

He put his hand on her shoulder, reassuringly. At least he thought it was reassuring. A moment later, he wasn't so sure. His hand rested on smooth bare skin, silky and warm. He smelled lavender and rose and hints of wine. And she was watching him with those eyes—rich, dark brown, like chocolate kisses.

All of a sudden, he felt a little dizzy. He leaned forward, almost without thinking. She rose slightly to meet him.

Her lips were soft, warm. He inhaled her sigh, tasting wine, then angled his mouth against hers. Her mouth opened beneath his lips, but he wasn't going to do anything about it. This was just a quick kiss, an intro as it were. Nothing serious yet.

And then it was.

Morgan's mouth opened wider and his tongue plunged deep, tasting, sensing. Warmth and smooth deep wetness. Without thinking, he raised his hand to her breast and felt the hard pebble of her nipple against his palm. Heat flashed again at his groin.

Somewhere his brain went on red alert. *Danger, danger, Will Robinson.* His body surged right ahead, hardening almost instantly. The warm weight of her breast filled one hand and he rubbed his palm against the other, her faint moan raising prickles on his scalp.

She held her hands at the sides of his chest, then smoothed them around his body, pulling herself tight against him. Erik heard a melodic chirping and wondered if it was him or her.

Until he realized it was his cell phone.

He stepped back, eyes closed, trying to catch his breath. His face was damp with sweat. "Sorry," he whispered, clicking open the cell with one hand.

A routine traffic call, fender bender on Highway 16. But by then he knew he had to go anyway. He turned back to her, tucking his cell in his pocket, trying not to think about what had just happened.

And what had almost happened.

Her eyes were huge, her mouth a thin line. "I didn't..." she stuttered, then stopped.

"I'm sorry about the call," he said quietly. "I'm not sorry about the kiss. Not hardly."

She still watched him, as if she were trying to make up her mind about something. Then the corners of her mouth edged up, slowly. "Drive carefully."

"I will." He smiled back at her, breathing again. "Sleep well."

"I will."

Erik headed for his truck, listening to the voice screaming in his head. *What was that? What the hell was that? You've got more than enough on your plate, Toleffson. You've got two months to prove yourself. Keep your mind on your freakin' job. You're supposed to be in control here, remember?*

No question. He was definitely going to concentrate on his job and nothing else. He was going to make this work. Definitely. But the smell of lavender and roses and dry white wine lingered in his head all the way back to town.

Chapter Five

By eleven the next morning, the glow of Morgan Barrett's kiss was a distant memory. Erik sat in the monthly meeting of the Konigsburg Merchants Association trying to avoid death by boredom. Technically, he had no business there since he wasn't a merchant, but Arthur Craven, the association president, had asked him to come, and he'd thought it was a good idea at the time. "Chief Olema never came," Craven explained, "and Chief Brody..." His ears turned slightly pink. Nobody in town wanted to say much about Brody. Now Erik sat in the back of the room and wondered if there was any way he could catch forty winks without being noticed while Hilton Pittman droned on for what seemed like eternity.

Pittman was a problem. If he didn't keep Pittman happy, the mayor would complain to the council and it would be a mark against him. So he had to make an effort. He was making one now, but it wasn't easy, given what a jerk Pittman was. He'd always managed to avoid crap like this as a working cop. Now he was an administrator, and apparently he was supposed to be fascinated by Pittman's latest version of the World According to Hilton.

Instead, he looked out the window of the restaurant and let his mind ramble back to Morgan.

He had a feeling she'd been as shocked as he was by that kiss last night. As a rule, he didn't go around making out with women he barely knew, no matter how appealing they were. It was also one of the more memorable kisses he'd had in his fairly routine romantic career. Most of the women he knew were practical about what they expected from him, and he pretty much gave them what they wanted. A lot of them had been cops like him—they understood each other. Of course, his last relationship in Konigsburg had been a disaster, given that the woman in question turned out to be a psycho bitch, but she wasn't exactly par for the course.

A picture of Morgan's face popped into his mind—her stunned expression when his cell phone had brought them both up for air. That definitely hadn't been par for the course. For either of them.

He liked the way her chin came down in that rounded point. She had a slight widow's peak too, that emphasized the heart shape of her face. A sprinkle of freckles scattered across the bridge of her nose, like cinnamon on sugar.

Cinnamon on sugar. Lord have mercy. Toleffson, you really are losing your mind. And your focus.

Morgan Barrett was obviously a very dangerous woman.

At the lectern, Pittman was finally wrapping up. "We have some big weeks ahead of us here, leading up to the Wine and Food Festival at the end of August. Y'all got your tickets to sell now." He gave them a wide, professional smile that probably should have had cameras clicking in front of it. "And don't forget the annual motorcycle rally this weekend. Bigger and better than ever."

Erik stared at him. Motorcycle rally? This weekend? *What motorcycle rally?* He looked around the room. Most of the faces looked resigned. A couple looked downright mulish.

Pittman's smile became even broader as he tried to warm up the audience. "According to the latest figures I have, we can expect over three hundred bikes. How about that, folks! That's a hundred more than last year!"

Pittman's assistant began to clap enthusiastically. After a moment, a few more people, like Tom Ames, the owner of the Faro tavern, joined him. Erik glanced at Allie Maldonado. Her arms were folded across her chest—she was very pointedly not applauding.

After a moment, Arthur Craven raised his hand. "I thought we'd agreed to limit the registrations to two hundred this year, Mr. Mayor."

"Limit registration?" Hilton raised his eyebrows theatrically. "We've got people who want to come to Konigsburg, Arthur. Why would we want to limit their numbers?"

Erik heard a few grumbles from behind him. Apparently,

that question wasn't as rhetorical as Hilton thought it was.

"C'mon, folks!" he cried. "Let's all work together and make this the best rally we've ever had. Go, Konigsburg!" Pittman pumped his hand in the air like a cheerleader. His assistant clapped even more enthusiastically. Some of the merchants joined in, but if they were excited, Erik thought they were doing a great job of hiding it. Even Ames looked like he'd rather be someplace else.

After Craven gaveled the meeting to a close, Erik headed for the front. Pittman glowered at his assistant, maybe because he didn't seem to be surrounded by nearly as many enthusiastic supporters as he might have expected. In fact, the unenthusiastic non-supporters were all heading in the opposite direction, toward the exit.

"Motorcycle rally?" Erik managed to keep his voice mild. Yelling at Pittman was not currently part of his job description and would be an example of gross stupidity.

"Annual event." Pittman began tossing notes into his briefcase, watching the disappearing hordes at the exit without making eye contact.

Erik gritted his teeth, feeling the slow burn deep in his gut. *Cool it.* "Three hundred bikers, you say? Shouldn't you have passed this news on to the police department, Mr. Mayor?" He gave Pittman his best viper-getting-ready-to-eat-the-sparrow smile.

Pittman finally turned to look at him. He seemed far too pleased with himself all of a sudden. Erik felt a sense of approaching doom.

"Well now, Chief, I told the police department. I even passed on the permit application from the rally organizers. Several days ago." Pittman narrowed his eyes slightly. "Seems like you've got a failure in communication over there in your department. Better look into that. You wouldn't want to miss anything important."

Erik's smile didn't waver. He'd spent a lot of time learning to hide how pissed he was about anything. "I'll have to check that permit, then, won't I? Make sure it's all in order."

"You do that, Toleffson." Pittman's voice became arctic. "Those bikers bring in several thousand bucks' worth of business with this rally. I wouldn't want anything or anyone to screw it up. Bad for the town, you know." He turned and stalked toward the exit, his assistant trailing behind him.

"Right." Erik watched Pittman's retreating back as he unfisted his hands. "Nothing bad for the town." At the moment, he felt like torturing Ham Linklatter in some particularly lengthy and excruciating way, which might be bad for the town but would be great for his own disposition.

Morgan watched Nando Avrogado step carefully into the tasting room. He seemed to be doing his best to be inconspicuous. Given his size, that might be difficult, and given Carmen's bloodhound abilities, avoiding her would probably be impossible.

The three people at the tasting room bar glanced up as he came in, then ignored him. They looked like yuppies from Austin, people who assumed they knew a lot more about wine than any small-town cop. They were, in fact, dead wrong about that, as Morgan knew only too well. Like all of Ciro and Carmen's kids, Nando had been drinking wine since he was in middle school, and he could probably tell the difference between sangiovese and syrah with a single sniff.

Nando caught sight of her and smiled, looking faintly embarrassed. "My dad around?"

"In the barrel room. I can call him."

He shook his head quickly. "Nah. I'll just leave him a note."

Kit was doing another one of her sales jobs on the Austinites. "This next one is our primitivo. Genetically, it's the same grape they use for Zinfandel, but we do it a little differently."

Nando's eyes narrowed as he watched her pour. Morgan fought to keep from grinning. No doubt visions of TABC officers invading the place were dancing through his head.

"I'll be with you in a moment, sir." Kit smiled at him, her teeth sparkling against her olive complexion. "Would you like to do a tasting today?"

Nando folded his arms across his chest and gave her a definite Officer of the Law look, then turned back to Morgan.

Morgan smiled. "This is Kit Maldonado—she's Allie's niece."

"So? You think that'll cut any ice with the TABC?"

"Now why exactly would the TABC be interested in Allie's

niece?" She gave him a wide-eyed look, her lips curving into a demure smile. "Why, officer, you don't think I'd use an underage pourer, do you?"

Nando frowned, his lips thinning.

"Relax, Ace." She put a hand on his arm. "She's twenty-one. I saw her driver's license. So did your boss, for that matter."

"Toleffson?" Nando gave her an incredulous look. "He was checking IDs?"

Morgan beckoned toward the cash register, where Kit was ringing up the wine purchases. "Hey, Kit, this is Nando Avrogado, Ciro's son. Got your ID handy?"

Nando shook his head, backpedaling. "That's okay. I'll take your word for it."

But Kit pulled out a black leather purse and retrieved her billfold without looking at him. "Here." She handed her driver's license across the bar. "Everybody seems to be checking it these days."

Nando cleared his throat, as he glanced at the license. "Doesn't do you justice."

"Thanks." Her voice was still slightly sharp. "Maybe I could have a T-shirt made up that says *Twenty-one as of May 23.*"

"How long have you worked here?"

He gave her his killer smile, what Morgan thought of as the Nando Special. She felt like shaking her head. *You'll need to do better than that, Ace.*

Kit narrowed her eyes again. "I started after May 23. Believe me, I've always been legal."

His jaw tensed. Morgan would bet he was always the "good cop" in any interrogation. He probably wasn't used to hostility. Particularly not from good-looking women.

"Glad to hear it. 'Legal' is something I'm always in favor of."

"Oh knock it off, both of you." Morgan took the driver's license out of his hand and gave it back to Kit. "You're as bad as Arthur and the pups."

He seized on the change of subject. "So where is the mountain lion, anyway? Out doing a little hunting?"

"Probably. I haven't seen him all day." She frowned. "Come to think of it, he didn't come in for lunch."

"Probably found himself something tasty on the hoof, so to

speak."

She shook her head. "He doesn't usually eat what he catches. He's a picky eater anyway."

Kit raised her eyebrows. "Arthur is picky?"

"Believe it or not. He chews on things, but he usually just leaves the carcass lying around with some strategic puncture wounds."

Kit grimaced. "Way more information than I wanted, boss."

Nando grinned again, charm oozing from every pore.

Kit glanced at him and then grinned back. Morgan suddenly felt like she should find something urgent to do in her office.

"About time you got here," Ciro's voice boomed from the doorway.

Nando managed not to roll his eyes, but Morgan guessed it was a near thing.

Ciro strode into the room. "Didn't you get my message?"

Nando nodded. "I got it, Dad. Didn't think I'd see you. I was gonna leave a note with Morgan."

Ciro shrugged. "No need now. Let me take you over to get a look at that property of Powell's."

"I'm on duty right now, Dad, I just stopped by to ask Morgan a couple more questions."

"On duty?" Ciro snorted. "Driving around in that sorry excuse for a police car?"

Morgan watched Nando's shoulders stiffen. As a veteran of more than a few family battles herself, she could sympathize. But judging from Ciro's face, she didn't think Nando would win this one.

"I don't have time now. Maybe later." Nando sounded like he was talking through gritted teeth.

"Later?" Ciro's face darkened.

"Ciro?" Morgan's voice was soft, but both men turned toward her. "We need to talk some more about that land before we do anything else about it. Erik Toleffson said there's a possible water problem up there."

"Toleffson? How does Toleffson know anything about that land?"

"Mr. Powell said some of his goats got sick. That's why Erik and Cal were up there the day I fell. We need to have him test the water before we go any further with leasing the land."

Ciro's eyes narrowed. "Powell won't like that."

"Probably not. But I don't think we'd want to lease someplace where the ground water is tainted."

Nando shook his head. "That's not likely. From what I understand, it's just the stock tank."

"And if it is, we can go ahead. But we need to see the results first."

Ciro shook his head slowly. "We might lose the chance to lease the place if we push Powell too hard. You sure about this, Morgan?"

She kept her voice level, but her fingernails cut into her palms as she clenched her fists. "I can call Dad if you want me to. I'm not asking you to give up the lease completely. Just get the water tested." *And stop acting like everything I suggest is suspect.*

"There is a problem up there, Dad. It may not be serious, but Powell does have some dead goats."

Ciro glanced at his son, then back at Morgan, his expression still dubious. "I'll think about it." He turned and stalked toward the work area in back.

"Thanks," Morgan murmured.

Nando gave her a dry smile. "No problem. It got me out of driving up to Powell's goat pasture, at least for the time being."

Ham Linklatter wasn't at the station when Erik got back from the Merchants Association meeting because it was his turn on night duty. Helen Kretschmer dug through Ham's desk without a qualm and unearthed the permit application for the motorcycle rally from the back of a drawer, along with the log Linklatter was supposed to be keeping to record any night calls.

The log was blank. The application wasn't.

Helen recommended some creative uses for Ham's entrails, which Erik promised to consider. She watched him as he scanned the permit application, her arms folded across her chest.

He sighed and dropped the application back onto the desk. "Looks okay to me. This thing goes on every year?"

"No sir. Not every year. Sometimes they go to Big Bend or

somewhere like that. But we get them every couple years or so."
She raised her chin, regarding him through narrowed, gunmetal
gray eyes.

"They give you any problems?"

Her expression suddenly became as blank as Ham's log.
"Brody didn't have any. But Brody was Brody."

Erik studied her. Helen was the only person besides
Linklatter who'd been with the department when Brody had
been chief, but no one had ever implied that she'd known
anything about his schemes. He'd never thought she was one of
Brody's fans, but maybe he'd been wrong. "What's that mean,
Helen?"

She shrugged and turned back toward her desk. "Brody
had ways of taking care of problems before they got to be
problems."

He took a breath, ready to grill her for details.

She gave him a narrow look over her shoulder. "I figure
you'll have to find your own way of doing that, Chief."

Great. A ringing vote of confidence there. Maybe Nando
would know something about the way Brody had handled the
bikers. He'd see if he could find him later tonight. After he'd
eviscerated Ham Linklatter.

Ham came in at five, ready for the evening shift.

Erik was waiting, the permit application in his hand. He
held it below Ham's nose. "You forget to pass this on to me,
Linklatter? Lucky we found it in your desk."

Ham's face, already one of the whitest Erik had ever seen,
turned the color of a snowdrift. His mouth opened and closed
several times without a sound. His pale blue eyes seemed to
sink even deeper into his skull.

"Yes sir," he muttered. "I guess I did forget."

Erik folded the paper and put it into his jacket pocket.
"Like I said, lucky Helen was able to find it for me. Otherwise,
we might've had some problems this weekend. Seeing as how I
wouldn't have known we were due to have three hundred bikers
camping in the city park."

"No sir." Ham cleared his throat, dropping his gaze to the
floor. "I mean, they won't all be in the park. Only twenty spaces
there."

Erik raised an eyebrow. "So where will the rest camp?"

Behind him, Helen snorted. "Camp? They don't camp. Not them boys. You check the B and Bs. My guess is you won't find a vacancy in town for the weekend."

Erik frowned. What the hell kind of biker stayed in a bed and breakfast? "That right, Linklatter?"

Ham swallowed, his Adam's apple bobbing up and down his skinny throat. "Some of 'em will be there, sure. Some of 'em will stay at the motels too. But some of 'em have their own hunting property up here. Lots of 'em stay out in the hills."

"Hunting property?" Erik had known a few Bandidos in his time. He tried to picture them hunting anything legal. It did not compute.

Helen grinned from her desk. "Not like the old days, huh, Chief?"

Erik frowned. He had a sudden mental image of Helen on a Harley wielding a tire iron. Not outside the realm of possibility. "Guess not."

Ham nodded, smiling now. "Yeah, those old boys come up here to have themselves a good time. No trouble. Just a lot of bikes up and down Main for a couple of days. Sounds like thunder sometimes."

"No drunks?" Erik skewered Linklatter with a glance, just to let him know he wasn't exactly home free yet.

"Oh, well, yeah, I mean I think they drink some, sure." Linklatter swallowed hard.

"You 'think'?" Erik had that same approaching doom feeling he'd had with Pittman at the luncheon. "Weren't you here when they came through the last time?"

Linklatter slid a finger between his collar and his neck, as if it were too tight for comfort. "Well, I was here, yes sir, but the chief had me directing traffic on Main most of the weekend."

"*All* of the weekend." Helen's voice was sharp. "Linklatter was out on the street. Brody and Morris handled everything else."

"You weren't here either?" Erik frowned.

"Chief said he didn't need me. Gave me the weekend off. Just as well—I had people coming in."

Oh, yeah, Helen on a hog with a tire iron, riding at the head of a pack of Bandidos. Made perfect sense. "Anybody else here then?"

Helen shrugged. "Don't know. I guess Peavey was part-time then. He probably was out on the streets too."

"Traffic," Ham whined. "Lots of traffic problems all weekend. We had our hands full. No time for anything else."

Erik considered a range of possibilities for the motorcycle rally, most of them unpleasant. "So who kept track of the campground—Brody?"

"Maybe, maybe not." Helen shrugged. "May not have been anybody keeping track of it. Campgrounds and bars sometimes run themselves around here."

Erik tried not to jump to conclusions. Just because Brody and Morris had both been crooked didn't mean anything had been going on at the motorcycle rally. Or would be at this one "He didn't have anybody keeping track of what was going on in town? Making sure they didn't have any problems?"

"I tell you, there was lots of traffic." Ham's face flushed to a dirty pink. "We had to look after that. Chief told us to keep a lid on it."

Erik nodded. No way was he going to get anything useful out of Ham, and Helen didn't seem willing to fill him in. Nando might have a better memory, but Nando hadn't been in the department then, so it would just be what he'd heard in town.

Of course, Nando wasn't the only one who might have heard things. Time to visit the Dew Drop.

Chapter Six

The Dew Drop was frozen in a time warp, Erik reflected. Nobody ever seemed to change their seats—or maybe he just didn't get there often enough to see them switch around. Terrell Biedermeier still sat on the same barstool, his rear end protruding into the walking space. Ingstrom still leaned his elbows on the bar, watching a dart game in the corner. Cal and his wife Docia still sat in what had become the Toleffson booth.

For an odd moment, Erik wondered what it would be like to have a table with somebody like Morgan Barrett that he could call his. To have someone who actually looked forward to seeing him walk in. *Jesus, get a grip, Toleffson.*

"Evening, Chief, have a seat." Cal grinned at him. "Rescued any more damsels in distress since I saw you yesterday?"

Erik shook his head. "Nope. Found any more poisoned goats?"

"Nope."

Ingstrom arrived at Erik's elbow with a glass of Dr. Pepper. "On the house?" he asked, raising a hopeful eyebrow.

Erik sighed. "Nope. Nothing's on the house, Ingstrom. Ever."

"My kind of lawman." Cal lifted his bottle of Dos Equis in salute.

"Gee, you two are just loads of fun. You sound like a pair of John Wayne impersonators." Docia waved at Ingstrom. "Bring me some more mineral water, Ingstrom. Preferably on ice."

Docia hadn't been coming to the Dew Drop much lately, now that her pregnancy made her take up an even larger space on the opposite bench. Erik hadn't exactly been keeping count, but he figured she was close to eight months. She definitely seemed bigger than she'd been the last time he'd seen her, which was only a few days ago. Considering that she'd started off at six feet and a healthy size, that was saying something.

Ingstrom shook his head. "Don't know if I have any more of that stuff. You're the only one who drinks it. How about some iced tea?"

"Can't do caffeine." Docia's lower lip jutted forward in a pout. "You have any Fresca?"

"Nope."

Docia's eyes narrowed. "Okay, Ingstrom, what *do* you have?"

Ingstrom counted off on his fingers. "7UP, Dr. Pepper, Mountain Dew and Coke."

"Okay, 7UP." Docia sighed. "Just buy some Topo Chico or some Perrier or something, okay? I promise I'll drink it all."

Ingstrom shrugged and headed back toward the bar.

Docia regarded Cal balefully. "Gee, being pregnant is fun. I'm the size of a baby whale, I can hardly walk and I can't drink anything naughty."

"How long now?" Erik asked.

"Five weeks and counting. I might even deliver before the Wine and Food Festival if I'm lucky."

"After which you'll be nursing so most of the same general rules will apply." Cal grinned at her.

"Crap." Docia's lower lip stuck out farther.

"Hey, Red, you're gorgeous. And you're going to be a fantastic mother." Cal put his arm around her shoulder, pulling her close. "And you'll have lots of time to drink wine down the road."

Pete thumped Erik on the shoulder. "Scoot over, or better yet let's grab a table. I see more people headed our way and Docia needs all the room she can get."

Docia narrowed her eyes at him, but Pete was already looking around for more chairs.

Erik helped him slide two tables together as Allie dropped into a chair. "Ingstrom, what wine do you have from Cedar Creek?"

Ingstrom glanced behind the bar. "Sauvignon blanc and a bottle of Morgan's Blend."

"We'll take it. And a bunch of glasses."

Cal settled Docia into a chair as Ingstrom placed a bottle and glasses on the table in front of Allie.

Erik stared at the bottle. The label had a woodcut of roses. "What's Morgan's Blend?"

Allie poured two glasses, pushing one toward Pete. "Morgan's father started doing it in her honor after he sold his first year's production. I don't know exactly what's in it. Ask Morgan—she might know, assuming her father told her."

"Ask me what?" Morgan slid into the chair beside Docia. Erik had a feeling she was deliberately not looking his way.

"What's in the wine—Morgan's Blend?" He nodded toward the bottle, as Ingstrom plunked more glasses on the table.

Morgan glanced at him, then looked quickly at the label. Yep, definitely avoiding him.

"Syrah, merlot, cabernet franc, a little bit of sangiovese. Dad varies the proportions depending on what kind of grapes we've got a surplus of." She picked up a glass and poured. "This is from four years ago when they had a lot of merlot. It's probably mostly that."

"Good stuff." Allie sipped her wine, narrowing her eyes at Morgan. "Are you okay? Cal said you fell."

"Yeah, sort of. Just a few scrapes and bruises. I'm okay." Morgan glanced at Erik and blushed.

A woman who blushed. Over him. Would wonders never cease?

Janie breezed in the front door, followed by Wonder, creating a general realignment of bodies around the table. Somehow Erik ended up next to Morgan, feeling the warm brush of her thigh against his.

"So." Janie poured her own glass of wine and nodded at Morgan. "You're okay? No breaks or sprains?"

Morgan shook her head. "Just skinned hands and knees, and bruised pride. The chief here pulled me out of the gulch."

"Erik," he said, automatically, trying to get a glimpse of Morgan's fathom-deep brown eyes.

Morgan blushed again, and Janie glanced at him, the corners of her mouth inching up.

Aw crap! He did *not* want to become another of his sisters-in-laws' projects. The last time Janie and Docia had gone into the matchmaking business, Lars had ended up married to

Jessamyn Carroll. Now, of course, Jess would be helping them try to fix Erik up. Time to get down to business. He cleared his throat quickly. "So tell me about this motorcycle rally Pittman's got going this weekend."

Allie and Docia groaned, Wonder grimaced, even Janie looked glum.

"What?" Pete's brow furrowed. "I wasn't here for the last one either. What's the problem?"

"The motorcycle rally." Wonder took a swallow from his glass of wine. "Begun by our illustrious mayor as a way to boost the pleasures of Konigsburg ever higher on the list of most popular tourist attractions in the state."

"Biker tourists?" Erik tried to do a quick mental recalibration, but it didn't work. The two words wouldn't fit together in his mind.

"Yuppies." Wonder's voice was dry. "Pittman's favorite type of tourist. Lots of money and limited good sense. Believe me, this is no outlaw biker get-together. Keep in mind, we're talking about Konigsburg. We don't hold with loud talk and riffraff."

"Like hell we don't," Allie growled. "Those guys may make more in a week than I do in a month, but that doesn't mean they don't behave like a bunch of six-year-olds when they get on those damn bikes."

"That's an insult to six-year-olds everywhere." Docia sighed, taking a sip of her 7UP. "And they do spend a lot of money."

"Right. They'll all come into Sweet Thing for lunch in their leathers and their bandanas with their old ladies. Only the old ladies are size zero model-types who won't wear helmets because it messes up their hair." Allie stared glumly at the wine bottle.

Erik frowned in confusion. "Would you rather have Bandidos or Hell's Angels?"

"I grew up in Brownsville. I know all about Bandidos, believe me. No, what I'd really like are some grown-ups who ride because they like riding motorcycles not because they're looking for a ten-thousand-dollar penis extension."

The entire bar seemed to fall silent for at least ten seconds. Wonder choked on his wine.

"Nicely said." Janie grinned at Allie.

Erik picked up his Dr. Pepper glass and hurriedly signaled

to the barmaid for a refill. "So what's the worst I can expect?"

"Drunks." Wonder nodded decisively. "They won't try to burn down the town or ravish the women, but they will get shit-faced at the Silver Spur or the Faro and then try to ride down Main. Or stagger down Main. Or crawl down Main. It really sets the tone for the weekend, believe me. Nothing like a few drunks puking in the city park to send the family tourists back home, and make them think twice about coming here again in the future."

Janie grimaced. "I swear they start drinking at breakfast. Either that or they really tank up at lunch. You can't walk down the street without seeing them by mid-afternoon."

Erik pinched the bridge of his nose, thinking. Maybe Brody had a reason for putting two of his three cops on traffic patrol, but at least one of them should also have been picking up the staggerers and stowing them in a cell. He'd have to figure out some way to police both the traffic and the drunks.

Docia groaned. "That's another thing—riding down Main. You can't believe the amount of noise these guys make."

"Because, of course, all of them have the biggest bikes they can buy." Allie splashed more wine into her glass. "This wine is really good, Morgan. Did I forget to tell you that?"

"Like thunder," Wonder muttered. "Chrome-plated thunder, that is."

Pete looked slightly dazed. "The wine?"

"The noise. Chrome-plated thunder is right. If you look at one of those babies in the sunlight, you're likely to go blind." Docia took a final swallow of her 7UP.

"Three hundred bikers, according to Pittman." Allie's lips became a thin line. "All of them riding down Main, flat out. Day and night. No conversations for three days. And no driving the highways unless you want to become part of an obstacle course for some idiot going eighty on a 500-pound bike."

"They do buy a lot of wine," Morgan mused. "They come out to the tasting room and load up. But we get drunks too. Ciro has Esteban hang around the patio to keep them in line. They also complain. Constantly."

"About what?" Erik watched her face. The spray of freckles across her nose. The way her lower lip protruded slightly. Unbelievably, he felt his groin tighten. *Fantastic timing. Control, Toleffson, control.*

Morgan shrugged. "In our case, they complain about the dirt road. They don't like the bumps or the washboard. One guy told me he'd only come back if we graded the road to the tasting room."

"They can't handle dirt roads?" Erik pictured the bike riders in Lander, Iowa, sliding down the hillsides in clouds of dust. But those had been dirt bikes, not big, chrome-plated monsters. Still, what kind of biker complained about dirt roads?

"They also don't like rain, mud or potholes. Nothing that might smudge the finish. Getting a feel for it now, Chief?" Wonder grinned.

Erik nodded. "Not *The Wild Ones.*"

"Nope. Forget Brando." Docia counted off on her fingers. "Forget *Easy Rider.* Forget Peter Fonda on any form of bike in any movie you can remember. Forget Dennis Hopper. Forget Steve McQueen. Forget any visions of big hunky males on king-sized hogs." Her gaze darted to Cal for a moment, and she grinned. "Present company excepted, of course."

Janie grinned too. Morgan suddenly became fascinated by the label on her wine bottle.

"Why the interest?" Cal tipped back his Dos Equis. "You gathering the troops?"

"Just trying to be prepared." Erik took another sip of Dr. Pepper, willing his body to settle down. "Since I've only got three officers, I need to figure out how to spread them around to take care of three hundred bikers." He ran through his mental checklist—drunks, noise, reckless driving on the highway.

Oh, a really fun weekend was coming up here.

Wonder frowned. "I guess Linklatter counts as a police officer. Personally, I'd deploy him as a speed bump."

"Ham's not so bad," Allie said. "You just have to tell him exactly what you want him to do."

"Sounds like you've got your work cut out for you, Chief." Pete poured himself another glass of wine. "Any established policies to fall back on?"

Erik shrugged. "Olema never had to deal with them—he wasn't here long enough. From what I hear, Brody didn't have any problems. Or none he talked about."

The table suddenly fell silent. Cal's face was dark as he stretched his arm around Docia's shoulders.

She put her hand on his knee, smiling gently. "It's okay, you know. His name doesn't make me break out in a cold sweat."

"Decent of you, given that the SOB tried to drown you," Wonder muttered.

Cal's mouth was a thin line. "You can't be sure of anything about Brody. Even now I don't think we know all the things he was up to when he was chief."

"Well, he didn't do much with the bikers." Morgan ran her finger down the side of her glass. "I don't even remember any drunks getting arrested the last time they were here. Ciro and Esteban took care of getting them off our property. I'll bet Hilton was ecstatic that nobody got picked up, seeing as how the whole rally was his idea. Arrests tend to make people feel unwelcome, you know."

"With Brody's leftovers, you're always waiting for the other shoe to drop." Wonder drained the last drops of his wine. "I wouldn't get too comfortable if I were you, Chief."

"Believe me, I'm not." Erik shifted his body so that his still-hardened groin was in a slightly less visible position. Just then the last thing he was thinking about was comfort.

Morgan followed Allie and Wonder out the door of the Dew Drop, trying not to show that she was aware of Erik Toleffson behind her. She hadn't felt this self-conscious around a male since middle school. Come to think of it, Erik Toleffson bore a certain resemblance to Brent Peters, the object of her affections in eighth grade.

All the Toleffsons were gorgeous—it was a well-known Konigsburg fact. Tall, broad, dark hair and eyes, killer smiles. Like every other Konigsburg female, she'd perked up when Cal had joined Horace Rankin's veterinary clinic, but he'd taken one look at Docia and been a goner. Then Pete had come to town for Cal's wedding and fallen hard for Janie Dupree almost before anyone else had had a chance at him. Lars had moved himself and his daughter down the following year, and lots of Konigsburg women had suddenly developed a need for a really good accountant, but he'd taken up with his babysitter, Jess Carroll, and married her a few months ago.

That left Erik. Nobody seemed to be rushing to catch him,

even though he was just as handsome as his brothers. Maybe because he was both handsome and sort of, well, scary.

That kiss last night hadn't been scary, though. Just hot.

She took a deep breath, feeling the warm evening air fold around her like a blanket. *Steady, Morgan.* As she turned left, she found that Erik had fallen into step beside her.

"Thought I'd get some dinner." One end of his mouth edged up in a lopsided smile. "Care to join me?"

Beside her, a cast-iron streetlight had switched on, casting a warm glow in the twilight. "Sure." The word came out a little more breathy than she'd intended.

Steady, for god's sake!

"What's your favorite place?" Erik asked.

"Let me think." Morgan folded her arms across her chest as she walked so that she wouldn't bump into him. Although, in reality, bumping into him didn't sound bad at all. "I need to go to Brenner's, if that's okay. I've got to talk to Ken about a wine shipment anyway."

"Which one is Ken?"

Morgan might have imagined that slight edge to his voice. Or maybe not. "The sommelier. He and Lee, the chef, own the restaurant. They're major customers at Cedar Creek, and the restaurant's so popular it's good for our business." She didn't bother explaining that Ken and Lee were partners in more than just the restaurant. He'd been here for a couple of years—he should know that already.

"I know Lee. I guess I know Ken, too, by sight anyway. The redhead, right?"

"Right."

The lights were already lowered at Brenner's. Candle lanterns gleamed on the tables, illuminating the pale mauve tablecloths. For a moment, Morgan stood in the doorway, drinking in the essence of Konigsburg.

"Morgan, sweetheart, welcome! I don't suppose you brought a case of primitivo with you." Ken hurried across the dining room and hugged her enthusiastically, his slightly plump face stretched in a broad grin.

"Oh, I'm sorry, no. We haven't released the new vintage yet." A band of tension began to stretch across her shoulders. Again. Her father was the one who'd have to decide about the release date for the wine with Ciro's recommendation. Another thing she wasn't authorized to do.

Ken frowned. "Honey, we get requests for it every night. People have loved it ever since we put it on the menu, and they get pretty annoyed when we don't have any. If we can't get more soon, we may have to take it off the wine list."

Morgan nodded quickly. "I know, believe me, I know. I'll call Dad tonight and see what I can do. We've got some nice sangiovese left and some Morgan's Blend."

Lee approached from her other side and slid his arm across her shoulders. "Personally, I love Morgan's Blend. Come and sit down, babe. You can work this out later."

Morgan managed a smile that was almost sincere. "You know Erik, right?"

Lee gave him a dry grin. "Oh, yeah, the chief and I go way back. He kicked Otto Friedrich's ass in our parking lot. Made us the stuff of legend."

Erik dipped his head. "Glad to oblige."

Two minutes later they were at a side table, the one where Lee usually put Cal and Docia. Morgan wondered about the significance. Probably just a coincidence. She flipped open her menu and tried to pretend she was hungry.

"Okay." Erik's voice was low. "What are you upset about, and why are you trying to pretend you're not?"

She blinked at him. How on earth had he noticed? Nobody else ever seemed to. Or maybe they just didn't care. She let herself slump back against the banquette. "Like I said, Brenner's is one of the winery's best customers. I don't want to lose them."

"Doesn't sound like you will." His lips thinned slightly. "Everybody calling everybody 'sweetheart' and all."

"That doesn't mean anything. We like each other, the three of us. But they're in business, just like the winery. If I can't get them the wine, they'll drop Cedar Creek off their wine list. And they may not be too excited about putting us back on it if they can't rely on us to keep them supplied."

"The wine's not ready?" He leaned forward, watching her face.

"I don't know. Maybe, maybe not. Dad's the one who decides. He's the wine master." Dad—who hadn't been to the winery in three months. And who still wouldn't be able to come for a few more weeks, according to his doctor. The band of tension drew tight across her shoulders again. "He hasn't been healthy enough to come back to Cedar Creek yet."

"Is the wine still in the barrels?"

Morgan shook her head. "It's been bottle-aging for a while."

"So take him a bottle."

She sighed. A sensible thing to suggest that would work fine with a sensible man. Her father, on the other hand, was a wine master. *Sensible* was not in his vocabulary. "Maybe I'll try that. He's pretty much bored out of his skull by now. Maybe he'll agree to release it without actually being at the winery when we do." *But I doubt it.*

"Morgan, my love." Lee put a plate on the table between them. "Mushroom empanadas with a touch of manchego. No frowning. No sighing. Eat." He grinned, his dark eyes dancing. "Ken wants to bring you some wine, but he's nervous. Tell me you're not upset about all of this stuff with your wine. Trust me—it's going to be okay."

"I'm not upset." Morgan tried to make herself sound perky. Erik narrowed his eyes at her. Apparently, she didn't do perky very well. "Honestly."

Across from her, Erik snorted in disbelief and broke off a piece of empanada. "Good stuff," he said, chewing.

"Thanks." Lee raised an eyebrow. "Dinner?"

"Right." Erik's gaze seemed to bore a hole into her chest. "Bring us something she'll eat every bit of, okay?"

Morgan saw Lee's mouth edge up in that same kind of knowing smile she'd gotten from Allie. God, could people be any more obvious? He was just a guy, after all. *Right, Morgan, and Chateau Margaux is just a red wine.*

Ken slid a glass onto the table, smiling apologetically. "I know it's not yours, Morg, but it's still good. I thought maybe you'd like to give it a try. New Zealand sauvignon blanc." He poured pale golden wine into the glass in front of her, then set a glass of iced mineral water with a lime slice in front of Erik. "Here you go, Chief."

Morgan took a sip, letting the cool, slightly citrus taste fill her mouth. She closed her eyes. Maybe it was easier to talk if she didn't see Erik Toleffson's deep molasses gaze. "Good flavor." She glanced in his direction again. "Would you like a glass?"

Erik shook his head. "I'll pass. Thanks."

Morgan blinked at him. "You don't drink?"

"I drink water." He took a sip. "Also tea, coffee and more Dr. Pepper than is good for me. It's hard to find in Iowa—did you know that?"

Morgan opened her mouth to ask him why he didn't drink wine, but he cut her off. "Tell me about your father." He watched her, eyes half-closed.

Looking at him definitely made it hard to think. "What do you want to know?"

"How did he get hurt?"

"He fell off a truck." She rubbed the back of her neck to release the tension. "He was riding in the back with some equipment and the truck hit a rut in the road. It was just a freak accident. They weren't even going that fast."

"But he's still laid up?"

Morgan propped her elbows on the table, resting her chin on her fist. "His leg was badly broken. He had surgery. Twice. Now he has physical therapy, and I think my mom wants him to stay in Austin."

"Your mom. The non-wine drinker. You said they were separated."

"Yeah, but I don't know if it's permanent. The winery was always a big issue between them, and now Dad's not out here running it. Maybe Mom can talk him into cutting down on his hours when he's back on his feet."

"Which would mean what for you? Running the whole thing on your own?"

"I'm not ready for that. Ciro runs things. I'm trying to learn the business."

"Looks like you're running yourself ragged while you do."

She looked up, directly into that deep brown gaze. Like lava. She felt a quick jolt of heat between her thighs. *Steady, Morgan.*

"I'll be okay, Chief. You do what you have to do, right?"

Erik decided his goal for the evening was to get Morgan to look at him for more than two seconds at a stretch. She was as skittish as a teenage driver in a license exam. He felt like the two of them were veering all over the road.

"So how long have you known the dynamic duo here?" He nodded at Lee and Ken, conferring next to the wall of wine cases that backed the bar.

"Since they opened up, which was about five years ago now. I started stopping in for dinner whenever I visited Dad at the winery. They were one of the winery's first restaurant sales. I got them to try some of our sangiovese, and I gave them a pitch on stocking wine from Texas."

He willed her to look at him. "You do the marketing for the winery?"

She grimaced. "My dad doesn't believe in marketing. He says the wine sells itself."

"That'd be a first. I've never seen anything that sells itself."

Morgan shrugged. "I didn't do much marketing for them before, but I've done a little promotion since I moved here last fall. Some winery dinners. A brunch for the volunteer pickers. A newsletter. I haven't had time for much more." She met his gaze for a few seconds, before her eyes skittered back to her wine. "I'm a good marketer. I'm only a passable winery manager."

"I'd say you're doing fine. Everyone who's mentioned your wine has been enthusiastic about it." Erik watched her long, slender fingers slide along the stem of her wineglass and told himself not to think about what else they could be doing under other circumstances.

Morgan's lips twisted. "My dad made the wine we drank at the Dew Drop. He's very good. I'm still learning."

"What does Nando's father do at the winery?"

"Ciro is Dad's partner. He runs all the vineyard operations, and oversees the crush." Morgan shook her head. "He probably could have taken over when Dad was hurt, but Dad wanted somebody from the family at Cedar Creek, and I wanted to do it. So I quit my job in Austin and moved up here to learn how to run the winery. Ciro tolerates me, but Carmen always reminds me how little I know about what I'm supposed to be doing."

"Is that what you want to do—the winery business?"

"Yes. But I want to do it right. And I want to get us more widely known beyond the limited distribution we've got now." She took another gulp of her wine and settled back in her chair, her lips pulled into a tight smile. "Let's talk about *your* family for a while."

"Okay. What do you want to know?"

"You all come from some little town in Iowa, right?"

He nodded. "Lander. My dad teaches high school biology there. My mom's an administrator at a nursing home."

"How big is it?"

"Smaller than Konigsburg." He sipped his mineral water. "It's a few miles west of Des Moines. Out in the corn fields."

"Did you all grow up there?"

"Yep."

Morgan narrowed her eyes. "Come on, don't go all western on me."

Erik sighed. "Lander is the most boring town in the world. My folks are straight-up, true-blue, salt-of-the-earth types. There's not a whole lot to say about either of them."

Morgan raised a questioning eyebrow. "And their son's a cop? Seems logical. Isn't it?"

Lee Contreras appeared tableside before Erik could think of a good answer. He watched Contreras bustle around Morgan, putting a plate of chicken and rice in front of her with stern orders to eat it all. His own bowl of paella smelled like nothing he'd ever tasted before. Not that that was a problem.

Conversation became a series of yums, mmms and blissful slurping. As meals went, this one rated up near the top of anything he'd ever tasted that wasn't covered with barbecue sauce. He noted with approval that Morgan's plate was also mostly empty.

Finally, she leaned back in her chair. "So tell me, Chief, how did you become a lawman? And this time I won't let you slide around answering."

Her eyes danced. For a moment, Erik considered coming up with a polite lie, one that would keep that sparkle going. But he'd decided a long time ago to stick to the truth whenever he could. Or at least a part of it.

"It was a good alternative to jail."

Chapter Seven

Morgan blinked at him but stayed silent. *Okay, so far so good.*

"I said my parents were true-blue, salt-of-the-earth types. I didn't say I was." Erik took another sip of water, settling back in his chair. "In point of fact, I was a punk. And not even a smart one, not that most punks are."

It had been the logical next step after his bullying had come to an end once his brothers had begun fighting back. Moving on from simple assault to bigger crimes. He felt like wincing at the memory of his seventeen-year-old self—greasy hair down to his shoulders, black shirt, black jeans, chain wallet, Doc Martens. *Oh, yeah. Mr. Cool is in the house.*

"Most of what I did would fall under the heading of stupid crap." He counted off on his fingers. "Stealing a couple of six-packs from a Stop-N-Go, drag racing on the highway, vandalizing the bleachers at the high school football stadium. The high school where my dad taught, you understand. I had a real genius for screwing with my family."

He glanced up. Morgan was watching him with narrowed eyes. *Terrific.* At least he'd finally managed to get her full attention. "But I had some friends who weren't so small-time. I had a part-time job as a mechanic at a garage in West Des Moines that doubled as a chop shop, not that they ever told me what was happening straight-out. I had a pretty good idea what was going on, though. And I didn't try to do anything about it or tell anybody."

Morgan frowned. "Why?"

Erik sighed. "It was good money. And the guys who were running it didn't care if I knew or not. I wasn't what you'd call a poster kid for ethical behavior even though I came from the kind of home where ethical behavior was a big part of life. I was sort of odd man out in my family." As his brothers could all testify. With any luck he wouldn't have to talk about the complicated dynamics of that relationship. At least not tonight.

"What about your brothers?"

Erik managed to keep his expression flat. So much for vain hopes. "What about them?"

"How did they feel about you?"

"We didn't have much to do with each other. I was older—they mostly stayed out of my way. Except for Pete." Who had, of course, been the big brother Erik should have been, the one who looked after his younger siblings and took the brunt of Erik's violence. "We went at it a lot of times when he was growing up. If you really want to know what kind of kid I was, ask him." Only he profoundly hoped she wouldn't. At least not yet—not until he'd had a chance to prove that Mr. Hyde was currently under control.

Morgan's forehead furrowed. "What happened?"

"The guys at the chop shop got caught, and I got dragged in with them. The cops couldn't prove I had anything to do with it, but I couldn't prove I didn't. And they didn't exactly care what they could prove—they just wanted all of us in the slammer."

"Did you go to jail?"

He shrugged. "I would have, but I caught a break. Technically, I was still a juvenile, albeit a dangerous one, so they sent me to juvie court. The judge there was a friend of my father's, and he had some leeway. He pulled me out of the courtroom and sat me down in his office. Told me I was headed for jail if I didn't get my act together. And if I went to jail, it would destroy my parents, who didn't deserve it. For some reason, I listened to him. He suggested the military as a way out of Iowa, since by then my rep would have made it impossible for me to get any kind of honest work around Lander, plus I was considered one of the up-and-coming criminals in town. I took him up on it."

She gave him a half-smile. "Army or Marines? Somehow I don't figure you as the Air Force or Navy type."

"Army." He tore off a piece of bread and dipped it into the bowl of olive oil Lee had dropped off earlier. "I did two tours with the MPs."

"Did you like it?" She was frowning slightly, maybe worrying about his worthless young self. Maybe.

"Yes and no. It helped me get my shit together, but I'm not big on authority figures. Which is to say I'm good at giving orders but not at taking them." He shrugged. "On the other hand, I figured out I liked police work, weird as that seems. And I got a GED and some college hours out of the deal, so that helped."

Plus he'd convinced his parents he wasn't quite the miserable excuse for a son they must have thought they'd produced. He remembered his father's expression the first time he'd come home in uniform, that strange mixture of fear and pride flashing across his face.

Sorry about all the crap, Pop. I'll try to make up for it someday.

"When I got out, I went to work for a private security company in Davenport while I finished my degree in Criminal Justice. Then I went to work for the cops there."

Morgan reached for her wineglass. "So did you like that job any better than the army?"

He picked up another piece of bread, trying to decide how to answer. "Yeah, I did. But it was still Iowa."

"Why do I feel like there's more to the story than you're telling me?" She narrowed her eyes. "Why is Iowa a problem?"

Erik shrugged. "I've sort of done Iowa." *And I needed a real second chance. With my family.* They'd been the ones he'd hurt most, the ones he had the most to make up to. He wasn't sure he'd really been able to do that yet.

"So you came down here." Morgan gave him a dry smile. "I'd say you hit Konigsburg at the right time. The whole police department was an unholy mess after Brody took off. The place was a shambles as far as law enforcement was concerned. And Olema didn't strike me as much better, even if he was more honest."

"Olema wasn't the brightest bulb on the tree, but he had his points. He hired me, after all."

"And now you're in charge."

"For the time being. I've got two months to prove I can do the job. That I've got the experience and the will."

Morgan's eyes narrowed. "So this is your chance to prove yourself?"

"Yep, more or less." *Again.*

"But you've done so much already. You're the one who arrested the person who tried to kidnap Jess Carroll's baby—even if Olema did screw up and let her go. And you're the one everybody calls if they've got trouble. You or Nando. You've had over a year to prove yourself, and you've done it. People around here trust you."

Erik sighed. "Honey, law enforcement is a lot like show business—most people only remember what you did last week."

She leaned forward, so that her hand was only a couple of inches away from his. Surreptitiously, he moved so that he was touching her, feeling a little jolt of heat in his fingers.

"So you're trying to be the perfect chief of police?"

"Yeah, maybe I am. But maybe that way I'll at least get some things right."

"And that's why you're so worried about the bikers."

He leaned back again, letting his hand slide along hers as he regarded her through half-closed eyes. "That's one of the reasons."

Her mouth spread in a slow smile. She slid her hand over his so that their fingers were lightly interlaced.

Erik felt himself tighten all the way down to his heels. *Lord above.*

"What's the other reason?"

It took him a moment to remember what she was talking about. *Bikers. Right.* "Something feels off about that rally, but I'm not sure what. I've just got a gut feeling. It's bad news."

"You're a good cop, Chief Toleffson, at least as far as I can see. You're a hell of a lot better than what we've had to put up with around here for the last few years. My guess is whatever you do with the bikers, the town will be behind you in a big way."

"Thanks." His voice felt rusty in his throat, and he tossed back the rest of the water in his glass. Unfortunately, that finished everything on the table.

He considered ordering more food just to keep her sitting there with him, her hand covering his. But he figured it wouldn't be a good idea for the chief of police to be seen spending the entire evening at a *tête-à-tête* in Brenner's restaurant instead of chasing criminals. Never mind that there weren't any criminals around to be chased at the moment.

Morgan frowned slightly, her deep brown Bambi eyes narrowed in thought. "I never liked Brody. Even before I knew he was a crook. He always looked sort of like an actor who'd been hired to play the part of a small-town chief of police. More style than substance, if you know what I mean."

He shook his head. "He had a lot of substance, just the illegal kind. This town was in trouble after Brody, and it definitely needed somebody to come in and take care of things. But Olema wasn't the best person to be in charge of the cleanup. He was a good ol' boy, but he sucked when it came to running a department. And I'm probably as bad as he was at administration."

"You've got Helen." She grinned. "Helen is the Attila the Hun of administration."

He had a sudden picture of Helen in a wolf-skin and a horned helmet. *Yep.* Another good role for her. "The personnel are solid here. Well, most of them anyway."

Her grin turned wry. "Ham will come around. Eventually."

"Here's hoping I can keep from throttling him before he does."

He tried not to stare into her deep chocolate eyes. A gorgeous woman, sitting at a table with him. Not exactly a run-of-the-mill event. "Want some coffee?"

She nodded. "After two glasses of wine, I feel a little wobbly. I'm sort of losing my head. Must be the hours."

He could think of a lot of comments to make about that. Unfortunately, none of them were the kind of thing he wanted to share on a first date.

After they'd finished the espresso Lee insisted on giving them for free to make up for the wine problems, Morgan let Erik walk her down the darkened street toward her SUV. She could hear music from the beer garden next to the Faro, guitars and a distant drumbeat.

"Konigsburg nights." She smiled, shaking her head. "Lordy, it makes you want to sit and put your feet up on a front-porch rail someplace."

"You have a front porch?" He sounded faintly amused.

She couldn't see his eyes in the darkness, but she knew they'd be riveted on her. They had been all during dinner. Every time she'd looked at him, she'd found that smoldering gaze following her. It made her feel itchy and hot and altogether unsettled. Chief Toleffson was way too much man for a disheveled novice winemaker like her. He should probably be pursuing somebody slightly larger than life, like Calamity Jane. Somebody who matched him in size and reputation.

"We've got the patio outside the tasting room. That's as close to a porch as I get." Morgan stopped beside her SUV and tried not to fumble as she looked for her keys. Now came the tricky part—getting away without getting too close to him. She had a feeling getting too close would lead to complications. And she really didn't want complications.

Did she?

"Let me." He took the keys from her suddenly limp fingers and pressed the button to unlock the front door. Then he handed them back, not moving from his position between her and the SUV.

Morgan took a deep breath. "Look, I don't want you to get the wrong idea about me. I mean I'm not..." She groped through her vocabulary trying to find a word that worked.

What exactly aren't you, Morgan?

He was smiling at her, that same small lopsided grin he'd had in the Dew Drop. She wondered if he ever grinned completely.

"You're not..." He arched an eyebrow.

"I'm not...loose."

Oh lordy, she was a moron. *Loose. What are you, the Church Lady?*

At least she'd answered her own question—Erik Toleffson was definitely grinning on both sides of his mouth now. "Loose?" His eyebrow arched again.

"I mean..." She waved a hand, helplessly. Why had she suddenly lost all ability to speak in coherent, adult sentences? If this was the kind of effect the chief had on her, she needed to run for cover while she still could.

"You mean you don't usually allow somebody you know only slightly to kiss you for an extended period of time without punching him in the jaw." His grin slid back to lopsided.

"I've never punched anyone in my life." But then she'd also

never had a kiss like the one with him at the winery last night. Of course, punching him probably wouldn't have been her reaction of choice.

"I could show you how to punch somebody, if you want." He folded his arms and leaned back against her SUV. "It's all in how you make a fist. Don't ever tuck in your thumb—you may break it if you do."

"I don't really need to know that. I'm a nonviolent person." She stood still, wondering how she could ask him to move aside so she could get into her SUV and go home.

Wondering if she really wanted him to move aside.

He reached toward her, running his index finger along the ridge of her cheekbone. A thin streak of heat followed his fingertip. Morgan worked on not whimpering.

"For what it's worth, I don't go around kissing almost strangers either." His voice was soft, like a caress in the darkness. "But it seemed like a good idea at the time."

She swallowed. Was that disappointment she heard in his voice? "It *was* a good idea," she blurted. "Just a sort of unusual one."

She took a deep breath. *Morons. Morons on my team.*

He grinned again. "I thought so, too. Still do."

She exhaled slowly. Her body felt tight, as if she'd been holding herself taut for far too long, like a stretched string. "What do we do now, then?"

He pushed himself up straight, sliding his fingertip along the edge of her ear, then sinking his hands into her hair. His fingers wrapped around the back of her head, pulling her toward him.

And then she was resting against his chest, caught in the warmth and closeness of his body.

"We pick up where we left off," he murmured.

She smelled the faint tang of mingled sweat and aftershave as he lowered his mouth to hers. Then she opened her lips and breathed in his warmth.

She slid her tongue against his, feeling the edge of teeth, while a jolt of excitement seemed to spread from her breasts downward to her belly and thighs. He tasted spicy, with a lingering savor of coffee. She angled her head slightly to take the kiss deeper and felt his hands slide from her shoulders to her hips, pulling her tighter against him.

She could feel the hard ridge of arousal jutting into the joining of her thighs, making her want to move. His fingers dug into her buttocks, kneading, pushing her to ride the heat kindling between them.

She pressed her body tighter against his, rubbing slightly. Tension built in her belly, the heat spreading. She was inching closer and closer toward the edge. A small moan built up in her throat. She wanted him. However she could get him. Right now, right here.

In front of the Millsburger Building in downtown Konigsburg where anybody could walk by at any moment.

She lurched back, gasping for breath, wondering just where she'd left sensible, no-nonsense, exhausted Morgan Barrett, who sure as hell would have been smarter than this.

Erik gave himself a quick mental kick. He'd pushed her too far, too fast. He should have known better after that whole "loose" thing. She wasn't ready for this.

Hell, *he* wasn't ready for this!

One minute it had been a sweet, hot goodnight kiss, and the next he'd been ready to, well, climb on top of Morgan Barrett in the middle of downtown Konigsburg. Clearly, he'd been without a woman way too long.

Equally clearly, he couldn't go around kissing Morgan in public anymore. Next time it had to be in a place where they could keep going, provided they were both ready to take it to the next level. And the next. And the next. Because the one thing he'd learned after two kisses was that neither of them was crazy about stopping.

"Are you okay?" he murmured, brushing the hair back from her forehead.

She still stared up at him, her eyes a little dazed, as if she were trying to figure out exactly how she'd ended up in the middle of downtown Konigsburg with bruised lips. Then she sucked in a breath. "Yeah. Okay. I think."

"Should I apologize?"

She suddenly broke into a grin. "Was it that bad?"

"Only if you're going to conk me with something if I don't

say I'm sorry."

"I keep telling you I'm not the violent type." Her grin widened. "I promise I'm not going to punch you or conk you with anything."

"Not even if I kiss you again?" He felt another ripple of heat in his groin.

Her smile faded slightly. "Probably not. But I really don't think you should. At least not on a downtown street where half of Konigsburg might walk by at any time."

He rubbed his jaw. "Okay. I'm open to suggestions for where I *could* kiss you again."

The corners of her mouth edged up. "I'll give it some serious thought."

"Good." He leaned back against her SUV, more to keep her from getting in and driving off than anything else. "When can we get together and discuss it?"

Her gaze was suddenly wary. "I could make you dinner sometime. If you're free, that is."

He fought to keep from grinning. He had a feeling she might move him away from her SUV bodily if he did. "I'm free. Believe me."

Or anyway, I'm easy.

"Tomorrow night?" She smiled again, faintly.

"Sure..." Erik started. Then he remembered. "Hell, the bikers."

Morgan groaned. "Oh, god! They'll start coming into town tomorrow afternoon and they won't leave until Sunday. Neither of us is going to have a spare minute tomorrow."

"And I'll be on duty all the time they're here." He sighed, stepping aside from the SUV. "Rain check?"

"Definitely." She opened the door and climbed in. "Believe me, after the bikers, we'll both need something."

He already needed something, preferably within the next five minutes. But he knew a lost cause when he saw it. "See you in the Dew Drop?"

She gave him a dry smile. "Yep." She pulled the door closed.

Erik stood watching the taillights of her SUV disappear down the road to Cedar Creek. He considered how much he'd prefer having dinner with Morgan Barrett to riding herd on a bunch of yuppie bikers. Three hundred of them. With no one enthusiastic about the prospect except their sleazeball of a mayor.

Eventually, he was going to have to do something about Hilton Pittman, even if it did get him in trouble with the city council. It might almost be worth it.

Chapter Eight

It took Erik significantly longer to fall asleep that night than it did normally. Morgan Barrett had definitely gotten under his skin—or between his sheets in this case. She didn't exactly dance on the ceiling, but he kept seeing her deep brown eyes whenever he began to drift off, along with the spray of freckles across her nose and the way her lips seemed to turn up naturally at the ends. He finally drifted off to dream about Disneyfied deer tripping through grape-laden vineyards.

BRRRRRWAAAAAPPPPPP!!!!

The sound brought him half off the bed before he'd even opened his eyes. Erik stumbled toward the living room window that faced Main, belatedly grabbing some underwear before pulling back the curtain. The sound from the street intensified—he could almost feel the vibration through the floor. He peered down at the four-lane expanse of Main Street, rubbing sleep from his eyes.

A quartet of motorcycles roared down the street, their throttles wide open. Chrome gleamed on the front forks, the engines, the exhaust system. The bikes seemed to shimmer in the sunlight. Or maybe it was just the vibration that made everything seem to shake.

Erik sighed and stumbled back to grab his uniform. He had a feeling he had a long weekend ahead of him.

Ham Linklatter was the only one at the station when he walked in. Maybe that was why Ham was sitting at Helen's desk at the front counter instead of his own in the main room. If Helen had been there, Ham would have been a dead man.

Linklatter gave him his usual baleful glance, doubly baleful today since it looked like Ham had come straight from the shower. His lank hair was plastered across his skull like pond scum.

"About time somebody else got here," he grumbled.

Erik stared at him for a count of three, watching Ham's face turn the usual unpleasant shade of pink, then he glanced at the clock. "I'm on duty in twenty minutes. Figured I'd get here early."

He heard the door open and close behind him, then watched Ham's face change from unpleasant pink to pale green.

"Linklatter," Helen's voice rumbled from the doorway, "what the hell are you doing sitting at my desk?"

Ham gathered a stack of papers from the desktop and started to slink toward his desk at the back of the room. Helen placed herself squarely in his path, resting fists the size of softballs on her broad hips. She pointed at the papers. "What are those?"

"They're mine," he whined. "I'm just taking them back to my desk."

She extended her hand in front of Ham's nose. After a moment, he placed the stack of papers on her flattened palm.

"Don't be messing with my stuff, Ham." Her voice sounded like an underground volcano getting ready to erupt.

Ham moved swiftly to his own desk.

Nando walked in, yawning. "You hear the arrival of The Mild Ones?"

"Oh yeah. Unfortunately, the noise ordinance doesn't kick in until sundown."

"By then they'll all be drinking at the Silver Spur or the Faro. So what's the plan?"

Erik hung his hat on the rack at the door. "I talked to DPS. They'll be keeping an eye on FM 1822 from here to Oltdorf." Oltdorf was a wide spot in the road about eighteen miles from Konigsburg. The highway that went there was a series of curves through picturesque Hill Country scenery, some posted at twenty-five.

Nando nodded. "Okay, sounds good. What else is going on?"

"I called Friesenhahn." And of course that had been one swell conversation—only the second week Erik had been in office and already he needed help from the sheriff. "He's sending over a couple of deputies to help with patrol this afternoon. And we can transfer prisoners to the county lockup if we fill up here."

Ham scowled. "Prisoners? We never had no biker prisoners in the jail when Brody was in charge."

Erik, Nando and Helen all turned to stare at him. Ham ducked his head and pretended to read the memos on his desk.

Erik nodded at Nando. "Make sure you take a run by the campground when you do your patrol. And keep an eye on the Silver Spur and the Faro. Anyplace else they're likely to be drinking?"

"Rustler's Roost," Helen rumbled, naming a roadhouse a few miles west of town.

"That's outside the city limits. Friesenhahn's problem."

Nando nodded. "Not too many in town yet. More tonight. What about…"

The rest of his question was drowned out by a vibrating roar from the parking lot, followed by a series of explosive *pop*s. Moments later, a man who could only be the bike's owner stepped in the door.

He was encased in black leather from shoulder to heel. His jacket was covered with shiny zippers. Erik wondered briefly if he'd had them chromed along with his bike. He wore a crisp black bandana knotted around his head and black aviator sunglasses that probably cost more than Erik's entire uniform, including badge. Either he'd spent his childhood watching motorcycle movies, or he was one of the bigger idiots Erik had yet encountered in Texas, which was saying something.

The biker pulled off his sunglasses with a practiced devil-may-care swipe, smiling with teeth that gleamed almost as brightly as his zippers.

"Morning, gents, how's it hanging? Great to be back in Konigsburg."

Beside him, Erik felt Helen stiffen. Apparently, the biker hadn't realized not everybody in the group was a gent. Always a dangerous mistake. "Morning. What can we do for you?"

"I'm here to see the chief." The man glanced around the room, his eyes lighting on Ham. "Hey there, Officer, good to see you again. Remember me? Mel Hefner?"

Ham spread his lips in a thin imitation of a smile, carefully not looking at Erik.

Mel Hefner tucked one bow of his sunglasses into the top zippered pocket on his jacket. "Where's Chief Brody?"

The deafening silence that followed that question finally seemed to dim Hefner's smile slightly. He glanced from face to face.

Erik kept his voice bland. "I'm Chief Toleffson. What can I do for you?"

Hefner's forehead furrowed. "Brody retired?"

The details of Brody's disappearance from Konigsburg after his unsuccessful attempt to murder Docia and the subsequent search for him by the Rangers had been published in every major newspaper in the state, as well as a national news service. Erik upped his assessment of Hefner's idiot status. "Something like that. Now, what can I do for you?"

Hefner's smile blossomed again. Wonder Dentist would probably be green with envy at his incisor caps. "Just wanted to work out the details for the weekend. Most of the TBA are due in tonight."

Erik sighed. He knew he had to ask. "TBA?"

"Our group—the Texas Bikers Alliance. Of course, I like to think of them as Mel's Angels, seeing as how I'm the president." Hefner looked inordinately pleased with himself.

Behind him, Nando succumbed to a coughing fit.

Erik carefully avoided looking at Helen. He had a feeling he'd lose it totally if he did. "So what details do you need to set up with us?"

Hefner glanced around the room again, looking slightly less sunny. "Maybe we could talk about that in private."

Erik frowned. All his instincts were immediately on high alert. "We can use my office." He jerked his head at Nando, who fell in step behind him.

In the office, Hefner gave the two of them a doubtful look. He swallowed quickly, then resumed his dazzling smile, settling into the chair across from Erik's desk. "I assume the arrangement we had with Chief Brody still stands even though the chief has retired."

Behind Hefner, Nando moved slightly, leaning one shoulder against the wall so that he had a better view of Hefner's face.

Erik kept his own face expressionless. "What arrangement was that?"

Hefner moved his shoulders against the back of his chair, restlessly. "The...ah...arrangement. About the rally visitors."

Erik took a careful breath. Grabbing Hefner by the throat probably wouldn't speed things up, satisfying though it might be on other counts. "Mr. Hefner, this is the first rally I've seen. What arrangement about the visitors are you referring to?"

"Well..." Hefner's smile was definitely beginning to wobble around the edges. "Chief Brody arranged for us to sort of, you know, pay our fines in advance. So that we wouldn't have to go through the whole posting-bail-and-returning-for-trial thing."

Erik sat very still, watching Hefner sweat and trying to decide if he was actually that stupid. Maybe he should just give him the benefit of the doubt and assume that he was. "So you paid the fines in advance. Did Chief Brody return the money for people who didn't do anything that warranted a fine during the weekend?"

Hefner was definitely squirming now. "Well, no, not exactly. I mean we agreed anything left over in the end would be donated to the Konigsburg Police Benefit Fund. Sort of our thank-you gift to the town for being so hospitable and all."

"And how much did this payment amount to?" Erik felt the beginning of a headache somewhere behind his eyes.

Hefner exhaled quickly. "Oh, it varied. Usually around a hundred dollars a person. I mean the fines for the kind of thing our members might get picked up for aren't all that big, right? You know, jaywalking, stuff like that."

"A hundred dollars a person?" Erik kept his voice bland.

"That's what it came to." Hefner nodded vigorously. "We really appreciated the consideration too."

Nando whistled softly.

Erik leaned back in his chair and studied the other man for a long moment. "Okay, Mr. Hefner, you've just basically admitted to bribing a public official. And since you were trying to continue the deal with me, that's another count of attempted bribery. Potentially, your weekend just got a lot shorter."

Hefner's mouth moved soundlessly, like a beached trout. His eyes were suddenly the size of golf balls. "But...but...Chief Brody was the one to suggest this. He said it was a convenience he offered for groups like ours, to keep us from being hassled. He said it was perfectly legal."

Erik leaned forward, propping his elbows on his desk.

"Chief Brody is wanted for assault, attempted murder and burglary, among other charges. He's currently unavailable, seeing as how he's a fugitive. I wouldn't appeal to his reading of the law if I were you."

Hefner sank down in his chair like a deflated balloon version of himself. For a moment, Erik almost felt sorry for him. On the other hand, stupidity was frequently its own reward. He sat back in his chair, switching into his Voice of Authority mode.

"Here's the deal, Mr. Hefner. I want you to go back to your group now. Tell them the town noise ordinance is in effect from sundown to sunrise. Tell them officers will be picking up anybody guilty of public drunkenness and tossing them in the county lockup. Tell them the Highway Patrol will be watching for speeders on the county roads. In other words, tell them to behave themselves. If nothing nasty happens this weekend, I'll overlook what just transpired here. If anything goes down, I'll throw the book at you. Got it?"

Hefner took a deep breath. His zippers trembled. "Yes, sir. That sounds quite reasonable."

"Good enough." Erik let one corner of his mouth inch up. "You have a nice day, now."

He spent the rest of the morning patrolling the streets, watching yuppies pretending to be outlaws on bikes that were almost too much for them to handle.

Unlike Hefner's, Erik's bike back in Davenport had been over five years old and looked pretty routine. It lacked chrome. It could, however, move like a son of a bitch thanks to the time he'd spent working on it. As he turned the cruiser up West Street, he profoundly wished he still had his bike and could use it now, rather than driving the standard piece-of-crap cruiser that the city of Konigsburg provided to its law enforcement officers. On the bike, he could have taken any of these hotshots. In the cruiser, it was a toss-up.

Every time he thought about the conversation with Hefner, he wondered what the town would have faced if Linklatter had gotten the chief's job. Ham would probably have accepted those "pre-paid" fines from Hefner without a qualm, although he might have been a little confused when he found out there was no Konigsburg Police Benefit Fund. Erik figured the only Konigsburg policeman who'd benefitted from Hefner and the boys had been Brody.

After a couple of hours of watching bikers barrel around town while trying to avoid permanent hearing damage, Erik turned the cruiser toward the suburbs, such as they were. He told himself he was heading for Cedar Creek only to make sure the bikers weren't making trouble at the winery.

He definitely wasn't going there to check on Morgan, who definitely—most probably—didn't need his help.

The winery was surrounded by chrome-plated monsters taking up most of the parking spaces. The seats around the patio tables were occupied by men and women in leathers and vests and ponytails. Overall, the ponytails looked better on the women—of course, so did the vests. Esteban Avrogado dozed at a corner table. He opened one eye and raised a hand in salutation as Erik walked by.

Skeeter and Fred moved hopefully among the tables, tails wagging and tongues lolling. Occasionally someone took pity on them and tossed a cracker.

Erik strolled toward the tasting room, keeping his eyes peeled for Morgan and trouble, in about equal measure. In the doorway he paused.

Morgan stood behind the tasting room bar, staring fixedly at a far corner of the room. Three men in leathers sat on the barstools in front of her. It seemed to Erik that their gazes were all focused on her breasts. Maybe it seemed that way to Morgan, too, judging from the stiffness in her shoulders.

"C'mon, sweetheart," one of the leathers cajoled, "just one glass. We'll pay for it. Pick your favorite so we'll know what's fit to drink."

Morgan's voice was sharp. "I'm sorry, sir. I'm not allowed to drink when I'm pouring. State regulations."

"Well, it's just us here," another man said. "Who's going to know? Besides, we want to buy you a drink."

Erik walked farther into the room. Hefner wasn't currently taking up a jail cell. There was plenty of room there for three obnoxious yuppie bikers. Halfway to the bar, he caught Morgan's eye.

She shook her head slightly and he stopped.

"Gentlemen," she said, briskly, "I'll be happy to make wine recommendations for you. That's what I'm here for. But as I said, I can't drink on the job. Now, what can I pour for you?"

The men glanced at each other, then one of them shrugged. "Some of the syrah. And don't be stingy, baby."

The others snickered. Erik resumed walking across the room, letting his boot heels strike the floor more noisily than usual. The leathers glanced at him without much interest.

"Afternoon, officer," one of them drawled. "Checking IDs?"

Erik ignored him. "Everything okay here, Ms. Barrett?"

Morgan's smile seemed frozen. "Great, Chief. We're having a terrific afternoon."

"Yeah, only Ms. Barrett here won't even have a drink with us. What fun is that?" One of the leathers turned around, propping his arms against the bar and attempting a sneer. In Erik's opinion, his Brando impersonation left a lot to be desired.

"Ms. Barrett is obeying the law when she refrains from drinking on the job. Perhaps you weren't aware of it." Erik rested his hand on the top of his baton. Not that he'd use it. Not that he wasn't tempted.

One of the leathers snickered again. "Oh we know all about the law. Fact is, Officer, you're talking to three members of the bar right here."

"Right," another leather chimed in. "Members of the bar at the bar, as it were."

"Interesting." Erik let his mouth edge into a half-smile. "That should save time if I have to lock you up. You can just call each other."

One of the leathers cleared his throat. "No need for threats, Officer. We're here to have a good time, spend a little money. No harm done."

Erik raised his gaze to Morgan. "Ms. Barrett?"

Morgan's smile looked pasted on. "No harm done, Chief. I believe the gentlemen were going to buy some syrah. I'll call Ms. Maldonado to help."

Erik watched her shoulders slump as the leathers moved to the other side of the room to give Kit their wine order. "I could have handled it," she muttered.

"You did handle it." He shrugged. "I just added a little firepower. Jerks like that sometimes need a little prodding."

Morgan raised her gaze to his. Her eyes looked more like good bourbon than chocolate today. "Thank you anyway. They'd been sitting there for thirty minutes. I was about to call

Esteban."

There was a burst of laughter from the leathers. One of them shook Kit's limp hand. She didn't look any more impressed than Morgan.

The Brando impersonator walked back across the room while the other two headed out the door. He gave Morgan a somewhat oily grin. "So...Ms. Barrett, is it? Would you care to join me for dinner tonight?"

Morgan's mouth stretched in something that looked more like a rictus than a smile. "No. Sorry. Other plans."

"Oh, well." Brando reached into his pocket and pulled out a business card. "If you ever need a good lawyer or a good time in Plano, look me up." He gave her a smoldering gaze that probably wowed all the ladies at the Friday happy hour.

Erik watched him saunter toward the door to join his friends. "That man is possibly the biggest asshole in the state of Texas. Maybe I should do everyone a favor and shoot him now."

Morgan chuckled, leaning forward on the bar. "Nobody in Konigsburg would convict you." She cleared her throat. "What are you doing for dinner this evening?"

Erik shook his head. "I'm going to be on duty most of the night."

"Which doesn't mean you don't get to eat, right?" She looked up at him from beneath luxuriant eyelashes.

"Yeah, I'll probably grab something at the Dew Drop around seven, unless somebody else does something stupid I have to deal with." He raised an eyebrow. "Want to join me?"

"I'll give it my best, Chief. Try not to shoot any assholes between now and then, okay?"

Erik allowed himself a full-sized grin this time. "No promises, ma'am, no promises."

Three hours later, he sat in the Dew Drop sipping what was probably the worst cup of coffee he'd ever tasted. And given his army experience, that was saying something. The Dew Drop's food was only marginally better than its coffee since it was all microwaveable. He gazed at the limp slice of pizza in front of him and sighed.

He'd spent the rest of the afternoon making sure Hefner's troops had gotten the message about the "behave yourself" policy. Most seemed to be fairly quiet, although a few had shown some *Wild Bunch* tendencies that he and Nando had managed to tamp down. Unfortunately, he discovered that the story about Hefner and Brody had gotten out somehow—he suspected that Linklatter had been listening at the door since neither Erik nor Nando had told anybody. Now he was having to answer questions he didn't really want to deal with.

And Morgan hadn't come to the Dew Drop with everybody else.

"You realize this means Brody was clearing somewhere between twenty and thirty thousand dollars per rally," Docia said. "He had four rallies, so we're talking about something in the neighborhood of a hundred thousand overall." Even in the darkness of the Dew Drop, he could see outrage in those wide green eyes. He suspected that getting pissed was not good for somebody as pregnant as she was. Cal had his arm around her shoulders, looking a lot like a compassionate grizzly bear.

"He probably used the money to head for Brazil." Erik made the mistake of sipping his coffee again, then tried not to grimace. "Or Bermuda. Wherever your better class of fugitive heads these days. I don't know much more about it than you already know—we turned everything over to the Rangers who've got the file on Brody."

"Damn. I was hoping for some juicy details I could pass on to Allie when she finishes selling bread to the bozos." Wonder squinted at Erik's plate. "You shouldn't be eating Ingstrom's food, Chief. He's applied to have it added to the historic registry."

Allie slid into the chair beside Wonder, leaning over to kiss his cheek. Wonder might have blushed, but it was too dark in the Dew Drop to tell. She glanced at Erik's pizza. "You poor man. If I'd known you needed dinner, I'd have brought you some soup and a kolache."

The thought that he might have had Allie's soup rather than Ingstrom's pizza was enough to kill what little of Erik's appetite remained. He heard the door swing open and turned, hoping for Morgan. Instead, Nando walked in with a stunning brunette who looked vaguely familiar. Across from him, Allie's expression soured.

"Is that Kit?" Docia frowned.

"That's Kit." Allie narrowed her eyes. "With Nando Avrogado. Another thing I didn't know about until now."

"Kit?" Erik recognized her now—the pourer from the tasting

room at Cedar Creek.

"My niece." Allie sighed. "This *in loco parentis* business sucks."

"Allie, she's twenty-one." Docia grinned at her.

"Yeah. Tell that to my brother Tony. If he finds out she's dating Nando Avrogado, he'll have my head."

Nando stopped beside Erik's chair, nodding at the group. "Everything quiet?"

Erik shrugged. "So far. Any problems at Cedar Creek?"

Kit grimaced. "Obnoxious yuppies. And we ran out of sangiovese. Morgan and Ciro are slapping some labels on bottles tonight so we'll have more to sell tomorrow."

Which at least explained Morgan's absence. Another reason to be pissed at the bikers—he wouldn't even have the pleasure of seeing Bambi this evening. And he still had to check out the bars on Main, the campground and the city park. Erik took one last shuddering sip of coffee and pulled his hat from underneath his chair.

Time to go put the fear of Texas justice into some half-assed motorcycle clowns who'd had the temerity to ruin his weekend.

Chapter Nine

Morgan figured her Saturday would have to be better than her Friday night. She and Ciro had put foil tops and labels on fifty bottles of sangiovese, along with another fifty of syrah. At least she had a machine to help her instead of doing it by hand like her father had in the early years. Still, by the time they'd finished, she was well-nigh giddy with boredom.

Of course, as Carmen had helpfully pointed out, her father wouldn't have waited until the night before the bottles were needed to finish the labeling. He would have checked the inventory and realized that more bottles should be on hand for a big weekend like the motorcycle rally.

Once again, Morgan wished Carmen would go back to torturing Nando and Esteban and leave her alone. It didn't help that Carmen was absolutely right.

She'd missed the Dew Drop. And Erik. She hoped the freakin' bikers would at least order a few more cases of wine to make it up to her.

Skeeter clicked happily around the tasting room, looking for any leftover tidbits of cracker and cheese he could gobble. Morgan shook her head. "You know it's not good for you to eat people food. Go find some dog food."

Skeeter gave her his most soulful starving-puppy look. "Forget it," Morgan snapped. "I know you, remember? Go find Fred."

Skeeter sniffed around the bar one more time, then trotted disconsolately toward the door as Kit walked in.

"Morning," she yawned. "Got enough wine for the troops?"

"Let's hope." Morgan started to slide bottles into the bin under the counter. Behind her, Skeeter whimpered.

Morgan turned as Arthur pushed through the pet door and limped into the room. He gave Skeeter an ominous glare as he moved toward his food bowl, favoring his left front foot.

Morgan put the bottle she'd been holding back on the counter and approached him gingerly. At his best, Arthur wasn't particularly sociable. When he was sick or hurt, he could be a real pain. "What have you done to yourself, cat?"

Arthur flicked an ear in her direction but kept limping to his usual spot beside the door.

"Rough night, huh?" Morgan knelt beside him and reached for his paw.

Arthur batted her hand away, showing the tips of his claws.

Morgan sighed. "Okay, okay. I won't bother you now. But later today I'm going to have a look at that paw, cat."

"Something's wrong with his paw? What did he do?" Kit opened the office door and tossed her purse inside.

"Dunno. He was limping, but he won't let me get close." Morgan stood up, brushing off her hands. "I'll check him again later when he's had time for a nap and hasn't been on his feet for a while. Maybe he'll be in a better mood."

"Poor kitty." Kit started to lean down, then took a good look at Arthur's glowing golden eyes and thought better of it.

Arthur gave them both a malevolent glare.

Morgan stroked him lightly along his spine, then rubbed her fingers. "You've got some gunk on your fur, cat. Been rolling in the muck, have we?"

Arthur stretched and collapsed into a loose ball, paws curled under. Morgan rubbed him behind his ears, and he rumbled.

"You're kidding." Kit raised an eyebrow. "He purrs?"

"Sure. Deep down he's a sweetie." Morgan stood up, squinting toward the parking lot. The rumbling wasn't just coming from Arthur. From outside she could hear the sound of bikes bouncing up the drive. "Crap. They're here ten minutes before opening time. Why do I have the feeling today is going to be a bitch?"

Kit grinned, giving Arthur's head a cautious scratch. He opened one topaz eye but didn't move. "Batten down the hatches, skipper, looks like we're in for a bumpy ride."

The bikers came in waves, Morgan discovered. Sort of like

107

locusts.

They did buy a lot of stuff, she'd give them that—wine by the glass, by the bottle, by the case. They also ordered the pre-made cheese plates that were the only food Cedar Creek sold. By one o'clock, she'd had to send Esteban to Allie's bakery to get more cheese and bread.

Being this busy was actually a great way to keep from thinking about Erik Toleffson. Not that it really worked, given that she seemed to be thinking about him even when she wasn't. She hadn't really needed him to protect her from the jerks in the tasting room yesterday—she'd been doing her job long enough to know how to protect herself, with Esteban's help of course. But there had been something sort of...reassuring about his presence in the room. She liked knowing he was there, and knowing he was ready to do whatever needed to be done to keep her safe.

Not that she hadn't been safe, surrounded by customers and winery workers. But still.

She had a feeling that interesting things could have happened between them last night if she'd only been able to make it to the Dew Drop. The stupid bikers had a *lot* to answer for.

She and Kit took turns running the tasting bar and serving cheese plates. One or two of the bikers complained because they didn't sell any other food, but most of them were happy to sit on the patio and drink wine in the cool shade cast by the awning and the live oaks at the edge.

Esteban still sat at his corner table, looking massive and sleepy. He only had to get up once, when a couple of the bikers got into a loud argument over the relative merits of Napa versus Sonoma. One look at Esteban's biceps and they'd subsided into grumbling.

Business finally began to slack off around four as the bikers headed back to town for a motorcycle show and dance in the city park. Kit and Morgan collected stray wineglasses and swept up crumbs and trash on the patio.

"How'd we do overall?" Kit tied up the trash bags and added them to the stack already waiting for garbage pickup on Monday.

"Good, I think. I haven't added everything up yet." Morgan wiped her arm across her forehead. "I know we sold a lot of cases. We'll have to call FedEx on Monday to arrange for the shipping."

Fred waddled past, glassy eyed. Morgan shook her head. "Damn it. Those dogs are going to be sick as...well...dogs. They did nothing but beg all afternoon."

"Puppy eyes," Kit mused. "Works every time. How's Arthur?"

"Oh geez." Morgan turned back toward the tasting room. "I got so busy I forgot to check on him."

Arthur lay where they'd left him, curled in a listless heap near the doors. Morgan knelt beside him. "Hey, cat, how's it going?" As she reached toward his paw, Arthur lifted his head.

His mouth was wet with foam. "Oh, Jesus, Arthur!" Morgan gasped.

Kit knelt beside her. "Looks like he threw up."

Morgan's shoulders tightened. "I've got to get him to town. I'll take him to Cal Toleffson's clinic. They've got an emergency service."

"How exactly are you going to get him there? Has he ever ridden in a car before?"

Morgan's brow furrowed. "I got him to Horace for his shots a couple of times, but he shredded the plastic crate. I've got the carrier I used when I brought Fred from Austin. Arthur might fit in that."

Kit stood. "You're going to put Simba here in a pet carrier? One that smells like a dog?"

Morgan stared up at her, trying to tamp down the panic. "I've got to try."

"Right." Kit sighed. "Just wait a minute until I find the iodine and bandages. Then we can have at it."

After the five drunks Erik arrested on the first night, the bikers began to settle down. He had a feeling the first five were sort of test cases, to see if he'd really throw them in the clink.

He did. With relish.

Given that he might actually need Konigsburg's cells later on for more prisoners, he'd transferred the drunks to the county lockup later in the evening and then let their assorted friends, relatives and legal representatives sort it out. One of the biker-lawyers—it turned out there were several—gave him a lengthy speech about writs of habeas corpus until Erik gave him his best I-eat-lawyers-for-lunch look and told him to take it up with the judge on Monday. The lawyer, who was half-pickled himself, wandered away grumbling.

After a while, Erik even began to get a kick out of the situation in a kind of sour way. Among other things, dealing with the bikers was a great test for Konigsburg's cops.

Linklatter was pretty much a wash, of course. Erik sent him to direct traffic, which he hadn't yet managed to screw up and which kept him out of everybody's way.

Nando was as good as Erik had figured he'd be—calm, efficient and just menacing enough to keep the drunks in line. Peavey turned out to be a lot better than he'd expected—slow-moving but steady and incapable of panic. Those qualities might be the result of a complete lack of imagination and humor, but Erik would take what he could get.

And one glance from Helen seemed to sober up even the most thoroughly plastered biker. Since he didn't have enough cops to run the station and patrol the streets, Erik put her in charge of the building while the rest of them drove around in the cruisers. Somehow just having Helen stroll by the cell doors made the five prisoners much more enthusiastic about moving to the county lockup.

Bert Rodriguez and another of Friesenhahn's deputies showed up the first day and drove through periodically after that, checking out the campground and the more active bars, but they hadn't been needed as much as Erik had feared they might be. Mel Hefner was apparently able to convince his troops to be on their best behavior.

For the Saturday afternoon parade down Main, Erik had Peavey and Linklatter close off the intersections and then sat back to watch the line of bikes move up the street. For once, the noise didn't make him feel like punching somebody in the face.

The bike show that evening was relatively peaceful, along with the dance afterward. Linklatter and Peavey took care of the routine patrolling. Erik and Nando were stationed in highly visible positions at opposite sides of the park. Erik considered having Helen do a walk-through, but decided it would be overkill.

The band for the dance specialized in fifties rock, yet

another nod to the biker mystique. It didn't even annoy Erik too much anymore, although the whole Brando thing was getting fairly old at that point.

He leaned his butt against the side of his cruiser and listened to the band play "Rock Around the Clock". The bikers were dancing on the cement square in front of the bandstand. Some of them had had enough sense to remove their leathers, but a lot of them were staying true to their personas until the bitter end. Erik wondered if he should have had an ambulance standing by for the inevitable cases of heat prostration.

A sheriff's patrol car pulled in behind him and Bert Rodriguez stepped out. His khakis looked freshly starched, as opposed to Erik's drooping gray cotton. Erik liked the county uniforms better than Konigsburg's, but it wasn't his top priority at the moment.

Bert had been one of the interim chiefs who'd filled in while the town figured out what to do after Olema had finally agreed to go. On the whole, he'd been a good substitute, although neither he nor Fred Olmstead, the other fill-in, had bothered to do much of the paperwork that had piled up in the chief's absence. That was now Erik's problem, which he'd have to deal with as soon as the bikers returned to their real lives.

Bert leaned his six-foot-two-inch hulk against the cruiser beside him. "Quiet night."

Erik nodded. "Unless you count Sha Na Na over there."

Bert grinned. "They're not so bad. It could have been country, after all."

"Not with this crowd." One of the bikers flipped his partner over his shoulder, staggering only slightly. Erik wondered again about ordering that ambulance.

He stared up into the dark canopies of live oaks overhead. Some of the bikers were sitting at picnic tables, concealing their beer cans in koozies. Erik had decided to ignore them as long as they stayed at the tables. In the great scheme of things, violations of the city park regulations were minor.

"Nice town you've got here, Chief," Bert murmured. "Not bad at all."

"Yeah, it's got its points." Erik glanced back down Main, but no one seemed to be up to anything.

"Everything seems to be working out for you."

"So far. 'Course if the mayor gets his way that won't be how it ends up." Erik peered across the park. Nando lounged against his cruiser. As soon as the dance was over, he and Peavey would do a final patrol of the streets, and Erik could head back home to sleep for several hours.

"The mayor's an oily SOB, but from what I could tell he's not the most popular guy in town." Bert grinned. "This isn't rocket science here, Toleffson. Anybody who worked Baghdad and Kuwait City should be able to handle it."

"Baghdad and Kuwait City weren't exactly ideal preparation for Konigsburg. The city fathers might get upset if I started patrolling with an M-16." And the insurgents he'd run into in Baghdad had nothing on Pittman in terms of sneakiness. Erik squinted at the far side of the park. Was that actually Pittman talking to Hefner at the picnic table under a stand of pecans?

Bert shrugged. "Like I say, you seem to be handling it from what I hear. But you know, if you don't stick around, I may think real hard about applying for this job myself." Bert grinned again. "Somebody's got to save the town from Linklatter."

"I'll keep you posted," Erik growled.

The band swung into a middling version of "Not Fade Away". "Ever hear Joe Ely do this?" Bert asked. "His version is great. This version sucks."

Erik watched the dancers hopping around, feeling unreasonably annoyed. Why should it matter to him if Bert decided to apply for the chief's job? If he didn't hang on to it, he wouldn't have any stake in whoever took over after he left.

Except that he'd begun to think of Konigsburg as his town, for better or worse. And Linklatter would definitely be worse.

The dance broke up around nine, a lot earlier than he'd anticipated. Some of the bikers clearly needed to go back to their lush accommodations and collapse, assuming they had someone to help them out of their leather pants.

He watched the bikes move out, their engines making considerably less noise than they had when the first ones had rolled down Main. The noise ordinance was now being enforced, maybe for the first time in recent memory. He told Nando to get a cup of coffee and then check the campground one more time since that was where the serious drinking was liable to go on. Not that most of the bikers looked in any shape to be drinking anything stronger than iced tea. Bert and the other sheriff's deputy promised to make one more swing along the highway before heading back to their regular beat.

Erik drove back through town after the last of the bikers had left the park, stopping at the Silver Spur and the Faro to check for problems. Everything seemed relatively quiet. The Silver Spur had a folk singer in their outside garden who was putting the drunks to sleep. Not Erik's choice of music necessarily, but a nice option for the drunks. The Faro was livelier, but the Faro also employed Chico Burnside, a former pro wrestler, as their bouncer, to say nothing of the owner, Tom Ames, one of the few imposing men in town who wasn't also a Toleffson. Erik figured his own presence wasn't required.

He came to the end of Main and circled back on one of the side streets. The lights from Cal's animal clinic illuminated the parking lot. Erik slowed—he hadn't realized they were open this late. Normally, Cal was home in time for dinner, particularly on a weekend when Docia was due to deliver within the next month. The parking lot beside the clinic was empty except for an SUV.

Morgan Barrett's SUV.

He pulled his cruiser in beside it, locked up and headed for the clinic's front door.

Morgan sat huddled in a chair in the waiting room. When he walked in, she glanced up, her mouth edging into a small smile. "Hey, Chief. What are you doing here? I thought you had bikers to police."

"They're policing themselves right now. What's happening?" He took a seat beside her in a hard plastic chair that seemed designed to reject his butt. Probably Cal's secret weapon against anyone who might want to spend too much time at the veterinary clinic.

"It's Arthur." She stared at him with luminous eyes.

He was suddenly afraid she might start to cry. Then he'd have to do something about it, and he didn't have a clue what that should be. He usually ducked crying women. "Arthur?"

"My cat. You saw him a couple of times."

"Oh, yeah." He rubbed his jaw. "The bobcat. What happened to him?"

She shook her head. "I don't know exactly. He's been limping and throwing up. I was afraid maybe he'd been hit by a car. Cal's checking him over, but they had to sedate him to do it. Arthur's not exactly a good patient."

He figured that was an understatement—Arthur was probably a vet's worst nightmare. Better Cal than him. "How long have you been waiting?"

"It's been about a half hour since Cal got here. They had to call him in since it's after-hours." She blinked back tears again. "Poor man, I must have ruined his weekend."

She chewed her lip, and Erik felt a sudden, largely unwelcome flash of arousal. "Don't worry. Cal's probably used to it."

The door to the examination area opened with a whoosh and Cal walked toward them. Erik realized suddenly he'd never seen his younger brother actually being a vet. With his beard and shaggy hair, he looked like a grizzly in scrubs, sort of a professional grizzly.

"Hey, Chief." Cal grinned knowingly. *Great.* Now he'd probably go home and tell Docia his big brother was hooking up with Morgan.

Morgan stood up. "What's wrong with Arthur?"

Cal shrugged. "Bad case of motor oil, as it turns out. Looks like he must have rolled in it. And he walked in it too, which made his paws swell up. That's why he was limping."

"Motor oil?" She stared at him. "Where would he find that?"

"Maybe around some of the equipment at the winery. Tomorrow you might want to see if there's a pool of oil somewhere. You wouldn't want the dogs getting into it too."

"A pool of oil?" She still stared. "We wouldn't have anything like that around Cedar Creek. We have to be extra careful about contamination, what with the grapes and the wine. Particularly now that we've got the harvest going on."

"Well, maybe Arthur wandered into some oil at one of those ranches on the hillside. The thing is, it's all over his fur and his paws, and he tried to clean himself, which is what cats do."

She gasped. "Oh god, is it poisonous?"

"Not the way antifreeze is, but it's not exactly good for him." Cal pulled a plastic bin from underneath the counter. "That's what made him throw up. The main worry now is pneumonia, that and getting him cleaned up."

Erik frowned. "He can get pneumonia from motor oil?"

"When animals with oil on their fur throw up, sometimes they inhale the motor oil and that causes pneumonia. We'll need to keep him here overnight to make sure he doesn't develop respiratory problems." Cal rummaged through the bin. "Plus we need to give him a bath."

Morgan stared at him, aghast. "You're going to use water on Arthur?"

Cal smiled thinly. "Yeah. I'm not all that excited about it myself, but we need to wash the oil off. Armando's going to help. We can probably do it while he's still sedated." He pulled out a bottle of dishwashing liquid. "Here we go. Advanced grease-fighting properties."

"Should I wait?" Morgan was squeezing her fingers together, her eyes in full-on Bambi mode.

Cal's voice was kind. "It's okay, Morg, I think he'll be all right. But he does need to stay overnight, so we can keep an eye on him. You don't have to wait."

Her eyes filled with tears. "I don't want to leave him. He may be frightened."

Cal looked about as nervous as Erik felt, men confronting a potential weeping woman. "It's okay, we're used to frightened animals. We can deal. And you can come back first thing tomorrow morning to see him. I'll make sure Bethany knows to let you in early."

Morgan nodded, biting her lip again. Erik's body went back on high alert. He took a deep breath. "You can stay at my place. Then you can be here as early as you want to be. It's the apartment over Docia's bookstore."

Morgan smiled up at Erik gratefully. "Thanks. I'll take you up on that."

Cal looked like he was trying not to grin. "Yeah, that apartment is fairly close to the clinic. I used to hike over every morning when Docia was still living there."

Erik gritted his teeth. "Thanks for the tip." He really loved being an object of amusement for his little brother. On the other hand, his little brother deserved as much revenge on him as he wanted, given the amount of bullying he'd had to endure from Erik when they were younger.

"Okay." Cal let the grin break through. "I'll see you in the morning, then. Have a good weekend. What's left of it."

Erik ushered Morgan out the clinic door. Maybe there was only a little weekend left, but the chances for a good one were suddenly looking up.

Chapter Ten

Erik helped Morgan into the front seat of his truck, trying to pretend that he really was concerned about Arthur's health. He was also trying to pretend his temperature hadn't risen five degrees just from being in the same room with her.

True, they'd both had a demanding couple of days dealing with the bikers, and they both could probably use a little relaxation. Stress release could take a lot of different forms, including sex, and he could definitely provide something along those lines. Then again, taking the lady home so he could jump her when she was worried about her cat didn't exactly qualify as honorable behavior. And, he reminded himself, he was trying to be an honorable man.

Morgan leaned back against the seat, her eyes closed. Erik glimpsed her face in the reflected streetlights. Her eyelashes looked like smudged shadows on her cheeks. Her lips turned up slightly in that faint built-in v shape.

Looking at her wasn't doing anything for his honor, to say nothing of his willpower.

"Have you had any dinner?" His voice sounded rusty, like his throat needed oiling. At least he hoped she'd think that was the problem.

She opened her eyes, grimacing. "Sort of. I grabbed a hunk of cheese and a bag of chips before I took Arthur in to Cal's."

He shook his head. "Sorry. That doesn't qualify as dinner in my book." He checked down Main. Brenner's was closed, and the Silver Spur was likely to be packed with bikers.

"Try the Coffee Corral," she murmured.

He narrowed his eyes. "You in the mood for a burger?"

"They do sandwiches and salads along with burgers. That's

about all I'm up for right now anyway."

Erik parked the truck in front of the blinking neon coffeepot. Inside, a scattering of tables were spread across the floor in front of the counter. One wall was taken up with booths upholstered in red leatherette.

Horace Rankin, Cal's partner and the city council president, sat with his wife, Bethany, who was also one of the assistants at the clinic. His brownish walrus moustache contrasted sharply with his thinning gray hair.

Horace's age was a mystery. Originally, Erik had figured he was around sixty-five, but he didn't act like a senior citizen. Horace and Bethany had gotten married soon after Cal and Docia, and now they sat hip to hip in one of the booths. Every once in a while, Bethany touched his hand and smiled. That kind of behavior gave a man hope.

Horace wiped a napkin across his crumb-dusted moustache. "Evening, Chief, all quiet on the biker front?"

"Far as I can tell." Erik squinted at the menu posted over the counter. "Any recommendations besides burgers?"

"Hell, son, this ain't Brenner's. Stuff tastes like you'd expect it to." Horace took off his gold-rimmed glasses and polished them with an outsize pocket handkerchief. "Enchiladas are good, though."

Bethany grinned at him, then nodded at Morgan. "What's the word on Arthur? Armando said he was staying overnight."

Morgan shrugged. "Motor oil. Cal's giving him a bath and keeping him under observation."

Rankin shuddered. "Bathing the mountain lion. Better him than me. I knew I had a good reason for partnering up with your brother."

"Arthur will be okay, Morg. Cal's the best." Bethany grinned again, turning her bright blue gaze to Horace. "Present company excepted, that is."

Erik ordered a plate of cheese enchiladas and a tuna salad sandwich for Morgan from Al Brosius, the owner who also ran the kitchen. They took a table at the side.

The wall opposite them was painted with a mural of cowboys gathered around a campfire. Cowboys and one very familiar-looking cowgirl.

Erik squinted. Unless he'd lost his mind completely, the cowgirl looked a lot like Helen Kretschmer. He studied the mural more closely, examining the cowboys beside her. One was a dead ringer for Horace.

He shook his head to clear it. Obviously, he'd been working too hard. "That mural's new, isn't it? I don't remember seeing it before."

Morgan grinned, nodding toward Al, who was now flipping a burger on the grill. "He started putting it in last week. Al was an artist in Austin before he and Carol opened this place. He says he'll add somebody new from time to time. Like that." She gestured toward a distant corner of the mural where a pair of cowboys were inspecting a calf. The one checking its teeth bore an uncanny resemblance to Wonder Dentist, while Erik was pretty certain the one holding its rear end was his baby brother, Cal.

He shook his head again. Definitely Konigsburg.

Hilton Pittman was not a happy man, although he did his best to conceal it. He walked down Milam, his hand on Jonelle's elbow, nodding to the citizens who recognized him and ignoring the ones who didn't.

Jonelle narrowed her eyes as they approached the Coffee Corral. "I thought you were taking me out to dinner."

"I am." Hilton managed a smile, although it made the muscles of his jaw hurt. "This is an undiscovered gem, believe me."

Jonelle snorted.

Hilton paid her little attention—his mind was elsewhere. The biker rally had been one of his best ideas, a surefire moneymaker and an easy sell. The bikers came to town, stayed in the area hotels and B and Bs, ate in the area restaurants, and drank in the area bars. Everybody had a stake in keeping them happy and keeping them in Konigsburg. Brody had understood that.

Toleffson apparently didn't.

All weekend long, Hilton had listened to whining bikers. Or rather, one whining biker—Mel Hefner. Mel was a royal pain in the ass. Toleffson had threatened him, he told Hilton, actually threatened him with arrest. Toleffson had told him to keep the other bikers in line. Toleffson had warned he'd haul people to jail.

Hilton had assured Hefner he was shocked—*shocked*—that the chief of police would take it upon himself to threaten the town's honored guests. He promised he'd look into it directly and finally managed to pry Hefner out of his office.

Hefner was an idiot, but he seemed to be telling the truth. Toleffson had actually arrested five of the bikers for public drunkenness. Hilton had had to do some fast talking with Hefner and some equally idiotic biker lawyer who'd threatened to take the city to court.

He doubted that they'd have much of a case, given that the five bikers had been found puking in the city park, but that wasn't the point. The point was Toleffson didn't understand the importance of keeping the bikers happy. The man was moving from being a nuisance to being a liability. And dealing with the problems he'd caused had cut into time Hilton had reserved for the pursuit of Ms. Jonelle Montevista, who worked for the local beer distributor. For that alone, Hilton had decided to make Erik Toleffson pay.

He pushed open the door of the Coffee Corral, smiling his best trust-me-with-your-daughters smile.

Jonelle ran her gaze around the room. She still seemed unimpressed.

Hilton turned the smile in her direction. "A gem, trust me, a gem."

The sound Jonelle made didn't bode well for the rest of the evening.

Behind him Erik heard a brief flurry of voices as more people came in. He turned to see a woman with hair the color of sun-bleached hay checking the menu. Hilton Pittman stood beside her, furtively studying her breasts. They were worth studying, if only to figure out how she managed to walk upright with that much weight in front of her.

Morgan's lips thinned. "Unless that's Hilton's long-lost niece, he's stepping out on his wife again."

Erik watched Pittman scan the customers, stopping to stare at Horace Rankin and then at him. He wondered which of them Pittman would approach first.

Rankin, of course. Good indication of where Erik came in the political pecking order.

Horace looked like he was suffering from a sudden case of dyspepsia. He nodded a quick greeting at Pittman and then returned to his enchiladas. Pittman worked his way toward Erik's table, shaking a few hands along the way, but his smile seemed to lose some brilliance as he came closer. "Toleffson." He nodded toward Morgan. "Ms. Barrett. Quiet night."

Erik allowed himself a half-smile. "Looks like it, Mr. Mayor."

Pittman's eyes narrowed. "Heard you picked up some of our guests yesterday."

"Yes sir." Erik leaned back in his chair. "Some of our guests were drunk as skunks. Turning them loose on the streets with eight hundred pounds of motorcycle didn't seem like a great idea."

"Throwing people in jail won't make them or their friends want to come back here any time soon. Brody was always able to handle the problem without arrests."

"Brody also left most of the drunks wandering around the streets on their own," Horace growled from his table behind them. "Or ralphing in the parking lots. That wasn't much of a solution, Pittman. Anyway, the rest of us never thought so."

Erik studied Pittman. He wasn't sure how far the news had spread about how Brody had "handled the problem", but it might be interesting to find out. "Brody had some unique law enforcement methods. Do you know how he handled the bikers, Mr. Mayor?"

Pittman's tan turned a nasty shade of magenta.

Erik waited.

A smart man would stay quiet. Pittman, however, didn't. "Just because Brody was on the wrong side of the law doesn't mean he didn't do some things effectively."

"What things would those be?" Erik kept his expression blank.

Pittman leaned forward, resting his palms on the table. "He knew how to get along with people, that's what. Tourists are our lifeblood here, Toleffson."

Erik nodded. "Yes sir, they are. But drunk ones are likely to make the non-drunk ones unhappy. And if they drive around, they may make the non-drunk ones dead."

Pittman stood up again, his hands fisting at his sides. "You don't keep anybody happy by roughing them up, drunk or not."

Erik kept his bland expression in place. He'd dealt with better bullies than Pittman—compared to his commander in the MPs, the man was an amateur. "True enough. That's why we didn't rough them up. Unless you count Helen's comments concerning their manhood." Behind him, he heard Rankin snicker.

Pittman's color didn't improve. His voice came in a hiss. "You just keep in mind you're on probation, Toleffson. And if you keep screwing up when you handle the tourists, you'll be out on your ass before your two months are up."

Morgan's voice was soft. "Mr. Mayor, I think your lady friend is getting impatient."

Miss Straw Hair was looking at Pittman as if he'd crawled out from under a rock and could crawl right back as far as she was concerned.

"Miss Montevista is a business associate," Pittman snapped. "She is not a lady...er...friend."

Morgan looked like it was killing her not to say anything, and Erik had to admit it was hard not to grab a nice fat straight line like that. But she smiled sweetly.

"Better hurry, Mr. Mayor, she's waiting."

Pittman gave Erik one more narrow-eyed scowl, which he broadened to include Morgan and Horace, then walked back to join his business associate at the counter.

Al Brosius arrived at their table a few moments later, carrying some large platters on his arm. "Here you go, Chief, enchiladas, tuna salad, chips and salsa."

Erik frowned. "I didn't order the chips."

Brosius's mouth spread in a thin smile. "Had some extra lying around in the kitchen. They'd just go to waste. Enjoy." He glanced toward Pittman, then sauntered back slowly as Ms. Montevista expressed her general annoyance in a voice that sounded a lot like fingernails on a blackboard.

Morgan grinned at him. "You really do like jerking authority figures around, don't you? Of course, in Hilton's case it's totally justified."

"Hell, Pittman's too easy. He's already a walking politician joke." Erik glanced around the room. Morgan wasn't the only one grinning as Miss Straw Hair gave Pittman her opinion of his general competence. "If everybody thinks he's a jerk, why exactly is he mayor?"

Morgan peppered her tuna. "Mostly because nobody else wants to do it. The people who'd be good don't have time, and the people who have time are all as bad as Hilton." She sighed. "Maybe we'll get lucky next election."

Ten minutes later, the mayor left with a couple of bags of food and a clearly disgruntled date. Erik would be very surprised if Pittman got any action out of his adventure with Miss Straw Hair.

He wondered if he'd have any better luck himself. Not with Miss Straw Hair, of course.

Morgan chased a bit of ketchup around her plate with a French fry, careful not to look up at him. Erik had a feeling she wondered something similar.

He took a deep breath and pushed back from the table. Show time.

Morgan told herself she wasn't nervous. Several times. It didn't work. Her stomach was tied in knots. Maybe they weren't going to have sex. Maybe they were just going back to his apartment to sleep.

Maybe she'd be the next American Idol.

She tried to remember how long ago it had been since she'd last gone to bed with someone. Probably Christopher, who qualified as her last boyfriend. Nobody since she'd moved to Konigsburg, that was for sure.

But then again, Erik Toleffson wasn't like anyone she'd ever known before, so what made her think that being with him would be like being with someone else?

Erik parked near the side door to his apartment, around the block from the bookstore. Docia had lived there for the first three years she'd owned the shop, until she'd moved in with Cal. Morgan had been to Docia's apartment lots of times, and she told herself that going there now wouldn't be that different.

Right, Morgan.

She climbed the stairs behind Erik, carefully keeping her eyes away from his really great-looking butt, and watched him unlock the apartment door. Then she stepped through while he held the door for her.

The rooms seemed oddly bare without Docia's furniture. A

slightly battered couch sat in front of the limestone fireplace, a faded rag rug on the floor beside it.

Erik shrugged. "Pretty barren, I know. I haven't bothered to buy much furniture, but there's an extra bed in the spare bedroom. I'll take that. You can take the main one."

Morgan felt a quick stab of disappointment. What did she expect? That he'd ravish her on the planked pine floor? *Interesting idea.* "Okay."

Erik leaned back against the fireplace, propping his elbows on the mantle. "Tired? Hungry? Thirsty?"

"You're offering to take care of all my needs?" Her cheeks blazed. She should learn to think before talking around him. Of course, thinking around him seemed to take her in a lot of interesting directions.

The corners of his mouth inched up. "Whatever I can."

"Oh, hell." She sank down on the couch. "You know, I really don't make an idiot of myself around anybody else. You have the most amazing effect on me."

Erik straightened, then moved to sit beside her on the couch. "What's up, Morgan?"

"Why did you ask me to stay here?" She turned slightly so that she could watch his face. "Why not just send me back to Cedar Creek?"

"You mean besides my tremendous concern for Arthur's health?" He shrugged, gazing back toward the fireplace. "Why do you think?"

"I asked you first."

"Because I wanted some time alone with you." He turned back to look at her. "With no distractions."

She swallowed. "Time to do what?"

Erik watched her for a long moment, his eyes the color of dark coffee. Coffee too hot to drink, but too good not to. He slid his arm behind her shoulders, coaxing her closer. "What do you think?"

"I asked you first," she whispered as his mouth came down upon hers.

He tasted her for a moment, running his tongue along her lips, the edge of her teeth. Faint spirals of heat seemed to dance across her skin, and she lifted her hands to his shoulders and higher, running her fingers through his cropped hair, surprisingly soft against her fingertips.

Erik's hands rested at her waist, moving slowly across the small of her back. Then he lifted her into his lap, settling her bottom between his legs. She could feel the swell of his erection against her hip. Her hands tightened against the back of his neck.

Morgan tried to pull her reeling mind back into focus again. Did she remember how to do this? Maybe she needed a quick review.

His fingers brushed across her temple, pushing back the curls spilling across her forehead. "Are you scared, Bambi?" he whispered.

Bambi. She hadn't a clue what he meant by that. "No, I'm not afraid of you. I'm just... It's been a while for me."

He nodded. "Me, too. We can take it slow."

She took a breath, then began pulling open the buttons of his uniform shirt, slowly, one by one. She slid her hand across the hard muscles of his chest, feeling the slight rasp of hair against her palm. He caught his breath with a sharp hiss.

Morgan raised her gaze and gave him a half-smile, the mirror image of his own. "What makes you think I want it slow, Chief?" she murmured.

Erik stared at her. All of a sudden she looked less like Bambi and more like the kind of predator that ate deer for breakfast. Her fingertips felt cool upon his chest, but they left trails of heat as they brushed across his skin.

He wanted her naked. Hell, he wanted them *both* naked. Immediately.

He tugged her T-shirt up to her shoulders, and she pulled it off in a swirl of brown ringlets. He stared down at a bra that was designed more for display than coverage—flame-colored lace and satin, pushing her breasts together in deeply shadowed cleavage. Her nipples were dusky circles enhanced by the lace.

Bambi had left the building. Tempest Storm was on the case.

He moved his fingers to the catch at the center of her bra, willing them not to tremble as he opened it. Her breasts spilled out, full and perfect, like ripe peaches. He filled his hands, rubbing his palms against the hard buttons of her nipples, feeling them peak.

Her breath came faster. She reached for his shoulders, pushing his shirt down his arms, then smoothed her hands across his pecs, in a movement that mirrored his own.

"Jesus," he breathed, dropping his hands.

She came to her knees, straddling his lap. Her breasts brushed against his chest. Draping her arms around his neck, she leaned forward, running the tip of her tongue along the edge of his collarbone, sending wetness and heat in a thin seam across his skin. The whispering touch of her lips, like rose petals, brushed over the hollow at the base of his throat.

Erik plunged his hands into the soft tangle of her hair, pulling her head back gently, then sank into her mouth again. He tasted desire, heat and a mild hint of tuna. He dropped his hands to her back, feeling the bumps of her spine, the faint dimples at the top of her hips. Together they began to slide down to the floor, his body covering hers, arms out to keep from landing all his weight on her.

For a moment, he considered tearing off her jeans here and now, going at it on the rag rug. One part of him really wanted that.

One very swollen and currently almost-painful part.

But he knew what happened here was more important than that. He had to make it right for her. Morgan Barrett deserved better than a hard floor and rag rug imprints on her ass. Slowly, reluctantly, he raised his head.

Morgan's eyes drifted open. Her swollen lips parted in protest.

He stood up, reaching a hand down to her. "Come on, Bambi. There's a better place for this."

She blinked up at him, then took his extended hand.

The bed looked huge, although Morgan understood that she might not be able to judge size too accurately right then. Erik was momentarily silhouetted by the light from the window, his upper body a perfect triangle, broad shoulders narrowing to flat hips. His chest was covered in dark hair, lightening over his stomach to arrow down at the waistband of his uniform pants.

God, he was big. Probably the biggest man she'd ever been with. And right now, a little unsettling, hulking in the darkness, looming over her. She remembered, briefly, that he was the scary Toleffson, the one no one wanted to mess around with.

Of course, right then messing around was exactly what she had in mind.

He still held her hand tight in his warm grasp. His gaze held her too, dark and brimming with heat.

Then he ran his hands over her body again, sliding from her hips to the side of her breasts. His touch was gentle, soothing. As if he knew she was a little...well, not frightened exactly. Maybe unnerved. He cupped both breasts in his palms and dropped his head to take a nipple into his mouth.

Morgan tangled her fingers in his hair, biting her lip to keep from crying out. A line of electricity flowed from her breast to her mons, leaving her wet and aching. She tried to remember if this was the way she usually felt before she had sex with somebody. She really thought it wasn't, but she was in no condition to remember exactly.

His mouth moved to the other breast, and her nipple puckered in the cool air. She felt his hands move to the waistband of her jeans, unfastening them, pushing them down.

She fought the impulse to cover herself—why on earth would she want to do that? She stepped out of what remained of her clothes and faced him, taking a deep breath.

This was what she was—smallish breasts, ribs and hip bones sticking out, and freckles. And if he didn't like it...

God, she really hoped he did.

She stood in a puddle of moonlight, silver and gleaming, her skin like white silk, her fathomless brown eyes luminous in the darkness.

Beautiful! Couldn't he come up with something better than that? Something she hadn't heard before? Stunning! No—that sounded like some half-assed fashion consultant.

"God, you take my breath away," he murmured. It wasn't great, but it was the best he could do, given that his brain barely had enough blood left to form a coherent sentence. Besides, she did take his breath away, literally. He had to remind himself to inhale.

He put his hands on her hips, pulling her closer, watching the corners of her mouth edge up in a slightly dazed smile. Dazed was good. At least he was on the right track.

She leaned forward, her lips almost against his ear. "I want to see you too," she whispered.

He felt her fumbling at his belt buckle and stilled her hands, then pulled down the zipper and stepped free. Delaying wouldn't make things any better. He knew what he looked like without clothes—the missing link walks again.

Morgan stared, eyes wide, then she reached for him. Her hands were cool against his chest, sliding downward, fingertips trailing across his stomach and abdomen.

He closed his eyes as her fingers encircled him, gliding along the length of his shaft, then cupping his balls.

He would die where he stood, and it would be worth it.

He felt her lips against his chest, her fingers moving again, and his control shattered like an eggshell.

He pushed her across the bed, covering her body with his own. For a moment she looked heartbreakingly young, vulnerable, her eyes as wide as some greeting-card child. He was suddenly afraid of hurting her, doing something wrong that would ruin it for both of them.

Then the corners of her mouth edged up into a grin that was way too wicked for jailbait. "Go for it, Chief," she whispered.

He fumbled in the drawer beside the bed, opening the foil packet with his teeth and sheathing himself in near-record time. Then he touched her, running his fingers through her folds, wet with her own arousal. He slid one finger into her scalding heat. Morgan moaned, and her body arched beneath his hand. Erik kept his gaze riveted to hers, willing her to keep her eyes open as he slid another finger in, stretching her, moving slowly.

Morgan threw her head back, eyes glazed. He rubbed his thumb across her clit, and she gave a strangled cry, her hands flying up to grasp the back of his head and pull his mouth down to hers.

He drank in her sounds, her moans, her gasps, moving himself between her thighs. Then he thrust slowly into her heat, enveloping himself in her.

He felt it through every inch of his body, everything on fire, burning to her touch. Someone groaned in pleasure. A remote, still-functioning part of his brain confirmed it was him.

"Oh sweet," he moaned. "Sweet Morgan!"

He drowned in her then, lost in her heat, the fragrance of roses and lavender filling his head like a memory. Somewhere he felt her arms around him, pulling his head to her shoulder.

He thrust himself against her, again and again, hearing her whimper. He was beyond whimpering himself, so dazed with desire he could hardly remember to breathe. The climax, when it came, washed over him in a wave, taking him under, his body crashing against hers.

He wanted to say something, needed to say something about what had just happened between them, how he felt. How he wanted her. But for the life of him he couldn't remember the words he was supposed to use. "Morgan," he whispered, finally. "Morgan."

And then he closed his eyes and let himself sink into the exhaustion of pure bliss.

Chapter Eleven

Erik woke at his usual six in the morning, feeling very, very satisfied. He wasn't sure why he felt that way, just that he did. And then he became aware of the smooth female shoulder nestled beneath his left arm.

Oh. Morgan. *Holy shit.*

He lay still, careful not to wake her. Mornings after were a bitch. In point of fact, he usually managed to avoid them since he preferred to head back to his own place after sex. Easier all around that way—no awkward "good mornings", no watery coffee and vanilla yogurt, no trying to come up with a polite way to slip out without committing yourself.

His last two girlfriends had been perfectly willing to let him go home. Since they were both cops themselves, they had their own schedules to keep.

Of course, right now he was already *in* his own place, so Morgan would be the one coming up with the excuses for slipping away. He felt a sudden tightness in his chest. He wasn't sure why that idea bothered him, but it did. He didn't want Morgan slipping away from him.

Unprodded, his thoughts drifted to the night before. He wasn't a particularly demanding man, as far as sex was concerned. Usually, sex was sort of like an itch that got scratched periodically. That's what last night should have been. A relief from all the tension that had built up between them over the past few days. A quick roll in the hay, good for both parties, then up and off the next morning.

That's what last night decidedly hadn't been. He couldn't recall ever feeling quite like this before. Sated. Replete. Every part of him satisfied. Happy. *Dear god—happy?*

Morgan Barrett was a very, very dangerous woman.

Because he didn't have time for this. He had two months to prove himself, while the mayor did his best to screw his chances. And now he had the new chore of finding all the time bombs that Brody might have planted around town with his extra-legal activities. If he screwed up any of this, he'd be back to square one. Hell, he might even be back to Iowa.

Erik told himself the clenching in his gut wasn't panic, and it wasn't. More like...regret. He wished he had more time, and not just for Brody. She deserved more time. In fact, she deserved a lot better than him.

Morgan turned over then, still half-asleep. Her hair was a mass of brown ringlets—she looked like a drowsy cherub. Until she opened those amazing brown eyes that drew him into the depths.

"Morning," she murmured.

Suddenly, all thoughts of mornings after were buried under memories of the night before. He spread his hand across her breast, feeling the nipple pucker against his palm. One silky thigh slid along his flank, and he was suddenly as randy as a fifteen-year-old.

"Morning." He grinned and covered her mouth with his own.

They spent a lazy forty-five minutes in his bed before duty called. It might be Sunday, but they both still had to work. Erik dug out the coffee while Morgan showered, then found a loaf of bread for toast. Fortunately, Docia had left her toaster behind when she'd moved out of the apartment, not that he'd ever used it before. Also fortunately, the controls weren't too complicated. His brain didn't seem to be functioning on full power yet.

He watched Morgan in the golden morning light as she sat across from him at the round oak kitchen table. Her brown hair coiled damply around her head in corkscrews, and her cheeks were still pink from the shower.

He really wanted to drag her back to the bedroom. Or possibly onto the kitchen table, although that might mean breaking some dishes. Breaking dishes with Morgan would be one great way to start the day, the week. Maybe the rest of his life.

Whoa! Back off there, bubba. No time for dalliance, remember? Anything long-term is strictly off-limits.

Instead, he offered to drive her to Cal's clinic after they'd cleaned up the kitchen.

Morgan blinked at him. "Oh. Arthur. Right." She grinned, slowly. "To tell you the truth, I'd sort of forgotten about him."

Erik grinned back. For some reason, the idea that he'd been enough to make her forget about Arthur was a kick. He wasn't used to being memorable.

Since it was Sunday morning, the parking lot at the clinic was empty, except for Morgan's SUV and Cal's truck. Morgan had called Cal to check before they left the apartment, and he'd said he'd meet them at the clinic. Erik found that a little odd, given that last night he'd said he'd let Bethany take care of things, and Horace and Bethany lived just down the street.

Cal opened the door as they came up the walk. "Come on in. Armando's bringing Arthur up now."

Morgan's expression was immediately anxious. "Does he have pneumonia? Is he okay?"

"He's fine." Cal frowned slightly. "Well, more or less."

"More or less?" Morgan arched an eyebrow.

"He had a lot more oil in his fur than I realized." Cal was still frowning. "We had to shave some of it off."

Armando emerged from the back of the clinic, carrying a rolled-up towel in his arms. As he got closer, Erik realized the towel was growling.

"Better put him down, but be careful." Cal grabbed one end of the towel to help lower the entire package to the floor. The towel fell free, and Arthur sat glaring at them, eyes bright with indignation.

Erik stared. The cat's hind end was entirely bare, along with three-quarters of his long plumed tail. A tuft of golden fur waved at the tip. He looked like a mutant cross between a puma and a poodle. He was also the most outraged animal Erik had ever seen. And he had every right to be.

"We did try to clean him up." Cal sounded apologetic. "But the fur was really saturated. This was the only way to get rid of all the oil."

"Oh, Arthur." Morgan dropped to her knees beside him. "I'm so sorry!"

Arthur looked unconvinced. He gave the tuft on the end of his tail a furious swipe.

She raised her gaze to Cal. "How do I take care of him?"

Cal sighed. "That's the hard part, Morg. You'll have to keep him inside. If he gets any more oil on his skin, it could cause serious problems. You can't let him out until some of the fur grows back. A few days, at least."

Her eyes widened into Bambi mode. "But people are constantly coming in and out at the tasting room where he lives. I can't close him in my apartment—it's tiny! He'd be miserable. And he'd probably tear it to shreds."

"You could board him here." Armando grinned at her. "I'll keep an eye on the cage to make sure he isn't tunneling out."

"Arthur in a cage?" Her brow furrowed. "I don't think I can do that. He'd be so unhappy."

Cal scratched the back of his neck. "I'd take him home with me, Morg, but he and Docia's cat would probably tear each other apart. After the two of them had my dog for dinner."

"Right. I don't think Docia's Nico would like sharing his space."

"I'll take him." For a moment, Erik felt like checking behind him to see where that voice had come from. He'd just volunteered to babysit a mountain lion.

"Oh, thank you!" Morgan gave him the kind of grin that made his groin turn to solid rock. "I'll help you get him settled in."

"You can visit him. He'd like that." Erik didn't glance at Cal. He had a feeling his brother would be grinning again.

Morgan's eyes were bright. "Oh that's great, really great. Thank you so much! Now let's see if the four of us can get Arthur into his crate."

Arthur was not, needless to say, a happy traveler. His growls reached a crescendo as Erik carried his crate up the stairs, and he could swear he heard scrabbling sounds, as if the cat was trying to tunnel out the side.

Fortunately, the crate was made out of polystyrene. No matter how tough Arthur was, Erik figured it would take him a couple of days at least to dig through.

He put the crate in the bathroom, while Morgan carried in a cat box and a bag of dry food she'd bought at the HEB three blocks over.

"This should be enough," she said. "He's not going to be

here that long."

Erik felt like knocking on wood.

"Thank you so much for offering to cat-sit." Her natural smile deepened into a clear v. "I hope he won't be any trouble."

"I think I can handle him." Actually, he wasn't all that sure he could, but he figured he and Arthur could reach some kind of understanding. Hopefully, before the cat reduced the apartment to rubble.

"Well, I guess I'll get going." She smiled again. "I should get to work."

He nodded. "Yeah, I need to check to make sure the bikers have cleared out."

"Well," she repeated. She looked slightly self-conscious.

Erik reached toward her carefully, running his finger down the slope of her nose. "Come up and see him whenever you like. I'll swing by and give you a progress report."

"I'll look forward to that." Her voice sounded a little breathy, and he felt himself hardening yet again.

Enough. They both really did have work to do. He grinned at her. "Come on, Bambi. I'll walk you to your car."

Since Nando and Peavey had taken patrol on Saturday night—for which, praise be since it had freed Erik for other pursuits—he spent the day doing paperwork and checking on Linklatter, the only other officer on duty. He took over patrol himself in the evening.

Not that there was all that much to do. Most of the bikers had limped off by mid-afternoon, leaving the town with its usual complement of retirees and families checking out the souvenir stores.

He stopped off briefly at dinnertime to open a can of the cat food Morgan had left for Arthur. The cat's burning golden eyes regarded him malevolently. Erik had the feeling only Arthur's lack of opposable thumbs prevented his assassination.

"It's okay, cat," he murmured. "You just have to put up with it for a few days."

Arthur settled down to chew morosely at his mixed grill.

Erik drove the cruiser up Main, stopping briefly at the Faro. The inside looked only half-full, if that, with the owner, Tom Ames, working the bar himself. The outdoor bandstand was empty. The bouncer wandered around the grounds, picking up trash.

"Everything quiet?"

Ames shrugged. "Looks like it. The major part of the asshole contingent took off last night."

Erik grinned and headed back up the street. The Silver Spur wasn't any more lively, although the folksinger was still earnestly putting the audience to sleep on the patio.

He climbed back into the cruiser and headed along a side street, wondering if he could somehow justify a quick trip to Cedar Creek. The older residential streets in Konigsburg were lined with live oaks and pecans, the white limestone and clapboard houses gleaming faintly in the deepening twilight.

He drove up the street slowly, looking at nothing in particular and thinking about Morgan, until he got to the elementary school with its grassy playground. Four or five boys were hunched together on the merry-go-round at the side. Erik surveyed them idly, ready to drive on, until they saw the cruiser.

And took off running.

He pulled to the curb quickly, climbing out as soon as the car came to a stop. The runners were too far away by then, dashing into the yards surrounding the school, but they hadn't all managed to escape. One boy stood jerking at the tail of his shirt that was caught between the bars of the merry-go-round. He stared up at Erik, eyes wide with panic.

Erik folded his arms across his chest, trying not to scare the kid into a faint. "Looks like your friends had things to do."

The boy took a shuddering breath and nodded, slowly. Now that he got a closer look, Erik pegged his age at maybe fifteen, but most likely younger. "What's your name, son?"

The boy's expression shifted from panic to something closer to misery. "Kent," he whispered.

"Kent what?"

He swallowed. "Kent Brosius."

"Al and Carol's son?"

Kent nodded, his Adam's apple bobbing as he swallowed. His toe moved in the dirt and Erik saw the glint of an aluminum can. *Well, hell.*

"Want to tell me what was going on here?"

"We..." Kent's eyes darted around the playground, looking

hopelessly for rescue. "We were just hanging out."

Erik reached down and picked up the can. "Who brought the beer? Was it you? From the restaurant?"

Kent shook his head so hard his hair went flying. "No sir, not me. My father would skin me alive."

Al might still do that if Erik took the boy in. He paused, staring at the beer can in his hand. He had a sudden vision of himself at age fifteen, already sneering, bad to the bone, at least in his own imagination. Trying so hard to impress the worthless bunch of losers he hung out with, the friends his parents wished he'd give up. *Jesus.*

Kent stared down at his shoes, his hands fisted at his sides. "Do you have to tell my dad?" he whispered.

Erik regarded the top of the boy's head. All in all, he'd rather be dealing with the bikers. "Okay, Kent, here's what I'm going to do. You pick up all these cans." He gestured toward the tangle of smashed cans lining the wire fence. "Get your friends to help you if they come back. Which they probably won't since you're the one who got caught. I'll swing back here in a half hour. If the area is clean, your record stays clean too. If I find any cans left, I'll have to talk to your dad."

Kent gave him a mildly mutinous look. "These aren't all ours."

Erik shrugged. "Like I said, you're the one who got caught. Take it or leave it."

After a moment, the boy nodded stiffly. "I'll do it."

"Good." Erik tossed him the beer can. "Better get started. The thirty minutes begins as soon as I'm in the cruiser. And Kent?"

The boy looked up at him, silently.

"You also need to keep out of trouble. Keep your nose clean for the rest of the summer, and nobody knows about this but us. But if I find you doing anything else, your dad will find out about everything after I take you in."

Kent's Adam's apple bobbed again. "Yes sir."

Erik blew out a breath and climbed back into the cruiser. With any luck, this would be the worst thing he'd have to deal with tonight.

Kit had another date with Nando Avrogado, so Morgan let her go early. Allie probably wouldn't be pleased, but Morgan wasn't a babysitter. And Kit definitely wasn't a baby.

She ran the sweeper around the tasting room, then straightened the merchandise on the rough wood shelves along the walls. It looked like they were running low on peach salsa—she'd have to call the company in Austin, although "company" sounded a little highfalutin for a two-man operation. The flavored vinegars and olive oil dipping sauces were both doing well, although they came from California rather than Texas. Maybe she'd e-mail the Texas Olive Oil Council sometime in the next few weeks to see if anyone had products they wanted her to sell.

She stood in the middle of the tasting room, rubbing a hand across the back of her neck, trying to think of other things she needed to do before she called it a night. Erik might still drop by, and she'd like to be out here if he did rather than in her apartment watching the news with her feet up. It made her seem more in command somehow. Not that she was in command of much where Erik Toleffson was concerned.

She had no idea what kind of future they had together, or even if they had a future at all. Probably best not to think in those terms—keep focused on what she could control, like olive oil for the tasting room.

She'd been totally out of control last night, for one of the few times in her life. But Erik was that kind of man. Even if she was out of control, she knew he'd protect her.

Morgan sighed, gathering up the cord to the sweeper. Erik hadn't exactly promised to drop by. He was probably on duty anyway, making sure the town had survived the biker rally. She shoved the sweeper back into the closet.

Skeeter and Fred boomeranged restlessly around the room. She wondered if they'd noticed Arthur was gone or if they just sensed something was different. Neither of them was big on different. She wasn't that big on it herself. "C'mon, boys. Time for your last visit to the outside world before lockup."

She opened the front door, letting the dogs scamper around her ankles. Frogs creaked in the twilight, adding a soprano note to the buzzing cicadas. Skeeter and Fred visited their favorite live oaks, sniffing at the roots as if they'd never seen the trees before.

Somewhere in the distance, Morgan heard the sound of a truck. "C'mon boys," she called. "Time to wrap it up."

Skeeter trotted toward her, but Fred moved to the next live oak trunk. "Fred, c'mon, enough." Morgan began to herd him back toward the door.

The truck sounded closer now, although she wasn't sure where it was. It sounded too far east to be on the highway. *Oh lord, please don't let it be a grape delivery.*

She closed the door behind the dogs, then raised the curtain to peer down the road. Grapes would be coming on the highway. They didn't have any deliveries scheduled, but sometimes the grapes showed up without a lot of advance notice. She heard the brief grinding sound as the truck downshifted. It almost seemed to be coming from the back of the winery, but no delivery would be coming down that hill after dark.

Morgan reached to the side of the door and switched on the yard lights, illuminating the patio and the area behind the winery where the deliveries came in.

The truck sounds stopped abruptly.

She peered out the back window, staring up the hill beside the Cynthiana vineyard. A dark shape was silhouetted toward the top. Maybe it was a truck. Morgan narrowed her eyes, trying to see beyond the brightness of the yard lights.

After a moment, she heard the sound of the truck motor once again. She peered at the shape on the hillside, but it seemed to have blended into the darkness. The truck sound faded slowly in the evening air, leaving only the crickets, the cicadas and the creaking frogs.

And some troubling questions. Why would a truck come down the steep hill beside the vineyard at night? Why would it turn back when the winery lights went on?

And was any of this worth calling Erik about?

After a moment, Morgan shook her head. She could imagine what he'd think if she called about something so feeble. *God, Morgan, you are pathetic.*

She turned the lights off again. But just before she headed for her apartment, she checked the locks one more time.

Chapter Twelve

Erik was having a heart attack. The pressure nearly suffocated him. His chest heaved as he gasped for breath. The heat was stifling, and the rumbling in his ears...

Rumbling? Since when did heart attacks rumble? He opened his eyes.

Two malicious amber orbs glared back. Arthur might be purring, but he clearly didn't want Erik to think he was entirely happy about the situation.

"Okay," Erik wheezed. "Off."

Arthur ignored him, settling his hindquarters more firmly over Erik's abdomen.

"Arthur," Erik snarled through gritted teeth, "get off!"

Arthur pushed his front paws down against the sheet, letting the tips of his claws graze the top of Erik's chest. A clear message, if he needed one, about who'd lose in any pitched battle.

He sighed. "What do you want, cat? Besides your missing fur, which I can't give you."

Arthur began to knead his upper chest, lightly, the points of his claws just enough to prickle. His rumbling purr seemed to resonate all the way to his heels.

He reached up to the back of the cat's neck, scratching the side of his head absently.

Arthur closed his eyes, pushing his chin against his fingers. So the wildcat liked to be petted. Who knew?

Slowly, Erik sat up. Arthur slid down to his lap, blinking. "Don't even think about putting your claws there," he snapped.

Arthur raised his amber gaze again.

Carefully, he slid out from under Arthur's paws, then stood up. He tried to remember if he had any more cat food. Yes. Morgan had given him a couple of cans before she'd reluctantly driven off to Cedar Creek yesterday. Along with a cat box.

He'd have to empty the cat box. *Jesus.*

Arthur hit the ground beside his feet with a thud, then looked up with a throaty "Mwrorwr!"

Erik stumbled toward the kitchen, wondering exactly how he'd gotten himself into this. His mind conjured up a quick memory of Morgan's silvery body lying beneath him. Oh, yeah—that was how.

An hour later he headed for the station, having locked a growling Arthur in the apartment. He'd probably have hell waiting for him when he got home, once Arthur figured out there was no escape.

Helen glanced up as he walked in. "Somebody waiting for you."

"Who?" He thumbed through the pile of mail that had come in while he'd been patrolling over the weekend.

She shrugged. "TCEQ. Powell's water samples."

Erik tossed the mail back in the inbox and started for his office. The Texas Commission on Environmental Quality probably didn't like to be kept waiting.

A blonde in khakis was sitting in his metal visitor's chair, glancing through a copy of *Law Officer Magazine* that likely dated back to Brody. She glanced up at him through wire-rimmed glasses and smiled. "Erik Toleffson, I presume. I'm Andy Wells."

"Ms. Wells." He shook her hand. "Thanks for coming all the way out here from Austin."

"Call me Andy. No problem coming to Konigsburg. My grandma lives here. I try to get down to visit her every couple of weeks."

Andy Wells had a nice smile and warm green eyes. As he sat at his desk, Erik wondered if he might have been interested if he'd met her when he worked for Olema. Probably. He didn't want to think about why he wasn't interested in her now except in a professional sense. "So what made Powell's goats sick?"

She frowned, dropping the magazine back into the rack beside her chair. "We found a mixture of things in the sample. Chlordane, perchloroethylene and motor oil. Hard to say which one had the most effect. None of them would do the goats much good."

"Motor oil?" He tried to remember if there had been any farm equipment around the tank. He didn't think so.

"Yeah." She shrugged. "A layer on top. That might have been what the goats swallowed when they drank the water."

"What's the other stuff—chlordane and perchlorowhatever?"

"Insecticide and dry-cleaning fluid."

Erik narrowed his eyes. "How the hell would dry-cleaning fluid get into a stock tank?"

"How would any of it get into a stock tank?" She gave him a faint smile.

"Motor oil could be accidental—spilled from farm equipment." He rubbed the back of his neck, thinking. "Could insecticide be from runoff?"

She shook her head. "Not this stuff. It's strictly for residential use—termites. And it's been banned since the late eighties because of environmental problems. Some people still use it illegally, though. It's nasty but it does the job."

Erik felt that prickling along his spine he got whenever a particularly troublesome situation seemed to be looming. "So none of the stuff could have gotten there accidentally?"

"I'd say not. I suppose something like used motor oil could have been stored at the ranch, but you said the stock tank was up in the hills."

"Yeah." He rubbed his neck again. "Way back."

Wells sighed. "Sounds like dumping, then."

"You mean somebody went up there and dumped all of this into Powell's stock tank? Why the hell would they do that?" He rubbed harder.

She grinned. "No idea, Officer. I'm just a lowly environmental scientist, not a law enforcement type. We do see this kind of stuff occasionally, though."

"What kind of stuff?"

"Illegal dumping. All of those substances are supposed to be disposed of in particular ways—they're potentially harmful to the environment, and they're regulated. But you've always got people who try to get around the regulations." Her smile dimmed slightly. "Usually, they dump it down the drain somewhere and we trace it back from the dump site."

"But you wouldn't be able to trace this." He dropped his hand, slowly.

Her grin faded altogether. "Not if they dumped it back in the hills. My guess is you've got somebody using the stock tank as what my dad used to call a 'target of opportunity'. If you can't dump something into the sewer, dump it onto the ground."

"Well, crap." He stared down at the water report, not that the numbers meant much to him.

"Exactly." Andy Wells dug around in her briefcase and pulled out her Blackberry. "Now I need the contact information for this Mr. Powell so I can get in touch with him."

He blinked at her. "Get in touch with him? You don't think Powell dumped stuff on his own land, do you?"

She shook her head. "No, but the thing is, he's got a truckload of problems to take care of now—the tank will have to be cleaned out and he'll have to dispose of the water somewhere. TCEQ will have to monitor it to make sure the situation doesn't get worse. But we'll also help him out."

Erik closed his eyes. He could imagine what Powell would say when he heard about all of this. A day that began with a cat-induced heart attack didn't show many signs of improving.

Mondays were the slowest days at Cedar Creek—few people felt like drinking wine on a Monday morning. Morgan had even suggested closing the tasting room on Mondays to give them a day to regroup, but Ciro had vetoed the suggestion. "If somebody hauls themselves up to the hills on a Monday, the least we can do is pour them some wine to celebrate," he explained.

Nobody seemed to be celebrating this Monday, though. Kit wiped water spots off the glasses, while Morgan restocked the wine racks. Thanks to the bikers, they'd had a big weekend— over a hundred cases sold—which was good and bad. Good because they needed the money. Bad because now they were close to being out of sangiovese along with being altogether out of primitivo. They had a few cases of syrah and moscato, but not many. They were even running low on Morgan's Blend.

Pretty soon they'd be down to their generic red and white,

along with the sweet wine, Bluebonnet Sue, which sold well enough but weren't the kinds of wine that would keep people coming back for more.

Ciro walked up behind her, juggling a case of syrah. "Tell Cliff he needs to do another release, Morg. I won't go ahead with it until he agrees, but he needs to get on it now."

She sighed. "I know. I'll talk to him, Ciro. I promise."

She glanced around the tasting room. Kit was wiping off the bar, lining up glasses where the sunlight caught them. She had faint blue shadows under her eyes, Morgan noted. Kit and Nando were probably up to something interesting in their spare time.

Not that she had time to think about anybody's sex life right then, including her own.

She sighed again. She might as well stop putting it off. She had to talk to her father, and it would be better to do it in person than over the phone. She swung through the door to the storeroom and walked over to the unreleased bottles of primitivo and sangiovese that lined the back wall, ready to be labeled.

She tucked a couple of bottles into a gift box, then headed for the front door. "Okay, Kit, you're on your own for the day. I'm going to Austin."

Kit grinned, leaning back against the counter. "Great. A chance to work on my plans for world domination."

Morgan grinned back. "Better you than me, toots."

The drive to her parents' house always took longer than she expected, but that was par for the course with Austin traffic. She thought about the morning rush hour jams she'd struggled with when she'd worked in North Austin. She usually arrived at the office feeling harried and irritable and lucky to be alive, given the general lunacy around her.

For a moment, she pictured rush hour in Konigsburg when the tourists were in full swing. It was never as bad as this. And she could always duck into the Dew Drop with her friends.

Did she really miss Austin all that much? True, she was tired to death from working twelve- to fourteen-hour days. But in a weird way that was better than feeling harried and irritable. She was still musing on the possibilities—and dodging madmen in BMWs—when she pulled into the driveway.

Every time she'd seen her father since the accident she felt the shock all over again. He'd never been a big man, but after the injuries he'd seemed to shrink even more. Now he sat straight in his chair at the kitchen table, his pant legs loose around his ankles, his shirt hanging from his shoulders, hollows around his collarbone. Still, his eyes had the same gemstone brightness they'd always had.

He glanced up as she walked in, his mouth spreading in a grin. "Well, this is a nice surprise! Hi, baby, what's new?"

"Oh, this and that. Some things I needed to talk to you about." Morgan poured a glass of iced tea from the pitcher in the refrigerator, giving herself time to pull her thoughts together, then settled in the chair opposite him. "We had a really great weekend with the motorcycle rally, Daddy. I haven't tallied everything up yet, but it looks like we sold at least twenty cases more than last year."

Her father reached across the table to squeeze her hand. "Good, sweetheart, that's good to hear. That's always been a profitable weekend, even if the people are a pain in the rear."

Morgan took a deep breath, keeping her voice as matter-of-fact as she could. "We've got some supply problems, though. We're almost out of sangiovese and we're all out of primitivo. Ciro thinks it's time to release the new wine."

Her father waved his hand impatiently. "We can talk about that later. What about that vineyard site Ciro found—Joe Powell's pasture?"

"There may be some water problems there. Some of his goats have gotten sick."

"From drinking the water? When?" Her father leaned forward.

"Just a week or so ago. There was something wrong with his stock tank."

"Where does he get the water for the tank? Is it ground water or does he bring it in? Are they sure it was the water and not something else?" Her father tapped the table in front of him, eyes bright. "Tell Powell to get a water analysis done before we sign the lease. That way we can see if there are any ongoing problems or if it was a one-time thing."

Morgan nodded, pushing the hair back from her forehead. "I've already suggested that to Ciro. And the police are investigating the whole thing. About the sangiovese and the primitivo, if we could do an early release..."

"Too soon." Her father shook his head, dismissively. "It won't be ready for another month at least. Did you talk to DeMarco about that shipment of roussanne grapes from Lubbock?"

"Yes sir." Morgan moved her stiffening shoulders. She could feel a tension headache starting near her eyes. "They'll deliver them next month. Daddy, I tasted the sangiovese last week, and it tastes ready to me. Ciro thinks so too."

Her father looked up at her, frowning. "Morgan, it's too soon. Believe me, I've been doing this a lot longer than you have."

"I know you have, Daddy." She stared down at the bottles at her feet. Yelling at her father wouldn't get him to do the release. "But we're almost out of wine. We may lose the Brenner's account if we can't supply them with some more primitivo."

Her father shrugged. "If we lose them, we lose them. There'll be other restaurants. That's better than letting wine go out before it's ready. We've got our reputation to consider."

There'll be other restaurants. Morgan took another deep breath, forcing her hands to unclench. "Brenner's is the most popular restaurant in Konigsburg, Daddy. It gets reviewed in the Austin and San Antonio papers. It's got a blurb in *Texas Monthly.* A lot of people come to the winery because they tasted the wines at Brenner's. And it took us months to get them to put our wine on their list in the first place. We need to keep our wines in there, and to do that we need wine to sell them. It's the only advertising we've got right now." Seeing as how her father refused to do any advertising directly since the wines could sell themselves.

Her father stared at her in silence for a few moments. "You say you tasted the sangiovese?"

"Yes sir. And the primitivo."

"And Ciro tasted them, too?"

"Yes, Dad, he did. He thinks they're ready. I brought a bottle of each one with me." She picked up the bottles from the floor. "Would you taste them for me, please?"

"What exactly did Ciro say?"

She tried not to sigh. Of course, he trusted Ciro's judgment more than hers. Ciro had been in the business as long as her father had. *So why not let Ciro make the decision?* "He thinks they're good."

Her father leaned back in his chair, staring at the bottles in front of him. "That's how we used to do it, you know. Me and Ciro, sometimes Carmen. We'd sit down and try two or three bottles, figure out if it was right yet. If we needed to try a different blend. It's all a matter of taste, you know. You can't do it by machine."

Morgan pushed her lips into a smile. Ciro and Carmen would never do that with her, or if they did, they'd never listen to her opinion. Why should they? Even her own father didn't trust her judgment. "Yes, Dad, I know. And your palate is better than anyone's. But we really need this wine now."

Her father sighed. "Pour me a sample of each, then. But I'm not making any promises."

The ache that had begun in her throat eased slightly. "No, Dad, I know you're not. Just give it a try."

Leila Barrett arrived at her husband's house, which had once been her house as well, at five forty-five. The closing on the latest McMansion in the new development she was selling had been delayed for a couple of days and she'd gotten off early. She recognized Morgan's SUV in the driveway and felt a quick surge of concern. What had gone wrong now?

The first thing she saw when she walked in the kitchen door was her husband and her daughter, sitting together at the table with two open bottles of wine between them.

Wine. Of course. It had to be wine.

Leila managed not to frown quite as ferociously as she wanted to. Ever since Cliff had developed his obsession with wine, she'd been trying to find a way to talk him out of it. The fact that he'd spent more time with the winery than he had with her over the past few years had led to their current separation, which might or might not become permanent, depending on whether the old coot could bring himself to appreciate his wife as much as his latest release. Now he'd managed to drag their daughter into this insanity, this endless money-sink of a winery. Every time Leila thought about it, she started grinding her teeth. Her dentist had threatened to fit her with a harness to keep her from grinding them down to nubs in her sleep.

She stared critically at her daughter's profile, just visible through the kitchen door. She had dark circles under her eyes, and she was developing crow's feet. Leila adjusted the jacket of her Talbots suit over the slight spread of her hips. She'd also be willing to bet Morgan wasn't eating right.

After a moment to let her exasperation settle, she walked into the kitchen, smile firmly in place. "Sweetie! How wonderful to see you! I thought that was your SUV out front."

At close range, she thought Morgan looked worse than she had from a distance. She had hollows under her cheekbones, and her eyes were tired. Silently, Leila cursed Cedar Creek, Cliff's accident and wine in general. She didn't care how good the stupid vintage was, it wasn't worth wearing her daughter to a frazzle.

"You'll stay over tonight, won't you? Too late to be heading back to the hills today, especially since you've been imbibing." Leila waggled her eyebrows in what she hoped was a comical way. Given Morgan's current weight, a half bottle of wine would boost her over the blood-alcohol limit in two seconds flat. "If Cliff can't put you up here, you can stay at the condo with me."

Morgan hugged her, and Leila swore she could feel every bone in her daughter's body. "Hi, Mom. I didn't really drink all of this. Dad did most of it."

Leila narrowed her eyes at her husband. Cliff wasn't in much better shape than Morgan was. She'd tried to ration him to two glasses of wine a night.

He shook his head, grimacing. "Don't worry, warden, I spat most of it out. Merely sipping for test purposes."

"So what's the verdict, Dad?"

Beneath Leila's hands, Morgan's shoulders seemed awfully tense for a family visit. Leila raised an eyebrow. "What are the two of you up to now?"

"Wine business." Cliff kept his gaze on Morgan. "Okay, Morg, I agree on the sangiovese—it's ready to go. But the primitivo needs at least a couple more weeks."

Morgan's shoulders relaxed, and she gave her father a brilliant smile. Leila felt her heart contract. Her daughter really was a beautiful woman.

If only she didn't look so tired! At this rate she'd be worn down to a wisp before she found Mr. Right. Leila put her arm around Morgan's shoulders and nudged her toward the refrigerator. "Just give me a chance to fatten you up a little, sweetie. Then you can go back tomorrow. Cedar Creek can survive without you for a night." Cedar Creek could survive without Morgan indefinitely if Leila had anything to say about it.

Across the room, Cliff stood slowly, reaching for his cane. Leila looked away quickly. Seeing him limp across the kitchen always twisted her heart. And she couldn't afford to feel sorry for him—it might cloud her judgment so that she'd end up living with him again, taking second place to that damned winery. "Cliff, do you want anything special for supper?"

He sighed. "Nope. I'm going to take a nap for a half hour or so. That should give the two of you time to discuss me."

Leila stifled the impulse to help him up the stairs. "Take as long as you want. Once we finish with you, we'll move on to something more interesting." She heard his snort as he moved through the door. At least the old coot still knew how to laugh.

Morgan didn't, judging from her expression as she watched her father hobble toward the stairs.

"Believe it or not, he's doing much better now." Leila turned back to check the freezer. "His doctor says he can start driving in another few days."

Morgan gave her a dry smile. "Which means he'll be coming up to Cedar Creek the day after the doctor lets him start."

"Exactly." Leila pulled out a frozen pizza, along with a bag of lettuce from the hydrator. "We'll have some pizza, baby. Lots of cheese and pepperoni. At least when Cliff starts going to that damned winery again, he can take over some of the work you're doing. Anything that doesn't require moving around too much, that is."

Morgan shrugged. "I'm okay, Mom. Don't worry about me."

Leila felt her jaws tightening again. Harness time. She turned to look at her daughter, hands on hips. "Morgan Elizabeth Barrett, you are not 'okay'. You look like you're ready to drop in your tracks. And you've lost so much weight they're going to start putting your picture on the cover of the tabloids along with all those damn fool starlets who starve themselves. Don't you dare tell me not to worry. I'm your mother."

For a long moment, Morgan stood, blinking. Then she sank into one of the kitchen chairs, rubbing her hands against her temples. "All right, I'm tired. And I need to be more careful about what I eat. I told Dad I'd manage the winery until he was back on his feet, and that's what I'm doing."

Leila considered whether to hug her or shake her until her teeth rattled. She decided on the hug, just a quick one across Morgan's shoulders. "You can let other people do things, you know. As a matter of fact, Ciro and Carmen could probably run that place on their own. Your dad just wanted to keep his hand in, so he picked on you. But I don't think he realized what he was asking you to take on, baby. You've had to learn things in a year that it took him ten years to learn himself."

Morgan looked up at her, smiling with tired eyes that made Leila's heart ache. "Why didn't Dad just let Ciro take over the whole operation in the first place? He's a lot more qualified than I am."

Leila blew out a breath. "I'm not sure, baby. He may have wanted you to get involved in the day-to-day routine of the place. I think he hopes you'll take over his share of Cedar Creek some day, that you'll love it as much as he does."

Leila glanced at Morgan in time to see the panic in her eyes. *Oh good lord.* Was Cliff's vision of her daughter's future that much of a nightmare?

Leila patted her on the shoulder, leaning back against the counter. "Let's not think about your father and what he wants for a minute. What do you want to do, sweetheart? Do you really want to run Cedar Creek?"

"I'm not sure anymore. I thought if I took over as manager, I could finally show Dad I wasn't a complete lightweight. I know he's always been disappointed that I didn't major in chemistry or agriculture—something that could have helped at the winery."

Leila picked up the bag of lettuce and started for the sink. It kept her from grinding her teeth again. "You've never been a lightweight, Morgan. And you did major in something that could help at that damned place. Lord knows Cedar Creek could use some marketing. It's not your fault your father's too pigheaded to see it."

"Thanks, Mom."

Morgan smiled and Leila felt her heart contract again. *Damn you, Cliff Barrett. And damn Cedar Creek.*

She pulled the pizza out of its plastic bag. Time to shift gears. "So what's new in Konigsburg? Any interesting people?"

Behind her, she heard Morgan yawn. "We had a bunch of

bikers last week for a rally, but I wouldn't call them interesting exactly. Other than that, not much is going on. Except for Arthur, that is."

"What about Arthur?" Leila turned on the oven for the pizza and began dividing the lettuce into bowls.

"He got into some oil somewhere. The vet had to shave off some of his fur to clean him up."

"Mercy." Leila was operating on autopilot now, half listening while she looked for a tomato in the refrigerator. "So who's keeping track of him while you're gone? Ciro and Carmen?"

Morgan didn't answer for a moment. Leila looked up and caught her expression—guarded, maybe even a little guilty.

"No, he's staying with a friend of mine until some of the fur grows back. The vet said it may take a few days."

"A friend?" Leila's radar shifted into high beam. "You mean that nice lady who owns the bakery?"

Morgan picked at her cuticle, just as she had when she was little and wanted to avoid direct eye contact with her mother. "No. Just a friend."

Just a friend. Interesting. "Anyone I know?"

Morgan lifted her gaze for a moment, her expression deliberately bland. "I don't believe so."

Obviously subtlety wasn't working. "A male friend?"

Morgan's mouth narrowed to a thin line. "Yes, Mom, and that's all I'm going to say about it. Okay?"

Leila laid the pizza onto the oven rack jauntily. All of a sudden she felt a lot more optimistic than she had only a few moments before. "Of course, honey. My lips are sealed."

She walked to the kitchen table and the two bottles of wine left over from Cliff's taste test. Normally, she refused to drink wine as an expression of her dislike for the whole Cedar Creek experience. On the other hand... She picked up a glass.

"Which of these bottles did Cliff decide was good?"

Morgan stared at her openmouthed, then pointed to the bottle on the left. "You're drinking wine, Mom?"

Leila smiled, pouring herself a healthy tipple. "Yes, ma'am. All of sudden I feel like having a little celebration." She lifted her glass. "To Arthur. And his speedy recovery." *Only not too speedy, please.*

Chapter Thirteen

The TCEQ officer, Andy Wells, left early in the afternoon to break the uniformly bad news to Joe Powell—who then spent twenty blistering minutes on the phone with Erik. At five, he tried calling Cedar Creek, only to have Kit tell him that Morgan was in Austin.

He ate dinner with Arthur, not exactly the evening he'd planned.

The next day he spent the morning talking to various state agencies about illegal dumping, then devoted the afternoon to nosing around Powell's pasture with Nando. They found a lot of limestone, cedar bushes, nopal cactus and goat crap.

"Remind me again, what are we doing out here?" Nando asked him.

Erik wasn't entirely sure, but he thought he'd know the answer when he saw it. "Looking for oil," he muttered. "Or something that resembles it."

They finally found it near a sharp limestone outcropping around a hundred yards from the stock tank—a large irregular black circle on the ground.

Nando stared down at it, eyes narrowed. "Smells nasty."

Very nasty. Erik walked carefully around the edge. Double tire tracks ran across the far side. He knelt beside them. The last big rain had been a couple of weeks ago. Something heavy had driven through the mud. If he'd been working for a big-time department, he could have had a lab tech take impressions, but in Konigsburg he was on his own, unless he wanted to get Pittman to pay for the county lab.

Right. When they're ice-skating in hell. He pulled out his camera and began snapping shots.

Nando stood at his shoulder, staring down at the tracks. "Heavy sucker."

"Yeah. Fair-sized truck, most likely." Erik knelt down to get a better angle for the camera.

"You suppose they drove that thing up here over the same road we used?"

Erik thought about it. Anybody who drove a large truck over that road ran the risk of being seen by Powell or one of his ranch hands. "Maybe at night."

Nando shuddered. "Scary thought."

"Yeah. Maybe they do it in late afternoon or evening. After Powell's hands head for home." And then he stopped, staring at the black spot.

Morgan had been pushed down the hill in late afternoon. He rose slowly to his feet, staring back at the hillside where he'd found her.

Damn! She must have been walking around the pasture while the dumper was still up there. Maybe she'd scared him. Maybe he'd tried to get rid of her so he could get away without being seen.

Erik felt his gut clench. *Tried to get rid of her.* He scanned the steep limestone outcroppings at the back of the pasture. "There must be another road up here."

Nando frowned. "Lots of roads all over these hills."

"Yeah, but this one has to lead up here from somewhere other than Powell's ranch." Erik followed the scar running through the grass, the mark of the double tires.

They found the break between the limestone cliffs a few hundred yards farther on. The road dropped down steeply on the other side.

Nando whistled softly. "Hell of a drop."

Erik nodded. "But it doesn't run directly by Powell's place. Less chance of being seen. And it looks a little smoother than the one we took."

Nando shrugged. "Even if the driver didn't go by Powell's place, somebody might still have seen him. Big truck to be rolling around the back country."

Erik surveyed the countryside. Clumps of cedar and live oak, limestone crags, white dots that could either be boulders or goats. To the east, neat cultivated rows and a distant building. A familiar distant building.

Cedar Creek Winery.

"Well, hell," he muttered.

Nando grinned. "Hey that's good. Maybe somebody down there saw the truck."

"I hope so." Better than the other possibilities that had occurred to him.

They drove back down on the road they'd driven up rather than trying to follow the dumper's steep path. "He must have come up here at least twice," Erik explained as he negotiated around some truck-killer potholes. "The first time he dumped a load in the stock tank. The second time he dumped it on the ground—maybe because Powell had chicken wire around the stock tank by then."

And Morgan had almost seen him the second time. In fact, maybe she actually had seen him without realizing it. So the bastard had thrown her down the hill.

Erik would find that goddamned truck if it took him the rest of his time in Konigsburg. And then he would turn the driver over to Helen Kretschmer for re-education after he'd undertaken some general ass-kicking of his own.

As he pulled into the winery parking lot, he realized he was looking for Morgan's SUV—and not seeing it. He felt a quick stab of disappointment.

Nobody was inside the tasting room when they first walked in, but the door to the office swung open and Kit Maldonado walked out.

Nando grinned. "Hey, *chica.* You seen any big trucks coming down from the hills within the last couple of weeks or so?"

"How big?" Kit frowned, one wrinkle marring her smooth forehead. "You mean like those extended cab things?"

Nando shook his head. "Not a pickup. More like delivery trucks, commercial stuff."

Kit shrugged. "Not that I recall. But I can't really see the main road in here, just the hills."

Erik turned to look out the window with its view of the vineyards. He could just see the line of the dirt road from Powell's pasture across a hill to the left, alongside what Morgan had called the Cynthiana vineyard. "Have you ever seen anybody driving way back there above the vineyard?"

Kit frowned again. At this rate, those wrinkles were going to make her look at least nineteen by the end of the day. "A truck coming down over there? No. Not that I remember."

"What truck? Where?" Ciro Avrogado walked in carrying a case of wine. He glared at his son. "What are you doing here?"

Nando grinned back easily. "Being a cop. You seen any trucks come down that road from Powell's during the last couple of weeks, Pop?"

Ciro squinted toward the window. "That road? What damn fool would take his truck down that? It's a goat track."

Ciro scowled in Erik's general direction. Erik smiled back. "This particular damn fool went down it twice. The second time was the day Morgan got hurt at Powell's pasture."

Ciro's gaze sharpened. "Was he the one who hurt her?"

Erik shrugged. "Maybe. We'll know when we talk to him."

Ciro looked back out at the hillside, then shook his head. "I haven't seen anybody up there, but I might not notice. We're pretty busy this time of year getting the grapes in. You might ask Esteban, though. He's out in the yard more than I am. He might have seen something."

"Who did what to Morgan?" Kit was frowning again. "I thought she fell down the hill."

"She did. But she might have had some help."

Kit stared at him wide-eyed as the tasting room door swung open and the subject of the conversation walked in. Four pairs of eyes immediately swung her way.

"What?" Morgan's eyes widened and she glanced down at her hands. "Did I spill something on myself?"

Ciro walked over to her, ignoring Erik and Nando. "What's the verdict on the wine?"

"The sangiovese is a go. He wants to wait a couple of weeks on the primitivo."

Ciro nodded. "Right. I figured that would be it. Labeling time." He rubbed his hands together, smiling as he turned to Nando. "Good thing you're here. We'll need all the help we can get."

Nando shook his head. "I'm still on duty, Pop. And I need to go back to town for my truck."

Ciro narrowed his eyes, then turned to Morgan.

She groaned. "Not this afternoon, please. I just got back from Austin. I'll work on it tomorrow, I promise."

Erik glanced at his watch, then put an arm around her shoulders. "C'mon. I'm off duty in ten minutes. You can come and visit Arthur."

Three pairs of eyes nailed him to the wall. He suddenly felt like ducking.

"Where is Arthur that she needs to go visit him? Why isn't he here where he belongs?" Ciro's voice was heavy with suspicion.

"Arthur's staying at Erik's place until his fur grows back. I haven't seen him in a couple of days. Let's go." Morgan turned back toward the door.

Kit gazed up at Nando with enough heat to start a small bonfire. "You want a ride back to town?"

Nando's lips spread in a slow grin. "Sure."

Erik glanced back at Ciro. "If you think of anything..."

"Yeah. Right." Ciro was staring back and forth between Nando and Kit, his brow furrowing. Finally, he turned back toward the winery and shrugged. "I'll get that labeling run set up. Maybe Esteban can start on it tonight."

Checking on Arthur took maybe five minutes, largely because Arthur wasn't much interested in being checked on. He glanced drowsily at Morgan, allowed her to scratch his ears, and then fell noisily asleep again. At that point, Erik realized he didn't have any food in the house and his stomach was growling almost as noisily as Arthur was snoring. Not exactly the road to romance.

The Dew Drop was surprisingly empty when Morgan and Erik got there—Docia and Cal sat at a side booth, Biedermeier and a few other men hunched over their stools at the bar.

Morgan frowned as she slid in beside Docia. "Where is everybody?"

Docia shrugged. "Pete and Janie went to San Antonio for the weekend. Lars and Jess never come in anyway since they've got the kids to take care of. And ever since Kit moved in, Allie's been spending most of her time at Wonder's. She even cooks for him. I hear she got him to clean up his kitchen."

Cal grinned. "Figures. Wonder will do anything to get Allie to cook. Besides, she'll be living there full-time after they get married, right?"

"I don't think they've decided where they're going to live. Allie's got a fantastic kitchen at her house. I don't think Wonder will want her to give that up."

Cal sipped his Dos Equis. "Wonder's yard is better. Maybe they can alternate."

Docia rolled her eyes but said nothing.

Erik raised an eyebrow at Morgan. "Hungry?"

"No, I had a sandwich with Mom before I left Austin. But I'd love something to drink."

"Wine?"

Morgan's lips curved upward. "Beer. I think I'm wined out."

Erik got a Shiner and a Dr. Pepper from Ingstrom, along with a dubious-looking Frito pie. Good thing his stomach was used to crap. He settled in beside Cal, handing the Shiner to Morgan.

She smiled her thanks. "Why were you and Nando out at the winery this afternoon? Any trouble?"

Erik narrowed his eyes, trying to decide how much information to pass on in a public place. "We were doing some checking out at Powell's. Do you remember a heavy truck up at the pasture the day you fell? I thought you said you heard one."

Morgan frowned, shaking her head. "I heard a motor, something driving away, but I didn't see anything. It could have been a heavy truck."

Erik turned to Cal. "How about you?"

Cal shrugged. "Too busy carrying Morgan back up the hill. I didn't see any truck there except yours."

"Was someone there?" Morgan leaned forward, her brow furrowed.

"Maybe. Somebody had been there earlier, messing with the stock tank."

"Somebody poisoned Powell's stock tank?" Cal's voice rose slightly. A couple of heads turned toward them from the bar.

Erik grimaced. "I don't think it was somebody out to hurt Powell." Although now that he thought about it, finding Joe Powell's enemies might be easier than finding a dumper who'd chosen a "target of opportunity". Given Powell's tendency to fly off half-cocked at everybody who crossed his path, he must have left some disgruntled people in his wake.

Morgan's eyes widened. "Was somebody actually trying to

hurt me?"

Heads turned again. Erik gritted his teeth. "I don't know. I'd guess not—I'd guess he was just trying to get away without you seeing him. So far as I can tell, nobody was trying to hurt anybody." Except maybe some goats and the occasional cat.

Docia leaned her swollen body back against the booth, rubbing the small of her back. "Gee, this is getting interesting. Also totally confusing."

Erik sighed. "Look, I can't say much more about this. I just wanted to know if either of you saw anybody driving around out there."

"No, but there's more traffic back around Powell's place than you'd think." Cal sipped his beer. "Powell has his goat feed delivered, and hay for his horses. His ranch hands live in town, so they're always coming and going. Hell, he gets FedEx and UPS just like the rest of us."

Erik frowned. "So if you saw a truck back there when you were working with the goats..."

"I wouldn't think anything about it. A Rolls-Royce I'd notice. A truck?" Cal shrugged. "Nah."

The Frito pie was about as bad as Erik had feared. He ate half of it before giving up. Powell's animals might not have been deliberately poisoned, but Ingstrom's customers were in mortal danger.

Morgan smiled. "If you want, I can fix you something back at Cedar Creek. I think there's some soup in the freezer."

Erik dropped the remains of the Frito pie into the trash can on his way out. Ingstrom scowled at him.

The road to the winery was familiar by now. Erik drove on autopilot and spent most of the time watching Morgan when she wasn't looking—and sometimes when she was.

"Can you tell me what's going on at Powell's, or do you have to keep it a secret?"

He sighed. "It involves you too, potentially. Somebody dumped some chemicals back in Powell's pasture—stuff that's supposed to be disposed of in a particular way."

"So it was an accident? But why would someone be back there with chemicals?"

He shook his head. "Not an accident. Illegal dumping. Instead of contracting with a company that's licensed to dispose of nasty stuff, you pay a dumper to take the stuff off your hands. Then the dumper takes it somewhere and gets rid of it."

She stared at him, eyes wide. "But if it gets into the ground water, it could poison the water supply."

"Yep." He turned his gaze back to the road ahead. "Which is why I'd like to find this SOB. That and the fact he pushed you down that hill at Powell's."

Morgan sat frowning beside him. Her eyes looked dark again, like she'd just had another weight added to her shoulders. One more thing the dumper could take responsibility for. And Erik too, since he'd passed on the news.

She closed her eyes for a moment. "We'll need to check at Cedar Creek. If he dumped at Powell's pasture, he might have dumped at the vineyards too. Right at harvest time."

He shrugged. "Maybe. Looks like he used a fair-sized truck, though. Could something bigger than a pickup get into the vineyards?"

"Some of them." Her eyes were still closed. "Depends on the road and the location. I'll have to tell Ciro. He knows the vineyards better than I do. He can start checking them."

Erik decided he might as well talk about all the unpleasant possibilities at once. "Would Arthur range as far away as Powell's pasture?"

Morgan's eyes flew open. "Arthur? You mean the oil?"

He nodded. "Oil was part of what was dumped at Powell's. Would Arthur go that far?"

"I don't know." She touched the tips of her fingers to her lips. "Usually he sticks around the vineyards—lots of rodents and lizards to catch."

Erik pulled into the parking lot next to the winery. Sunset turned the vineyards gold, casting long shadows along the vines. "Up for a walk?"

She sighed. "Sure."

They started up the drive behind the winery building toward the equipment sheds and the nearest vineyard, scanning the ground.

"What am I looking for?" Morgan asked. She turned up the hill toward the Cynthiana.

"At Powell's it was a big black circle. Is this Arthur's favorite vineyard?"

"Sometimes. This one and the one to the west." She turned in that direction and stopped. "Oh crap," she whispered.

Erik stepped beside her. A drainage ditch ran between the road and the vineyard. They stared down at a black stain running half the length of the ditch.

He blew out a breath. "Easy for him to use. All he'd have to do would be to run a hose down into the ditch and then use it to pump out the chemicals."

She pressed a hand to her mouth. "We'll have to test the ground water—and the grapes from this vineyard before we harvest them. We'll have to destroy the grapes if they've been affected. Crap, crap, crap!" She closed her eyes for a moment.

"You probably won't have to do that. This drainage ditch is downhill from the vineyard. Chances are runoff would flow away from the grapes, not toward them."

"I should have thought of that, shouldn't I? I'm such a great winery manager! I can't even tell the difference between uphill and down." Her lips trembled slightly.

"C'mon, Bambi," he murmured, sliding an arm around her shoulders. "Give yourself a break."

She sighed. "Who should I call about this?"

"Ciro." He began walking her back toward the winery. "And a woman named Andy Wells at the Texas Commission on Environmental Quality. But you can't do anything now—TCEQ will be closed for the day. It'll still be here in the morning."

"Damn it all, who could do this?" She turned to look at him. "And when? Skeeter and Fred aren't good for much, but they do make a lot of noise if anybody drives up after dark." She stopped for a moment, staring back toward the vineyard. "Erik, I may have heard him, myself."

"When? You mean up at Powell's?"

She shook her head. "Two nights ago. After I was at your house." Her cheeks blazed for a moment, and he suppressed a totally inappropriate grin. "I heard a truck up in the hills. I thought it might be a grape delivery and turned on the yard lights."

"Did you see it?"

She shook her head again. "After I turned on the lights I heard it stop and then go back up the road."

Erik studied the road that ran alongside the vineyard until

it turned back toward Powell's pasture. "Is this a main road in from Konigsburg?"

"Not really. It goes back into the hills, then intersects with a farm-to-market road. Some people use it when they're heading to Johnson City." She climbed the steps to the tasting room entrance, then stood still for a moment, resting her forehead on the door. "Oh lord, just what I need—another cheery thing to complicate my life."

Morgan ran through her mental checklist. Call Ciro. Call TCEQ. Call Dad. Her chest felt tight. Her shoulders ached.

Maybe she was cursed. That would explain why every time things seemed to be working out, something else went haywire. The wood door felt cool against her forehead. *You'll get through this. Just open the door.*

Beside her Skeeter and Fred nudged against her leg, whimpering to be let inside.

Suddenly she felt Erik's fingertips sliding across the back of her neck, smoothing away the damp hair. "C'mon, Bambi, let's go in and get something to eat."

Right. She'd promised him dinner. And that wouldn't happen as long as she stood there feeling sorry for herself. She raised her head as she opened the door. The palm of Erik's hand rested, warm and strong, against her nape.

He pushed her gently through the door, then closed it behind them. Twilight shadows played along the walls as the dogs clicked to their food bowls.

Erik's arms slid around her waist, pulling her against the hardness of his chest as his lips brushed across her forehead.

Morgan let herself be embraced, fitting herself between his thighs. Heat and wetness began to build at her center.

"You're using sex to distract me," she murmured, rubbing her face against his collarbone.

"Yes, ma'am." Erik grinned down at her. "That's one purpose."

"What are the others?"

"To pleasure you, Morg. And me." He ran his finger along the swell of her lower lip, sliding the finger inside her mouth. Morgan sucked quickly, tasting salt as she ran her tongue across his fingertip.

He pulled back again, staring down into her eyes, like predator and prey. "Is it working?"

She swallowed. "Is what working?"

He threw back his head and laughed. "C'mon, Bambi, time for you to show me where you live."

She narrowed her eyes. "Why do you keep calling me that?"

He leaned down to run his tongue along the ridge of her ear.

She felt a sudden jolt of heat. "You're trying to distract me again."

He turned to flip the latch on the front door, then began to herd her gently toward the door to her apartment. "This is your place, right?"

"Right." She shook her head once as if that could clear it. "Aren't you hungry?"

"Later." His voice rumbled against her ear.

"But..." Her breath caught in her throat as one of his hands cupped her bottom.

"Pleasure first, Morg." He had her T-shirt off before they reached the living room, his fingers sliding down to unfasten the snap of her jeans. Morgan began to pull at the buttons on his shirt, trying to unfasten them. Her fingers didn't seem to be working right.

"Easy," he murmured, "I've only got two uniform shirts and the other one hasn't come back from the laundry yet."

Morgan began to giggle, leaning against his shoulder. Her head was spinning—her breath caught in her throat. "Help me then."

He pushed her hands away, then pulled the shirt over his head. She heard a button bounce away on the floor. "Damn it!" Erik growled.

Morgan felt breathless again; her laughter died away. Shouldn't she be worrying about the winery right now? Trying to figure out what to do next?

Nah!

She reached for his belt buckle as he unfastened her bra in front.

He caught her around the waist again, pulling her tight against him, her breasts pressed to his chest, so that she felt crinkling hair rubbing her nipples.

"Slow down, Bambi," he murmured, "we've got all night."

Morgan stared up at him, the fog in her brain suddenly clearing. *All night.* She had him all night.

He raised an eyebrow. "Trouble?"

She shook her head. "No. Anything but."

He gave her a slow grin that made her want to pull him down on the floor where he stood. "Good. That's just the way I feel."

Chapter Fourteen

Erik sat cross-legged in Morgan's bed, eating mango ice cream out of the carton. Morgan lay stretched beside him on her back, her head resting on her folded hands. He tried not to notice how that position raised her breasts and made her nipples look tantalizingly hard. She was watching him, those luminous brown eyes running quickly over his chest.

She looked hungry. He hoped it wasn't just for food.

"Want a bite?" He extended his spoon, careful not to drip melted ice cream on her belly.

She grinned at him. "You mean ice cream?"

Erik felt a quick jolt of heat, blood running straight to his groin. The woman was pure aphrodisiac. "Unfair. You're supposed to give me time to recover here."

After what they'd been doing for the past hour, he'd half-expected her to drop into an exhausted nap. Hell, he should have needed a little rest too. Instead, he could already feel the arousal beginning again.

"How long does it take you to recover, Chief? Personally, I'm feeling fine."

He squinted at her. "You look overheated to me." He turned the spoon so that it dribbled a few drops of melted ice cream over her navel.

Morgan arched her back, squeaking. "Geez, that's cold! At least you could have warned me."

Erik placed the ice-cream carton on the bedside table next to the plate of cheese and fruit from the tasting room refrigerator. Handy thing, tasting rooms.

"Let me take care of that." He leaned down, running his tongue into her navel. She tasted of cream, salt and woman, with hints of fruit. "Nice vintage you got here, ma'am."

"Fair is fair." She sounded slightly breathless. "I get to dribble some on you, too."

He handed her the carton. "Go to it."

Morgan pushed his shoulder lightly until he was lying flat, her hand cool against his skin. Then she picked up the spoon. "Let me think..."

He watched her hand move over his stomach, silver spoon flashing in the lamplight, then felt an icy thread from his breastbone to his lower abdomen. A moment later her tongue rasped down his body, turning ice to fire.

Every muscle in his torso went rigid. Recovery time was officially over. "Holy crap!" he gasped.

She grinned at him. "Definitely seems to be some revival going on here, Chief."

He grabbed her shoulder and pushed her down on her back again, reclaiming the carton and spoon. Scooping up some melted cream, he held the spoon above her left breast for a moment, until he had her complete attention. "Ready?"

Her lips tightened. She nodded.

He turned the tip of the spoon down. Peach-colored cream dribbled in a spiral around her areola.

Morgan sucked in her breath with a hiss.

Erik leaned over, taking the areola into his mouth. His tongue slid across beaded skin and a nipple as hard as a diamond. He sucked, tasting her again, feeling her fingers dig into his shoulders. He was rock hard already, but he had a feeling she was just getting started.

Time to suck it up, so to speak. He reached toward her hips, only to find himself rolling onto his back.

Morgan pushed hard against his shoulder. She moved to straddle the top of his thighs, her legs brushing the underside of his shaft. Curls danced around her face in wild disarray, a sexy, brandy-haired Harpo Marx. She pulled the carton and spoon out of his hands. And then she was dribbling ice cream across the top of his groin.

He caught his breath. "Watch it, there, Bambi," he croaked, "that's cold. You don't want to undo all that recovery, do you?"

She looked down at his rampant cock, grinning. "You don't look in any danger of wilting, Chief."

Well, damn. He felt a sudden thread of cold against the top of his pubic hair and braced himself. Then her mouth was sliding down his shaft, her tongue encircling the head, running down the cleft. Her cool hands cupped his balls, while her warm mouth engulfed him.

Erik dug in his heels and gritted his teeth. If he didn't want to explode, he should probably think about something else.

Right. Like that was even a possibility.

"Morgan," he gasped. He could feel his body tightening, feel himself at the edge, moving closer and closer to the cliff. "Sweet Jesus, please..."

She raised her head again, her smile an impish v. "Begging?"

He blew out a breath. "Oh, yeah."

"Good." Morgan sat up slowly, batting his hands away as he reached for her. "Just wait."

"Wait?" he panted.

She pulled a condom off the bedside stand and sheathed him, before raising her body slightly. After a moment, she lowered herself over his cock, inch by agonizing inch.

He suddenly had an idea of what Chinese water torture must have felt like. He closed his eyes, concentrating on breathing. In. Out. In. Out.

Inch by inch by inch...

"Morgan, dear lord above!" he groaned.

He felt her palms brace against his chest, and then she was moving up, then down, still slowly, her inner muscles pulling him in and releasing him as she moved.

"Witch," he gasped.

"Come on, Chief," she whispered. "Hang in there. Make me proud."

He slid his fists into her hair, pulling her mouth down to his, ramming his tongue deep, in and out in the same rhythm she moved against him.

She moaned against his mouth, her hips moving more quickly.

He dropped his hands to her buttocks, squeezing.

She moaned again. "If you keep doing that you'll mess up my concentration."

"God forbid." He slid his hands around her thighs and

between them, rubbing his thumb across her clit and downward to press against the place where they were joined.

She cried out, her body spasming around his shaft. Erik rolled her gently onto her back, thrusting home as he moved above her again. Her heels pressed against his buttocks, her feet sliding down his legs. Then he was coming, his body thrusting deep within hers, release like a wave rising up his backbone.

His breath came in gasps, his body moving without any rhythm, wild thrusts into her heat and wetness until his bones seemed to liquify. He collapsed over her in a loose heap, so limp he could hardly leverage himself off her body before he crushed her.

After what seemed like a long time, he was able to pull himself up so that he could drop beside her and feel the cool night air against his damp chest. "Holy mother of god."

After a moment, she snuggled against him, her cheek pressed to his shoulder. "Still hungry?"

He had enough breath left to laugh—barely. "No ma'am. I do believe you've taken care of it." He took a deep breath and blew it out. "For the time being, that is."

At eight the next morning, Erik walked into the station to find that Helen and Nando had beaten him there. Nando sat at his desk tapping at the keyboard of his computer.

Technically, it wasn't his desk or his computer. It was a desk that was available to any of the police officers who needed a desk. And since there were only three computers—Helen's, Erik's and everyone else's—that meant any officer who wanted to use a computer had to use that one, unless they wanted to risk Helen's wrath.

Only a fool wanted to risk Helen's wrath.

But Erik had banned Ham Linklatter from touching the computer without supervision after he'd almost wiped out a year's worth of data. Peavey was always afraid he'd screw something up and just used it for occasional word processing. The desk and computer were Nando's whenever he was in the office.

Erik knew he looked sort of rumpled—he still hadn't had time to get his other uniform back from the cleaner's. A button was missing on his shirt and his pants needed pressing. He suspected Nando was hiding a smirk.

Helen gave him a once-over and raised her eyebrows. "Got the paperwork on the Wine and Food Festival for you to look over."

Erik frowned. "What Wine and Food Festival?"

"The one at the end of the month." She shrugged. "So far as I know, that's the only one there is."

He took the papers from her hand, glancing through them, his face grim. "Doesn't this town ever have a month when there isn't a festival?"

Nando grinned. "Better hope not, Chief. We're in the festival business here. A month without a festival is a month without suckers, also known as tourists."

Erik sighed. "Is this another one like the biker rally?"

Nando shook his head. "More people but quieter. Wine drinkers don't usually end up barfing in the parking lots or picking fights, and it's only one afternoon, not the whole weekend. Plus it's all in the park—food booths, wine tent, bandstand. People mostly sit around and get mellow."

"Everybody'll need to be on duty, then." Erik rubbed the back of his neck. "More overtime."

Helen gave them both an evil grin. "Pittman's gonna shit blood."

"Don't tell me. Olema didn't police it, right?"

Helen shrugged. "He sent Linklatter over. Same thing, I guess."

Briefly, Erik wondered if the festival honchos had bribed Brody like the bikers had. He'd have to ask around—his brothers most likely wouldn't know, but Nando might be able to find out from his winery contacts.

"Low-stress job, Chief." Nando grinned again. "Lots of people sitting around in the sun, listening to Frankie Belasco play his accordion and drinking wine."

Erik dropped the papers back into his inbox. "You find anything more about dumpers?"

Nando grabbed a stack of printouts. "Yeah, Texas Commission on Environmental Quality has a bunch of stuff. There's a number to call."

"Good." Erik pinched the bridge of his nose. "We've got

another one.”

Ciro demonstrated his command of both Spanish and English obscenities when Morgan showed him the dump site.

“I called TCEQ. They’re supposed to be here later this morning.” She stared down at the black oval, telling herself it hadn’t gotten any bigger overnight while she was frolicking with Erik.

Ciro’s lips thinned. “You should have asked me first.”

“Sorry. I thought we’d want them here ASAP. Wasn’t that a good idea?”

He shrugged. “The more people who know, the more likely news is to get out. Might make customers think twice about our wine.”

She took a deep breath. *One problem at a time.* “We might need to test the grapes, make sure they haven’t been affected.”

His scowl was instantly darker. “Nothing’s wrong with the damn grapes, Morgan.”

“I know. Probably that’s true. But if we have the official okay, we can counter any bad publicity.” She tried to keep her voice soothing.

He raised an eyebrow. “And if we don’t get the okay?”

“If there’s a problem with the grapes, we’ll have to destroy them, won’t we?” Morgan felt her hands balling into fists at her sides. “We can’t take any chances with turning out bad wine.”

“Right. You’d know all about that. You’re a goddamn winemaking expert.” Ciro’s mouth was a hard line. He turned on his heel and stalked back toward the winery.

He was going to call her father. And Dad would climb all over her for this even though she had nothing to do with it. And it didn’t matter a damn what she thought about any of it.

Morgan rubbed the back of her neck again, trying to block the headache that was starting at the base of her skull. She wondered idly if a good rainstorm would take care of all the problems. Wash it all downhill for somebody else to deal with.

Right, Morgan. Very responsible of you.

She dropped her hands, suddenly. When had the last rainstorm come? Surely the dumping had to have been after that. If they’d had rain, the ground wouldn’t still be so black, would it? If they knew when it had rained maybe they could pinpoint the time the dumper had been on the property. And whether it had really been two nights ago.

"Morgan?" Kit stood on the stairs outside the tasting room. "Phone call for you. I think it's your dad."

Morgan sighed. Oh yeah, this day was going to be a beaut.

At least her father listened quietly while she explained the situation, then told her to call him as soon as the TCEQ had left. He also told her he'd be driving to the winery by the end of the week.

Of course he would. Obviously, she'd reached the tipping point. Her father wouldn't stay away any longer, wouldn't leave her to make any more mistakes. Morgan couldn't decide if she was resentful or glad. Maybe some of both.

The TCEQ team arrived an hour later. Andy Wells, sturdy and blonde, like somebody's mom, took soil samples. She gave Morgan a reassuring smile. "We'll get these analyzed. It'll take a little more time than the water samples from the stock tank did. My guess is, though, you've got the same mixture as Mr. Powell—it smells the same."

Morgan leaned down and sniffed the soil, then stood up quickly. "Pew! Don't know how I missed it."

"The smell dissipates. Eventually." Wells began packing up her equipment.

Morgan took a deep breath. "What do we do now? Should we have the grapes tested?"

Wells shrugged. "If you want—for your own peace of mind. But I'd be very surprised if you find anything. The ditch is downhill from the vineyard, so unless you're pumping water uphill, the ground water should flow away from the field."

"What about cleanup?"

"That's tougher. You'll probably have to have this excavated, depending on what we find when we test. There are grants available to help with the expense—you won't have to pay for it all yourselves."

Morgan's lips thinned. "Good news, bad news I guess." Her hands clenched at her sides again. "God, I'd like to know who did this to us."

Wells nodded. "Believe me, you're not alone. When we find this guy, we'll throw the book at him."

Hilton Pittman sat in his office pretending to do paperwork. In reality, he was thinking about the police problem. Hell, in reality, he was thinking about Erik Toleffson. Correction—he was thinking about how to get rid of Erik Toleffson.

Sheriff Friesenhahn probably fell all over himself laughing whenever he thought about how he'd dropped Toleffson on Konigsburg. Of course, it wasn't like Hilton had had much choice—the city council was clearly not ready to accept Ham Linklatter as the new chief of police.

Hilton sighed. Linklatter might be a moron, but he followed orders just fine. Toleffson didn't appear to take orders from anybody. Hilton had to figure out some way to get rid of him, preferably without waiting through the entire two-month probationary period. Preferably, in fact, before the Wine and Food Festival. Firing Erik Toleffson within the next couple of weeks would definitely make Hilton's summer.

The office door swung open, and Hilton frowned. His secretary, Doralee, really needed to learn how to knock. Somebody else who didn't follow orders.

"Mr. Pittman, Mr. Powell wants to see you."

Hilton frowned harder, trying to remember if Powell had contributed to his campaign. Before he could check the contributors list that Brinkman had prepared for quick reference, Powell barreled past Doralee.

"Goddamn it, Pittman, you got to do something about that pissant Toleffson!"

Hilton sat up straight, instantly giving Powell his full attention and his most dazzling smile. "Come on in, Joe. Tell me all about it."

At noon, Erik snuck home and changed his uniform. Clara DeWitt at the laundry told him she could sew the button back on his shirt, which meant he'd at least have a change of clothes later in the week. He probably needed a third uniform, but he hated to spend the money until he had the job for real.

In two months. More like one, when you considered time served.

For a few moments, Erik allowed himself to wonder what it might be like to be the full-fledged chief of police in Konigsburg. He could buy a house, settle down. Or something.

He shook his head. Two months. No telling if they'd keep him on after that. And if they didn't, he'd have to move on to someplace else. Because there was no way in hell he was serving under Ham Linklatter.

Someplace else. The chief in Davenport had told him he could come back anytime. Back to Iowa. Back to what he used to be. He shook his head. *One problem at a time.*

He checked over the paperwork for the Konigsburg First Crush Wine and Food Festival. At least the winery association was paying for private security in the wine tent. He and his men would have to keep an eye on the rest of the park and the downtown traffic, but the rent-a-cops could take care of any drunks at the source.

Erik stared down at the permits, wondering if he could make up an excuse to go out to Cedar Creek. He'd left Morgan early in the morning, when both of them were still half-asleep. Maybe he could take her to dinner at Brenner's or something.

Loud voices from the outer office snapped him out of it. He stepped through the door to see Joe Powell and Helen, more or less nose-to-nose.

"And I say I gotta see the chief now," Powell was snarling. "You tell him to get on out here."

"What can I do for you, Mr. Powell?" Erik kept his voice quiet. It usually made people drop their own voices down an octave so that they could hear him.

Powell's face was the color of a wicked sunburn. His jaw looked like granite. "Nothing you can do for me, goddamn it! You already done it!"

Erik took a breath. He had a feeling Helen would have been using her baton if he'd ever given her one. "Let's step into my office, please."

Powell strode into the office and stood facing him. Erik closed the door. "What's the problem, Mr. Powell?"

"The problem? I'll tell you the problem." Powell's voice began to rise again. "You told the people at Cedar Creek Winery my water was poisoned. You probably lost me a long-term lease on my pasture! Now they want me to get the goddamn water tested."

Powell's voice apparently had two settings—loud and deafening. Right now he was on deafening.

Erik sighed. "Mr. Powell, I didn't tell anybody your water was poisoned. Ms. Barrett had an accident at the pasture when I was up looking at your stock tank—at your request. When I took her down to her winery, she wanted to know how I came to be there, and I told her."

Powell's face had gotten significantly redder. Erik began to wonder if he'd have an attack of something, and if he did, whether he could get Helen to do the mouth-to-mouth. No way was he doing it himself.

"You had no call telling anybody anything about my property," Powell bellowed. "Bad enough you sent them TCEQ people up there. Now I got to get my stock tank cleaned and I can't even dump the water out of it!"

Erik's patience began to wear thin, not that it had been all that thick to start with. Powell's voice could give anybody a headache. "Powell, the situation with your stock tank isn't exactly a secret in town. And you've got another dump site up there now."

"Another one? What the hell?" Powell's mouth opened and closed soundlessly, as if his outrage was too great to express.

Erik sighed. "Instead of yelling at me, why don't you help me figure out who's dumping chemicals on your land?"

Powell flexed his jaw, his eyes flashing. "Why should I figure it out? That's your job, ain't it?"

Erik nodded. "It is. But I don't know who uses the roads back there, and you do. You and your hands could help me find this SOB before he comes back and dumps more poison on your land. Or on other ranches out there. If we all get together on this maybe we can do something about it."

Powell stared at him a minute longer, then sat heavily in the chair opposite Erik's desk. He looked like a man who'd had a very rough month. "What do you want to know?"

By the time Powell left a half hour later, Erik had a list of people who regularly drove heavy trucks around his land. Erik glanced at the clock—five thirty. Time for the Dew Drop.

On his way out, he dropped some letters off at Helen's desk. She glanced at him. "You know Powell went to Pittman before he came here?"

Erik raised an eyebrow. "Did he now?"

"Yep." Helen gave him a sour grin. "Powell was down there when he was still mad as a bee-stung rattler, before you calmed him down. You better figure old Hilton's gonna be on your back by tomorrow at the latest."

Definitely time for the Dew Drop.

Chapter Fifteen

The Dew Drop was full of shadowy bodies, Biedermeier and the other drinkers all bellied up to the bar. The usual suspects were gathered at their table at the side—Allie and Wonder, Cal and Docia, Pete and Janie.

Correction. One suspect was missing. Erik felt a quick pang of disappointment. He should have gone out to Cedar Creek to get Morgan after all.

She showed up five minutes later, tucking a stray curl behind her ear. Her T-shirt hung loose around her shoulders, and there were shadows under her eyes. Erik had a momentary pinch of guilt for making her lose sleep—even if it was in a good cause.

"Sorry," she muttered, sliding in beside him.

He cocked an eyebrow. "What for?"

Morgan stared at him for a moment. "I don't know exactly. I guess I'm just used to saying 'I'm sorry' before I say anything else. It's been that kind of day."

"Get this woman a drink, immediately!" Wonder waved at the barmaid. "Wine?"

She shook her head. "Not after the afternoon I've had. Margarita. Straight up."

Erik was suddenly very aware of the heat of her hip next to his on the seat and the faint scent of lavender and roses. "What's happening at Cedar Creek?"

"What isn't? TCEQ is testing the dump site, but it looks like the grapes are probably okay, and Dad's coming to check things out later this week."

Allie leaned forward, frowning. "Dump site? What dump site?"

Morgan sighed. "Oh gather round, children, it's a fun tale for the whole family."

Pete shook his head after Morgan had given them a brief outline. "Who the hell is doing this? First Powell and now you? And how do they get there?"

"Drive, most likely. All three sites are close to a road." Erik took a swallow of Dr. Pepper, glancing around to see if anyone at the bar was listening to their conversation.

Cal grimaced. "I wouldn't call that goat track at Powell's a road, exactly, but I guess anything with four-wheel drive could get up there. What kind of truck do you think it was?"

Erik watched him silently for a moment, the corners of his mouth edging up. "Privileged information."

"Sorry. It's easy to forget you're a cop sometimes."

Wonder shook his head. "No it's not. Erik looks more like a lawman than anybody else in the room."

Erik took another swallow of Dr. Pepper. He thought of Ozzie Friesenhahn, his paunch hanging over his belt buckle, his uniform pants straining every time he sat. "What exactly does a lawman look like, Wonder?"

Wonder grinned at him. "Check the mirror."

Erik glanced up at the mirror behind the bar. He looked pretty much like he always did—his hair was a little mussed from his hat, and his eyes were tired from not having slept a lot the night before. Your basic-model Toleffson, sort of a domesticated missing link.

Compared to him, Morgan looked a lot better even if she was exhausted. Her brown hair hung in soft curls over her forehead and the deep purple of her T-shirt made her eyes seem even darker than usual. Their gazes met for a moment in the mirror, and Erik felt a shot of heat to his groin.

Another sleepless night was definitely called for.

"Why do policemen wear hats?" Janie's voice interrupted the beginning of a really hot daydream.

Erik turned to look at her. "Is that a straight line?"

"No, it's a real question. All the cops in town always wear Stetsons—so do the sheriff's deputies. Why?"

Erik took a moment to regroup, then he took a deep breath. "To protect us from ice storms."

The crease deepened between Janie's eyes, then slowly her

mouth spread in a grin. "So now I'm supposed to say we have no ice storms in summer. And then you say…"

"See, it's working." Erik grinned back.

"Jokes are my department, Toleffson," Wonder growled. "And you didn't answer her question."

"I don't know the answer to her question. Tradition?"

Erik sensed a movement to his left and caught a glimpse of Terrell Biedermeier's face in the mirror. Biedermeier was staring at him. As he saw Erik glance his way, he dropped his gaze and hunched back over the bar. Erik tried to remember if he'd ever said more than three words to Biedermeier in the past.

"So is it a special hat?" Docia leaned back against the booth. "Lead lined, say?"

"Lead lined?" Wonder raised an eyebrow. "To protect him from cosmic rays? Or is that aluminum foil?"

"Would you like to see my hat, Docia?" Erik picked up his hat from the bench and handed it to her.

Docia squinted at the crown in the dim light of the Dew Drop. "Darn! Looks normal."

Erik smiled again, trying to pay attention to the conversation while he glanced carefully into the mirror. Biedermeier was still staring into his beer.

"At least it doesn't smell like goats. Unlike Calthorpe's hat." Wonder grimaced in Cal's direction.

Erik couldn't quite see Biedermeier's face in the mirror anymore. Too bad. He wanted to check the expression.

Cal shook his head. "I'm a goat doctor, Wonder—part of the time anyway. At least it gets me outside. I will never have to spend the morning gazing at Rhonda Ruckelshaus's tonsils."

Wonder shuddered. "I avoid tonsil-viewing. Molars are bad enough."

Janie giggled and poured herself more wine. Docia said something about the Wine and Food festival. Erik tried to listen while he watched the mirror.

He concentrated on the segment of Biedermeier's face he could see, willing him to look up again. After a moment, Biedermeier tossed down the contents of his shot glass and headed toward the men's room, turning his back on the booth.

Erik frowned. He still hadn't been able to see Biedermeier's face clearly. He might have been mistaken, but he was pretty sure he wasn't. From the one brief glimpse he'd had earlier, he'd swear Terrell Biedermeier was a very nervous man. Or a frightened one.

Arthur was not a house cat. Morgan had known that when Erik had offered to take him in, but she hadn't thought to mention it. Now she wondered if she should have. Erik's living room looked as if it had been hit by a very focused hurricane. Every tabletop had been cleaned off. Books, magazines, pencils, and the assorted detritus of life were tossed around into corners and under furniture where Arthur had seen fit to chase them. A couple of sofa cushions trailed threads, marked by Arthur's claws.

Arthur himself sat in the middle of the kitchen table, glaring at them both.

"Evening, cat." Erik's tone was mild.

"Arthur, what have you done?" She shook her head in disbelief. Arthur squinted at her, then dropped his chin back on his paws.

Erik began picking things off the floor, putting them back on the surfaces Arthur had cleared. "Don't worry about it. He does this every day. Very efficient. Lets me know how bored he is until I get home."

"What happens when you get home?" She considered pushing Arthur off the table, but he looked like he wouldn't go quietly.

"He eats dinner and we negotiate where he's going to sleep."

Arthur's head shot up as Erik opened a can of cat food. He rose majestically to his feet and jumped to the floor with a significant thump.

"Here you go," Erik grunted. "Bon appetit, you old bandito."

"Oh, man." Morgan sank down in a kitchen chair. "I had no idea what a pain he'd be. I'm sorry I got you into this."

Erik turned to face her, resting his hip against the edge of the kitchen counter. He looked long, lean, and very dangerous. "First of all, you didn't get me into this, I volunteered. Second of all, why are you apologizing again?"

"I guess...I just..." she stuttered to a halt. "I don't know exactly."

He stepped beside her, running his fingers lightly through her hair. "Ease up, Morg. Not everything is your fault. And you can't fix it all. Trust me, ol' Arthur and I get along just fine. He hasn't done anything I haven't seen a cat do before."

She closed her eyes, enjoying the feel of his fingertips rubbing against her scalp. Warmth spread through her body, as if her muscles and bones were liquefying. In another minute, she'd fall asleep.

"Don't you dare fall asleep on me, Miss Morgan." His voice whispered against her ear. "I have plans."

Her eyes popped open. "Do these plans involve ice cream?"

One corner of his mouth inched up in his half smile. "Maybe. But I thought we'd start with dinner first." He walked back toward the counter.

She rose to follow him. "You cook, too?"

He pulled open the refrigerator door. "Nope. I defrost. There's lasagna. And I can manage to put a salad together."

She considered volunteering to whip something up out of whatever he had around but decided not to be the perfect guest for once. "Lasagna's great."

She watched him move through the kitchen, every gesture measured and precise. He seemed to concentrate totally on whatever he was doing, whether it was chopping lettuce or making her moan in ecstasy.

Her body began to warm at the memory of what that concentration had been like in bed.

Oh, Morgan, watch it. He's absolutely not the long-term type.

If he had been a long-term type, would she be interested in something long-term herself? Her chest tightened.

Don't go there, Morgan.

He slid the frozen lasagna pan into the microwave, then set the timer. "Should be ready in ten minutes or so. Can you last?"

Can we last?

"Sure." She worked on keeping her voice level. The tightness in her chest was almost painful.

He stepped beside her, running his fingers through her hair again. "I've been wanting to do this ever since you walked into the Dew Drop tonight."

She raised an eyebrow. "Hair fetish, Chief?"

"Curl fetish." He grinned, leaning against the table beside

her. "Soft corkscrews are my favorite. Hard to keep my hands off them."

She turned her head so that her cheek rested against his palm, rubbing along the roughness of his calluses. "Mmmm."

Erik cupped her face in both hands, then leaned down to press his lips to hers, a soft whispering brush that began to ignite almost as soon as she felt his touch. Morgan opened her mouth slightly, nibbling at his lower lip, then felt his tongue slide in, rubbing against hers. Closing her eyes, she ran the tip of her tongue along his teeth, tasting a faint reminder of the soda he'd had at the Dew Drop.

His hands slid down her sides to her waist, circling her, then pulling her to her feet. He moved to cup her buttocks, dragging her hips against him so that she felt the hardness at the front of his pants.

She draped her arms around his neck and pushed her body against his, riding the electric charge that seemed to play between them.

At which point, the microwave timer went off.

Erik raised his head. "Damn! That was a short ten minutes."

Morgan tried to speak, then settled for nodding. Her throat had closed up again.

He stood looking down at her, ignoring the *ding* of the timer behind him. "Goddamn, woman, you are really something else! If I weren't so hungry, I think I'd let that lasagna turn to dust."

She swallowed, letting out a shaky breath. "Thanks. I do give rain checks, though."

He leaned down and kissed her nose, running the tip of his tongue across it. "Count on it, Bambi. This may be the world's fastest dinner."

The next morning, Erik leaned against the counter in the main room of the station, inhaling his third cup of coffee. A few more nights with Morgan and he'd be a zombie. A highly satisfied zombie, of course.

Nando had worked the night shift and wasn't due in until noon. Helen was doing something mysterious with her computer that involved multiple backups to an external hard drive. Linklatter sat at his desk looking...just looking like Linklatter.

Erik sighed. Technically, Linklatter should be on patrol and Erik needed to prod him into it. But these days Linklatter seemed to be going out of his way to exasperate him, and he didn't feel like playing games with him right then. He took another sip of coffee and wondered if there was any way to get Ham to be less of an asshole.

His lank hair drifted across the front of his head, revealing a small bald spot. He was writing something on a yellow legal pad, his ballpoint moving furiously across the page.

Erik pushed himself to his feet and ambled in his direction, giving him lots of time to hide whatever the hell he was writing. He watched Ham glance up and color the usual unhealthy shade of pink, then shove the legal pad into his middle desk drawer.

Probably a report to Pittman. Somebody in the office was obviously Pittman's snitch, and Linklatter sure seemed like the best candidate.

Erik leaned his hip against the desk next to him, allowing one side of his mouth to drift into a faintly sour grin. "Morning, Ham."

Linklatter nodded stiffly. "Chief."

Erik folded his arms. "What can you tell me about Terrell Biedermeier?"

Linklatter blinked. Clearly not the question he'd been expecting. "Terrell? Why?"

"Just curious." Erik half-smiled again. "You've lived here a long time, right?"

Linklatter gave another stiff nod, but his eyes were no longer narrowed. "All my life."

"So tell my about Biedermeier. Is he a local?"

"Terrell?" Linklatter paused to think. "Nah, he moved here about the time I finished school, ten years or so ago."

"Businessman?"

"Owns his own business—pest control. Does that make him a businessman?" Linklatter looked confused.

"Sort of. So how's he doing?"

"Okay, I guess. Don't know much about it."

"He's fighting with the big guys." Helen had stopped

tapping at her keyboard. "Big chain of exterminators moved in a couple years ago. Biedermeier's trying to compete. Not doing too well at it from what I hear."

Erik nodded. Business troubles. That could account for Biedermeier's expression in the Dew Drop. Except that it had been directed at him, and he had no connection with Biedermeier's business that he knew of.

"Does he spray for bugs here at the station?"

Helen snorted. "Pittman won't authorize any money for an exterminator. You see anything moving, stamp on it!"

Right. Erik picked up his coffee cup and headed back toward his office. Behind him he heard the door open.

He half turned and watched Friesenhahn's bulky form move through the doorway. The man had to weigh at least three hundred, most of it packed into his substantial gut. He took off his cream Stetson and reached into the pocket of his khaki pants, then pulled out a large white handkerchief to wipe his forehead.

Erik leaned back against the doorway to his office. *Well, goddamn. There goes half the day.* "Morning, Sheriff, how're things at the county?"

Chapter Sixteen

Friesenhahn started to put his hat back on when he caught sight of Helen sitting at her desk. He nodded, tucking his Stetson under his arm. "Ma'am."

Helen's expression was guarded. "Sheriff."

He turned back to Erik. "Morning, son. You got yourself an office somewhere around here?"

"Yes sir." Erik pushed himself up from the doorway. "Right this way."

He could hear Friesenhahn walking behind him. His leather belt creaked beneath his paunch and the heels of his boots thumped heavily against the linoleum. The sheriff was long past the days of sneaking up on the bad guys. Erik slid into his desk chair, while Friesenhahn subsided into the visitor's chair in front of him.

"Well, son, you seem to have settled in." The sheriff glanced around the office.

Erik could see no evidence of his settling in, given that the only thing on his office wall was a generic picture of the old Lutheran Church on Main, but he figured he'd let Friesenhahn play it his way. He nodded. "Yes sir, I guess I have."

"You and the locals getting along okay?" The sheriff's beady eyes, like black peppercorns, regarded him steadily.

Erik suddenly had a hunch where this conversation was heading. He rested his elbows on the desk. "Most of them, yeah."

"Not all of them?" Friesenhahn raised a shaggy eyebrow.

"No sir. I've had one or two run-ins. Par for the course."

The sheriff blew out a breath. "Figured as much. Heard a

rumor you'd been stirring up the local ranchers—mayor claims he's had complaints."

"Ranchers? Plural?" Erik leaned back in his chair again. "I had one angry rancher in here yesterday, but we smoothed everything out. He's had some illegal dumping on his land."

Friesenhahn's eyes narrowed. "Dumping? You call TCEQ?"

Erik nodded. "We're on it. I've got a list of the trucks that drive across his land, and we've got another dump site in the same area we're checking out. Now people around there know what to look for, we should be able to track the guy down."

"Keep me posted. We'll need to check if other people in the county have been hit. Now what about Pittman?"

Erik sighed. The sheriff was a bulldog when he had a question he wanted answered—he never let loose. "Pittman's one of those mayors who gets in the way a lot."

Friesenhahn's laugh rumbled from his considerable gut. "Might as well call him by his rightful name. Pittman's an asshole, son."

"He is that. You have any idea how much trouble I may be in over this?"

Friesenhahn shrugged. "He wants to get rid of you. My guess is the city council's not inclined to let Hilton Pittman tell them what to do. However, it'd be a good idea to peel him off your back, or you're not gonna get much done around here."

Erik kept his expression bland. Given his choice, he preferred to ignore Hilton Pittman and his complaints. But he had a feeling he didn't have any real choice if he wanted to keep this job. "Any ideas about how I might do that?"

"Well—" the sheriff scratched his chin, meditatively, "—in your place, I'd probably apologize for any misunderstandings. Tell him you got off on the wrong foot. That won't make Pittman altogether happy, but it'll at least give him the idea that he's won one. For somebody like Pittman, that's a big deal."

Erik's stomach knotted briefly. Apologizing to Pittman struck him as a great way to develop an ulcer. "What would be your second choice?"

"Son, apologizing is the best way to take care of this situation. You know it as well as I do. Pittman may be an asshole, but part of this job is working with assholes."

Erik's jaw hardened. There were a variety of responses he could make, most of which would piss the sheriff off. He didn't do apologies all that well, not even with his family—who deserved them more than Hilton Pittman did.

Friesenhahn's grin began to fade as he waited. "You know something, Toleffson? In a lot of ways, you're one hell of a cop. You had a good record before you came here, and you've been outstanding in this shithole job. I don't know why you're here exactly, but the town is damn lucky to have you."

"Why do I feel like there's a 'but' coming up here?"

The sheriff grinned again. "But...you got a tendency to go off half-cocked when you get pissed at somebody. Like your relationship with Pittman. You been stirring him up when you didn't need to. That's just pure stupidity on your part, son."

"I think we're agreed on that. I haven't exactly handled it well."

"But you've managed to keep things going here so far. So far." Friesenhahn cocked an eyebrow in his direction. "Basically, you need to improve your people skills. Or your dealing-with-asshole skills. Part of a job like this is learning how to work with 'em because believe me you'll never get rid of 'em. You got a chance for some on-the-job training here. Don't blow it."

"Dealing with somebody like Pittman's not an easy skill to develop."

The sheriff sighed. "It's something you've got to do, Toleffson. If your relationship with the mayor gets too bad, the city council is likely to decide since they can't fire Pittman, it's easier to fire you, hire Linklatter and save themselves the hassle."

A band of tension began to form across Erik's shoulders. They both knew the corollary to that. Linklatter took over and Erik left Konigsburg. For good. *Apologize to Pittman or find yourself a new job somewhere else. Like Iowa.*

Friesenhahn hauled himself to his feet in stages, pushing up against the arms of his chair. "But I don't think that's gonna happen. I got confidence in you, son."

"Well, thanks for that, anyway."

The sheriff placed his hat firmly on his head, then turned back toward Erik again. "Just don't do anything that would make them fire you, Toleffson. It would really frost my butt to let Pittman think he'd won this one."

As Erik considered that possibility, he had to admit it

would frost his butt too.

Hilton Pittman sat in his office, waiting for Ozzie Friesenhahn to arrive. He knew Friesenhahn was in town because his assistant, Brinkman, had seen him drive by. And he knew why he was there. To warn Erik Toleffson about the need to play along.

All Friesenhahn needed to do now was drop by Hilton's office and confirm the obvious—Toleffson was back in line, Hilton was back on top, and all was right with the world once again.

On reflection, Hilton could have kicked himself for waiting so long to complain. If he'd just made his unhappiness known the first time Toleffson made trouble, he could have been spared the whole biker debacle.

An hour later he was still waiting for Friesenhahn and beginning to feel seriously pissed off. After all, Friesenhahn needed his help almost as much as he needed Friesenhahn's. They were both elected officials. Hilton could help Friesenhahn round up support with the Konigsburg Merchants Association. Friesenhahn really couldn't afford to annoy Hilton too much.

Could he?

Friesenhahn finally showed up around one, about the time Hilton was planning to head off to the Coffee Corral for lunch. Hilton might have asked the sheriff to join him under other circumstances, if he weren't so seriously annoyed.

Or, given Friesenhahn's size and probable appetite, maybe not. Feeding the sheriff might put a strain on the city's budget.

"Sheriff." Hilton extended his hand for a quick shake, then directed Friesenhahn into one of the overstuffed leather chairs he'd gotten the city to purchase for his office.

Friesenhahn sank down against the chair cushions, which subsided beneath him with an audible hiss.

Hilton waited for the sheriff to tell him he'd talked to Toleffson and then depart, but Friesenhahn gave him a benign smile as he glanced around the room. "Nice office you have here, Mayor. Real comfortable."

Hilton nodded, trying to keep his impatience in check. "We try to make visitors feel real welcome in this town, particularly in the mayor's office. My door is always open."

The sheriff's smile flickered for a moment, and Hilton felt himself flush. Okay, so he couldn't use the same lines with the sheriff that he used with the Merchants Association. His jaw firmed. "I assume you're here about Toleffson."

Friesenhahn's smile turned dry. "Good man, Toleffson."

Hilton's jaw clenched for a moment. Then he pulled himself together. "Maybe in some situations. He's had problems here."

The sheriff nodded slowly. "I spoke to him about that. Unfortunately, these misunderstandings do happen."

Misunderstandings? Hilton gritted his teeth. It was all he could do to restrain himself from grabbing a handful of Friesenhahn's shirt front. "This is more than a misunderstanding, Sheriff. The man's created several problems around town."

Friesenhahn narrowed his eyes, leaning his head against the leather chair back. "What problems were these? You mentioned some ranchers—if you could give me their names, I could follow up on that. Go have a conversation with them. See what the trouble is, maybe smooth down some feathers."

Hilton swallowed. He didn't know how reliable Powell would be if Friesenhahn talked to him. The man was already beginning to waffle about filing a complaint against Toleffson. In fact, he'd told Hilton to forget the whole thing. He figured he'd have to spend some time stoking Powell's wrath again in order to get him down to city hall. "I prefer to keep their names confidential, Sheriff. But I can assure you he caused several problems with the visitors during the motorcycle rally last week."

"Problems?" Friesenhahn raised an eyebrow. "Such as?"

"He arrested several of our guests. Chief Brody always managed to avoid arrests. Bad for the town's reputation as a tourist destination."

The sheriff narrowed his eyes and Hilton did a quick backtrack. "Not that Chief Brody was a model policeman by any means."

"I didn't see any sign Toleffson was doing anything wrong at that rally. The people he sent over to the county jail were plastered. If I'd been here, I'd have picked them up myself. They needed to sleep it off before they hurt somebody."

Clearly, the sheriff wasn't going to do what he was supposed to do without some major prodding. "Nonetheless, if we continue to have problems with Chief Toleffson, I'm afraid I'll have to take this matter to the city council and ask them to reconsider his appointment."

"I've suggested that Toleffson work out his problems with you. I'm sure he'll talk to you about it soon. He knows it's important."

Hilton drew himself up. "Well, perhaps we can avoid any public unpleasantness. But if not..." He spread his hands and tried to look like a reasonable man, which meant concealing just how pissed off he was at the moment.

Friesenhahn didn't look particularly impressed by Hilton's gesture, but, of course, there wasn't much he could do about it.

Hilton smiled again, getting to his feet. "Thanks for dropping by, Sheriff."

Friesenhahn hauled himself out of the chair's depths with some difficulty. "I'll keep track of how things are going here, Mayor. You can be sure of that. After all, if the police department doesn't function, the county may have to take over again." He gave Hilton another predatory smile.

Hilton narrowed his eyes. "Surely we won't have to go that far, Sheriff. A change in personnel might take care of the problems."

"It might, Mr. Mayor, depending on who gets changed for who. On the other hand, we can't have a town the size of Konigsburg without effective law enforcement. Believe me, I'll keep an eye on things here."

Somehow neither his words nor his smile made Hilton feel even slightly better. He stared after Friesenhahn's retreating bulk. It seemed that the ammunition he was currently using wasn't going to blow Toleffson out of the water. Which meant new ammunition was definitely called for. He'd turn that little rat fucker Brinkman loose on Toleffson's records tomorrow and see what he could dig up.

Erik put off talking to Pittman until the end of the day. He figured the taste it would leave in his mouth would demand a trip to the Dew Drop at the very least, possibly the Dew Drop and Brenner's, if he could run Morgan down. Of course, no matter what happened with Pittman, he intended to run Morgan down.

Pittman's secretary, a tiny, birdlike woman named Doralee, looked up at him with narrowed eyes as he walked in the office door. Erik could read her thoughts—it was four forty-five and he was going to make her stay late.

"It's okay, Doralee." He managed a smile, but it wasn't much of one. "This isn't something you'll need to stick around for." *Hell, the fewer witnesses the better.*

Doralee gave him a better smile than he'd given her. "Thanks, Chief. I'll let him know you're here." She gathered up her purse and lunch sack, then walked over to Pittman's door and flung it open.

"Goddamn it, Doralee." Pittman's voice filled the outer office. "Can't you learn to knock on the goddamn door?"

Doralee treated that as a rhetorical question. "Chief of police is here to see you. I'm going home."

Erik took a deep breath as Doralee brushed past him. *On-the-job asshole experience. Right.*

He stepped into Pittman's office to find the mayor industriously writing something on a notepad at his desk. Erik was fairly sure Pittman had picked up a pen for his benefit. The mayor made a great show of ignoring Erik's existence for a few moments, then looked up, unsmiling. "Yes, Chief. What is it you want?"

To be at the Dew Drop with Morgan Barrett. "Just a minute of your time, Mr. Mayor." Erik sat abruptly in one of Pittman's overstuffed leather chairs since otherwise he figured Pittman would leave him standing for however long this particular meeting took.

Pittman drew his brows together in a scowl. "I'm very pressed for time, Chief. Please get on with it."

Erik took a deep breath. "We seem to have gotten off on the wrong foot, Mr. Mayor. I apologize for any misunderstandings that might have occurred over the motorcycle rally." His stomach was clamped tighter than when he'd faced a teenage drug dealer with a four-inch knife. At least he'd gotten to kick the teenager in the gut. Not that he wouldn't have liked to do the same to Pittman, who was currently giving him his best imitation of a pissed-off high school principal.

"'Misunderstandings', Chief? I'd say the situation went considerably beyond misunderstandings. You harassed our guests."

The clenching in Erik's stomach moved to his jaw. "No, sir. We did not. We arrested five drunken bikers. None of them chose to challenge the citations." Considering that they'd probably have gone up in front of Judge Calhoun, who had a reputation for giving drunks lots of hours of community service on the county road crews, the drunks had gotten off easy.

"But none of them will come back to Konigsburg for another rally." Pittman leaned forward, thumping his finger against his desk pad for emphasis. "None of them will be spending money in this town again."

Erik sighed. He knew a no-win discussion when he got into one. "No sir, probably not, and that's unfortunate."

"We need that motorcycle rally, Toleffson. It's one of the biggest events the town has. We can't afford another debacle like this last one." Pittman began scribbling furiously on the notepad again, his mouth a thin line. "From now on, I've told the rally organizers to work directly with the mayor's office. My staff and I will be taking care of all problems ourselves. I'll be in charge of the city's response to any disturbance." Pittman gave him a tight smile.

Erik felt a vague prickling along the back of his neck. "How will you do that, Mr. Mayor? Your office doesn't have any standing as a law enforcement agency."

"My office will serve in an administrative capacity, as it always has." Pittman began moving papers around on his desk, a busy man currently being distracted by trifles. "The police department will discuss any arrests with me before they're undertaken. To make sure they're strictly necessary."

Erik's jaw clenched again, hard enough this time that he thought he felt a muscle pop. "The police department may have some problems with that idea...sir."

Pittman's face flushed slightly. "The chief of police—whoever he is—won't have any say in the matter. That's simply the way it will be done from now on."

"Have you consulted the city council about this particular policy?" The words slipped out before Erik could think about it. Oh well, he could only stomach Pittman for so long anyway.

The slight flush on Pittman's face turned much darker. Erik could see a vein throbbing at his temple.

"The council will do what I say," Pittman snarled. "And I say the police department is under my jurisdiction from now on."

Erik willed himself not to respond. He knew his expression betrayed him, but he couldn't do anything about that.

Pittman's mouth stretched in a grim smile. "You really think you can take me on, Toleffson? You really think the council will be on your side? Think again. I've been working in this town since before you were running bare-assed in the cornfields. When push comes to shove, I know how to make the council do what I want it to do, no matter what Horace Rankin thinks. If you don't like the way I run this town, maybe you should check out some job opportunities somewhere else. Because believe me, if you get in my way, I'll crunch you like a tree roach."

Erik got to his feet slowly. It wouldn't do to let Pittman think he was running anywhere. And his other option, punching Pittman in the mouth, would only cause more grief. "As I said, Mr. Mayor. I'm sorry for any misunderstandings between us. From now on, I'll be very clear about whatever I intend to do. Have a nice evening."

He placed his hat back on his head and nodded at Pittman before he walked out the door. He didn't trust himself to say anything more without calling Pittman something that really would get him in trouble with the town council, no matter how good it might make him feel otherwise.

Hilton popped a couple of antacids as soon as Toleffson disappeared. It looked like he'd have to put Brinkman on overtime to find something that would boot Toleffson out the door. And he'd be willing to bet there would be something, somewhere. Men like Toleffson didn't get where they were by being nice guys.

His office phone rang just as he was picking up his briefcase. Damn Doralee! She hadn't put the phone onto voice mail before she left. Hilton grabbed the receiver. "Pittman."

"Mr. Mayor?"

The woman's voice sounded vaguely familiar, that slightly exaggerated drawl like someone doing a bad Scarlett O'Hara imitation. "Ms. Hastings? Is that you?"

"Why yes. What a great memory for voices you have, sir."

Hilton gritted his teeth. Margaret Hastings was one of the

most irritating of Konigsburg's shop owners. Doubly so because behind that simper was a mind like a steel trap and a vindictive streak that was even wider than Hilton's. "I'm the only one here right now, so you might want to call back tomorrow morning, Ms. Hastings. I'm afraid I can't do much without my staff." Tomorrow at least he could foist her off on Doralee.

"But it's you I need to speak to, Mr. Pittman. After all, you're the ultimate authority to appeal to in Konigsburg."

Hilton recognized soft soap when he heard it, but he wasn't averse to being flattered, particularly after the day he'd had. "Well, I'll help you if I can, Ms. Hastings. What seems to be the problem?"

"Corruption." Her voice dropped a half-octave. "Police corruption. It may not seem like much now, but I thought it was my duty to bring it to your attention. Before we had another...situation like we had before with Chief Brody."

Hilton closed his eyes. Margaret Hastings had once dated Ham Linklatter. If this was going to be a little post-breakup revenge, he wanted out now. "Now, Ms. Hastings, I'm sure all of our officers try their best. Perhaps you misunderstood the situation."

"Oh, but it wasn't an officer. It was the chief himself. And I didn't misunderstand anything."

Hilton lowered himself slowly into his desk chair, allowing himself a brief shit-eating grin. *Thank you, Jesus!* "The chief, you say? Well, of course that's different. You go right ahead, Ms. Hasting, and tell me all about it."

Chapter Seventeen

The Dew Drop was empty when Erik got there, after he'd changed out of his uniform. Just his luck—the one time he really wanted to listen to Wonder bitch about something, he wasn't around to do it.

He slid onto a barstool and waited for Ingstrom to bring him his Dr. Pepper. For the first time in a couple of years, he felt like getting roaring drunk, but he didn't want to give Linklatter any excuse to pick him up.

He stared down at the dark brown liquid in his glass and imagined it was bourbon. Ingstrom wouldn't even blink if he ordered a shot of Maker's Mark to go along with the Dr. Pepper.

A bright ball of rage burned just below his rib cage like a glowing ember. A shot of bourbon was all he needed to fan the flames, turn the ember into something hotter, something a lot more dangerous. He knew those flames. He knew what they could do, what they would consume.

Stop it, Erik, that hurts! No, Erik, don't! Leave me alone, just leave me alone! The soundtrack of his childhood.

Erik closed his eyes, breathing slowly. He wished mightily that at least one of his brothers was around, just to reassure him that those times were over. Even if he wasn't ready to tell them about what was going on. Although he knew he'd have to. Eventually. If he was going to screw up again, he wanted to give them some advance warning.

Not that it would be much of a surprise. It would simply convince them he was the same person he'd always been—the nightmare big brother. The bully who didn't know enough to protect his own kin. The half-assed punk who'd blown every opportunity that had ever come his way. The loser.

And deep down, he knew that punk still lurked inside him somewhere. He'd done everything he could to make him go away. Maybe it hadn't been enough.

Erik sighed. Obviously, he wasn't in any shape to be sitting in a bar right then. He dropped a dollar bill on the counter and headed out the door.

He swung by the Coffee Corral on his way home to pick up one of Al's burgers and some fries, and on the off chance that somebody from his family would be in the dining room. His lousy luck held. Nobody was around, and the food did nothing to calm the burning in his gut.

Back at the apartment, he shared the kitchen table with Arthur, who wasn't interested in hearing about his troubles. Just as well. By then Erik was thoroughly sick of self-pity.

Around nine, after he'd had the time to watch a couple of witless TV shows and read the *Austin American-Statesman*, the doorbell for the outside door rang. He glanced out the window to the street and saw Morgan.

"What's up?" Erik herded her in the door, feeling a quick rush of adrenaline. Maybe the day could be salvaged after all.

Morgan picked up a large pet crate from the doorstep. "We had a break in the labeling. I thought I'd come get Arthur."

Correction. The day was just as sucky as it had seemed.

He followed her up the stairs, keeping back so that the pet crate wouldn't connect with his nose. Arthur thumped down off the table as they walked in the door, regarding her with suspicious eyes.

"You don't have to take him home." He reached down to scratch Arthur's ears. "He's doing okay here."

"Okay? He's creating chaos. And enjoying it."

He shrugged. "So?"

Morgan's lips spread in a faint grin. "Besides, he's already grown back some fuzz. I think it's safe to bring him back home now."

Erik regarded Arthur critically. A fine layer of yellow fluff coated his rear quarters. "That's not much fuzz."

"It's enough. Anyway, I thought you'd be glad to get rid of him." She opened the pet crate.

Arthur promptly scuttled under the couch.

"Oops." Erik tried not to grin. *Way to go, cat!*

Morgan blew a curl off her forehead with an irritated breath. "Arthur, you're not helping."

"On the contrary," Erik murmured, sliding an arm around her waist. "He's helping me a lot."

She raised her gaze to his, eyes narrowing. "Ciro and Esteban aren't finished labeling the sangiovese yet. I should get back. They need me." Her perfect teeth nibbled on her lower lip.

His breath caught in his throat, and he felt an ache deep in his groin. "They're not the only ones. I could use a little help here myself."

Morgan's eyes widened. She placed her palms on his chest. "Keep talking."

"I've got some mint chocolate chip ice cream." He swallowed, feeling the warmth of her hands move through him, then reached down to gather her into his arms, pulling her taut against his body, feeling the fire in his belly slowly change from burning to heat.

Her mouth was a warm, wet delight. His hands dropped to her buttocks, feeling the tight muscles contract. *Oh, yeah. Definitely the best way to go.*

She pulled back for a moment, staring up with eyes the color of night. "You think I can be had for a dish of ice cream?"

"Nope." Erik took a deep breath. "But I can."

Morgan sat cross-legged on Erik's bed, watching him eat ice cream. Lit by the dim bedroom lamp, his profile looked carved from stone, his nose and chin sharp and craggy. His hair, grown slightly longer than his usual military cut, brushed across his forehead in a dark wave. Naked he looked like something primal—the slabs of muscle on his chest covered with a thick pelt of dark hair that extended down his belly. She loved the feeling of his body against hers, the sense of both danger and protection in those broad shoulders, those long arms, those narrow, supple fingers.

Something was bothering him. She didn't know how she knew, but she was sure. She'd never seen a man more skilled at keeping his emotions under wraps than Erik Toleffson. Even in bed, he held something in check. He was the most amazing lover she'd ever had, but she wasn't sure she'd had him, really. And at the moment something was going on beneath that deceptively calm exterior.

She reached for the ice-cream carton and his spoon. "Did you go to the Dew Drop after work?"

He nodded. "For a little while."

"Anybody there?"

"Nobody I wanted to talk to."

"You didn't stay?"

He shook his head, his lips moving into a dry smile. "I go for the people, not the atmosphere."

Morgan took a breath, wondering if now was really the time to dig deeper. "Could I ask you a really nosy question?"

His smile became guarded. "Ask away."

"Are you an alcoholic?"

He watched her for a moment, his eyes flat. Then he shrugged. "Not in the usual way, I guess."

"What do you mean?"

"I'm not a binge drinker. I can stop and start. And I could go without drinking if I needed to—I did in Iraq."

"But you've stopped drinking altogether now."

He shrugged again. "I decided it was better for me not to. I went through AA, and the process worked for me."

"Oh." She stared down at the mint chocolate chip, trying to form her questions into something coherent.

"I'm what you call a mean drunk." His lips twisted slightly. "Like that guy in the story, the one with two personalities."

"Dr. Jekyll and Mr. Hyde?"

He nodded. "That's the one. Only when I drink, the ol' Doc goes missing sometimes. I'd rather stay in control."

Control. It was the right word, now that she thought about it. He'd need to be the one in control. Always. "What's bothering you, Erik? Did something happen today?"

His gaze fastened on the spoon in her hand, but she had the feeling he wasn't really looking at it. His lips thinned as he thought. Maybe as he decided whether to tell her what was going on. "I went to see Pittman," he said finally. "Friesenhahn warned me he was after my butt, told me to go in and make nice with him to see if I could head him off."

She tried to picture Erik making nice with anybody, least of all Hilton Pittman. She couldn't see it. "What happened?"

"Friesenhahn's right. He's after me. But there's no way I

can head him off or settle with him. He's going to keep digging through my life until he finds something he can use, and then he's going to sink me."

Morgan stared at him. He still wasn't meeting her eyes. "He's going to *try* to sink you."

He took a breath, finally looking at her straight on. "No. He'll do it. There's enough stuff in my background to give him all the ammunition he needs. All he has to do is look, and he'll find it."

She swallowed, careful not to look away. "You mean the stuff you did when you were a teenager?"

Erik turned away again, staring out the window at the darkness. "More than that. I'm not a nice guy, Morgan. The rest of my family—my brothers, my father—they're all nice guys. I'm not. I've made my living pushing people around. Most of them deserved it, but it wasn't pretty. You do what you have to do, but it's not...like people think it is. When you start dragging that stuff into the light, it gets messy."

She stared at him for a moment, trying to see what was happening behind the blankness of his expression. "You're a cop. It's not like you work with a great class of people."

His lips moved into a dry smile. "Still, most people don't like to see what it takes to stop the bad guys sometimes. And I've always got Mr. Hyde looking over my shoulder. Waiting for an opening."

Morgan shook her head. "I've never seen you lose control, Erik. Ever. I mean, I've seen Ham Linklatter have hissy fits more times than I've seen you get angry. What are you so afraid of?"

He turned back to her, running his fingers lightly along the side of her hip. "Mr. Hyde is a tricky son of a bitch. You think he's gone—you think you've got him licked. And then all of a sudden he's right there breathing down your neck." He closed his eyes. "All through my childhood I just let him run. Whenever I felt like pounding somebody, I did. Ask my brothers—they'll tell you I was the big brother from hell. What I mainly remember about it was being angry most of the time, and letting that anger run whenever it suited me. In the army I learned how to control it, but it never goes away. I mean, I could happily have pounded Pittman into the carpet this afternoon. Mr. Hyde was panting to go."

She rested her hand on his. "But you didn't. You walked away."

He turned toward her, his eyes fathomless again. "This time I did. Tomorrow, who knows? It's always there, Morgan. Mr. Hyde—he's always there."

Morgan moved her hand to his face, tracing his jaw with her fingers. "But so is Dr. Jekyll. Maybe you're not a nice guy, but you're a good man, Erik Toleffson. I believe that."

His eyes closed as he turned to kiss her fingertips, lightly. "Thank you, Ms. Barrett."

"For what?"

"For being somebody I can talk to." Erik gave her one of his half-smiles, one corner of his mouth moving up.

"Anytime, Chief." She leaned forward, brushing her lips against his. "Anytime at all."

Erik wrapped his arms around her waist, pushing her back against the softness of the bed. She could feel the hardness of his arousal, nudging between her legs. Apparently, conversation was over for the night. And she didn't mind a bit.

Erik managed to get to the office by eight thirty the next morning, but it was a struggle. On the other hand, thanks to Morgan, he no longer felt like using Linklatter for target practice.

Nando had left a pile of printouts about illegal dumping in his mailbox before taking his day off. Erik figured he'd read through them at some point if things ever slowed down enough in the office to allow him some reading time.

Peavey had picked up a teenage graffiti artist who'd marked up the middle school basketball court. Helen passed on a handful of permits for his signature. Linklatter, wonder of wonders, found a stolen car on Milam. True, the car was parked, and there was no sign of the thief. But it was still the most actual police work he'd ever seen Linklatter do.

Erik himself fielded calls from TCEQ and Powell, who had information from his ranch hands about mysterious trucks in the back country. All in all, a busy morning.

A few minutes after noon, he got a call from Pittman's secretary, Doralee. "Chief, I thought you'd like to know you're on the agenda for the city council meeting next week." She sounded like she was keeping her voice low on purpose.

"On the agenda?" He frowned. "I didn't ask to be on the agenda."

"No sir," Doralee muttered. "You're not on as a speaker. I mean you're an agenda item. He asked me to put your name on."

Erik didn't need to ask who "he" was. Pittman. *Busy man, our mayor.* "Thanks, Doralee. I appreciate it."

"No problem. You might want to talk to Horace Rankin, Chief."

He sat staring at the phone after Doralee hung up. He had a very good idea why Pittman had put his name on the agenda. He'd found the smoking gun he'd been looking for—Erik was even fairly sure he knew what it was. And of course Pittman would make it work. He was going to be fired.

Friesenhahn would *not* be pleased.

Nando was sitting in the tasting room at Cedar Creek watching Kit when Morgan got there a little after noon. She assumed it was his day off, given that he was out of uniform. Hard to believe he'd spend the day watching Kit pour wine. Of course, "watching Kit" was the operative phrase there.

Right now she was pouring a glass of red for a tourist dressed in jeans and a bright green Konigsburg T-shirt. The tourist's eyes seemed fastened on Kit's breasts, and he was grinning. Nando looked like he was considering how satisfying it would be to push the tourist's nose through the back of his head.

Morgan placed the plastic pet crate next to the office and opened the wire mesh door. After a moment, Arthur emerged, giving her a dark look. He really hadn't wanted to leave Erik's apartment. It had taken both of them to capture him in a towel and then pour him into the carrier. He'd spent the entire drive back to Cedar Creek complaining loudly.

After a moment, he stalked across the room, sauntering by Nando's foot, sending Skeeter and Fred skittering to the far corners. *Wimps.* Right now, Arthur didn't look like much of a threat. His hind quarters were covered with a fine yellow down, extending up his tail to the puff of hair at the top. Morgan couldn't believe any self-respecting dog would be frightened of a cat who looked like that.

She ducked into her apartment to get a bag of dry cat food. Arthur gave his bowl a sniff, then moved to his traditional spot on the doormat.

"Afternoon." Nando shifted on the barstool as she approached, draping a paper napkin across his lap. Not much in the way of camouflage.

"Hi. So what do you think? Doesn't Arthur look a lot better?"

Nando blinked at her. "He looked worse before?"

"Well, he's had a few days of pampering. Erik's been keeping him until he regrew some fur. Chief Toleffson, I mean. He was keeping Arthur. I brought him back this morning, but he has to stay inside until he grows back a little more fuzz." Morgan felt her face flush pink. Geez, could she be any more obvious?

Nando grinned. "Hard to picture Toleffson pampering anything."

"He did an excellent job. He really took care of him. Arthur looks like he's gained another five pounds." God, now she sounded like the world's prissiest Sunday school teacher.

She glanced up. Nando had gone back to watching Kit. Oh well, she'd probably be doing the same thing if Erik were standing behind that bar.

Erik waited until late afternoon to head for Cedar Creek. He hadn't done anything about Pittman and his plans yet—he didn't know what he could do, if it came to that. Talking to Horace Rankin might help, but he didn't want to go to the animal clinic to do it, where he'd be seen by half the town as well as his baby brother. He wasn't ready to involve the family in this. Hell, he might never be ready for that, although he needed to let them know what was happening.

Cedar Creek was a viable alternative.

He had a variety of very good reasons for going there. He wanted to check for tire tracks leading to the dump site, although finding any was pretty much a lost cause, given the amount of traffic on the roads around the winery. He wanted to look over the winery's trucks to rule out the very unlikely chance that one of them might have been used to dump illegal chemicals. And he wanted to see Arthur.

Embarrassing, but true. He'd missed the cat's crushing weight on his lap at breakfast that morning, along with his ability to precisely clear every flat surface in the apartment by evening. He even missed Arthur's steadfast refusal to cut Erik any slack. It was the first time he'd ever felt he and a cat had a lot in common.

Morgan had insisted on taking him home because she was sure Arthur had worn out his welcome, and Erik hadn't been entirely sorry to see him go. It was only when he wandered up the stairs after lunch and found everything just where he'd left it when he went to work that morning that he realized he sort of liked having the old bandito around.

To say nothing of having Morgan around. He wasn't sure why he'd unloaded on her last night. He wasn't the kind of man who confided in people. In fact, he couldn't remember ever confiding that much to any single person, not even the shrink his chief in Davenport had made him visit. And he'd felt better after talking to Morgan than he had after talking to the shrink.

All in all, given all the crap coming down in his life, he was definitely in the mood for another night with her. Maybe some hot, raunchy, mindless sex. Or some warm, soft, all-night-long sex. He didn't really care which, as long as Morgan and sex were involved.

Of course, first he had to check for the dumper, just so he could tell himself he had a legitimate reason for being there.

He parked the cruiser at the side of the tasting room, then walked back toward the equipment shed. A couple of men in dusty jeans and T-shirts passed him, heading from the winery building toward the parking lot.

Erik recognized one of them—Nando's big brother Esteban, emphasis on *big*. Erik figured Esteban must weigh at least as much as Friesenhahn, and he was almost as tall as Cal. He looked more like a linebacker than a grape farmer.

"Can I help you, Chief?" Esteban pulled off his hat and rubbed his arm across his forehead.

The afternoon sun blazed overhead. Erik nodded, balancing his sunglasses on his nose. "Are those the only trucks the winery has?" He could see a pickup and a trailer for hauling grapes.

Esteban shrugged. "The only ones we own. But people who work here drive some."

"Anything heavy duty?" Erik glanced around the yard, but he couldn't see anything besides a tractor and a flatbed trailer near the vineyard fence.

"Nope." Esteban grinned at him a little sourly. "We didn't dump anything, Chief. Trust me, if any of us did it, we'd have headed off to somebody else's vineyard."

Erik sighed. "Yeah, I figured as much. I don't suppose you saw anybody driving a big truck around here lately."

Esteban shook his head. "Dad asked everybody about that, but nobody's seen anything out of the ordinary. No heavy trucks we didn't expect. Maybe they came at night."

"Maybe." Erik thought of Morgan at the winery by herself while an outlaw dumper poured toxic waste outside. It wasn't a picture he liked much. He walked toward the vineyard where the dump site was located.

After a moment, Esteban put his hat back on and followed him. "You think this is the same guy who poisoned Powell's goats or somebody different?"

Erik grimaced. Just his luck to have two of them "Yeah, I think it's the same guy. I hope so anyway."

They rounded the corner of the vineyard. The long black oval of the dump site was now surrounded by an orange plastic temporary fence.

"TCEQ says the vineyard's okay." Esteban's lips thinned. "We were lucky. If the bastard had dumped on the other side, he might have poisoned the ground water."

"Glad to hear it." Erik climbed a small rise where the road began to wind up into the hills. Then he turned back to look over Cedar Creek from the top.

A cluster of cars still sat in the parking lot beside the tasting room. A few trucks were scattered at the side, probably the ones that belonged to the vineyard workers. One of the workers hosed down the concrete slab at the back of the winery.

"Grape delivery?" Erik raised an eyebrow at Esteban.

Esteban grinned, shaking his head. "Don't even think about it. They're big trucks, but they're already full of grapes and they head out of here like bats out of hell as soon as they unload."

"Back to Lubbock?"

"Or Garland. We buy from both."

"Well, hell." Erik wiped his sweaty forehead on his arm. The setting sun was brutal—the temperature must be hovering around the high nineties. He was close to being off duty. Maybe it was time to find Morgan and head back to town for a little Dr. Pepper and some recreational booty.

A flicker of light near the tasting room caught his attention—somebody's rearview mirror. He could hear the rumbling sound of tires on the road.

As he watched, a midsize truck pulled up in front of the building. Heavy duty, with double tires and a tank fastened to the back.

Erik strained to read the printing half-obscured by dust on the side. *Easy Kill Pest Control.* He stood very still, feeling the muscles in his shoulders tense. One of those moments when a series of pieces clicked into place.

Esteban sighed. "Looks like Terrell's gonna spray the tasting room for bugs. At least it's the end of the day. Most of the tourists have already left."

"Terrell?" Erik asked. But he already knew the answer.

"Biedermeier," Esteban explained. "It's his company. He does the tasting room every month or so."

"You spray the winery for bugs?"

"Just the tasting room. It's not close to the production area. You know South Texas—if you don't spray, you get critters in the house. And the last thing we need is for a roach to go crawling across some tourist's foot."

"Every month." Erik watched him.

"He's got two or three customers out here. Us and Castleberry. And he does my folks' place while he's out here since they live so close." Esteban's forehead furrowed for a moment. "I guess he does Joe Powell's house too, now that I think about it."

Erik took a deep breath. "Powell."

Esteban nodded.

"Goddamn it to hell," Erik muttered. Without turning to look at Esteban, he headed down the hill at a fast trot.

Chapter Eighteen

Morgan looked up as the door swung open. On the other side of the tasting room, Nando leaned against the bar while he talked to Kit. The two of them were so far gone they didn't seem to be aware that anybody else had entered the room.

Terrell Biedermeier had his metal insecticide tank strapped to his back, his sprayer in his hand. "Afternoon," he mumbled.

He wore a dirt-colored baseball cap low on his forehead, while his chin prickled with beard stubble. He looked as if he'd prefer to be sitting on his barstool at the Dew Drop.

She nodded at him. "Hey, Terrell. I didn't realize you were coming out here. Is this the day you usually spray?"

Biedermeier shrugged. "Had another building in the neighborhood. Saves me a trip."

She sighed. She wasn't crazy about spraying insecticide around the wine. If nothing else, it interfered with the smell. But most of the businesses and a lot of the homes in Konigsburg got sprayed once or twice a month to discourage the tree roaches from taking up residence indoors. Fortunately, since it was so close to closing time, the only people in the room were Nando and Kit. They could go ahead and close early. "Okay, go to it."

Across the room, Kit stowed several bottles in the refrigerator and used the vacuum pump to cork two or three others. Biedermeier spraying the baseboards probably wouldn't have any effect on the open bottles, but it never hurt to be sure.

"Hey, boss, mind if I take off? It's only ten minutes until closing time." Kit gave Morgan a hopeful grin.

She shrugged. "Sure. No problem."

Biedermeier began squirting along the side of the room,

ignoring everybody else, as usual. Morgan wondered if dispensing poison had a particular effect on your personality or if he was just naturally surly. She wrinkled her nose at the faintly peppery smell.

Nando stood back as Kit came around the counter then slung his arm across her shoulders. They ambled toward the door, heads together and murmuring. Biedermeier glanced up at Nando as he walked by, then moved more rapidly toward the other side of the room. Nando didn't take his eyes off Kit long enough to notice.

Morgan did. She frowned. Why exactly would Biedermeier want to scuttle away from Nando?

Outside there was the thud of someone hurriedly mounting the stone steps to the tasting room. She checked the clock—four minutes until closing. Whoever it was would only have time for a single quick taste of something or other, and they'd probably have to drink it on the patio because of the faint insecticide smell from the spray. It didn't really matter. She wasn't up to keeping the tasting room open late today anyway.

Then the door swung open and Erik stepped into the room. Behind her, she heard Terrell Biedermeier inhale noisily. He sounded slightly bronchial.

The first thing Erik saw as he entered the tasting room was Morgan. The second thing he saw was Terrell Biedermeier standing directly behind her with an insecticide sprayer in his hand and an expression of pure terror.

Erik felt a quick prickling up his spine, and his hands balled into fists. He forced himself to relax and smile. "Hey, Terrell, got a minute?"

Biedermeier edged farther away from him, but he was still too close to Morgan for comfort. "What do you want?" he growled.

"Just a moment of your time." Erik gave him the good ol' boy grin he usually reserved for little old ladies and Cub Scouts.

"Why?" Biedermeier kept moving back, centering himself behind Morgan.

Erik placed his hands on his hips, resisting the urge to grasp the handle of his baton. "Just a couple of questions. Won't take long. Why don't we go outside and talk?"

Morgan put the glass she'd been polishing back on the

shelf and started to move away. Biedermeier stepped in front of her.

"Terrell?" Her brow furrowed.

Erik walked toward them at an angle, slowly, trying to draw Biedermeier away from her. "Come on, Terrell, it won't take long, I promise. Morgan's got stuff to do in her office. Let's leave her to it." With luck, she might catch the hint and move away toward the office door.

Biedermeier's glance darted toward him and then back to Morgan again. "I ain't done nothin'."

"Didn't say you had." Erik kept moving, more slowly now.

Biedermeier edged closer to her. "You stay back, Toleffson. I got nothin' to say to you."

Morgan turned, finally beginning to move away toward the office.

Biedermeier dropped the sprayer quickly, dragging it behind him on the floor, and wrapped one hairy arm around Morgan's neck, jerking her back against his chest. "You stay back, I said." His voice rose dangerously. Erik could see the whites of his eyes. "I don't want to hurt her."

"I don't want you to hurt her either." Erik kept his voice level, trying to remember all the lessons he'd had about dealing with hostage situations. Unfortunately, nobody had ever discussed hostage situations where your girlfriend was the hostage and where your dearest wish was suddenly to kick the hostage taker into the stratosphere.

"Come on now, Terrell, you haven't done anything yet that qualifies as a felony," Erik soothed. Not entirely true, but he didn't feel too bad about lying under the circumstances. He worked on keeping his voice calm. "Let Morgan go before you screw up big-time. If you let her go now, I won't add this to my report."

Morgan jerked against Biedermeier's arm, "Terrell, what in god's name is wrong with you? Let me go, you idiot!"

Something metallic flashed in Biedermeier's hand, jabbing at Morgan's side. Erik heard her hiss.

Biedermeier's glance darted around the room, checking the exits. "I don't want to hurt you, Morgan, but I need to get out of here. You tell your boyfriend to stay out of my way."

Erik wondered just how far away Nando was. Not that either of them could do much with Biedermeier holding a knife at Morgan's side. His chest felt tight, the muscles flexing hard in his arms. A mixture of adrenaline and rage churned in his belly as Biedermeier's arm tightened around Morgan's neck.

He began edging for the door, dragging her along with him.

She stumbled once, then caught herself. "What's going on?" she gasped, jerking against his arm again. "I don't understand."

Erik moved parallel with Biedermeier, careful not to get too close. "He's the dumper, Morgan. He's the one who almost poisoned your vineyard."

"Terrell!" Morgan cried, half turning toward him. "How could you!"

"Didn't hurt nothin'," Biedermeier mumbled. "Just that old drainage ditch out there."

Morgan's eyes were wide, the pupils dilated. Erik was suddenly very aware of her thinness, her fragility. She looked as if her bones could crack if Biedermeier jerked too hard.

He flexed his hands again. "What have you got in mind, Terrell? You haven't got much room to maneuver here, you know."

"Just stay away from me," Biedermeier growled. "Just stay back."

He stumbled toward the tasting room door, still dragging Morgan with him.

"Damn it, Terrell, move your arm! I can't breathe," she muttered.

Biedermeier ignored her. "Open the door," he snapped, nodding toward Erik.

Erik stared at him. Opening the door would bring Erik directly alongside Morgan. Obviously, Biedermeier wasn't big on foresight. Maybe he could do something with that.

"Open it! Now!"

Erik shrugged. "Sure. Don't get excited, Terrell." He moved carefully toward the tasting room door and Morgan.

"Get back!" Biedermeier squeaked.

Erik rested his hands on his hips, trying to sound reasonable. "Terrell, I can't do both. Either I open the door or I get back. Which is it?"

"Lemme think!" Biedermeier's forehead looked clammy. He stumbled back toward the bar again, still dragging Morgan in front of him. As he did, his heel ran into a large yellow lump on the floor near the door.

The lump promptly reached up and took a substantial bite out of Biedermeier's calf.

Several things happened more or less at the same time. Biedermeier howled and grabbed his leg. Morgan pulled away from him, staggering back to the bar. Arthur, the lump in question, arched his back, hissing.

Erik dodged around Arthur and threw Biedermeier to the floor. There was a ringing in his ears; spots danced before his eyes. His hand drew into a fist almost automatically. He drove it hard into Biedermeier's face.

"Erik, no!" Morgan's voice came from somewhere behind him.

The sound of his blood pounding in his ears almost blotted her out. The need to slam his fist into Biedermeier's face again was almost painful. He drew back his fist.

"Erik, please."

He stood frozen, feeling Morgan's hands on his arm, cool against the heat of his skin.

"Please stop now," she murmured. "I'm okay."

Erik closed his eyes for a moment, letting his heartbeat slow down again, then jerked the handcuffs off his belt and threw Biedermeier onto his stomach. He yanked his wrists behind him. "Don't you fucking move."

Biedermeier's face was smeared with blood. The sound of his sobbing breaths seemed to fill the tasting room.

The door flew open, as Nando, Kit and Esteban tumbled in on top of each other.

"What the hell?" Nando stared at Biedermeier, sprawled on the floor, arms pinioned behind his back.

"He's the dumper. Read him his friggin' rights," Erik growled. He forced himself to move back, away from Biedermeier, breathing hard as he did. His heart was still pounding so loudly he could barely talk.

Nando pulled his Miranda card from his pocket.

Biedermeier whimpered. "My nose hurts. Prob'ly broke. And that thing bit me. It might have rabies."

Arthur stalked majestically across the floor, ignoring the chaos behind him. The pom-pom at the end of his tail whipped back and forth furiously.

Erik silently promised him the biggest can of tuna he could find. He looked down at Morgan. She stood beside him, one hand clenched at the base of her throat. Her pupils looked so large it was difficult to see the color of her eyes.

Shock. He needed to do something about that. Right now. "Come here," he murmured, pulling her into his arms.

Nando droned through the Miranda warning, then raised an eyebrow. "Care to tell me what just happened here."

"Like I said, Biedermeier's the dumper." Erik rested his chin on the top of Morgan's head. "He tried to take Morgan hostage. Arthur's a fucking hero. That about covers it." He willed himself not to check out Biedermeier's bloody face.

"A pen!" Morgan's voice was muffled against his shirt front.

Erik glanced down at her. "It's okay, Morg. It's all over."

Morgan pushed back from him. She bent over and picked something shiny off the floor. It looked like a silver ballpoint. She held it up, staring at it. "It was a pen he had jabbed in my side. Not a knife. He poked me with a stupid pen!" Morgan moved past Erik before he could stop her and kicked Biedermeier in the rump. "You held me hostage with a ballpoint, you freaking moron!"

Erik grabbed her around the waist, pulling her back before she could kick Biedermeier again, although it killed him to do it. "Easy."

Morgan twisted in his arms, trying to get back to her target. "What were you going to do," she yelled, "autograph me to death? A freaking ballpoint, for god's sake!"

Erik closed his eyes, holding Morgan tight against him. "Take this asshole in to the hospital and get him checked out," he told Nando. "Then take him to the station. The cruiser's outside. I'll be there as soon as I can."

"Right." Nando took hold of Biedermeier's belt, jerking him to his feet. "Come on, Terrell, your reign of terror is over."

Biedermeier stared at him woozily. "He broke my goddamn nose! He can't do that. I got rights."

"Hell, Terrell, if he'd broken your nose, you'd have a lot more blood on you than that. Come on." Nando pushed him toward the door.

Erik slid his arms tighter around Morgan's waist, pulling her back against him again. "It's okay, Morg. We're both okay. Ease up now."

Morgan's breath was ragged; her shoulders began to tremble. "A ballpoint."

"It's okay," Erik whispered. He turned her so that her forehead rested on his shoulder. "It's over. Let it go, Morg."

"I'm not going to cry," she muttered against his collarbone.

"No," he agreed.

"I'm not going to let that asshole make me cry."

"No." Erik rubbed his face against her hair. "I know you won't."

Her shoulders began to shake. "I'm not crying," she gasped.

"Of course not."

"Oh hell, hell, hell," she moaned, her shoulders heaving with sobs.

"It's okay." He rubbed small circles on her back. "Let it go now."

Over Morgan's shoulder, Erik saw Kit move toward them tentatively. He shook his head.

Esteban leaned against the back wall, his brow furrowed. "You need any help there, Chief?"

"No." Erik turned toward him. "I'm going to take her back into town with me."

"Okay." Esteban watched him with narrowed eyes, as if he were seeing the chief of police in an entirely new light.

Erik knew that look. He'd seen it before. Somewhere Mr. Hyde was cackling.

Morgan had worked her way through Erik's refrigerator in less than ten minutes. The man didn't even have orange juice. After a quick survey of the equally empty kitchen cupboards, she'd called Athenos Pizza for a large with everything, paying for the delivery when it came with a twenty and a handful of change she'd grabbed from the tasting room cash register.

She had found one thing in the cabinets—three cans of salmon-flavored cat food, the premium variety. If that was Arthur's normal dinner at Erik's place, it helped to explain why the cat seemed to be so unhappy about leaving.

Chewing on a piece of pepperoni, she wondered when he'd make it back. When he'd dropped her at the apartment, he'd told her he might be a couple of hours getting Biedermeier

Long Time Gone

locked up. Not that she was exactly anxious to hear about Biedermeier. Morgan shuddered. She could still feel Terrell's arm across her throat, the rasp of his arm hair against her collarbone. She could still smell him—panic sweat and the faint chemical smell of his clothes.

Suddenly, her skin felt clammy. She really could smell Biedermeier. Still.

She tossed her piece of pizza back in the box and headed for Erik's bathroom. Shower time.

Erik climbed the stairs to his apartment, trying to decide if he felt elated or depressed. Some of each, as a matter of fact.

Biedermeier had a bruised nose and a black eye, but nothing serious. He and Nando had taken him back to the station from the hospital, surprising the hell out of Peavey, who had night duty. Biedermeier didn't have much to say, particularly since the doctor in the ER had given him a couple of industrial-strength painkillers. Erik figured questioning him could wait until tomorrow, but he had Peavey start the paperwork for a search warrant on Biedermeier's house.

Most of the businesses who'd used his services would probably claim they thought they were dealing with a legitimate waste-disposal firm. Of course, the fact pickups had been done by a guy driving a pest control truck might have been an alarm for someone who'd had any real concerns in that area.

Erik smiled a little grimly. TCEQ and the sheriff were going to have a lot of fun with this one.

But he wouldn't. Friesenhahn had called him a few minutes after they'd locked Biedermeier in a cell to let him know he was going to the County Judge in the morning for a writ. Erik could question Biedermeier and search his house, but anything he found would end up in the sheriff's property room eventually, and the sheriff would be by to pick up his prisoner tomorrow afternoon.

He unlocked the door to his apartment and stepped through, scanning the empty living room. "Morgan?" As he turned down the hall, he heard the sound of running water. The shower.

For a moment, he debated whether to join her or not. She'd had a bad afternoon, what with Biedermeier deciding to play master criminal for five minutes. She might not want to do much besides have some dinner and go to sleep. A decent man would probably leave her alone until she'd indicated her preferences.

On the other hand, he did need a shower. And his afternoon hadn't been much better.

Who was to say she couldn't indicate her preferences while wet and naked?

Chapter Nineteen

Morgan stood in the shower, letting the last traces of Terrell Biedermeier wash down the drain. She closed her eyes and felt the warm water pulse against her face as another layer of tension dissolved along with it.

She only half-heard the bathroom door open and close. "Erik?"

"Were you expecting anybody else?" His voice sounded muffled, and she heard a boot hit the floor.

"Not really." She turned slightly, letting the water trickle down her spine.

"Want company?" His voice rumbled beneath the sound of running water.

"Sure." She smiled against the warm stream, then turned her head again to let it soak into her hair. "Do you have any shampoo?"

The shower curtain rings scrapped against the metal rail. "Sure I have shampoo. You think I'm a savage?"

Cool hands slid along her flanks, pushing her aside so that he could climb in behind her, then pulling her body back against the warmth of his chest. Morgan brought the backs of her thighs against him, feeling the warmth of his skin beneath the cooling water. Incredibly, she began to feel a warm flush of desire growing in her belly. Good to know Biedermeier hadn't traumatized her all that much after all.

"Are you okay with this, Bambi?" Erik's voice rumbled against her ear. "Or would you rather I back off?"

She leaned her head against him. "Don't. You. Dare."

He chuckled. "Want me to wash your hair?"

A quick jolt of desire flickered beneath her skin. She kept her eyes closed, reveling in the heightened feeling that rolled through her body "Yes, please."

After a moment, she felt the cool slide of liquid, then his fingers rubbing against her scalp. The air filled with a clean, powdery scent. "You use baby shampoo?"

He turned her so that her breasts were pressed against him, moving her head back beneath the spray. "You want to make something out of that, ma'am?"

"Nope." Morgan grinned, eyes closed against the water pouring across her forehead. His chest brushed against her nipples, sending small spikes of excitement down toward her mons. His lips pressed against the wetness of her throat, his tongue licking along the line of a tendon to her collarbone. Her breath rushed out in a whoosh. "No fair."

"Why not?" His voice was muffled against the top of her breast. She felt the brief nip of his teeth, then his hands cupping her buttocks, pulling her tighter.

"There's soap around my eyes. I can't open them until I'm rinsed."

Erik's chuckle whispered against her throat again, and then his hands were running through her hair, cupping the water so that it spilled across her forehead and down her face. "You're done."

"Not yet." She opened her eyes, grinning wetly. "But I think I will be soon."

"Definitely." His molasses eyes danced with heat. Tiny drops of water clung to his eyelashes and the dark beard stubble across his cheeks, giving him a moist shine.

Morgan wrapped one leg around his thighs, as he spread his knees slightly to support them. She leaned back against the wall, letting the water from the shower flow along her side, dividing into channels where their bodies touched. She could feel the head of his erection pressing against her opening.

"We're going to kill ourselves doing this here," she murmured. "One slip and we're toast."

"Just have faith, Bambi." He braced his hands on either side of her head, leaning forward so that he slid partway inside.

Morgan moaned, half protest, half need. He leaned forward again so that he slid further inside her—slowly, slowly inside. She curled her toes against him, then wrapped her leg more firmly around his waist, tucking her heel against his rear. "Do it, Chief," she gasped.

"Patience, ma'am."

She heard the grin in his voice. His face was buried in the crook of her throat, his teeth nipping at the edge of her shoulder. She groaned, thrusting herself against him, and he slid to her core, all heat and wetness and wicked delight.

He arched above her, pushing himself away from the wall. She watched the muscles of his arms and chest bunch and strain as he moved. His hips thudded against her, driving deep.

Her knees seemed to dissolve, all strength leaving the leg she was balancing on. A bubble of heat and light rose inside her, expanding through her body, and she cried out, looping her arms around his neck to keep herself from slipping.

He pushed her flat against the wall, pounding hard but still not hard enough, not deep enough. She groaned, trying to move closer, and he took her breast in his mouth.

The pull on her nipple sent a line of sensation straight down to her toes. She gritted her teeth and jutted her body toward him again, their hips slapping in the water that streamed over her head. Heat erupted through her, shattering her. "Oh lord, Erik."

His body hammered on top of her, once, twice, again, harder, deeper, riding it out until he was gasping for breath against her cheek.

She whimpered, her body shuddering with aftershocks.

"Easy, Bambi," he whispered. "Easy now."

She slumped against his arms, sliding down the wall to the tub, and Erik slid with her, pulling her on top of him. They lay together in the pooling spray that cooled the heat of their skin.

"Nice shower," he muttered.

"Yeah." Morgan looked down from above him. "I think I've been in here too long, though. I'm all wrinkly."

Water beaded on his forehead, his cheeks, matting his eyelashes. His lips spread in a soaking grin. "Sorry, I'm too wiped out to think of a comeback to that." He sat up slowly, carrying her until she straddled his hips, then reached to the end of the tub and turned off the water. "I'd say you're done."

Her lips spread in a lazy smile. "Ooh, am I ever!"

Erik pushed the shower curtain open and pulled a bath

sheet off the towel rack across from the tub. He wrapped it around her body, rubbing gently against her skin. "Time to dry off, Morg. Wouldn't want you to dissolve. Not yet, anyway." His teeth flashed against the dark gold of his skin.

Morgan felt a sudden clench as she looked up at him. *So much man. So scary gorgeous.* And still somehow she didn't know him at all. She reached for his shirt. "Come on, Chief. Pizza's getting cold."

Erik sat cross-legged in the middle of the living room floor and considered the last piece of pizza in the box in front of him. He'd put on a pair of jeans, but that was it—they weren't dressing for dinner. Morgan sat across from him in one of his T-shirts, which reached to the middle of her thighs. He was trying not to be too aware of the fact she wasn't wearing any underwear.

A true gentleman would offer that last piece of pizza to his lady first. A hungry cop would race her for it. He sighed. "Want the last piece?"

Morgan shook her head, wiping a napkin across her mouth to pick up a smear of tomato sauce. Her brown curls stood up in corkscrews around her head. She looked like a very sexy Shirley Temple. "I'm full. Go for it, Chief."

He picked up the last piece and watched her stretch across the floor. It was a good thing he had his hands full or he'd have jumped her again. Better to focus on other things, at least until they'd had time to digest dinner. "So how are you feeling?"

Her forehead furrowed. "Feeling? After that shower and the pizza I'm feeling terrific, why?"

He shrugged. "I mean post-Biedermeier."

Morgan pursed her lips in a way that made his gut clench. "I guess I should still be traumatized, but I'm not. I mean, it was Terrell Biedermeier, for Pete's sake. The bug man. And he threatened me with a ballpoint pen."

He fought a grin. "It was still serious, Morg. He did threaten you, even if it was bogus."

She raised up on one elbow. "Well, you saved me and I'm fine." She gave him a dazzling—if somewhat guarded—grin, glancing around the room. "Kind of sparse in here, isn't it?"

Okay, we'll change the subject. He followed her gaze.

"Maybe. I didn't bring much with me." He hadn't had much to bring in the first place. His first home in Konigsburg had been a single-wide. Fortunately, Docia's old apartment had come available when Pete and his wife Janie had bought their own house. He'd picked up a couch and a kitchen table at a used-furniture store. And Docia had left her king-size bed behind when she'd moved in with Cal. It was the best piece of furniture in the apartment, and it had really come in handy since he'd met Morgan.

"What's that?" She pointed to the plastic display box on top of the television set.

He grimaced. "My Nolan Ryan autographed baseball."

She turned back to look at him, her mouth inching up into a smile. "You're a baseball fan?"

"Used to be." He sighed and took another bite of pizza. "My dad bought it for me when I was sixteen. I think he hoped it would get me to start playing again." His dad had taught him to pitch too. Maybe if he'd gone back to playing in high school, he wouldn't have turned into the town terror. But given his close association with Mr. Hyde, probably not.

"You were a ball player?" Morgan wet the tip of her finger with her tongue and began picking up crumbs from the box. He handed her the rest of his slice.

"For a while. Football, mostly, but I played baseball until my junior year. Then I decided being a punk was more fun." Not to mention it got more of a rise out of his dad. He gave himself a mental head-slap. Sometimes his younger self seemed like a complete stranger as well as a complete jerk. "That ball has been around the world with me, thanks to Uncle Sam."

"Do you still play?" She nibbled at the pizza, showing a flash of pink tongue that sent a jolt of heat southward to his groin.

He rolled onto his back beside her so that he couldn't look at her. "Yeah, I was in a recreational league in Davenport. The department had a team."

"Maybe you could start one here. I'll bet Nando would be good. Esteban used to be an athlete in high school. Maybe you could get your brothers involved. You could probably put a decent team together."

He glanced back at her bright smile. He let one corner of his mouth inch up. "Maybe."

They both heard what he didn't say. *If I can hang onto this job for more than the next week.*

She dropped her gaze. "Just a thought."

He felt a quick pang of something in his gut. Longing? He didn't want to examine it too much, not now at least. Best not to get any hopes up. "I'll keep it in mind if I can get around what the mayor's got planned for me."

"What's Hilton done now?"

"He's got me on the agenda for the next council meeting. Next week."

Her brow furrowed. "How can he possibly object to your performance as chief with what happened today? You caught the freakin' dumper."

"Not exactly. We caught the dumper's assistant."

"What do you mean?"

Erik sighed. It didn't seem like privileged information. "Terrell doesn't strike me as the type to set something like this up on his own. Somebody else was probably involved."

"Have you asked him?"

"Not yet. He's full of painkillers for his cracked nose." There was a beat of silence between them.

She took a sip of iced tea. "He had me in a choke hold. We both thought he had a knife. Nobody's going to hold that against you."

"Ah, Bambi, never underestimate my faulty interpersonal skills." He tried for ironic, but his tone was a lot closer to bitter. *Not good. Never let them see you sweat.*

"What will you do?"

He shrugged. "Go there. Tell my side of whatever Pittman's got to say. Hope for the best."

"When's the council meeting?"

"Day after tomorrow."

She stared down at him, eyes wide. "Erik, you should talk to Pete."

"Maybe." *Actually, no.* He hadn't earned the right to ask his brothers for help. Not yet. Maybe not ever.

"Erik..."

"Don't worry about it, Bambi, I can take care of myself." He reached out and pulled one of her corkscrew curls, letting it slip through his fingers.

She licked her lips, the tip of her tongue light pink against the darker burgundy of her lips. Her very full lips. Particularly the bottom lip, to which he'd paid a lot of attention in the shower.

Erik felt himself hardening again. Serious conversations could wait. Just as well since he didn't have any answers for her. What he was going to do about all of this was still a mystery to him too.

He picked up the pizza box, tossing in crumpled napkins. "Cleanup time, Ms. Barrett."

Morgan felt a dull ache somewhere around her stomach. Probably being held hostage, followed by late-night pizza, followed by later-night sex. All in all, a busy day.

More than enough to account for the hollow feeling in her chest, the grit behind her eyelids.

Of course, Erik might have to leave. When hadn't she known that? He'd always been straight about it, never tried to mislead her. Whatever they had was white hot and most likely temporary.

Oh, she might still be able to see him if he lost his job as chief, depending on where he ended up. Maybe he'd come by to visit his family occasionally, when he wasn't too busy. Maybe she could even visit him, if he didn't get that nervous, male, "are-we-this-serious?" look in his eyes when he saw her walk in.

But she wouldn't be able to find him in the Dew Drop anymore.

Knock it off, Morgan. She'd never been big on self-pity, and she wasn't going to give in to it now. After all, she'd only known him a few weeks and she wasn't the type to start active daydreaming just because she'd had sex with somebody. Or she never had been before.

And they didn't just have sex. They made love.

She exhaled a quick breath, looking around the sparse bedroom.

Behind her, she heard Erik's step. "Morgan?"

"I think I'll go back to Cedar Creek." She didn't turn as she began to pull on her clothes. "I've got stuff I need to do before tomorrow."

She turned then. He was watching her, his eyes dark. "Are you sure? You could stay over."

"I can't. Really. Thanks for a...great evening." Her voice sounded brittle, like one of those women in bad English movies.

"Any time." One corner of his mouth inched up again.

God, I'll miss his smile. Along with the rest of him. She started toward the door.

He reached for her, cupping her cheek in his hand. "You don't have to go, Bambi."

The hollow feeling in her chest throbbed painfully. "Yeah, I do. My dad may be coming back to the winery tomorrow and I need to get ready for him."

His gaze held hers for a moment longer. Then he leaned forward, brushing his lips against her forehead. "I'll call you."

She wanted to laugh but it hurt too much. *I'll call you.* Wasn't that what they always said?

"Sure. Later." And she was gone.

Erik got Biedermeier out of his cell as soon as he and Nando both made it to the station the next morning. They didn't have a room for interviewing suspects per se, but the break room housed the coffeepot, a refrigerator and a microwave, along with several cartons of paper towels and a mop and pail. He figured Terrell didn't exactly require special handling, but he read him his rights a second time just to be sure.

Biedermeier regarded him warily. The skin around his eye had blossomed into a dark purple, and the bridge of his nose was bandaged.

Erik shrugged. "You shouldn't have grabbed her, Terrell."

Biedermeier rubbed a hand across his stubbly jaw. "Yeah, I know. Lost my head there for a minute." He cast a longing look at the coffee pot on the counter. After a second, Erik nodded to Nando, who pulled a coffee can out of the refrigerator.

"Okay, Terrell." Erik leaned back in his folding chair. "Sooner or later some other people are going to show up to talk to you—Sheriff Friesenhahn to start with and maybe TCEQ. But for now, I've got some questions for you myself."

Biedermeier's eyes widened. "Why do I need to talk to all those guys? It was just a little dumping."

Erik pinched the bridge of his nose. "That 'little dumping' is a felony, Terrell, so eventually you'll end up in jail. I've got jurisdiction on you right now since I more or less tripped over you, but I won't keep it. Not on something high profile like this. On the other hand, if you talk to me now, I can put in a good word for you with the sheriff and later with the judge."

Erik let one corner of his mouth edge up in a smile that wasn't supposed to be reassuring. The idea of saying any good words about Terrell Biedermeier didn't rate high on his list. He hadn't asked for a lawyer yet. Erik didn't plan on reminding him that he could. If he couldn't remember the rights he'd just heard, he was shit out of luck.

Biedermeier peered up at him from beneath his bushy eyebrows. "What all you want to know?"

He put his recorder on the table in front of him. "Let's start with where you dumped around Konigsburg and when. And who helped you." He clicked the Record button and muttered the date, time and salient details into the mike.

Biedermeier glanced down at his folded hands. Behind him, Nando scooped coffee grounds into the ancient percolator, one eye on Terrell's tense shoulders.

"I got a list," Biedermeier mumbled finally.

Erik frowned. "A list. Of places around town where you dumped stuff?"

Biedermeier shook his head. "Nah. Places I picked up. He'd give me a list to use. Every time I did a pickup."

Erik sat very still. "He did? Who was that?"

Biedermeier shrugged. "Don't ask me. Only saw him a couple times. Most of the time he'd just phone when he had something and then drop the list in my mailbox."

"The list of people who wanted you to dispose of their chemicals?"

"Yeah. Never told me what it was I was picking up, though. Just to take it out in the hills and dump it. Used my truck. Motor oil, mostly, I guess. I'd hose the tank down when I was through."

Erik raised an eyebrow. "You added a little bit of leftover Chlordane of your own, though, right?"

Biedermeier frowned, shaking his head. "No sir, I don't use Chlordane. Don't have none around. It's banned."

Behind Biedermeier, Nando rolled his eyes as he plugged in the coffee pot.

"It's all banned, Terrell," Erik said dryly. "None of that stuff was supposed to be dumped. You're telling me the Chlordane didn't come from you?"

Biedermeier dropped his gaze to his hands again, then lifted one shoulder in a half shrug. "Might have been some in the truck, I guess. Left over, like you said. Best stuff there is for taking care of termites. Never knew why they banned it."

"It causes cancer," Erik said through clenched teeth.

"Hell, what doesn't?" Biedermeier settled back in his chair, squinting at the window.

"How did they pay you for those pickups, Terrell?"

Biedermeier rubbed his thumb across the back of his hand, staring silently at the tabletop. After a moment, he sighed. "Cash. It'd come in the mail a couple of days after I did a pickup." Behind him the percolator erupted with a loud *plop!* Biedermeier jumped.

Nando folded his arms across his chest, his face dark, as he walked around the table. "You're telling us you never met the guy who was running all this? That you got all your orders over the phone? Come on, Terrell. Even you aren't that dumb!"

Terrell's forehead furrowed, his eyes round. "Sure I am."

Erik gave Nando a *back-off* look. Nando turned around to pull some coffee cups out of the cupboard.

"You remember anything about the man, Terrell? What he looked like? He give you a way to reach him? A name?"

"No, sir. He'd just call every once in a while, tell me to make a run. Then the money would come. And I only saw him the one time when he set the whole thing up with me."

Nando's lips were a thin line. "How would you get the list of names? Would he give you that over the phone too?"

Biedermeier glanced back and forth between them, eyes wide. "He sends the list Priority Mail."

Erik rubbed his eyes, thinking about court orders for phone records, and then chasing down the man on the other end of those phone calls. Assuming the people behind the dumping had their heads so far up their asses they missed the news that Biedermeier had been arrested. He had a feeling that was something he'd have to leave to Friesenhahn, or possibly the Rangers.

"We'll need the list, Terrell. All the lists from all the jobs. You still got them all?"

Biedermeier swallowed, scratching around the edge of his collar. "I wasn't supposed to keep 'em. He told me to get rid of 'em after I made the drops."

"Did you keep any?"

Biedermeier's eyes darted around the room. "Dunno. I'd need to look."

"We'll look for you." Erik's voice was level.

"Maybe you could take us there now." Nando gave him an easy smile. Good cop, reborn. "You can pack your toothbrush while we pick up the lists. You don't mind if we go through your house, do you, Terrell?"

Biedermeier slowly shook his head. "Guess not. Might as well be you as anybody. Least I know you. Don't know the sheriff, do I?"

"Nope, you sure don't." Nando handed him a cup of coffee.

Erik pushed his chair back, getting slowly to his feet. "We'll talk again later, Terrell."

Nando followed him out the door, where Erik turned back. "Nice try, bubba, but seeing as how Pittman's already after my ass, we'll still need to get a search warrant."

Biedermeier's house smelled of sweat and old grease. Dust motes danced in the rays of sunlight that filtered through the Venetian blinds. Erik could see a few lumps of furniture in the dimness, along with a large-screen TV in the corner. Apparently, Biedermeier didn't deprive himself of all luxuries.

Nando sighed. "About what I'd expect Terrell to live in. What exactly are we looking for?"

"Lists of customers." Erik shrugged. "Cancelled checks. Business records. Anything that might give us a lead on who hired him."

"Assuming we buy into the whole 'mysterious mastermind' story." Nando sighed more deeply. "Where do we start?"

"You take the living room. I'll find his desk, assuming he didn't run his business out of the damn truck."

Two hours later, they'd found most of what seemed to pass

for Biedermeier's records—three banker's boxes full of miscellaneous junk. Erik had retrieved at least one list of customers from a battered desk in the back bedroom. If he'd hoped to get any leads from the list, one look told him to forget it—it was a photocopied printout in Courier.

He stared back at the house after they'd finished loading the boxes into the cruiser's trunk. A forties bungalow, like every other house on the block, with a live oak tree and an ancient rose climbing up the battered trellis at the front. If Biedermeier had been making a lot of money dumping outlaw chemicals, wouldn't he have moved to a better place?

And if Biedermeier wasn't making money on this deal, who was? Maybe the Master Criminal existed after all.

Around lunchtime, Morgan watched her father park his black SUV in the *Reserved* spot in front of the winery. As he pushed himself to his feet and began limping toward the tasting room, he looked almost like himself again. He was still thinner than he should be, and he leaned heavily on his cane. But his eyes flashed with the old fervor.

Wine snob alert!

She heard another door slam and glanced back at the SUV. Her mother stared up at the winery, thunderclouds in her eyes. So far as Morgan knew, her mother hadn't been in Konigsburg for the last two years. When her mom and dad had separated, her mom had sworn never to set foot in the winery.

Just past noon, and already things were off to an interesting start!

Her father nodded at her, smiling broadly, then headed toward Ciro, who stood in the tasting room door.

Her mother paused at her side. "Somebody had to drive with him. The old fool would have tried to come up and back in a day. Probably would have broken his neck in the process."

Morgan put her arm around her mother's shoulders. "Come on, Mom, let's get you a glass of something or other."

Inside the tasting room, her father was sitting at the desk in what was supposed to be her office, flipping through a series of notebooks. The barrel room records, the ones she'd spent hours keeping up to date. Ciro sat beside him, pointing to a page.

Morgan sighed. Shouldn't she feel more nervous about this? After all, they'd be checking over all the work she'd done for the last year.

But then it really wasn't her work. It was just what Ciro told her to do.

Her father glanced up at her. "Looks all right. Good job keeping the records up to date, Morgan."

"Thanks." She nodded, trying to feel pleased. Her stomach twisted again.

"My wine?" Her mother put her hand on Morgan's elbow, steering her toward the tasting bar where Kit sat studying them, her chin in her hands.

"Kit, this is my mom, Leila Barrett. Mom, this is Kit Maldonado. She runs the tasting room."

Her mother settled onto a stool in front of the bar, smiling at Kit. "That's the only job I'd want to have around here."

Kit grinned back. "Me too, ma'am."

Ciro and her father were flipping through more pages. Morgan heard Ciro mutter something about pH levels and acidity. He'd never told her anything about that. But what would she have done about it if he had? She still didn't understand all the wine chemistry her father and Ciro used when they did their blends.

Beside her, her mother sipped her viognier and watched, one eyebrow raised. "Are you all right, sweetheart?"

"I'm fine." Morgan rubbed a hand against the back of her neck. What she was feeling—or not feeling—had nothing to do with Erik Toleffson. Nothing whatsoever.

"Don't worry, honey, they're not shutting you out. Your dad knows how much this means to you."

Did he? Morgan doubted it, all of a sudden. A year's worth of scut work, of trying to prove herself to Ciro, to Carmen, to him, to herself. Did he know what that meant?

"Okay, Morg," her father called, "where's that Powell lease? And we need all that crap from TCEQ."

Morgan spent the afternoon finding files on the computer, bringing out bottles of wine for tasting, even bringing a cluster of Cynthiana grapes for her father to check. She began to feel like a cross between a gofer and a waitress, seeing as how she also kept them supplied with cheese, bread and fruit.

Carmen came in and swept her mother away for gossip and coffee. Her father and Ciro worked straight through lunch. Morgan chewed on a piece of baguette and watched Kit pour wine.

By late afternoon, she was ready to head for the Dew Drop, assuming her father didn't need her to dig up something from beneath the floor of the barrel room.

"Morgan!" She turned at the bite in her father's voice. He was staring at another piece of paper, but this time it looked like a letter. "Come here a minute."

Reluctantly, she walked across the room. This didn't look like fun. "What is it, Dad?"

Her father looked up at her again, one eyebrow raised. He held the sheet between his thumb and forefinger, as if it were contaminated. "Bored Ducks?"

Morgan looked over his shoulder. The letter from ATF. She scanned it quickly, grinning. "They approved the label? Fantastic! Esteban must have put it on my desk after he read it. Now we can release it at the Wine and Food Festival."

"Bored Ducks?" Her father's voice rose. "You want Cedar Creek Winery to produce a wine called Bored Ducks? Who the hell authorized this?"

"It's Esteban's blend." Morgan turned to Ciro. "You remember—the one he did a couple of years ago."

Her father turned to Ciro too, one hand fisted on the tabletop. "Since when does Esteban do blends?"

Ciro raised an eyebrow. "Boy's been taking viticulture and enology courses for a few years now. I gave him the okay." He turned a gimlet gaze on Morgan. "But I didn't okay that name."

Morgan's shoulders tightened. She forced herself to relax. "Have either of you been in a wine store lately? Lots of wineries are doing unusual labels. It gets people's attention. Sometimes they'll buy on the strength of the label alone. It's a good marketing strategy."

Morgan felt a hand on her shoulder. Her mother stood behind her, smiling a little too brightly. "I think it's a great idea. What does the label look like?"

Morgan pulled out another file and dug through it to find the artist's rendering. "It's clever. I found an artist in Austin."

Her mother took the sheet from her, grinning. "Look, Cliff, a woodcut, just like the other labels. The ducks really do luck bored. It's adorable."

Her father's lips were a thin line, his eyes like a stormy sky. "I don't do adorable wine."

"Why not?" Her mother's grin became more fixed. "Too likely to sell? Too likely to make the winery look like it's emerged into the twenty-first century? ATF approval means you can go ahead, right, Morgan?"

Morgan nodded. "We've got the labels printed up. All we need to do is slap them on."

Her father inhaled deeply, then blew out a breath. "Looks like I came back just in time. There is no way in hell Cedar Creek will put these labels on our wine. Or call it anything that stupid."

"Cliff, shut up." Her mother placed her hands on her hips, "You will not ruin your daughter's idea. She's the marketer. You're the winemaker. Leave her alone."

Her father's jaw tightened. Suddenly, Morgan felt like ducking.

"I didn't tell you to mess with the wines or the way we sell them!" he spat. "I sent you here to learn how the wine is made, so that you'd understand the business."

The muscles in Morgan's chest clenched so hard it was painful. Her breath caught in her throat. "You mean since I've never been able to understand business before?"

Her father regarded her silently, his jaw rigid.

Morgan exhaled hard. "Well, at least that's out in the open. For your information, Dad, we've already gotten approval to release Bored Ducks at the Wine and Food Festival. I still managed to do that even though I seem to be a shitty winery manager, based on the amount of crap I've had to put up with over the past year from everyone here, including you." She swallowed. Her eyes were beginning to sting. "I'm through for the day. I'm going to town. I'll see you all tomorrow. Maybe."

She thought she heard her mother's voice calling after her as she pushed through the door, but she didn't bother to look back.

Chapter Twenty

Hilton sat in his office, wondering how to get around the problem of Toleffson and Biedermeier. It was damned inconvenient for Toleffson to have caught the dumper, particularly when Hilton was this close to getting rid of him. Biedermeier's arrest might come across as a strong argument in Toleffson's favor.

Of course, whether it was a strong argument or not, Hilton should still be able to convince the council to fire Toleffson. He'd just have to lean heavily on the interpersonal-problems angle and drop the little bombshell Brinkman had dug up in Toleffson's record. He figured that would be enough to make the council somewhat queasy, particularly if he made some vague references to possible lawsuits. Maybe he wouldn't call it firing. "Reassigned" had a nice sound. That way Hilton himself wouldn't have to take any heat for getting a hero fired.

Hilton knew from experience that the city council members would agree to just about anything if it meant going home on time. And people would forget about Toleffson soon enough. They always did.

Still, he really wished there was some way he could give Friesenhahn the credit for catching Biedermeier instead of Toleffson. He wouldn't mind doing a grip and grin with Ozzie, who always managed to bring along some reporters when he cracked a case.

Hilton's irritation flared again as his office door swung open. Doralee still needed reminders about not walking in unannounced. He didn't bother to look up. "Goddamn it!" he snapped. "Didn't I tell you to knock?"

"Not that I recall, no." Horace Rankin stepped into the

office, his graying walrus moustache bristling.

Hilton swallowed. He'd always been able to deal with the other members of the city council through a mixture of charm, bribery and intimidation. But neither charm nor bribery worked with Rankin, and Hilton wasn't stupid enough to try intimidation. Rankin might gut him. "What can I do for you, Horace?"

Rankin sat uninvited in one of Hilton's padded chairs. "What's this thing about Toleffson? Why is he on the agenda tomorrow night?"

Hilton cleared his throat. "Personnel matter. We'll be in Executive Session."

"What kind of personnel matter?" Rankin took off his gold-framed glasses and polished them with a bright red bandana handkerchief. "You know he found out it was Biedermeier doing the illegal dumping out in the hills? Caught him out at the winery."

Hilton's jaw tightened. "I know."

"So you wouldn't be dumb enough to try to get rid of the man now, would you, Pittman?" Rankin breathed on his glasses and polished them again before replacing them on his nose. He turned magnified eyes on Hilton.

Hilton shook his head. "I'm trying to correct some problems Toleffson has created in his time here. And bring some facts to light about his past record in Iowa. Hopefully, tonight will take care of everything."

"Problems?" Rankin raised his eyebrows. "What problems would those be? Far as I can see, Toleffson has been the best thing to happen to the police department in years. And Ozzie Friesenhahn said his record was outstanding."

Hilton managed a chilly smile. "We'll have to differ on that, Horace. A closer look will show he has some definite problems both now and earlier."

Rankin settled back deeper into the padded leather chair, studying Hilton over his fingertips. "You're going to screw this up, aren't you, Pittman?"

"Screw what up?" Hilton began savagely unfolding a paper clip on his desk to keep from throwing something. "I'm doing my job here, Rankin. I'm running the city."

Rankin began to push himself up slowly from the depths of the chair. Hilton had never noticed how tall Horace was. Must be six feet or so. Remarkable really.

Horace leaned over the desk, planting his fists on either side of the desk pad. "Listen, Pittman, nobody has messed with you because it wasn't worth their time. Start screwing around with Toleffson, and it may suddenly become worth my time to do something about you."

Hilton raised his gaze from the desk to Rankin's face. His expression was enough to make a timid man recoil, but Hilton was made of sterner stuff. Besides, he knew for a fact Rankin didn't want to run for mayor. "I'll take your opinion under advisement, Horace."

"You do that." Rankin stood up straight, his eyes never leaving Hilton's face. "See you tomorrow night, Mr. Mayor."

Somehow when Horace said it, Hilton's title didn't sound nearly as impressive as it should have.

Morgan awoke at seven the next morning and listened for voices in the tasting room. When she'd returned to the winery after dinner, no one had been around. Ciro had stuck his head in to inform her tersely that her parents were staying at a B and B in town. At least her mother and father were back together for the moment.

Every time she thought about the future, she got a stomach cramp. Staying at Cedar Creek under the current arrangement made her insides burn, but going anywhere else, admitting to herself that she'd never be good enough to be part of the winery, hurt a lot worse.

She'd had dinner with Allie and Wonder at Brenner's, but she hadn't seen Erik all evening. Maybe he was on duty. Or maybe he'd decided to start easing back on spending time with her. After all, it was beginning to look like they both might be headed elsewhere soon enough.

All in all, the sight of the empty tasting room did nothing to make her heart feel any lighter. She put food out for Skeeter and Fred, along with some cat crunchies for Arthur.

By the time her father stepped onto the front porch, she was seated at the bar with a cup of coffee.

"Morning, Dad."

Her father climbed onto the stool next to her, narrowing his eyes. "I waited for you last night. You didn't come back."

"No." Morgan took another sip of coffee. "I had dinner with some friends."

"We need to get this straightened out, Morgan."

She glanced at his face for a moment, the hard look in his eyes. "I don't know if we can, Dad. We seem pretty far apart just now."

"I didn't mean to imply you haven't done your work here, Morg." Her father glanced out the window at the vineyards along the hillsides. "Place looks good. You and Ciro kept it running well." He turned back to her. In the early morning light, the shadows emphasized the hollows in his cheeks and the wrinkles surrounding his deep-set eyes. He looked older than he ever had.

He leaned forward, covering Morgan's hand with his own. "Considering how much you had to learn and how hard you had to work, you did a hell of a job, kid."

Morgan exhaled, suddenly aware of how tight her chest had been. "Thanks, Dad. It's not just about helping to run the winery, though. Not for me anyway."

Her father's brow furrowed. "What do you mean?"

"I have some ideas about Cedar Creek. About things we can do to increase our sales—to make us better known around the state. And maybe even outside the state."

The moment of silence seemed to stretch uncomfortably. Her father jaw grew tight. "We're already well-known. Those medals over there show how well-known we are."

Morgan's chest tightened again. "Some people know what we do, but a lot more don't. We're not as widely distributed as the other wineries around here. And we should be. Our wine is as good as theirs. Better, in most cases."

Her father shrugged, looking back up at the hillsides again. "Our sales are decent. About as much as our production can support. No point in trying for more sales when we don't have the capacity. I don't see that we need to make any major changes."

"*Decent* shouldn't be enough." Morgan swallowed hard. "We should be looking to the future, building on our customer base so that we can expand."

Her father shook his head. "We're fine the way we are. Don't mess with things you don't understand, Morgan. Just concentrate on learning the details of production. Don't waste your energy on all that marketing garbage. We don't need it. We never have."

Morgan closed her eyes. The ache in her gut was painful.

"You want me to just go on doing things the way you've always done them?" Her voice sounded flat to her own ears. "No changes? No using my expertise? You want me to just be a worker bee and keep out of the way?"

Her father grimaced. "Look, maybe it's natural for you to think you can come in and make everything bigger and better here. But that's not why I asked you to come. You're supposed to be learning the business. Not changing the way we've run the winery. It works, Morgan. It doesn't need changing. We're a premium winery. We're known and respected throughout the state. What you want—what you're suggesting isn't right for Cedar Creek."

"How do you know what I'm suggesting, Dad? You haven't heard me yet."

"I know what you've done so far—trying to release wine too soon just so we can get into some damn restaurant. And trying to have us produce this idiotic pop wine." Her father grimaced. "Jesus, Morgan! What were you thinking? Haven't you paid any attention over the past year?"

In the silence that followed, Morgan heard a mockingbird tuning up in the live oaks outside. She took a deep breath. "So that's it," she murmured, shaking her head. "That's how we end it."

Her father stared at her, brow furrowed.

"When I first came here, I thought I had something to offer. I thought I could take what I learned and apply what I already knew to make things better here. But the longer I've worked here, the more I understand—you never wanted me to do what I do best. And you'll never be satisfied with the way I do everything else. Face it, Dad. I'm lousy at being you. I just hope I haven't forgotten how to be me." She folded her arms across her chest, what there was left of it. Maybe she could market the whole experience to the model wannabes—the Slave Labor Diet.

"What you do best?" Her father's voice cracked. "What you do best is smoke and mirrors. All that useless crap you learned at business school." He thumped his hand on the oak cask below the counter. "This is real, goddamn it. This is what you should be thinking about. This is what you should be proud of."

Morgan closed her eyes again. "I *am* proud of it. But why the hell can't you be proud of me too?"

"That's a good question, Cliff. You have any answers for her?" Her mother's voice sounded remarkably calm as she walked across the room.

Morgan's head shot up. Her father started so violently that he spilled his coffee, then muttered curses as he mopped it up with a napkin.

"Morning, all." Her mother smiled blandly at them both. "Any more coffee there?"

"Yes, ma'am." Morgan couldn't decide if she felt relieved or worried that her mother had waited until now to walk in, but she poured her a cup of coffee anyway.

Her mother lifted herself onto a stool at the bar beside her father. "Well, this is interesting. I thought I'd be coming here for breakfast, not a Texas version of *King Lear*."

Her father narrowed his eyes, but said nothing. Morgan decided that was a good idea.

"So let me see if I've got the gist of the argument here." Her mother took a sip of coffee, gazing at the Cynthiana vineyard. "You, Cliff, want Cedar Creek to stay exactly the same as it's always been because it's just freakin' perfect as is."

Her father took a sharp breath, but her mother held up her hand to stop him. "And you, Morgan, would like to try to introduce some marketing to the winery because you actually know something about it beyond the blanket assumption that it's snake oil. Is that about right?"

Morgan nodded slowly. "That's about right."

"So what would it take to bring these two points of view together, Clifford? Aside from a miracle?"

Her father started to say something, then stopped, staring down at the floor, his mouth a grim line.

"Morgan? Any ideas?"

Morgan studied her father for a long moment. *Raise or fold, Morgan. Raise or fold.* "Bored Ducks is due to be released at the Food and Wine Festival this weekend. Use that as a test case. If people like it, if it sells, maybe Dad could listen to some of my other ideas. If it's a bust, I'll go quietly."

Her mother sighed. "Sounds fair to me."

Her father stared down at the coffee cup he still held, then glanced back up at her. "Okay. If you've already printed up the labels, you might as well go ahead. There's no time to print up more. But if it doesn't sell, from now on you will accept my judgment on things like this that you know nothing about. And you will never try anything like that again."

Morgan exhaled, suddenly aware that she'd been holding her breath. "Daddy, if it doesn't sell, trust me, I won't want to try anything like that again."

Erik sat in when the Rangers and Friesenhahn questioned Biedermeier. Not that they got anything new out of him. Erik had the distinct feeling that there wasn't much new to be gotten from Biedermeier. That well was pretty much dry.

The questioning had taken all afternoon and the drive back from Austin had taken over an hour, given the traffic. By the time he reached Konigsburg, he was hot, tired and more depressed than he had been when he'd left. He headed for the Coffee Corral, parking his cruiser out front.

Inside, he saw Lars and Jess at a booth with their children. Daisy, age three, was industriously coloring. Jack, age one or so, was industriously reducing a French fry to mush by pounding it flat. Jess gave him a distracted wave after he'd left his order with Al Brosius.

He liked all three of his sisters-in-law, but Jess was his favorite. Maybe because she'd known him first as a cop who'd helped her, not as her husband's slightly sinister big brother. And Lars, like Cal, seemed to have forgiven Erik for all the pain he'd caused when they were young. An evening with Lars and Jess would be low stress, even if they had to talk around the kids.

"Join us," Lars called.

"Sure." Erik started to amble their way.

"Chief?" Al stepped away from the front counter. "Got a minute?"

Erik glanced curiously at the kitchen to see who else could be cooking. Kent, the budding juvenile delinquent, was flipping burgers with ease.

"Sure." Erik followed Al to a table at the side. "What's on your mind?"

"I found out about Kent," Al blurted.

Erik waited. He wasn't exactly sure what to say to that.

Al stared down at his hands, then back again. "I wanted to thank you for giving him a break. He's a good kid. He'll keep his nose clean. I'll make sure of it."

Erik nodded. "I know. Teenagers. It happens. He'll be fine."

"I know you didn't have to help him. I appreciate it. Let me know if there's ever anything I can do for you."

Erik thought of all the breaks people had tried to give him when he was a teenager, and the lousy use he'd made of them. "Thanks. Don't worry about it." He clapped Al on the shoulder, then stood. "How did you found out about it? Did Kent tell you?"

Al grimaced. "Nah. Ol' Margaret angels-are-my-middle-name Hastings. She lives across the street from the school. Saw Kent picking up the cans and bullied him into telling her what was up. Couldn't wait to call me."

Erik felt a telltale prickling along the back of his neck. Something about that wasn't good. "Well, like I say, don't worry about it. It's water under the bridge now."

By the time he got to the table, Lars and Jess had switched into cleanup mode. Jess was swabbing Daisy's fingers with a wet wipe, while Lars worked on Jack. "What's new?" Lars grinned up at him. "Other than your heroic capture of the mysterious dumper, that is. At least we won't have to detour around Biedermeier's ass at the Dew Drop for a while."

Erik decided the question of what else was going on in his life at the moment wasn't one he wanted to tackle right then. "You on your way out?"

Jess nodded. "We've got to get these two home before they burn out. Why don't you come to dinner next week?"

"We've got family dinner next Friday," Lars reminded her. "We can catch up then."

Jess gave him a grin that showed her dimples, as Lars began unsnapping Jack from his highchair. "I don't think I ever congratulated you on being chief. Way to go."

Erik managed to push the corners of his mouth into a passable smile. "Thanks."

Jess's grin began to fade as she looked at him. "Troubles?"

"Just tired."

She studied him a moment longer, then shrugged. "You're a

lousy liar, Erik. We'll talk about it at the family dinner. I need to catch up on what's going on in your life."

By Friday, of course, they'd all know what was going on. Not that he'd be any more excited to talk about it. "Okay. We'll talk then."

He watched them stagger out the door, parents with their squirming children. Once he would have bet he'd never be like them. Now...

Now he had other things to worry about.

He headed back to the station and took a quick check through the Wine and Food Festival paperwork. This weekend. He sighed—he might not even be in charge by then. Ham Linklatter walked in a few minutes later, looking like death. Since Ham always looked like death, Erik didn't think much about it and left him to his night duty.

He pulled into his usual parking spot beside the bookstore, then walked back to the Dew Drop. He doubted Morgan would be there, but it never hurt to check.

And it might be better than calling her this late after not talking to her for a day and half. Even though he was a social halfwit, he knew that was not a good idea, even if he had a good excuse.

The Dew Drop was full of dart players and beer drinkers, but no Cal, no Docia, no Allie, no Wonder.

No Morgan.

Erik sighed. Another fence to mend. No, more than that. Morgan was definitely more than a fence.

He turned back up Main, heading for Spicewood and home. In front of him, the door at Brenner's opened and Morgan stepped into the street with the sommelier, Ken Crowder.

Erik stopped, his breath catching in his throat. She had her back to him.

"Okay, babe—" Ken chuckled, watching Morgan's face, "—two cases. We'll probably sell some glasses on the name alone. Plus it tastes great."

Morgan hugged him quickly. "Thanks. You'll love it. I promise."

Erik cleared his throat. "Morgan?"

She turned to look at him, all Bambi eyes and Harpo hair. Erik's throat felt even tighter.

"Erik?" A thin line appeared between her brows.

His voice sounded rusty again, the way it always did when he was close to her. "I was looking for you."

Ken glanced back and forth between them, grinning. "Okay, not that either of you is listening to me, but I'll want those two cases tomorrow so we have them by the day of the Festival."

Morgan nodded absently, not moving her gaze from Erik. "Sure, right. I'll do that."

Only when he heard the door close behind them did Erik realize Ken was gone. He ran through a quick list of explanations in case she was so pissed she wouldn't even talk to him. "Come home with me," he murmured instead.

Morgan blinked at him and smiled. "Okay."

His body tasted of caramel. The thought drifted through Morgan's mind as she licked her way down his chest. Her fingers caressed his rib cage, smoothing along his skin. Something inside her loosened, as if a string had been plucked, sending vibrations humming through her core.

"I missed you," he whispered, his fingers sliding through her hair. "All day I missed you, Morgan."

I missed you too. But she didn't say it. She was too busy running her tongue along the edge of his hip bones, grazing them with her teeth. Judging from the sharp hiss of his breath, he agreed her tongue had much better things to do than talk.

She reached between his legs, cupping him gently, running a quick fingernail across the silken puckering skin.

He gasped again. "Morgan, for god's sake!"

She opened her mouth over him, sliding her tongue along the shaft then back, taking him in slowly, slowly, like a ripe cherry sliding against her tongue.

The sound of his breathing seemed to fill the room. She skimmed her hands along the smooth, soft skin at the tops of his thighs. Reveling in the feel, the sense of him. His smell, his taste—salt and heat and caramel.

He plunged his hands into her hair, his fingers rubbing her scalp as she worked her tongue around his thickness.

Morgan concentrated on the sensations that swirled over her. She'd resigned herself—well, almost, anyway—to never having him in her bed again. But now here he was. Appearing on the street almost magically. She wasn't inclined to question her luck.

"Morgan," Erik gasped, his voice tight with need.

Morgan drew him deeper into her mouth, almost to the back of her throat, her hands sliding beneath his sac, cupping him again.

"Morgan," he gasped again, "I can't..."

"Then don't," she murmured.

"No." He pulled gently on her hair. "I want to be inside you, Morg. Now."

Morgan raised her head to look at him. His eyes seemed glazed, aching with need. She lay back, feeling him slide on top of her, his fingers touching her folds.

"You're wet for me," he whispered, the words brushing against her skin like petals falling in the wind.

"Yes."

He pulled a condom from the drawer beside the bed, sheathing himself in record time.

She arched her back as he slid inside, wrapping herself around him, taking him more deeply into her body. He sighed against her cheek.

"Oh, god, Morgan, it feels so good. You feel so good."

"Yes." Her voice broke on the word as he began to move.

Somewhere at the back of her mind a voice still told her to get away while she could. He might be leaving, and he wouldn't be back. And it would hurt so much when he was gone. And she was so close to loving him.

Close to loving him. No, not right. She loved him.

Morgan's eyes prickled with tears, while her body convulsed beneath him. Too much, too much. She fought to get her breath back.

"Morgan," he murmured against her ear, "okay?"

She gasped air into her lungs. She couldn't have spoken if her life depended on it. She nodded, gasping.

She could feel him inside her, still hard. She brought her hands up again, stroking the soft skin of his inner thighs, moving to cup him again, to move her fingernails lightly across the puckering skin. His motion became jagged thrusts as he moaned. She touched him again, and he broke, driving himself deep within her until he reached something that set her off again, her body shuddering helplessly.

Erik held her, his face pressed against her hair. "Sweet Jesus, Morgan."

Don't say it, the voice in her head screamed. *Don't, don't, don't. Keep quiet.* Morgan bit her lip to keep from saying anything at all, snuggling deeper into his arms.

They lay wrapped together for what seemed to be a long time. Morgan's eyes began to drift closed, her control began to slip. "What's going to happen, Erik?" she murmured. "Do you stay or go?"

The long pause before he answered brought her back to reality. *Oh god, oh god, too close. Too close to saying what I can't afford to say.*

Erik sighed. "I don't know. Even if I can get through tomorrow night, Pittman's not going away. And I don't know how I can change anything with him."

Morgan let her eyes drift shut again, fighting the tightness in her chest. Each time she gave him up, it hurt more. And she would not—would *not*—say anything about how she felt. She'd save herself from that kind of grief.

"What about you?" Erik pressed his face against her hair. "What about your father? And the winery?"

"I don't know." The tightness in her chest clenched harder. "It all depends on Bored Ducks now, on how well it does at the festival. Then he'll decide whether he'll let me do any of the things I want to do."

After a moment, his hands moved to cup her face, tilting her head back so that she was staring up into his molasses dark eyes. "This is it, Morgan," he whispered. "Don't think about anything else. Just think about now."

"Just now." The words seemed to stick in her throat. She reached up to run her fingers lightly along his cheek as he dipped his mouth down to hers again.

Chapter Twenty-One

Friesenhahn called Erik mid-afternoon. "I guess you know about that meeting tonight, son."

Erik sighed. "Yes sir, I'm going to be there."

"You got a strong point in your favor with Biedermeier. If Pittman's smart he'll back off."

Erik's mouth twisted slightly. "If Pittman was smart, none of this would be happening."

"True enough. I'd like to offer you a job with the county if Pittman forces you out, but we got a hiring freeze on. Texas ain't exactly a great place to find a job right now."

"That's all right. I've got some options."

Like Davenport. Erik closed his eyes, feeling his stomach clench. Two thousand miles and a lifetime away from his family. And Morgan Barrett.

He managed to grab a sandwich from the Stop-N-Go for supper. Right now, he rated his chances of staying in his current job at around fifty-fifty. Biedermeier's arrest could make Pittman's job slightly harder, but he didn't doubt the mayor's ability to rise above it.

Pittman was a politician, used to speaking before crowds and used to making his case, no matter how spurious that case might be. Erik was lousy at public speaking, and he hated explaining himself to anybody. If he had to judge between the two of them himself, he'd probably vote for Pittman. His only hope was that the facts might speak for themselves, because he sure as hell couldn't speak for them. On the other hand, he had a good idea what those facts would include. And they wouldn't say anything he wanted to hear again.

He arrived at the council chambers around five minutes

early. Helen had told him the meetings tended to end at nine on the dot, which meant they started precisely at seven.

But even though he was early, Hilton Pittman had beat him to it.

Pittman stared at him for a moment, as if he hadn't expected Erik to actually show up. He cleared his throat and started pushing papers around the table. "Sorry, Chief, it's an Executive Session tonight. No members of the public allowed."

"I'm not exactly a member of the public, Mr. Mayor." Erik gave him his most bone-chilling smile. "Besides, I understood I was on the agenda."

Pittman swallowed visibly. "You're on the agenda as an item, not a speaker, Chief."

"Toleffson has a right to be here, Pittman." Horace Rankin walked in behind Erik, carrying his usual dog-eared notebook. "The Texas Open Meetings law requires us to begin in open session so that you can announce what part of the session is closed." Rankin's glasses reflected the light so that Erik couldn't see his eyes. "You ought to look it up. Interesting reading. In fact, Toleffson here could request that the meeting be open if he wants to. And according to the council rules, a member of the Council could request that he be present."

Pittman looked like he was running through a string of obscenities in his mind, while keeping his professional smile in place. "Personnel matters are usually handled in Executive Session, Horace."

"The mayor doesn't usually bring personnel items to the city council, either." Rankin's lips spread in a grim smile beneath his walrus moustache. "I'm not for shutting anybody out if they want to be here. And I'm definitely not for keeping Toleffson from hearing whatever charges you plan to make against him. Consider this my official request for his presence."

Dan Albaniz, Portia Grandview and Arthur Craven, the other members of the council, walked through the swinging door behind Pittman. Albaniz glanced at Erik, his brow furrowing slightly. "Chief? Something going on?"

"I may have some input for your discussion tonight—thought I'd drop by." Erik was getting tired of smiling, particularly since his smile in this case was just a general lip stretch.

Albaniz gave him a blank look. "Well, thanks for your

input. We're always happy to hear from citizens."

Behind him, Portia Grandview was already seated, checking hurriedly through her agenda. She paused halfway down the page, then glanced up at Pittman. "We're discussing Chief Toleffson?" She turned toward Erik. "What's going on?"

"Let's get started." Pittman sat abruptly.

Erik pulled out a folding metal chair at the front of the small audience section. Given its butt-numbing qualities, he found himself hoping the meeting actually did end on time.

Behind him the door swung open once more as Doralee entered, steno pad in hand. "Sorry. Didn't mean to be late, but there's so much traffic these days." She smiled brightly at Erik. "Maybe you could look into that, Chief?"

Pittman cleared his throat noisily and Doralee took her seat at the other end of the table.

"I had originally intended this meeting to be in Executive Session." Pittman sounded more basso than usual, as if he were addressing the Supreme Court. "But Horace informs me that some Open Meetings law precludes that."

Pittman shot Horace a venomous glance. Horace smiled blandly back.

"At any rate," Pittman continued, "I suggest we proceed to the item concerning Chief Toleffson so that he won't have to sit through our routine business."

Albaniz and Grandview both glanced at Erik and then back at Pittman. Craven, who apparently knew a little more about where the power lay in Konigsburg, looked at Horace.

"Okay by me," Horace rumbled. "Everybody else all right with it?"

The three council members glanced at each other and nodded.

"My purpose in coming here tonight…" Pittman paused, glancing at his small audience and readjusting his rhetoric. "I'm here tonight to ask the council to remove Chief Toleffson from his position."

The three council members shifted their gazes from Erik to Pittman and back to Erik again in a kind of silent tennis game. Erik wondered if he was winning.

"Why would you do that?" Albaniz looked thoroughly confused. "I heard he caught Biedermeier. Somebody said the

Rangers took him to Austin."

He turned to Erik for confirmation. Pittman cleared his throat so loudly Erik wondered if he'd burst a blood vessel.

"This has nothing to do with Biedermeier. Biedermeier is beside the point."

"Now there I've got to disagree with you, Pittman." Horace leaned back in his chair. "The first of many times this evening, I imagine. Arresting somebody like Biedermeier is exactly the point. Toleffson is doing just what he's supposed to do, and he's already doing it a hell of a lot better than Brody or Olema ever did."

Grandview started to nod, then caught herself, glancing quickly at Pittman.

"One arrest doesn't make up for all the problems in other areas." Pittman looked like he was gritting his teeth again.

"What other areas?" Albaniz looked even more confused than before. "What problems?"

Pittman took a deep breath and blew it out. Erik had a feeling the meeting wasn't exactly proceeding according to plan.

"There have been complaints." Pittman's voice took on a sepulchral quality. "From our citizens."

"Which citizens?" Horace was polishing his glasses furiously. "Who complained?"

"I don't want to violate peoples' confidentiality..." Pittman began.

"Horseshit," Horace snapped, then turned briefly to Portia Grandview and Doralee. "'Scuse me, ladies." He swung back to Pittman again. "You don't accuse a man and then not even tell him who's complaining. Hell, that's unconstitutional!"

"Chief Toleffson already knows who's complained, at least in one instance." Pittman turned narrowed eyes toward Erik.

Horace raised an eyebrow. "So who was it, Toleffson?"

"The only complaint I had directly was from Joe Powell." Erik shrugged. "I thought we'd worked that one out."

Horace's eyebrows shot up to his hairline. "Powell? You want to fire Toleffson because Joe Powell complained?"

Albaniz stared at Pittman, wide-eyed. Craven grimaced and shook his head. Erik thought he saw Doralee smile, fleetingly.

Horace gave a disgusted snort. "Joe Powell called me a murdering quack when one of his goats got into some jimson weed and died. The next day he was on the phone calling me to come out and deliver a couple of kids his prize nanny was dropping."

Craven nodded. "Joe's gotten pissed off and resigned from the Merchants Association so many times we've stopped paying attention. He always comes back a couple of weeks later and pretends nothing happened."

"Oh, god, don't get me started," Albaniz moaned. "I sold him some drought coverage a year ago."

Grandview sighed. "Paint. We sold him the paint for his living room. And then he came back three times because he swore it wasn't the paint he'd wanted."

Horace narrowed his eyes at Pittman. "Joe Powell gets pissed off at everybody. It never lasts, and he's never serious. You're not going to convince me to do anything based on a complaint from Joe Powell."

"Me neither," Grandview chimed in. Beside her, Albaniz and Craven nodded silently.

Horace leaned back in his chair. "Okay, Pittman, who else you got?"

Pittman's face had turned a mottled pink. He inhaled a quick breath. "There was also a complaint from Margaret Hastings. Do you want to try to dismiss her too?"

The council members shifted uneasily. Pittman gave them the ghost of a smile. "According to Ms. Hastings, the chief has allowed underage drinking to take place on the elementary school playground. She suspected he'd been paid not to arrest the drinkers, probably by their parents."

Erik gritted his teeth. *No good deed goes unpunished.*

"Chief?" Horace turned toward him. "What do you have to say about that?"

Erik took a breath. "There was a group of boys on the playground one night when I drove by. They took off, but one of them got caught. He wasn't drinking when I got there, but there were beer cans on the ground by the fence. I told him to pick them up and keep his nose clean for the rest of the summer."

He glanced at the council members. Grandview stared down at her legal pad. Albaniz was frowning. Craven leaned forward in his chair. "Why didn't you take him to the station?"

"I couldn't have charged him with anything. What evidence there was was strictly circumstantial." *Assuming you didn't count Kent's confession.*

"What about a breathalyzer?" Albaniz asked.

"The boy wasn't drunk, and he was underage. I would have had to call his parents to test him for alcohol. I didn't want to do that."

Grandview looked up at him, her brow furrowed. "You didn't tell them?"

"No ma'am. I told him I'd tell his parents if I ever caught him in a similar situation again or if I heard reports of him causing trouble. As I understand it, Ms. Hastings called the boy's father and told him what happened."

Doralee muttered something that sounded like "She would."

The council members were all frowning now. Probably all parents, trying to decide if that's what they would have wanted done.

"What about Ms. Hastings' claim that you were paid off by the parents?" Horace asked.

Erik flexed his hands beneath his seat. "I've never taken a dime from anyone, certainly not from the boy's parents." *Just chips and salsa.*

Horace took off his glasses, pinching the bridge of his nose. "All right. Doesn't seem to be any evidence of misconduct here to me, just a difference of opinion about how a situation should have been handled. What's next, Mayor?"

"There were all those problems during the biker rally."

"What problems?" Albaniz shook his head. "I thought it went much better this year than the last one."

"He arrested five of our guests!" Pittman's voice rose. "No one ever got arrested at the rally before. How do you explain that, Toleffson?"

Erik looked back toward the council members. "When Brody was chief, a lot of violations never got prosecuted during the rally—public drunkenness, for example. Some fights. Nobody got arrested because Brody didn't pursue the people who were at fault."

"Drunk as skunks, most of them," Craven growled. "Had to hire some people to clean up my parking lot after they left."

Portia Grandview nodded. She owned a hardware store on the other end of Main. "Took us a day to sweep up all the beer cans and broken glass in the city park."

Erik turned back to Pittman. "It turned out Brody had an arrangement with the biker organization. He told them if they paid their fines in advance, he wouldn't pick them up." He glanced back down the council table. Rankin snorted. Even Arthur Craven, the original hometown booster, looked grim.

"As you might guess, the bikers thought this was a great deal. They kicked in around a hundred bucks per member in 'pre-paid fines' and Brody left them alone. This year the arrangement was no longer in force, so there were more arrests."

Horace turned back to Pittman. "Did you know about all this, Mr. Mayor?"

"Of course I didn't," Pittman snarled. "I'm not a crook."

"Arresting drunks doesn't sound like a problem to me," Craven mused. "Most of the merchants would be in favor of it—keeps the other tourists happy."

Grandview didn't look entirely convinced. "Still, the mayor has a point here, Arthur. We do want tourists to come back. Arresting them should be a last resort."

Erik managed a half-smile in her direction. "Yes, ma'am. I'd say that's our general philosophy."

Grandview narrowed her eyes slightly, then turned back to Pittman. "So Joe Powell and Margaret Hastings complained and the chief arrested some drunk tourists. Any other problems, Mr. Mayor?"

Pittman stared at her, tight-lipped. Then he reached into the briefcase at his side, pulling out some photocopied sheets. He tossed them on the table in front of the council members. "There, Portia. There's your problem." He turned toward Horace. "Try explaining that one away."

Horace picked up a sheet and scanned it carefully. The others followed suit. After a moment, Horace glanced up at Erik. He reached into the pile and handed him a copy of his own.

Erik didn't need to look at it—he'd seen it before. It was the page of his personnel record from Davenport that included his suspension.

After he finished reading, Horace looked up at him again. "Well, son, you want to tell us what happened here?"

Erik shrugged. "We were taking a prisoner in and he got

loose. He attacked my partner. I subdued him."

"What did you do?" Grandview's eyes were wide.

Erik managed a very thin smile. "I hit him. More than once."

"You sent him to the hospital with a concussion and numerous contusions." Pittman looked a lot more confident all of sudden. He was back to addressing the Supreme Court. "The other officers had to pull you off him."

Horace leaned back in his chair. "What happened to your partner?"

"She went to the hospital too. Skull fracture."

Grandview shook her head. "How do you explain this, Chief?"

"Basically, I screwed up." Erik blew out a breath. "The guy was out of control. I should have called for backup, but I didn't. I was afraid my partner was dead."

Pittman narrowed his eyes. "Nobody's arguing the man you beat up was a saint. But the examining board in Iowa ruled the force used was excessive. Somehow this suspension didn't get mentioned when we hired Toleffson." He gave Horace a fierce look.

Horace shrugged. "Friesenhahn reviewed the records. He didn't think it was important."

"Maybe he didn't think it was important because he didn't feel Konigsburg is important. Or maybe he just wanted to have his own man in charge here, in spite of the possible consequences." Pittman shuffled his papers, glancing at the council. "Can we take the risk with Toleffson? He's already dragged tourists off to jail. Can we afford it if he 'screws up' again?"

Albaniz licked his lips. "What do you mean?"

Pittman's lips spread in a very unpleasant smile. "I understand Terrell Biedermeier was taken to the hospital after his arrest. Care to explain that, Chief?"

In the silence, Erik could hear the clicking of Doralee's keyboard. More records. Just what he needed.

"Biedermeier took a hostage before we arrested him. He had to be restrained. After his arrest, I sent him to the hospital with Officer Avrogado to make sure his injuries weren't serious. They weren't. He spent the night in jail."

"Sedated, as I understand it." Pittman's voice had dropped to basso again.

"He was given painkillers for his bruises." Erik gritted his teeth. Apparently, Linklatter's report to Pittman had been thorough.

The silence in the council chamber seemed almost to echo.

"The man in Iowa sued the police department, didn't he, Chief?" Pittman's voice was almost a purr.

"Yes, sir. He did." Erik's hands fisted.

"I repeat." Pittman's voice was soft. "We need to replace Toleffson as chief. Immediately."

The council members stared down the table at Erik, eyes wide.

Horace began polishing his glasses, furiously. "I'm going to move that we table this decision for a couple of days to give us a better chance to study this information. We'll call a special session Friday night."

"Wait a minute," Pittman sputtered. "I object!"

"You got no room to object to a council decision. Do I hear a second?"

"Second," Albaniz muttered.

"Any dissent?" Horace narrowed his eyes at Pittman. "Other than the mayor, that is?"

The council members shook their heads.

"Then we'll take this up again on Friday. Now we got other business to take care of. You can take off, Chief, unless you've got something else you want to bring up."

Erik stood, settling his hat on his head. He nodded at Horace and the rest of the council members then turned toward the door, managing to get there without having to look again at Pittman's triumphant smile.

Chapter Twenty-Two

Morgan stumbled into the tasting room at around seven thirty the next morning still trying to wake up—not surprising since she hadn't slept for more than a few hours the night before. She figured she might as well put in her time selling wine rather than lying in bed thinking about Erik Toleffson.

When she'd gone to the Dew Drop yesterday afternoon, Erik wasn't there. She'd driven by the station on her way back to Cedar Creek, but his truck was gone. Morgan tried not to consider the very real possibility that Chief Erik Toleffson was now packing to leave Konigsburg, while Ham Linklatter prepared to take over the police department and the town prepared to go to hell.

He hadn't called her. She hadn't exactly expected him to. But still, after their last night together she'd sort of...wanted him to.

Morgan sighed. Her day was already threatening to stretch to fourteen hours since they needed to get ready for the wine festival Saturday.

Maybe because of all the preparations they needed to do, Kit was there early too, helping Esteban load Cedar Creek Winery glasses into cardboard boxes. She yawned as she passed a box to Esteban. "Is this festival as big a deal as I think it is?"

"Pretty much." Morgan took another box from Esteban and began loading glasses herself. "Usually they pull in several hundred people. It's a great place to pick up some new customers."

"Are we taking all the wines?" Kit pulled several more glasses from beneath the counter and began shoving them into another box.

"Maybe. What's the final decision?" She raised an eyebrow at Esteban.

He grinned. "We're pouring five wines. Sangiovese, viognier, Creekside Red and Creekside White, and Bored Ducks."

"Bored Ducks?" Kit frowned. "We have a wine called Bored Ducks? I never heard of it."

"We do now—or anyway, we might." Morgan pulled the flaps of the cardboard box closed. "We did the labeling last night. Was Ciro okay with putting it in the festival rotation?"

Esteban nodded. "Dad said the festival would show how interested people might be in a wine like that."

There was a cold weight in the pit of Morgan's stomach. If the wine sold well, maybe her father would believe she could do the marketing. If it didn't... She took a deep breath. No wimping out. Bored Ducks was going to sell like hotcakes, damn it! Or like mango sherbet, given the temperature.

Mango sherbet. Morgan closed her eyes. She was *not* going to think about Erik Toleffson.

The door to the tasting room swung open and Nando strode in, winking at Kit. He paused as his brother pushed past him with a load of boxes. "Whoa! Looks like work going on here." He glanced around the room, grinning. "Always great to see other people doing stuff."

Morgan chewed her lower lip, trying to decide how to ask him about Erik. *Casual, play it casual.* "How are things down at the station?"

Nando shrugged. "Same as always, I guess. Except for the thing with Toleffson."

Morgan felt as if someone had grabbed her heart and given it a quick squeeze. "What about him?"

Nando's eyes widened. "You didn't know? Geez, Morg, I'm sorry. I thought you and Toleffson... I mean, I thought he would have told you."

She worked hard on keeping her expression bland. "Told me what?"

"Pittman tried to get him fired at the council meeting last night, but the council tabled the vote until Friday." Nando shrugged again. "I hope they'll tell Pittman to stuff it, but with politicians, who knows?"

Morgan's stomach tied another knot. So he still didn't know whether he got to keep his job. She wished he'd called her anyway. Not that she could be much help under the circumstances. Still, she would have gone back into town and tried to do something. Maybe that was why he hadn't called her—he didn't want her to try.

She picked up a bottle of sangiovese and thrust it into a box as the winery door swung open.

"Morning, baby," her mother called. "Mercy, you all look busy today."

Morgan turned to see her father limping in the door after her mother. He squinted around the room. "Everything ready for the Wine and Food Festival?"

Morgan nodded. "We're working on it."

"Good." Her father propped himself against the tasting room bar. "We'll stay over a couple of days. Always a big day. I need to see how that Bored Ducks stuff pans out."

Morgan closed her eyes for a moment. *Terrific timing, Dad.* "Great. You'll be pleased, believe me."

"I hope so, honey." Her father reached out to pat her shoulder awkwardly.

Morgan decided Erik Toleffson could wait. She put an arm around her father and rested her head on his shoulder. "It'll work, Daddy," she whispered. "I promise."

"Cliff, this is all wonderful, but I've got clients." Her mother's voice sounded slightly choked as she dabbed at her eyes with a tissue. "Much as I'd like to, I can't stay."

"Call them." Her father grinned, watching the bustle around them. "Take a day off, Leila. Let's see what happens. I want to know how this is going to turn out."

Morgan sighed. *I do too, Dad, I do too.*

Erik managed to get to the Coffee Corral by seven thirty the next morning. He hoped he'd be awake enough for an early meeting. He stopped at the counter for a cup of coffee and some breakfast from Al before heading to the table.

Al gave him a half-smile as he plated a chorizo-and-egg taco and a side of home fries. "I tried to go to that meeting last night, Chief, but Pittman's stooge said I couldn't stay. I guess they talked about Kent."

Erik shrugged. "It was okay. I kept his name out of it."

"I heard. We'll be watching that asshole, believe me. Pittman's days as mayor are numbered."

Erik wasn't sure watching Pittman would do any good, but he thanked Al anyway. He found a booth near the window and sat to wait. Pete arrived five minutes later and slid in opposite him with a cup of coffee. "What's up?"

Erik took a deep breath. He'd spent half the night trying to figure out how to tell the family, but he still hadn't come up with a good way. He just knew it needed to be done. Maybe if he did it fast, it would hurt less. Like tearing off a bandage. "There's a good chance I'm going to be fired on Friday. I wanted to give you all a heads-up before it happened."

Pete stared at him, then placed his coffee cup carefully on the table in front of him. "What's going on?"

"Pittman took a longer look at my record than Friesenhahn did. When I was in Davenport, I got in trouble for unnecessary force. I drew a month's suspension. It was in my record and that was part of my application for chief, but either Friesenhahn didn't notice, or more likely he decided not to point it out to the council."

Pete stared at him, eyes dark. His expression flattened. "How did it happen?"

"My partner and I were bringing a guy in. He was high on something, probably crystal meth. The handcuffs must not have been fastened entirely—anyway, he got loose. He hit my partner in the back of the head with the handcuffs and she went down. He went on hitting her before I could get to him. He lacerated her scalp and there was a lot of blood. I grabbed hold of him and..." He took another long breath, but he didn't look away from Pete's icy gaze. "I lost it. A couple of the other guys had to pull me off him. He ended up in the hospital. So did my partner. Both of them made it, but it was a close thing with her. He fractured her skull."

Pete nodded slowly, his mouth a thin line. Erik had the feeling he was taking mental notes. "What happened afterward?"

"My boss went with the suspension instead of firing me, since Paula was hurt bad and the guy was out of control. He told me he might have reacted the same way under the circumstances, but that it was still a boneheaded thing to do. I had to agree with him on that."

Pete's face was still blank. After a moment, he shrugged. "You really think they'll fire you for that? You didn't try to conceal it—they just didn't notice."

"It's not just that. I took a swing a Biedermeier when he had Morgan in a hammer lock. He had a black eye and some bruises. And Pittman's still got a hair up his ass about the bikers I arrested. And then Margaret Hastings is claiming I'm soft on underage drinking." Erik managed a half-smile. "I think I'm in the clear on that one, though."

Pete leaned back in the booth, eyes narrowed. "How long have you known about this?"

"The hearing was last night."

"But you knew it was coming."

Erik shrugged. "I had an idea that it was, yeah."

Pete's jaw was rigid. "Why didn't you tell me it was coming—hell, tell all of us?"

"You couldn't have done anything." Erik let himself look down at his breakfast, spearing a piece of chorizo. "It wasn't something I wanted to share with anybody, particularly. It was my screwup. My problem. Another one of my problems."

He glanced up. Pete was staring out the window at the street.

"Anyway." He shrugged. "Horace tabled the vote until Friday. But I don't know which way it's going to go. I figured you needed to know before the news got around."

"Before the news got around to us." Pete looked back, his mouth a thin line. "Jesus, Erik."

He shrugged again. "I'd say I'm sorry, but we both know how little good that would do. It didn't help that much in the past either. You'll tell everybody else, though, right?"

Pete stared at him for a long moment, eyes burning. Then he grimaced. "Yeah. For what it's worth, I'll tell everybody else."

At the station, Erik hunted for the Wine and Food Festival paperwork. It wasn't on his desk where he'd left it, nor was it on Helen's desk where it might legitimately have ended up. Helen made a cursory check of the filing cabinets, glowering.

"Goddamn Linklatter," she muttered.

Erik sighed. "What about him?"

"When I came in, that Brinkman was here. The mayor's assistant. He and Ham were talking together about something. Ham looked like he'd just had a good meal or gotten laid. With Ham, I'd say the meal's more likely."

"Brinkman took the paperwork?"

Helen shrugged. "It ain't here. And Linklatter was the only one in the station last night."

"Okay. Let's keep going and assume we're policing it until we hear otherwise." Or until the mayor decided to try taking over the police department and running it himself, which might be imminent. Erik wondered who'd be in charge of the festival if they fired him. He sighed. *Please don't let it be Linklatter.*

At noon, Erik walked around the city park, taking in the bustle of preparations for the Festival. The central pavilion was full of booths, with banners floating from the ceiling, each with a different winery name. Alamosa, Texas Hills, Spicewood, Flat Creek, Crossroads, Lone Oak, the names reeled on as he peered down the length of the room. Near the middle on the left he saw Cedar Creek.

Morgan was stacking boxes at the back of the booth.

Erik took a breath. *Guts up, Chief. She's not even in your weight class.* He headed toward her, wiping his suddenly damp palms on his thighs. He should have called her.

Morgan glanced up at him as he neared the booth, her eyes suddenly wary. "Hi, Chief."

He nodded. And then he was stuck. *I meant to call but I didn't want to talk about it.* That sounded like he didn't want to talk to her, which wasn't exactly true. *I meant to call, but I didn't know what to say.* Closer, but it made him sound like a moron. *I meant to call, but I was afraid of how it would sound to you.* Oh yeah, that was a real winner.

"Getting set up for the festival?"

Morgan gave him the faintest of smiles. "Well, yeah, seeing as how it's Saturday."

Erik licked his lips. "Right. I like your banner." *Jesus, could you be any lamer?*

At least Morgan's smile was more pronounced, although he suspected it was inspired by his idiocy. "Thanks. We get them from the Texas Department of Agriculture."

He nodded, thinking furiously and coming up dry. "Want to have dinner tonight?"

Her smile dimmed. "I can't. We're knee-deep in preparations. I've got to stay at Cedar Creek tonight."

"Oh." Erik sighed. "Maybe tomorrow." Assuming he still felt like eating after the council meeting.

"Maybe."

He hadn't been this tongue-tied since he was a teenager. He managed one more smile and a nod before heading off toward the exit. *Oh yeah, that went well!*

He swung by the mayor's office around four. He didn't have much hope about his ability to pry the festival permits away from Pittman, but he figured he had to at least try. Doralee sat at her desk, ticking desultorily at her keyboard. She glanced up at Erik and shook her head. "He's gone for the day."

Erik frowned. Not having to actually talk to Pittman could be a very good thing, now that he thought about it. "Do you know if he's still got the paperwork on the Wine and Food Festival? I'd like to go over it again myself."

Doralee gave him a rueful smile. "Sorry, Chief, he always locks up before he goes. I think the file's still in there, though."

"Well, at least he didn't take it home with him. Thanks, Doralee."

He headed to the Coffee Corral for dinner, hoping for once he wouldn't run into any member of his family. The room was mostly empty except for some tourists at the back. Kent was running the counter.

He glanced up, giving Erik a small smile. "Evening, Chief."

He nodded. "You learning the restaurant business?"

Kent's smile turned wry. "Sort of. Dad decided I needed to spend more time here. Especially in the evenings."

Erik nodded again. "Not a bad idea."

After his cheeseburger, he headed up Pin Oak for one last look at Biedermeier's house as twilight began to descend. He had no reason to believe they'd missed anything significant among Biedermeier's personal effects, but he wanted to take another walk-through.

The house didn't look any better in the gathering twilight than it had earlier. With a coat of paint and some attention to the yard, it might actually have some charm, although *charm* didn't seem like a word that got applied much to Biedermeier. Now the place looked sort of like Biedermeier himself, like it had been a long time since anybody cared.

Erik fumbled in his pocket for the house key, studying the darkened windows. A fool's errand. He wouldn't find anything.

A light flickered across the upstairs windows.

Erik blinked. Had he really seen anything?

But there it was again—a moving beam, very dim, quickly extinguished. Like somebody with a flashlight was moving across the upstairs rooms in Biedermeier's house. And that somebody was emphatically not Terrell Biedermeier, currently locked up tight in Ozzie Friesenhahn's jail.

Erik slid from behind the steering wheel of the cruiser, opening and closing the door as quietly as he could, and started toward the house. Logically, he should have called the station for backup, but seeing as how backup would have been Ham Linklatter, he didn't bother. He unsnapped the top of his holster and climbed the front steps, keeping to the side to avoid any creaking boards. The front door was unlocked.

Inside, the living room was partially illuminated by the neighbor's yard light. Erik worked his way carefully to the stairs that led to the upper floor, then started up, listening for footsteps over his head. The person with the flashlight apparently wasn't concerned about making noise. Erik could hear the sounds of drawers being pulled out, the rustling of papers.

He slipped down the hall toward Biedermeier's office at the back. A thin line of light spread from the partially open door. Erik pushed the knob slowly, inching the door open enough so that he could peer through the crack.

A man was bending over Biedermeier's battered metal filing cabinet, dropping manila folders onto the floor behind him. Erik unsheathed his service revolver and threw the door wide. "Police. Hold it right there. Do not move."

The man froze, his hands gripping a folder. Erik took his stance, holding his revolver in front of him. "Whatever you're thinking about doing, don't. Stand up. Slowly. Hands in the air."

The man did as he was told, the folder dropping to the floor. "Look, Chief, I can explain."

"Turn around. Take it slow."

The man turned as Erik hit the light switch with his elbow. He stood blinking in the dingy room, manila folders piled at his feet. "I can explain," he repeated.

Erik's mouth edged into a slow grin. "Oh my, Mr. Brinkman. I'll just bet you can. But let me read you your rights, just in case."

As Erik pushed the handcuffed Brinkman through the door into the station, Ham Linklatter sat up straight at Helen's desk, staring. Ham was the only one there, which made sense since Ham was on night duty. Just Erik's luck—even Peavey would have been an improvement.

Erik put his hand in the middle of Brinkman's back, pushing him toward his office. "Linklatter, Mr. Brinkman here was apprehended in the commission of a burglary. I'm going to need your help." He nodded toward his office door, and Ham rose quickly to his feet.

Brinkman sank into the chair opposite Erik's desk. "Can't you take these handcuffs off now?" he whined. "They hurt."

Erik removed one cuff and refastened it to the side of the chair. "Stay there."

"Got no choice, do I?" Brinkman subsided with a pout.

Erik opened his desk drawer and pulled out his camera. "Smile, Mr. Brinkman."

"Fuck you."

Erik snapped the shutter a couple of times. Then he headed toward the door, where Linklatter stood spellbound. Erik pushed him back into the hall. "I've got a couple of things to do before I question him, Linklatter. Make sure he doesn't do anything stupid, like try to get out of those cuffs. And don't talk to him, no matter what he says to you. You understand me?"

Ham nodded, his Adam's apple bobbing as he swallowed.

Erik started toward Helen's desk, then turned back. "Ham, if any of this—and I mean *anything*—gets to Pittman, I swear to god I'll see you fired. Even if it's the last thing I get to do as chief. Got me?"

Ham's eyes narrowed. After a moment, he nodded again.

Erik sat at Helen's desk, fumbling through the cards in his wallet until he found the one he wanted, then punched the number into his cell phone.

The voice on the other end sounded more gravelly than usual, if that were possible. "Toleffson, this had better be good."

"Sheriff, I just picked up a guy tossing Biedermeier's house. I'm going to e-mail you his picture. You might want to show it to Biedermeier and see if he recognizes him."

Friesenhahn's voice sounded less pissed. "You think it's the guy who ran the dumping operation?"

"Possibly. I'm sending it now." Erik connected his camera to the computer and punched up the image, then clicked on the e-mail program. After a moment, he heard Ozzie's grunt on the other end.

"What the hell? That's Pittman's stooge. Wouldn't Biedermeier already know him?"

"Possibly not. This is Biedermeier we're talking about."

Ozzie sighed. "You got a point there. I'll get back to you."

Erik disconnected, then walked back up the hall to his office. Ham stood just inside the door, his arms folded across his chest. Brinkman slumped in his chair, glaring at him. "I take it as a personal insult that you left me with this moron."

Ham's eyes narrowed as he scowled. Erik figured he was discovering just who his friends really were. "I'm not particularly interested in your hurt feelings right now, Brinkman. What were you doing in Terrell Biedermeier's house?"

Brinkman stared back at him. "Terrell and I are business partners. I had a legitimate reason to be going through the files. I needed our records."

"What business would that be?"

Brinkman's mouth flattened. "Pest control."

"And the reason you were using a flashlight rather than doing your search with the lights on?"

"Didn't want to alarm the neighbors."

Erik leaned back in his chair. "Oh, very nice, Brinkman. Good save. I just sent your picture to Ozzie Friesenhahn. He'll show it to Terrell. If you're actually business partners, Terrell will confirm it. Of course, the business you were partners in may not be the one you just mentioned."

Brinkman swallowed, eyes narrowing. "It'll be his word against mine."

"True. Of course, you were caught burglarizing his office,

which may put some extra weight on whatever Terrell has to say. And I have a feeling searching *your* house could be very interesting. I'll make that argument to the judge first thing in the morning. My guess is the search warrant will be forthcoming in record time."

Brinkman stared down at his shoes for a moment, then lifted his gaze back to Erik. "I want to call my lawyer. And you might want to call the sheriff back too. Hell, call the Rangers. I've got stuff you all might like to hear."

Erik kept his expression bland. "Yeah? Like what."

"Like what you've been waiting for. I can give you Pittman."

Morgan and Esteban finished labeling the Bored Ducks around seven that evening and loaded the cases into the truck to be taken to the festival grounds. Carmen had placed a plate of something in the tasting room refrigerator before commandeering Esteban for a job in the barrel room. Now Morgan placed the mystery plate in the microwave without really looking at it. Whatever it was she'd eat it—she was that hungry.

Whatever it was tasted pretty good. Morgan had to restrain herself from wolfing it down. She thought about Erik Toleffson as she chewed, not that he helped slow down her metabolism. She wasn't sure what that episode at the fairgrounds had been all about. At least he'd asked her to dinner.

At least he still seemed to want some kind of relationship with her, even if that relationship didn't have much future for either of them.

Morgan rinsed off Carmen's plate in the sink, then loaded it into the dishwasher with the last of the dirty tasting room glasses. She cast a quick glance over the shelves, wondering if they'd have enough glasses to sell in the tasting room tomorrow what with all the glasses they'd taken to the festival. Oh well, they'd probably have more people at the festival than at the winery.

She flipped the lock on the door, checking to make sure both dogs were inside. No Arthur. She sighed. Probably out hunting—at least he wouldn't run into any new examples of Biedermeier's handiwork.

Wheels crunched on the driveway, and Morgan turned back

toward the door. Probably Esteban coming back from wherever Carmen had sent him this time. She flipped on the yard lights as a Konigsburg police cruiser pulled up in front.

Morgan's pulse immediately kicked up a notch. *Erik.* She stepped out onto the wide front porch as he emerged from the darkness into the pool of light on the bottom step.

"Hi." Her voice sounded ridiculously breathy. She moved toward him until they were almost eye-to-eye—if she stood on the top step she was level with him.

"Hi." His lips spread in a full, lazy grin that she felt all the way to her toes. "I just picked up Pittman's assistant burglarizing Biedermeier's house. My guess is, he'll give Pittman up to save himself. I wanted you to be the first to know."

Morgan stared at him blankly, her mouth opening and closing soundlessly. She must look like a trout. "What?"

Erik shrugged. "I'd say my chances of holding onto the job just went to slightly better than even." He reached up and cupped the back of her head in his hands, pulling her mouth down to his.

She tasted heat, desire, passion that made her knees melt. "Come inside," she panted, when he came up for air.

"Can't. I'm on my way to Friesenhahn's to see what they can get out of Brinkman. But I'll be back tomorrow, and the day after that. I may get to stay right here in Konigsburg after all, Bambi. I just wanted you to know."

He gave her one more fierce kiss, then turned on his heel.

She stood watching as the cruiser turned back up the drive, her hand against her heart. All of a sudden the night seemed much brighter than it had five minutes ago.

Chapter Twenty-Three

By ten the next morning, Morgan was up to her hips in wine, almost literally. Esteban and the vineyard workers were loading cases into the truck while she counted. They'd figured on five cases of sangiovese, five of viognier, another five each of the table wines Creekside Red and Creekside White, and three cases of Bored Ducks.

Morgan made a face. If she didn't sell any Bored Ducks, her father would never let her forget it. Plus he'd make sure she went on doing scut work for the foreseeable future, assuming she stayed at the winery.

She glanced at the label in her hand. The woodblock print of ducks stared back. They really did look bored. Or constipated. There was a thin line, after all.

Her father and mother had showed up at the winery again first thing in the morning. Her mother had even insisted on loading some boxes of glasses herself, which was the most support she'd ever seen her mother give to the winery. Her father said nothing, but he smiled.

Morgan blew out a breath. Maybe her parents' separation wasn't that final after all.

She looked around the patio. The winery seemed quiet at least. A couple of tourists sipped wine in the shade. Carmen could run the tasting room on Saturday while she and Kit took care of the festival table. It was one of her promotions, even if her father didn't exactly recognize her efforts.

At least Erik would be there. Maybe. Assuming the council decided Pittman's charges no longer had any merit. He was the chief of police, after all, and the festival was a major event in town. He had to oversee the security around the park.

Morgan's lips tightened slightly. Erik might be staying, but they hadn't really talked much yet about what that could mean. He might have a future in Konigsburg now, and she might have one too.

The question was, did they have one together?

The chaos surrounding Brinkman's arrest had been about as bad as Erik had anticipated. Since any crimes involving Pittman's office fell under the general heading of official corruption, that meant jurisdiction was up for grabs between Friesenhahn and the Rangers.

The dumping service seemed to have been Brinkman's personal operation, but he'd presented the mayor to Friesenhahn on a silver platter, complete with account numbers and transaction details, in hopes of cutting a deal.

According to Brinkman, Pittman had profited from the biker rally rake-offs for sure. His part of the money had been delivered in the form of a campaign contribution from the Police Benefit Fund. Brinkman also claimed that Hilton and Brody had managed to extort payoffs from several other groups. Groups that might well be willing to talk to the Rangers about their experiences with the right persuasion.

The Ranger forensic accountants had found the police fund as soon as the ever-helpful Brinkman had provided them with the location of the account, but they were still working on the others, some of which were apparently offshore and tougher to access.

Pittman hadn't yet been brought in for questioning, but Erik thought he might have more important things to deal with right now than the council hearing, namely consulting with the kind of legal representatives who could keep him out of the slammer.

Nonetheless, he figured he wouldn't take anything for granted. Pittman might show up. Erik arrived at the council chamber at five minutes before seven, his hat in his hand and his stomach in knots.

Horace nodded at him. The other council members glanced at him curiously, then went back to studying their papers. Erik couldn't decide if that was good or bad.

At seven o'clock, Doralee came in. She gave Horace a quick

shrug, then took her seat at the head of the table. Two minutes later, Pittman walked through the door.

He'd obviously had a bad day. His complexion looked like putty and his hair stood in spikes, as if he'd been running his fingers through it. He stood at the head of the table, yanking papers out of his briefcase. After a moment, he glanced down the length of the room at Erik.

Erik recognized that expression. He'd seen it before with cornered criminals before they started shooting. The expression of a man who knew he was licked, but who'd decided to take everybody else down with him.

Well, shit!

Horace cleared his throat. "Let's get started."

Pittman narrowed his eyes. "I'd like to make a statement if I may."

"Mr. Mayor, you had your say the other night. Now I want to get down to business. If we have any time at the end of the meeting, you can speak then. Anybody got any problems with that?" He glanced down at the other council members.

The way the three looked at Pittman gave Erik the feeling they knew exactly what Brinkman had been telling the Rangers. He wondered if that information had come from Horace or from Friesenhahn. Not that it mattered.

"Okay, then, let's proceed. Don't know if you had a chance to study the chief's personnel file, but I took a good look at it over the last day." Horace picked up a sheet of paper from the pile in front of him. "I assume you've all got the file with you. Very interesting reading. Would you turn to page twenty-two please?"

Albaniz stared at him blankly, but Craven shuffled through the papers in front of him. "Got it."

Horace nodded. "Starting from the top, you'll see four commendations for meritorious service, *for his dedication to duty and exemplifying the high standards of the Davenport Police Department.*"

Grandview shook her head. "No one was questioning his ability as a policeman."

"On the contrary." Horace's voice was clipped. "That's exactly what we were doing. Or anyway, that's what the mayor was doing. Now take a look at the date on that last commendation."

Grandview squinted at the page. "June twelfth."

"It's the year that's important," Horace said quietly. "Three months after his suspension, he earned his fourth commendation."

Albaniz and Grandview both turned toward Erik. Craven frowned slightly. "Interesting."

"The mayor mentioned that this perp, Kronhauser, brought suit against the county. Don't know how much he got out of that—records are sealed. But I got an e-mail here from the chief in Davenport. He says Kronhauser got ten to fifteen years for assault when he went to trial after he was released from the hospital. That was on top of his conviction for selling methamphetamine."

"Drugs." Albaniz's lips narrowed.

"Oh yeah, the mayor forgot to mention it, but Mr. Kronhauser was high as a kite from his own product when he attacked Officer Romero, Toleffson's partner."

"I didn't 'forget to mention it'," Pittman snapped. "It wasn't relevant."

"Wasn't it? I'd disagree with that idea." Horace picked up another sheet from farther down in the pile. "If you want some more relevant information we can look at Toleffson's military records. Davenport wasn't the only place he got commended. He's also got almost seven years of outstanding police work along with that single screwup with Kronhauser. We should all have records that good. I know for a fact you don't, Mr. Mayor."

Pittman's face turned a dirty pink that made Erik think of Ham Linklatter. "That was uncalled for, Rankin."

"Now there, once again, we disagree. But we can discuss it later."

Erik sat very still, afraid to say anything for fear of saying something wrong.

Horace began polishing his glasses again. "Anybody got anything else to add? Any questions for the chief?" He glanced around the table. The council members stared back blankly.

He nodded. "Okay, then, Chief. Why don't you step outside so we can vote."

"He doesn't need to step outside." Grandview sounded tired. "None of us wanted to fire him before except for Mayor Pittman, and we don't want to fire him now. Right?"

Albaniz and Craven nodded.

Horace cleared his throat. "All right then. I move we end the chief's probationary period and hire him on full-time. Any discussion?"

The council members all shook their heads. "Sounds good," Craven said.

"All in favor?"

Three hands rose simultaneously.

Pittman slammed his fist on the table. "I object! This meeting is a farce."

"No, Pittman." Horace turned to look at him, his jaw tensing. "Your charges were a farce. Play time's over. You got other things to worry about now. Any other business?"

There was a flurry of head shaking as the council members began gathering their papers.

"Meeting's adjourned then," Horace said, rapping his gavel on the table in front of him.

Pittman stared around the table, then jerked his briefcase open beside him. His complexion was back to putty again. "You'll regret this," he muttered as he tossed his papers back inside the case. "You'll all regret this."

None of the council members glanced his way. Doralee, on the other hand, gave him a triumphant smile.

Pittman stalked out of the room without looking at Erik.

Erik took a deep breath, trying to unclench his fists as his brain struggled to process everything that had just happened. The council members headed for the door. Albaniz clapped him on the back on his way out. "Good job, Chief."

Erik nodded numbly. "Thanks." He stood, watching them go, then turned back to the council table. "Thanks, Horace."

Rankin shrugged. "Don't thank me. Pete's the one who did it."

He picked up a sheet of paper and handed it to him. Erik stared down at the yellow highlighting and the notes scribbled in the margins.

"He went through your file and showed me a bunch of stuff he thought I could use. Turns out I didn't need more than a third of what he found, but it was enough." The corners of Horace's mouth inched up. "Congratulations, Chief. I didn't think we'd ever get rid of that asshole Pittman. You done good, son. Glad to have you aboard."

Erik wasn't entirely surprised to see Pete standing on the other side of the chamber door when he walked out.

"Well?"

He shrugged. "They went for it. Ended the probationary period. Looks like I get to stick around."

Pete blew out a breath. "Praise be. The good guys win one. Now will you tell me what the fuck you thought you were doing?"

Erik blinked at him. "Which time?"

"When you didn't tell any of us what was going on. When you decided to go it alone. Goddamn it, Erik, if you weren't two inches taller than me, I'd kick your butt. Hell, I might do it anyway." Pete's eyes were burning. He looked like he might actually take a punch at him.

"I thought..." Erik paused, trying to figure out just what he had been thinking. That he'd just as soon not talk about it? That it was better not to let his family know he'd blown something else because he couldn't control himself? That they wouldn't care?

"You thought you could do it all on your own. And that we wouldn't give a shit. You were wrong. On both counts."

Erik shrugged. "It was my problem. I just didn't want to pull you all into it." He blew out a breath. "Thanks for your help. I appreciate it."

"You're my brother," Pete said slowly. "You'd do the same for me. Hell, you have done the same for me, for all of us. You took out that asshole Friedrich when he threatened Janie and you caught that bitch who was after Jess's son. And you pulled the freakin' police department together and saved the town from Ham Linklatter. Come on." Pete gave him a shove toward the exit.

"Where are we going?"

"My house. Everybody's waiting. Not that we had many doubts about what was going to happen."

Erik licked his lips. The thought of walking into a room filled with people who were waiting for him, maybe judging him, made his stomach clench tighter.

"Come on, Erik," Pete said gently. "They want to congratulate you."

For a moment, he thought about dinner with Morgan. But it would have to wait. Seeing, talking to his family took precedence over everything else in his life right then. He'd make it up to her tomorrow. One way or another.

He pulled out his cell. "Go on ahead. I'll catch up."

The corners of Pete's mouth edged up. "Give her my best."

Chapter Twenty-Four

The news about Pittman and Erik had apparently spread around town at the speed of light. When he finally dragged himself out of bed around eight in the morning, he'd had to run a gauntlet of grinning citizens on Main, all of whom had wanted to shake his hand or buy him a cup of coffee, sometimes both.

All Erik wanted to do was go to bed and sleep for about sixteen hours, preferably with Morgan at his side. Unfortunately, he had a festival to police.

Breakfast was another interesting experience. He went to the Coffee Corral again, just as he had the day before. Al Brosius handed him his coffee and breakfast taco without comment, although Erik had the distinct feeling eyes were boring into his back as he headed toward his table. He sat where he usually did, facing Al's mural of Konigsburg and the hills. Somehow seeing Helen Kretschmer dressed as a cowgirl always started the day off right, not to mention the recent addition of Docia as a dancehall queen, apparently drawn from memory since Docia currently looked more like the Hindenburg.

He ran his gaze across the mural and its characters without paying much attention. And then he stopped.

A new figure had been added to the small western town in the lower right corner. He wore a white cowboy hat and a western shirt half covered by a leather vest. On the vest was a large gold star.

Erik blinked. The lawman's face was very familiar, largely because he saw it in the mirror every morning when he shaved.

Once again, he felt the heat of eyes watching his back. If it really had been the old west, he'd have been a dead man. He took the last bite of his breakfast taco and regrouped, popping a plastic lid onto his cup of coffee.

"Nice mural, Al," he muttered as he walked by the cash register. "Thanks."

"Any time, Chief. You earned it." Al didn't bother to look up.

Around noon, Erik took a quick tour around the perimeter of the city park. All three pavilions were in use. The largest had the winery booths. The varicolored silk banners dangled over each one, with the winery's name and logo. Across the front of the building was a table with the silent auction baskets full of wine bottles and gift-wrapped boxes with floppy ribbons. Hostesses from the Konigsburg Merchants Association milled around, dressed in cowboy hats and vests that made them look like waitresses in a kiddy restaurant.

He could smell meat sizzling in the food pavilion, along with peppers, onions and garlic. His stomach had started to rumble as soon as he'd set foot on the grounds. He'd eat something when he could grab a minute—assuming he had a minute when he wasn't being pulled from one crisis to another.

He wandered slowly through the winery pavilion until he saw the Cedar Creek banner again. Esteban Avrogado was stacking cases of wine behind the table, while Kit Maldonado set up a display of bottles.

Erik stood watching for a moment until Kit looked up and grinned. "She's in the parking lot," she called, "getting more wine."

He cut back through the crowd toward the parking lot, only to be waylaid by Arthur Craven. "Chief, are your men providing security in here or is it the private cops? I need somebody to watch the ticket booth."

"Who's supposed to watch the parking lots, Chief?" Curtis Peavey was at his other elbow. "I thought it was us, but the private cops are wandering around out there."

Erik sighed and mentally gave Morgan a rain check. *Wait for me, Bambi.* He headed back toward the ticket booth to straighten out the rent-a-cops.

Morgan started pouring wine at one thirty and didn't look up for an hour. People stood in line four deep, waiting for the chance to give her a couple of tickets in return for a third of a glass of sangiovese or viognier or table wine or—knock on wood—Bored Ducks.

She didn't have much time to do a sales job, just to explain what grapes were in Bored Ducks when people asked. She got some snickers on the name—about what she'd expected. Snickers were good, right? It meant they were paying attention.

After an hour, Kit tapped her on the shoulder. "Want to sell bottles for a while? Looks like it's letting up a little anyway."

Morgan glanced around and saw the crowds had thinned a bit. She could hear snatches of melody from the blues band playing out on the lawn. Some of the tourists were taking their glasses outside to sit in the shade and listen. The price of a full glass of wine got them a Cedar Creek wineglass as a bonus.

"Sure. I'll take a break." She looked back at the cases piled behind her, their remaining supplies. Once they were sold, the Festival was over as far as Cedar Creek was concerned.

Three cases of sangiovese were left. Around two and half for Creekside White. Three for Creekside Red. Two for viognier. One for Bored Ducks.

Morgan blinked. One?

Esteban grinned at her. "They've been selling hand over fist, Morg. People try it because of the name, and then they want to buy a bottle. I already sent Tito back to pick up another case. That's all we can spare right now, though."

Morgan's shoulders relaxed for what felt like the first time in weeks. "Thanks Esteban. Your blend did it."

"Don't thank me." Esteban grinned more broadly. "My blend. Your idea. Looks like we won on this one, Morg."

Morgan glanced out across the room. Her father was standing near the silent auction table, checking to see what the current bids were on their basket. She tightened her hold on a Bored Ducks bottle as he looked up.

He glanced at the bottle in her hand, his smile becoming dry. Then he walked over to the table. "How are the sales?"

"We're doing well. Up from last year." She took a breath. "We're almost out of Bored Ducks."

Her father sighed. "I still hate that freakin' name, but the wine's okay. A little heavy on the merlot, but good overall."

At the other end of the table, Esteban gave her a quick grin.

Morgan smiled back. "It's selling very well."

"So it is." Her father glanced at the cases stacked behind

the table. "Write up your marketing plan. We'll go over it next week."

Morgan's shoulders relaxed a little further. *One problem down. One to go.*

Erik kept waiting for the fights to break out. Given the amount of wine being consumed, he figured they were inevitable. He didn't put much trust in the private cops on duty in the pavilion either. If something broke loose, most of them looked like they'd either head for the nearest exit or join in the mayhem.

What with checking on possible problems among the drinkers and the rent-a-cops, he didn't make it back to the wine pavilion for a couple of hours.

But as the afternoon wore on, nobody took a swing at anybody. People lounged on blankets spread across the grass, listening to the music from the bandstand. Some had glasses of wine, and some were sipping iced tea or soda. Most had plates of food—fajitas, chalupas, the occasional burger. Erik himself had managed to grab a sausage kolache from Allie's booth.

Konigsburgers were everywhere, taking advantage of the wine and the food and the music. Horace shared a bottle of red with his wife, Bethany, at a picnic table in the shade and ignored everybody else. Cal and Docia waddled around the edge of the dance floor, cheered on by Wonder, who waved his bottle of Spaten. As he walked along the perimeter of the lawn, Erik glanced into a shaded area where the city had set up a row of park benches and blinked.

Ozzie Friesenhahn sat side by side with Helen Kretschmer, each of them holding a glass of white wine.

Erik shook his head to clear it. He hadn't had anything alcoholic to drink, and he was still seeing things.

Nando appeared at his elbow. "Everything quiet, Chief?"

Erik nodded. "Looks like it. So when do the fights start?"

"They don't." Nando grinned. "I told you. Wine festivals are mellow. And besides, everything closes down at seven so nobody has time to get too blitzed."

Erik nodded, glancing around the lawn. People lounged on the grass. Another band was setting up in the bandstand.

"Of course this could get a little raucous," Nando mused.

"What could?"

Nando gestured toward the band. "This. Frankie Belasco. Tex-Mex Zydeco. Like the Texas Tornados. Felix Burton will be doing his thing."

Erik pinched the bridge of his nose. "Felix Burton. That would be the banker, Felix Burton?"

Nando nodded. "That's the one."

"He's at least eighty. What kind of thing can he still do?"

"You'd be surprised. He's the dance leader. Not official or anything, but he usually takes on the duty."

Erik thought about asking Nando to explain what duties being dance leader entailed, but he decided against it. Whatever Felix Burton was going to do, he'd find out soon enough. "Long as it doesn't involve assault, it's okay by me."

On the bandstand a man with a silver ponytail and sunglasses who was probably Frankie Belasco lifted an accordion and played a quick riff. Behind him a fiddle player joined in, then a guitar, a bass and a drummer.

The crowd cheered a little woozily.

"Hey, y'all," Belasco called, "time to boogie."

People got to their feet around the dance floor, sliding across in ones and twos. Erik found himself tapping his toe to the rhythm.

He scanned the crowd, inspecting the faces along the edge of the wine pavilion for possible problems.

And stopped short.

Morgan was standing just inside the main entrance. She wore a white peasant blouse trimmed in lace and pulled down so that her elegant shoulders showed above the top edge. Her skirt was long and black, with panels of bright embroidery around the bottom. Her wildly abundant curls tumbled along her throat. Long, dangly earrings almost touched her shoulders.

He had a sudden overwhelming desire to nibble on her collarbone. He started wading through the crowd in her direction.

"Chief," Curtis Peavey shouted close to his ear. "You want me to patrol the parking lot again?"

Erik nodded. "Sure. Anywhere. Go for it."

He had an image of Peavey's startled face, but he kept

moving in Morgan's direction. If he didn't take his eyes off her, maybe she'd stay put.

Morgan turned to say something to someone behind her, then looked out again. Her gaze met his.

Erik half-smiled, but it probably looked more like a grimace. He needed to get to her. He really *needed* to get to her.

Morgan watched him for a moment, a slight furrow between her eyebrows. She pressed her fingers against her lips, staring at him, then absently slid the tip of her index finger into her mouth.

Erik felt every muscle in his body go rigid.

Suddenly, a crowd of people pushed in front of him, a line snaking across the dance floor. At the front of the line, Felix Burton, the eighty-year-old banker, wore a broad-brimmed straw hat, a Hawaiian shirt, and something that looked like pajama pants printed with huge blue flowers. He threw his hands above his head, and everybody in the line followed suit. He swayed back and forth, and the entire line became a swaying jungle. He pushed his hands up and down at the sky, while a dozen pairs of hands copied him.

"Go, Felix, go!" somebody shouted.

Erik looked back at the entrance to the pavilion. Morgan was gone.

Cursing to himself, he pushed through the crowd again. Behind him, Frankie Belasco and his band were playing something with a beat that resonated through the ground. Erik heard a roar that meant Felix Burton must have done something particularly popular.

He reached the entrance and started across the pavilion. A small cluster of tourists still hung around in front of the tables, drinking wine and talking to the pourers. Erik headed toward the Cedar Creek banner.

Kit Maldonado was pouring again. She looked up and grinned. "Out back, Chief." She nodded toward an opening between the booths.

He pushed the canvas aside and ducked through.

Morgan was perched on a picnic table three feet away. Her expression still looked faintly perplexed. "Hi."

"Hi yourself." Erik nodded toward her outfit. "You look like a gypsy." *A really sexy gypsy.* He pushed himself up beside her on the table.

"I'm sort of a Texas gypsy, I guess." She shook her head. "I just wanted to look like a girl. I haven't worn anything except jeans in so long I wanted to make sure I still knew how to wear a skirt." She looked away from him, staring down at the asphalt parking lot.

"You still know how." His voice sounded rusty again. He cleared his throat. "You heard about Pittman?"

She nodded. "So what's the verdict? Is he in or out?"

"The smart money's on out."

A smile quivered around the corners of her mouth. "Congratulations." She raised her gaze to his, great chocolate eyes pulling him into their depths. He felt an arrow of heat to his groin.

"What about you, the winery?"

"Looks like Bored Ducks is a hit. Dad's going to discuss marketing with me next week, god help me."

He nodded. "Congratulations to you, then. So you're staying at Cedar Creek?" He studied the smooth line of her throat, trying not to hold his breath.

"Yep. I like it in Konigsburg."

"Good." He drew a steadying breath. One problem taken care of.

His brain spun through a series of possibilities, trying to come up with the right set of words. *Want to have a drink in the evenings at the Dew Drop? Want to meet me after I get off this afternoon—and tomorrow afternoon and the afternoon after that? Want to try living together? Want to spend your life with me?* The words felt like sawdust in his mouth. He'd never been this nervous in his life.

"So where does that leave us?" she murmured. She looked back at him again, eyes wide.

Brown curls spilled down onto her shoulders, shadowing her ears. He realized suddenly her earrings were stars, thin chains of twinkling stars raining down from her earlobes.

"Want to hang out?" he asked, his breath lodging uncomfortably in his throat. "I mean sort of permanently?"

Which was probably the dumbest thing he'd said in his entire life!

The furrow reappeared between her eyes as she stared at him. Then she grinned, lifting the hair from her neck, sending a spray of starshine shimmering from her earrings. "That sounds good."

His breath left his body in a rush. "Glad to hear it." He nodded. "Can I have Arthur?"

Her forehead crinkled. "Do you *want* Arthur?"

He nodded again. "Yeah, he's a great cat. He seems okay in my apartment."

She grinned up at him, eyes dancing. "Then you can have him." Her grin faded slightly. "Of course, that's another interesting problem—where I'm going to live now. I can't stay in the winery apartment."

"Why not?" He reached out to pull one of the corkscrew curls. He loved to watch them spring back.

She shook her head. "Dad's going to be staying there off and on, now that he's coming back to work part-time. I'll need to find a new place."

He looked at her for a long moment. "Arthur could use a live-in sitter."

Her brow furrowed again. "Cat-sitter? Interesting professional possibility, but not exactly the career path I was thinking of pursuing."

"I could use a live-in sitter, too." He winced. This was his day for absolutely moronic statements. "I'm trying to ask you to move in with me, but I'm doing a lousy job of it."

She grinned, her stars shimmering. "You're not doing so badly. It's working, believe me."

On the other side of the pavilion a roar went up from the crowd. "Hell," he muttered, "what are they doing now?"

"Nothing serious." She turned toward the sound. "It's just Felix. He gets a little more outrageous every time he does this. He might be leading a group striptease this year. You really ought to go out there and watch."

"Come with me?" He reached to entwine his fingers with hers.

She nodded, gazing up at him beneath thick brown lashes. "If you'll dance with me."

He shrugged. "I'll give it a whirl. I'm not much of a dancer, though."

"With Frankie, everybody dances, trust me."

Erik stood up, tugging her to her feet, and then because he

couldn't help himself, he bent down to kiss her, opening his mouth against hers, running the tip of his tongue along her full lower lip.

She pressed her body against him, and he felt soft, braless breasts against his chest. He raised his hand to cup her, touching fullness and weight through the thin cotton, her nipple hard against his palm.

She purred against his lips and he leaned in farther, his hand sliding beneath the edge of her blouse.

Morgan pulled back slightly, her eyes alight. "This isn't exactly private, Chief."

He raised his head to see a couple of kitchen workers pausing to watch them. He gave them his best "move along" stare, and they went back to wrestling a large trash can toward the street.

She giggled. "Oh very good. I can see dating the police chief is going to be lots of fun."

He dropped his mouth to her throat running his tongue down until he nibbled on her collarbone as he'd been longing to do for at least the last half hour. Then he raised his head to look at her again. "Bambi, believe me, we are way beyond dating at this point."

"If we're not dating, what are we doing exactly?" She ran her fingertip along his lower lip.

He grinned at her. "We're going to live together, Bambi. We're in love. Haven't you figured that out yet?"

Her lips spread in a smile, the furrow between her brows disappearing. "Yeah. I had figured that out, believe me. Living together works for me."

He took a deep breath. "Me, too."

"You still haven't told me—why am I Bambi?"

He shook his head. "You just are. Come on, Bambi, let's dance."

Morgan glanced at the dance floor. Frankie had them all on their feet again, as usual. The dance line still snaked around the edges of the crowd—Felix Burton didn't even look winded. His wife, Arleta, sat on the far side of the pavilion with a large glass of red wine, regarding Felix with jaundiced eyes. She'd probably given up trying to rein him in by now.

Morgan's parents sat on lawn chairs in the shade. Her father had a bottle of Bored Ducks open in front of him. He was sniffing it carefully. Her mother took it out of his hand and poured herself a healthy glassful, then raised it in Morgan's general direction, grinning happily.

On the stage, the fiddle player ran through a familiar scale and everyone cheered. Frankie swung into "Jolie Blonde", bellowing the lyrics into his microphone.

Across the floor, Docia and Cal tried a swoop, which managed to clear a wide path on either side. Wonder and Allie twirled behind them, Allie in her bright red chef's pants with the green chilies running down the sides. Jess Toleffson clapped from the sidelines, while Lars pursued their giggling son toward the kids' pavilion.

The crowd ebbed and flowed around them. On the grassy lawn nearby, Andy Wells, the TCEQ investigator, stood next to an elderly woman in a walker. As Frankie's accordion trilled in the background, she began to move back and forth gracefully, resting the tips of her fingers on the walker's metal frame. The elderly lady swayed in time to the music, moving along with Andy and smiling.

Morgan shook her head. Konigsburg.

She felt a hand on her elbow and looked back. Janie smiled at her, as she pulled Pete toward the dance floor. "We have these family dinners on Fridays sometimes. Can you come over next week?"

Morgan glanced at Erik, currently muttering instructions to Nando. "Sure. I guess that's okay."

Janie's grin widened. "Oh, it's okay, believe me." She pulled on Pete's arm again to herd him toward the dance floor.

Erik held out his hand. "Shall we?"

"Oh yes," Morgan murmured. "We definitely shall."

She slid into his arms, moving with him to the music. People swirled around them like water around a stone, but she was safe and warm in his embrace.

"*Jolie blonde*," Frankie sang, "*ma chere 'tit fille.*"

Erik sighed against her ear, executing a gentle turn. "Thank god everything has finally settled down."

Morgan snuggled more tightly against him, humming along

with Frankie.

"Erik!" Cal's voice behind them sounded panicky.

Erik closed his eyes for a moment, then turned. "What's up?"

"Docia's water just broke. I'll never be able to get the SUV through the traffic. Could you... Is there any way you could..."

Morgan glanced at Cal. Docia was half-supported against his shoulder. She looked as if she was concentrating very hard on breathing. As Morgan watched, she took several deep breaths and blew them out in a series of quick pants. *Uh-oh.*

Erik sighed. "Come on. We'll take the cruiser." He turned back toward Morgan, his smile rueful. "Sorry about this. Raincheck, Bambi?"

Morgan's throat was tight all of a sudden. "There's nothing to be sorry for. They're your family, Erik. They need you."

Docia glanced at her, eyes wide. "What time is it? Was anybody checking on how long it was between those last two contractions?"

Cal gave her a look of absolute panic. "What? No, I forgot. Erik, can we get going now?"

"Sure." Erik began to move resolutely through the crowd, clearing a path for the clutch of Toleffsons—Cal, Docia, Pete and Janie—bobbing along behind him.

"Lars said he'd meet you at the hospital," Janie called, "after he takes Jess and the kids home."

All around them Konigsburg citizens began to gather, pushing aside the slightly woozy tourists to form a path to the parking lot. "Take Novarro to Main," someone called. "It's faster."

Morgan stepped beside Erik, helping him move through the curious Konigsburgers. "I'll come with you. You never know—you might need me."

"Always, Bambi." He glanced down at her, smiling again. "Always."

Morgan's heart gave a mighty thump. She was pretty sure she was smiling her idiot grin once again. Ah well, it might be a permanent condition. After a moment, she slid her arm around Erik's waist, heading toward the cruiser and the future.

About the Author

Meg Benjamin writes about South Texas, although she now lives in Colorado. Her comic romances—*Venus in Blue Jeans*, *Wedding Bell Blues*, *Be My Baby* and *Long Time Gone,* all from Samhain Publishing—are set in the Texas Hill Country in the mythical town of Konigsburg. When she isn't writing, Meg spends her time listening to Americana music, drinking Colorado and Texas wine, and keeping track of her far-flung family. To learn more about Meg, please visit www.MegBenjamin.com. Send an email to meg@megbenjamin.com or visit her on Facebook at www.facebook.com/meg.benjamin1, on Twitter at http://twitter.com/megbenj1.

There's no room in her life for love. Love has other ideas...

Be My Baby
© *2009 Meg Benjamin*
Konigsburg, Texas, Book 3

If Jessamyn Carroll had only herself to consider, staying in Pennsylvania after her husband's death would have been a no-brainer. Her vindictive in-laws' efforts to get their hooks into her infant son, however, force her to flee to a new home. Konigsburg, Texas.

Peace...at least for now. She's even found a way to make some extra money, looking after sexy accountant Lars Toleffson's precocious two-year-old daughter. She finds it easy—too easy—to let his protective presence lull her into thinking she and her son are safe at last.

Lars, still wounded from enduring a nasty divorce from his cheating ex-wife, tries to fight his attraction to the mysterious, beautiful widow. But when an intruder breaks into her place, and Jess comes clean about her past, all bets are off. Someone wants her baby—and wants Jess out of the picture. Permanently.

Now Jess has a live-in bodyguard, whether she wants him or not. Except she does want him—and he wants her. Yet negotiating a future together will have to overcome a lot of roadblocks: babies, puppies, the entire, meddling Toleffson family—and a kidnapper.

Warning: Contains Konigsburg craziness, creepy in-laws, a conniving two-year-old, a lovelorn accountant, a sleep-deprived Web developer, and lots of hot holiday sex.

Available now in ebook and print from Samhain Publishing.

To save one good man,
she'll have to let her inner bad girl out to play...

Just Right
© 2010 Erin Nicholas
The Bradfords, Book 1

ER nurse Jessica Bradford is a good girl. Okay, a reformed bad girl, but she's done her late father proud. Now she's one step away from landing Dr. Perfect, aka handsome, sexy, heroic Ben Torres—the hot fudge *and* cherry on top of her hard work scooping out a respectable life.

Ben learned the art of sacrifice from his missionary parents, but when a drunk driver he saved kills three people, he quits. To be precise, the fist he plants in the man's face gets him suspended. And the first dish he wants on his newly empty plate is Jessica—preferably naked.

Jessica can't believe the Ben she's found drowning his sorrows in a bar is her knight in shining scrubs. And he won't be pried loose until she bets 48 hours of her time in a game of pool. She loses. And the next morning she stands to lose much more.

The Chief of Staff's recommendation for the promotion she's been after rides on her ability to keep Ben out of trouble until things blow over.

Except "trouble" is all Ben wants. And despite herself, Jessica finds that she's more than willing to go down with him...

Warning: Contains hot love in a store dressing room and in the front seat of a car—at the expense of a very nice strawberry patch, unfortunately—oh, and hooker boots. Can't forget the hooker boots.

Available now in ebook and print from Samhain Publishing.